D1374687

The
Figurine

By Victoria Hislop

The Island
The Return
The Thread
The Last Dance and Other Stories
The Sunrise
Cartes Postales From Greece
Those Who Are Loved
One August Night
The Figurine

Maria's Island *(for children)*

Victoria Hislop

The Figurine

REVIEW

Copyright © 2023 Victoria Hislop

The right of Victoria Hislop to be identified as the Author of
the Work has been asserted by her in accordance with the
Copyright, Designs and Patents Act 1988.

First published in 2023 by
HEADLINE REVIEW
An imprint of HEADLINE PUBLISHING GROUP

Formula on p. 192 from P. W. Atkins, *Physical Chemistry* (Oxford: Oxford University Press, 1978)

Equation on p. 485 from R. E. Jones, with contributions by J. Boardman, H. W. Catling, C. B.
Mee, W. W. Phelps and A. M. Pollard, *Greek & Cypriot Pottery: A Review of Scientific Studies*
(Athens, British School at Athens, 1986)

1

Apart from any use permitted under UK copyright law, this publication may only
be reproduced, stored, or transmitted, in any form, or by any means, with
prior permission in writing of the publishers or, in the case of reprographic
production, in accordance with the terms of licences issued by the
Copyright Licensing Agency.

All characters in this publication are fictitious and any resemblance to real
persons, living or dead, is purely coincidental.

Cataloguing in Publication Data is available from the British Library

ISBN 978 1 4722 6393 3 (Hardback)
ISBN 978 1 4722 6395 7 (Trade Paperback)
ISBN 978 1 0354 1175 7 (Waterstones)

Typeset in Bembo MT Pro by Palimpsest Book Production Ltd, Falkirk, Stirlingshire

Printed and bound in Great Britain by Clays Ltd, Elcograf S.p.A.

Headline's policy is to use papers that are natural, renewable and
recyclable products and made from wood grown in sustainable forests.
The logging and manufacturing processes are expected to conform to the
environmental regulations of the country of origin.

MIX
Paper | Supporting
responsible forestry
FSC® C104740

HEADLINE PUBLISHING GROUP
An Hachette UK Company
Carmelite House
50 Victoria Embankment
London EC4Y 0DZ

www.headline.co.uk
www.hachette.co.uk

The
Figurine

For Ian

Μα πάνω απ' όλα σμίλεψαν
μορφή κυρίαρχη,
αυτή της γης-γυναίκας
. . . γυναίκας γόνιμης, καρποφορούσας,
παραγωγή της ίδιας της ζωής

Above all else they carved
one dominant form,
Earth-goddess mother
 . . . woman fertile, and fruitful,
and source of all life

Nikos Stampolidis
Director-General, Acropolis Museum

Foreword

Many great twentieth-century artists were inspired by the simple beauty and primitive form of the Cycladic figurine. Picasso, Modigliani, Brâncuşi and Henry Moore were among them. As a result, the appreciation of these third-millennium BC figurines grew. In 2010, for example, a single figurine, less than ten inches in height, was sold for more than $16 million in a New York auction house. This popularity, however, has also led to massive illegal excavation and clandestine trade.

The theft of cultural treasures and the falsification of provenance diminishes our understanding of civilisation. Every object illegally removed, smuggled and sold impoverishes the victim country and is often linked to broader criminal activities such as money-laundering and drug and arms trafficking. The war against perpetrators continues to be fought on an international scale.

Beauty has always cast its spell, but down the ages has always driven some to crime.

Part One

Chapter One

Helena stood at the top of the aircraft steps, blinking into the sunlight, a hot breeze blowing strands of hair across her face. Why was everything shimmering? So dazzlingly bright?

'*Páme mikrí*,' said the air hostess, holding her hand tightly as they descended onto the melting tarmac. 'Let's go, little one.'

At passport control, Helena's airline 'auntie' showed the child's stiff new passport to an official, before taking her to retrieve her brown plastic suitcase from the carousel. Helena was then handed over to a driver, who was parked directly outside the exit. As they approached the large black car, she noticed a silver statuette perched on the front of the bonnet. A shiny, winged lady.

The fifty-minute drive took her along the sea (so blue, so calm) and then into a network of busy, colourful streets, where she wound up her window to keep out the fumes. Twice when the car had to stop because of the traffic, a few children clustered round and peered in to look at her, and she shrank back into her seat, embarrassed. In another street, someone approached selling flowers. Everything seemed exotic and strange, the buildings tall, the roads narrow.

Finally, in an area where there were fewer people, much fancier dress shops and more trees, they stopped outside an elegant apartment block. '*Edó eímaste*,' said the chauffeur, speaking for the first time. 'We're here.'

5

The building was cream-coloured, and Helena could see grey marble steps leading up to a pair of glass doors. On either side of the entrance were big plants with large leaves that looked as if they had been polished.

This must be Evdokias 45 in Kolonaki, where her grandparents lived.

There was a small, stout woman with silvery permed hair standing on the pavement. She wore a blue skirt and a matching silky blouse with a bow at the neck. When Helena emerged from the car, the woman clapped her hands together in delight. She looked nothing like Helena's mother, but this must be her grandmother.

'*Koukláki mou! Koukláki mou!*' she cried, hugging Helena so tightly and for so long that the little girl wondered if she would ever let her go. She did not understand the term of affection but found it in her dictionary later. She had not been called a dolly before.

When she was finally released from her embrace, Helena followed her grandmother up the steps, past a brass plate with five buttons, into a gleaming foyer. A smiling uniformed man behind a desk stood up to greet her. The chauffeur had brought Helena's suitcase inside and the concierge picked it up and ascended with them in the mirrored lift, smiling and chatting all the way. By the time they got to the fifth floor, he knew Helena's name and age, her favourite colour and favourite ice cream, and she knew that Kýrios Manolis was going to be a good friend.

The apartment door was wide open, and Eleni Papagiannis led her granddaughter inside. Helena looked around her, wide-eyed, intimidated by the high ceilings and low lighting. The ubiquitous glint of gold, floor-to-ceiling windows and ornate framed mirrors in the alcoves reminded her of stately homes she had been taken to on school visits. She felt a long way from her parents and her plain but comfortable semi-detached home in Suffolk, but was determined to put on a brave face, just as she had promised before waving goodbye to them that morning. It was only for two weeks, she told herself, and even now her grandmother was speaking Greek to her, which meant that she was bound to be more fluent when she returned. This was one of the reasons she was here, but she might have to ask her grandma to slow down a little.

She was taken on a tour of the drawing room, dining room and kitchen. It was here that she met Dina, the maid, who was busy scrubbing the floor but sprang to her feet to welcome this important visitor.

'I'm so happy to meet you at last, little Helena!' she beamed. 'Your room is all ready!'

Helena was shown the spacious bedroom where she would sleep and understood that it was a special room for guests. They passed doors to four other bedrooms and three bathrooms. Finally her grandfather's study was pointed out, but she was not taken inside.

Most exciting of all was the large balcony, which had a spectacular view of the Parthenon. It was an image with which Helena was already very familiar and she suddenly felt more at home.

'We'll go there one day,' promised Eleni. 'But for today, I thought we would go for an ice cream? Would you like that?'

Helena nodded.

On the day she arrived, Helena's grandfather got home mid evening. General Papagiannis was in uniform and was at least a foot taller than her grandmother. If she had expected the same welcome from him, she would have been disappointed. Stamatis Papagiannis was noticeably unaffectionate. Her mother had warned her that his manner might be rather formal, but she had not really understood what this could mean. At this first encounter, he was clearly dismayed by the vivid colour of his granddaughter's hair. *Kókkino* was the first word she heard him say. Red. It was not meant as a compliment but as a criticism, and she felt her skin going crimson with shame. Her green eyes appeared to be even more offensive to him. '*Prásino!*' he spat, as if it was a swear word. She realised that he had only seen a photograph of her in black and white.

Fortunately, her grandmother poured such kindness on the eight-year-old that she began to savour each day, almost regretful at how quickly time went by. She discovered that they shared the same name, but in Greek it was pronounced 'Eleni'. Her grandmother renamed her Elenaki, little Eleni, and in return Helena was to call her Yiayiá.

The child was swept away by the thrill of being introduced to the colourful, dusty and flamingly hot city, and her grandmother helped dispel her homesickness with unlimited treats. Her first summer fortnight in the Greek capital seemed full of sweetness; not just her introduction to *zacharoplasteíon* specialities such as baklava and orange cake dripping in syrup, but also the fragrant lacquer that her grandmother sprayed in her hair, the scent of the jasmine flowers that blossomed profusely on the terrace, and the beeswax that Dina used lavishly in the apartment. And then there was her grandmother's name for her, *glykiá mou*, a term of endearment that Helena soon learned meant 'my sweetness'.

The excitement of the bustling city could not have been a greater contrast with her small town in Suffolk, where a bus only passed through twice a day to connect it with the county town, the local cinema only opened its doors on a Saturday, and a major event was the annual visit of a funfair.

Helena embraced the strangeness of everything in Greece, from the calls of the street sellers to the unfamiliar food she ate in local restaurants. She was unsure at first about the sharp-flavoured white cheese and the bitter black olives, but after a while she got used to all the odd flavours, even the way the water tasted. Her early days with her grandmother were safe and cloistered. On the first day, they went to Zonars, her grandmother's favourite place to meet her smart women friends, for ice cream. The following day they went to a beach, where the pale, fine sand was unlike any she had ever felt beneath her feet and the sea was warm and blue. She was allowed to swim as long as she kept her grandmother in sight, and as soon as she got out of the water, she had to sit in the shade of a big multicoloured umbrella.

Everyone who met Helena, whether they were known to Eleni Papagiannis or not, commented on the dramatic colour of her hair and usually lifted up one of her long bunches to examine it more closely.

'*Kokkinomálliko!* Little redhead!' they exclaimed, in tones that ranged from admiration to disdain. Helena was used to standing out from the crowd, even at home, but people were not usually so nakedly curious or rude. The only place where she blended in was Scotland, where all her cousins had similar colouring and even more freckles than her.

Her grandfather was mostly absent, sometimes for several days at a time, or he went out very early in the morning, returning late. Helena rarely saw him in anything other than his army uniform, and he remained a remote but intimidating figure. She could not tell her grandmother that she found him frightening, and only admitted to herself that she was happier on the days when he was not around.

One evening, however, he was home in time for dinner, and before he ate, he summoned her into his gloomy study, where he sat behind his desk and interrogated her in Greek about her day. She found the encounter terrifying, mostly because she was afraid of making errors and sensed his irritation when she did.

Before the ordeal began, Helena's grandfather (she was told to call him Pappoú but generally avoided it) picked a cigarette from the silver box next to his ink blotter, put it in his mouth and leaned forward. From his gesture, Helena understood that she was expected to light it for him with the table lighter, a heavy lump of solid metal engraved with his name, and she quickly worked out how to flick the lever to bring the flame shooting up from the base. As he took his first clearly satisfying inhalation, he sat back and listened to her struggle with her narration of the day, plumes of smoke rising between them. Every few seconds he interrupted her flow to correct her.

At the end of her account, his mouth curled into a smile but his eyes remained lifeless. Helena had never come across anyone with two separate parts to their face that seemed entirely independent of each other. After that, he got up without a word and she watched his towering figure leave the room to have dinner with her grandmother. She sat for a moment staring at the cigarette still smouldering in an ashtray.

When this process was repeated a few days later, he told her that the best way to learn was to fear failure. Every time she made a mistake, she had to put her hand out to be smacked. He only struck her lightly, but it was enough to leave a mark, and more than enough to humiliate her.

Helena was determined not to let these encounters with her grandfather sour her stay. Most of the day he was absent, and the joyful novelty of the outings with her grandmother more than made up for the sessions with him. Whenever they went anywhere further than a few hundred yards away, they travelled with her grandfather's driver in the well-polished Rolls-Royce, and the thrill of being driven around in the luxurious car was something she loved. She sat in the back with her *yiayiá* on the cream leather banquette and observed the city. There was always something to look at as they waited in the traffic: a man with an accordion, a bootblack, a shop with all its wares hung up for display outside, a priest who looked ten feet tall in a huge black hat. None of these things would be seen in Dellbridge.

The large numbers of soldiers and policemen on the streets puzzled her, given that nothing out of the ordinary was going on. She quizzed her grandmother about why there were so many, when in her own little town there was a single bobby who spent most of his day sitting in the station.

'Perhaps that's why England is such a lawless place, *agápi mou*,' said her grandmother. 'When you have plenty of men in uniform around, no one dares to steal.'

Helena did not respond. The only crimes she had ever heard of in Dellbridge were shoplifting from the Woolworths make-up counter and speeding on the new bypass.

Whenever she saw her grandfather in his army uniform, though, it was impossible to imagine anyone committing a crime in his presence, unless they cared nothing for their own lives. A teenager in Suffolk would certainly not steal a lipstick if there were people like him on every street corner. She found Stamatis Papagiannis quietly sinister, like a dormant volcano. If and when he was going to erupt was unknowable, but the threat felt constant.

On her first Sunday, the only day she saw her grandfather in civilian clothes, she was taken to the nearby church and told that this was a weekly outing. Both her parents were atheists, and Helena only went to her town's plain parish church a few times a year with school, so the Greek Orthodox traditions seemed very strange to her. There were no hymns for the congregation. All the singing was done by a group of men. Their other-worldly voices were beautiful and harmonised perfectly. Very little was spoken, and the priest swung a silver incense burner back and forth, back and forth as he chanted, filling the air with an intoxicating scent that lingered on her clothes for days. It was yet another part of the sweetness of Athens that she enjoyed so much. The priest was theatrical, with the longest white beard she had ever seen, ornate vestments trimmed with gold and a tall hat. He was nothing like the vicar who did the school services and was only distinguishable from the young teachers by his dog collar.

Helena was not bored even for a second, there was so much to absorb: the painted figures all around her with their big doleful eyes, the rows of silver charms representing prayers that hung on ribbons before some of the icons, the bundles of skinny candles that people planted into bowls full of sand, the sight of one old lady after another stooping to brush their lips against the glass-fronted image of a saint, passing their right hand in a triangular motion from head to heart, then right and left, over and over again. She loved the colour and ceremony of it all.

As they were walking home, her grandfather asked her who her *noná* was.

It was an awkward moment because she did not recognise the word.

'He means your godmother,' whispered Yiayiá.

'Oh, I don't have one,' responded Helena casually. '*Or a middle name like all my friends. I wasn't baptised.*'

'You weren't *baptised*?'

Helena recognised total incredulity in his voice. At first she mistook it for pity, but she quickly realised it was anger, and the force of it shocked her, given that he had emerged from a holy place only minutes before. She heard the word *noná* repeated, and then her mother's name, in Greek, of course, spoken many times over. Maria this, Maria that. He appeared to be furious with his wife, his daughter and his granddaughter in equal measure, though Helena could not quite work out the reason or what she could do about it.

Eleni Papagiannis tried to calm her husband down as Helena reddened with embarrassment at being the cause of this outburst. People on the street were looking at them and she was glad when they reached Evdokias 45. Her grandfather continued up the road, his stick tapping loudly and firmly on the pavement. The old lady was pale and her hand visibly shaking as she pushed open the door. She merely nodded at Kýrios Manolis as they stood waiting for the lift.

'He has a rendezvous with friends in a *kafeneío*,' she explained to Helena, 'and they will probably have lunch together after that. Army colleagues. Men he trained with many decades ago. Some of them have retired now, but many are still active. They love to meet up on a Sunday.'

Helena said nothing as the two of them went up in the lift. She was sure it was all a lie, and the more detail her *yiayiá* went into about her grandfather's social plans, the less Helena believed it or cared. She had a growing dislike of him: his uncontrolled temper, his apparent lack of feeling for his wife, the sour smell that hung around him.

Back in the apartment, they sat down to the lunch that Dina had very evidently made for three: lamb cutlets and salad. Neither of them ate much.

'It's a little too hot to eat, isn't it?' said Dina as she cleared the plates. Helena looked at her and thought how kind she was to pretend there was another reason for their lack of appetite. She wondered how many times the maid had needed to smooth over such a situation. Dina reminded her of the nicest teacher at her school, who was always encouraging children to be kind, teaching them that it was the only rule that really mattered.

After a long siesta, and when the day had cooled, they were driven up Lycabettus Hill so that Helena could see the view across the city. They sat for a while to have a cold drink in the café, and she tried to cheer her grandmother.

'I'm sure I can find a *noná*, Yiayiá,' she said, sipping her lemonade. 'I'll see if Mum can ask Mrs Wilson who works at her school. She's her best friend. Or maybe Dina could be?' she added as an afterthought, noisily sucking the last mouthful of lemonade through her straw. She was not sure if it was her words or the gurgling sound that was the reason for her grandmother's disapproving look.

She did not see Stamatis Papagiannis again that day, but when she was lying in bed that night, trying to sleep beneath the noisily whirring fan, she heard the sound of raised voices, mostly her grandfather's, from down the corridor. Angry shouting was not something she was familiar with, and she buried her head under her pillow.

When she got up the following morning, she found her grandfather already at the table, sipping coffee and reading his newspaper. She supposed that *Kathimerini*, as it was called, was equivalent to *The Times*, which was the one her parents had delivered each day. He looked up when she sat down and spoke to her in a voice unrecognisable from the one she had heard on previous days.

'You're in for a special treat later today, young lady!' he said, almost warmly. 'You should put on your best dress. *And* I want to see some smiles from you, *Elenáki mou.*'

Eventually, when her grandfather had left the table and disappeared into his study, her grandmother appeared, wearing a long-sleeved dress. It seemed strange for the heat of the day.

Around six in the evening, after a long and listless day, Helena excitedly ran down the stairs, beating her grandparents, who had taken the lift, to the foyer. The chauffeur was waiting in the street to take them to their destination. The occasion was a historical pageant, and Helena's grandfather was given privileged seating at the huge parade ground on account of his army status. The three of them had front-row places and a clear view of everything that took place.

Helena immediately noticed a group of men in throne-like seats on a decorated stage and asked who they were. Her grandmother explained that they were army colonels who had stepped in the previous year to run Greece properly. It was the child's first glimpse of the triumvirate who had staged the army coup.

It was left to Eleni, who seemed more deferential than ever to her husband that day, to give Helena explanations and commentary. Stamatis Papagiannis sat unsmiling, focused on the action and occasionally glancing across at the men on the dais.

Helena had never witnessed such a spectacle. She was spellbound by the action and the terrifying proximity of the performers. It began with a re-enactment of one of Alexander the Great's battles. Hundreds of men dressed as warriors of ancient times galloped into the sanded arena of the marble stadium and encountered the foe, leaping off their horses for man-to-man combat. The sound of clashing swords just yards from her face and the roar of the crowd was thrilling. At the end, an army tank disguised as a chariot trundled around the perimeter of the stadium parading the military junta's symbol: a phoenix rising from the flames.

'Those three men,' Helena's *yiayiá* told her in an interlude between battles, 'are doing an excellent job. The one in the middle is Georgios Papadopoulos, our prime minister; to his right is Stylianos Pattakos, to his left is Nikolaos Makarezos.'

Helena nodded out of politeness. Great Britain had a prime minister, Harold Wilson, and every time she saw him on television, he was smoking a pipe, so it was no surprise to her that his Greek counterpart was smoking one cigarette after another, rather like her grandfather. More surprising to her was the row of priests clad in black sitting immediately behind him. Some of them were smoking too.

Yiayiá's explanations remained bland and neutral, but Helena was conscious that her grandfather was listening in, ready to correct her, which he did once or twice, or to emphasise a point.

After an interval, during which Helena ate an ice cream, there were further battle displays. These were re-enactments of events that took place during the 1821 War of Independence against the Turks, 'the revolution' as it was known.

'The men with the baggy coloured pantaloons are the Turks,' explained Eleni Papagiannis. 'And those in the full white skirts – the *fustanélla* – are the Greeks!'

There was one horse, bigger than the others, that circled around the battle, ridden by a man with an impressive helmet.

'Kolokotronis,' the old lady said great pride in her voice. 'The hero of the revolution.'

From the Turks came blood-curdling screams as they waved their cutlasses in the air, but soon afterwards they were collapsing on the ground, slain by the mighty enemy. Finally, only Greeks were left standing. These men were the righteous winners. This was the clear and patriotic message.

Once the revolution re-enactment was over and victory declared, everyone stood as a vast flag, a blue cross on white, was paraded around three or four times to ever-increasing cheers from the eighty-thousand-strong crowd. It took eight men to carry it and eventually to spread it like a rug in front of the raised platform.

This was the cue for Papadopoulos to stand up and strut towards the microphone at the edge of the stage. There was a fresh surge of sound from his adoring supporters, who rose again to their feet and began to sing, apparently unprompted:

> *Vásta ta kleidiá, vástaxe gerá,*
> *To ónomá sou tóra pia aiónia tha meínei.*

The words had no meaning for Helena, but the enthusiasm of the crowd was rousing, and she liked the music and the jaunty rhythm.

'*Elenáki mou,*' said Eleni Papagiannis, 'I'll tell you what it all means later, but for now just join in with the chorus.'

Then came the words that were repeated every few lines. Hesitantly at first, but growing in confidence each time, Helena sang them out lustily:

'*Oré, Geórgio Papadópoule.*' Hurray for Georgios Papadopoulos.

For the first time that evening, her grandfather smiled.

'*Brávo, Elenáki mou! Brávo!*'

Her grandfather's pleasure at hearing her sing these words at the top of her voice appeared disproportionate to the effort involved. It seemed an easy way to earn praise from the severe octogenarian.

Georgios Papadopoulos spread his arms wide and high, a gesture of gratitude for the adulation. When the very last voice from the crowd was silent, he began to speak, his face partly obscured by the microphone, which was set a little too high for a man of his stature.

Neither his appearance (balding, thin moustache) nor his voice (high-pitched and hoarse, a screeching sound like fingernails on a blackboard) was what Helena had imagined for a leader of Greece.

They were sitting just beneath one of the loudspeakers, and the noise of the reverberations and the shrill amplified sound was worse than a dentist's drill. Instinctively she bowed her head and put her hands over her ears, hoping the speech would be over soon.

Her grandmother snatched her hands, pulled them down and firmly held on to them.

'Show some respect!' she scolded in a harsh whisper. 'And *don't* do that again!'

Papadopoulos ranted for what seemed like hours. Helena sat there rigid. The words were incomprehensible to her and Yiayiá no longer helped her out with any translation. She glanced at the old lady, who was fanning herself and listening with rapt concentration. It appeared that she was as avid a supporter as the rest of the audience, hanging on every word the man said.

Why, Helena asked herself, was everyone listening to this tirade? It seemed to her that the audience had been very polite from the moment they had entered the stadium, and yet they were being harangued as if for some misdemeanour. The tone of the address reminded her of when the headmistress made the entire school stay in at lunchtime because one person had written rude words on a toilet door. It seemed to Helena that he would never stop, and her eyelids began to feel heavy.

Eventually, though, he did finish speaking, and the audience stood once again. Out of respect or fear, Helena did not know. A military vehicle roared across the stadium, stirring up a cloud of dust. Papadopoulos climbed into it and then waved a regal farewell to the chanting crowd as he was driven away. The vehicle was followed by several more that came to collect others of sufficient seniority.

Soon the Papagiannis party was escorted to the exit. On the way, her grandfather paused to be greeted by many other men in uniform and their wives. Eleni Papagiannis shook dozens of hands too, and briefly introduced her granddaughter, who dutifully smiled each time, exactly as she had been instructed.

It was Dina rather than Yiayiá who came in to wake her the next morning, and sunshine flooded in as the maid threw open the curtains.

'*Ti óra eínai?*' Helena asked, blearily wiping her eyes.

'It's eleven o'clock, *agápi mou!*' Dina declared. 'And I have a lot to do today. Will you help me?'

Stamatis and Eleni Papagiannis were having an important reception that evening. Yiayiá was already out at the hairdresser's, and the maid was charged with getting the apartment ready and making everything spotless. From the door handles to the photo frames, nothing was going to escape Dina's duster. Helena was handed one too. They began with Eleni's collection of china figures on display in a glass-fronted cabinet in the drawing room. Helena had never been allowed to see them close to. Dina took every piece out and lined them up on various side tables.

'It's called Meissen,' she explained.

'What does that mean?' asked Helena.

'That it's very special china. And the way you tell if it's real is by this little pair of crossed swords on the underside.' Dina inverted a lady in a crinoline and showed her the symbol. 'Each one is worth many thousands of drachmas,' she concluded.

Very gingerly, Helena touched the head of one of them with a duster and then stood back and watched Dina.

There were dozens. A monkey band, allegorical figures, women representing the four seasons, classical gods and goddesses, a shepherdess, a shepherd grabbing a shepherdess, a sultan riding an elephant, exotic birds, several different breeds of dog, a lion, a leopard. And many ladies who danced.

Helena had a few china cats she had won at a funfair the previous year, but her parents had no such treasures.

While Dina very carefully tended to the figures, Helena was given the task of polishing twenty crystal tumblers with a special cloth and placing them neatly on the sideboard, next to decanters of various kinds of whisky. She lifted the stopper from one of them and recoiled at the smell.

'How do people drink that?' she shrieked. 'It's dis*gusting*!'

Dina laughed, putting her nose up to it as well.

'I have no idea, *paidí mou*, my child. It smells like poison to me.'

Helena spent a happy morning chatting and giggling with Dina. In the afternoon she watched her preparing trays of canapés, and was even allowed to help garnish them.

In the evening, she was instructed to stay out of sight.

Spying through a crack in the door on the arriving guests, she noted that they were all men. Some were in uniform and others not, and a few of them brought gifts, which were left on a console table in the hall.

Once the doorbell stopped ringing and the last guest had arrived, her grandmother came into the kitchen and watched Dina adding the finishing touches to her miniature tarts.

For an hour and a half, Dina came and went with platters, and every so often she refilled the ice buckets. All the while Helena stood on the little balcony off the kitchen. She counted the number of limousines that were parked in the side street below and watched the chauffeurs as they leaned on their bonnets, chatting to each other and smoking. One of them spent the whole evening shining his chrome wing mirrors.

At 9.30 precisely, the sound of male voices filled the hallway as the guests all left. Simultaneously, Helena heard the sound of car ignitions and engines purring. She looked down at the guests being magicked away in their luxury cars.

With both her grandparents in bed, she was free to stay up and nibble at some of the untouched platters of food. Chatting with Dina was a good way to practise her Greek. Dina was from a village in the Peloponnese and spoke very little English, so the two of them often found themselves giggling as they tried to communicate.

'*Mathaíno grígora mazí sou!*' Helena told her. 'I learn fast from you!'

The maid would be up for another few hours airing the drawing room, puffing up the cushions and clearing the over-filled ashtrays. There were also the vases to empty. Although the flowers had been fresh that morning, they had wilted in the heat.

There was more official entertainment for Helena that week. She was taken to a display of traditional dancing and song in the National Gardens. The night was as warm as ever, and she spent most of her time fighting off the midges that were attracted to her pale skin.

'This,' said her grandfather as the dancers gathered in a circle in front of them and the musicians struck up the first notes, 'is the essence of Greekness.'

Helena did not really know what that meant, but she tried to work it out during the display.

'*Tsámiko*,' he added, as if that would help her to understand.

The ten men in extravagantly pleated white tutus, the same style that Helena had seen at the revolution re-enactment and which her grandmother had described as *fustanélla*, and ten women, demure in headscarves, full white dresses and red aprons, began to dance. The patterns were complex and the dancers' steps were perfectly synchronised. The men had many opportunities to display acrobatic prowess, bending, limboing and jumping in the air to attract audience applause.

Helena was reminded of the Scottish dancing she had seen, and the kilt that her father kept in his wardrobe, but mostly she sat trying to suppress her giggles at the sight of the huge black pompoms on the men's shoes.

The dominant sound was the clarinet that kept up a constant wail above the din of drums and violins.

'Your grandfather used to be able to dance like that when I met him,' Eleni Papagiannis said with a sigh on their short journey home. She was sitting in the back with Helena, and her husband was in the front talking stiffly to his driver.

Helena found it hard to imagine.

'But after he was wounded, he never danced again.'

She had assumed that her grandfather used a stick because of his age.

The chauffeur was now parking outside the apartment, so it wasn't until the next day that Helena found the opportunity to ask more.

'He was shot,' said Eleni Papagiannis, sotto voce. 'During the war.'

Helena felt it displayed her ignorance to ask which war. Second? First?

'We had only been married a year, but he was so brave. He spent many months in hospital, but they managed to save his leg.'

'Poor Pappoú,' Helena said. 'It sounds like he was lucky, though?'

'He was, *agápi mou*. It happened during the Asia Minor campaign, and if there had been more brave men like him, we might have won against the Turks and the Catastrophe would never have happened. Who knows?'

She would ask her mother when she got home what this campaign was, and what Yiayiá meant by *the Catastrophe*. History had never really interested her very much.

'He was a hero, Helena,' Eleni Papagiannis said firmly. 'He *is* a hero.'

The word 'hero' was one she heard so often here, used for everything from Greek gods to the Colonels. Stamatis Papagiannis, with or without his limp, did not seem to fit the mould, but she nodded in any case.

Even though her homesickness had completely gone after the first week, Helena was excited when it was time to pack for her journey home. On the morning she left, Eleni Papagiannis took her out for a final ice cream in Kolonaki Square before the chauffeur drove her to the airport.

She had so much to tell her parents and knew how pleased her mother would be with the improvement in her Greek. Her grandfather was not there when she left, but both Eleni and Dina gave her firm hugs before she got into the limousine.

'We'll see you next year, won't we?' said Dina, sniffing into a handkerchief. 'Promise?'

'Of course!' Helena reassured her. '*Na metrísoume tous mínes.*'

They made a mutual promise to count the months.

When Helena landed back at Heathrow, the first person she saw as she came through the arrivals gate dragging her small case was her mother, elegant in a yellow coat, her dark hair wound up in a bun. Mary McCloud always stood out in any crowd for her eye-catching southern Mediterranean looks, oddly mismatched with her name, and she was often conscious that people could not quite place her. Hamish McCloud, tall and ivory-skinned with a thick head of auburn hair and steel-rimmed spectacles, stood next to her.

Mary grabbed her husband's arm as she spotted their daughter, looking healthily different from the day she had left, with a hint of colour on her pale arms and many more freckles on her face.

'Look! Look, Hamish! There she is!' she said, waving excitedly.

Both of them embraced Helena heartily.

The journey home went by quickly, with Helena doing her best to keep up with their questions.

Hamish noticed, even if Helena did not, that some of her answers displeased her mother. There were clearly a few things that Helena had done that did not meet with Mary's approval. Being taken to church was one of them.

'It was full,' she told her mother. 'As full as the church in Dellbridge when we have the school carol service. And it was just a normal Sunday. And Pappoú was shocked that I haven't been baptised. I don't know what he said exactly, but he seemed very annoyed about it.'

'Well, it's nothing to do with him.'

'But can I be? It would be nice to have a *noná*, Mum.'

'I think probably not,' interjected Hamish. 'It's not really something we believe in.'

'Typical of them to bring that up,' Helena heard her mother mutter before she changed the subject. Had Helena gone to any museums? Did she like the food?

Helena told them about the pastries, the ice creams and the pageant. Mary McCloud was keen to hear if her daughter had made any progress in her own mother tongue and chattered to her in Greek for a few moments. When Helena replied to her with a new fluency, Mary was impressed.

'And look,' Helena said, fishing something out of her bag and passing it to her mother in the passenger seat. 'Yiayiá gave me a school textbook. It's a simple reading book to practise with.'

Mary flicked through it and reached the page where there was a portrait of Georgios Papadopoulos. She had to overcome the desire to rip it out. Now that school books were published by the government, there was an image of him in every single one.

'And she said that next year I will have to start learning the formal language. It's got a funny name.'

'*Katharévousa*,' her mother said curtly. 'But I think the spoken kind is enough for now.'

Mary tried her best to hide any regrets over allowing her daughter to visit her parents. But when Helena described the cocktail party her grandfather had held, she found it very hard to contain them.

'I wasn't allowed to go,' Helena told her. 'Even Grandma didn't go into the room. But I spied on them standing about in the hallway. They all looked important and they all had big cars and chauffeurs, like Pappoú.'

Mary had read that there was a restriction on gatherings of more than five people in Greece. How typical that there was one rule for the well-connected and another for the rest.

When they got home, the postcard that Helena had written was lying on the mat. She picked it up and her parents smiled as she read it out, repeating much of what had been related in the car.

26 July 1968

I had chocolate ice cream with pieces of real chocolate and lemonade with real lemons. Went on a journey to the seaside, then went swimming. Watched boys water-skiing but Yiayiá says only boys can do it. Tomatoes very red here and melon is pink with huge black pips. Battle display with Pappoú and the prime minister talked. Went to National Gardens to see dancers. Lots of love, H xxx

She had written exactly the same words to her best friend, Jenny, squeezing them onto the back of an image of the Acropolis, a place she had not yet seen close to. Her grandmother had promised it for the following year.

'You'll have to send us a card as soon as you arrive next summer,' laughed her father.

'Next summer?' His wife shot him a look of irritation. 'We'll see about that.'

She knew that Helena's blandly worded postcard had probably been perused by the military regime. This first visit to Athens had been hotly debated before she and Hamish had agreed to it, and was the result of much compromise and negotiation. Eleni Papagiannis had written so many times inviting Helena to come, having accepted long ago that Mary herself would not return to Athens, at least not until her father had died.

It was the gentle Hamish McCloud who had persuaded his wife that it would be a terrible shame if Helena never met either of her grandparents, and that such a trip would be educational and confidence-building for their only child.

How could Mary, a teacher, deprive her daughter of perfecting a second language? The stifling conservatism of Greek society and the lack of space for dissent were already making the news in England, but ironically the military regime made it safe enough for a child to go, so Mary had relented.

'Please, Mum,' the child pleaded now. 'Yiayiá was so nice. And I promise I'll work even harder at my Greek next time. I'll come back fluent!'

'We'll see,' Mary said, hoping that the junta might be overthrown as unexpectedly as it had taken power.

A week or so later, they were in the car together travelling to Scotland, to see her father's side of the family. Helena mentioned all the soldiers and policemen she had seen in the streets and how her grandmother was always telling her how safe it was having them there.

'It depends what kind of world you want to live in,' her mother responded. 'Personally, I would rather live in a free one and risk my bag being pinched. But in any case, that's not a daily occurrence in our lives, is it?'

The last time anyone's wallet had been stolen in Dellbridge had been at the funfair three years earlier, and it had made the front page of the local paper.

The trip up to Scotland took longer than Helena's journey to Athens. They sang a few songs to pass the time, mostly rounds, and then Helena hummed the tune that had been stuck inside her head for a fortnight now.

'Oré, Geórgio Papadópoule . . . Oré, Geórgio Papadópoule.'

Her mother spun around in the passenger seat.

'Stamáta Élena! Amésos! Stop that right now! I never want to hear you singing that ever again. Do you understand?'

Helena had never seen her mother look so angry. And no, she did not really understand.

Up until now, Helena had never questioned her mother's simple explanation for not coming to Greece with her. She always told her that Athens was too hot in the summer and that she preferred to swim in the North Sea rather than in the Aegean, but Mary's irrational response to the song remained with her, even as the week passed in a chaos of barbecues on gale-swept lochsides and swims in the wild waves with her five red-headed cousins.

On their way home, they stopped for a night in Edinburgh.

'The Athens of the North,' said her father proudly, as they approached the city.

Helena made a zigzag with her forefinger across her misted-up window and peered through it. On this damp August day, she was baffled that the place was so named.

In the afternoon, Hamish McCloud led the way up Calton Hill in the drizzle to show his wife and daughter the National Monument. It was an incomplete copy of the Parthenon.

Mary McCloud read aloud from the guidebook. '"Unfinished through lack of funds, this nineteenth-century replica was built with local sandstone. The project was promoted by Lord Elgin, who wanted to link his name with the glory of ancient Athens."'

'I know it's not exactly the Acropolis,' said Hamish. 'But they did their best.'

'This was their *best*?'

Helena had never seen such scorn from her mother.

'Elgin?' she scoffed. 'The man who did his best to destroy the original? Outrageous vandal and thief!'

Mary McCloud turned away, muttering angrily in Greek.

'I'm going back to the car,' she said over her shoulder.

With rain trickling down her neck, her anorak already soaked through and her hair frizzing to double its normal volume, Helena lingered for a moment. She looked up at the twelve rain-streaked columns against the slate-grey sky, perplexed.

'Come on, Dad, let's go and find Mum,' she said. 'Maybe she feels a bit homesick.'

Holding her father's hand, she led the way back down the hill.

Chapter Two

The following summer, Mary took a call from her mother to say that Stamatis Papagiannis had had a fall. Helena was welcome to come, but she would be a bit preoccupied with looking after him. Her ticket was already paid for, however, and Helena reassured her mother that she was perfectly content to go. There would be a few outings with Dina, at least, and this time a language tutor had been hired to give her daily lessons.

She arrived the day that Apollo 11 was to land on the moon. The previous term she had won a prize for her project on space travel. Science excited her more than any other subject at school, and she had grasped the effects of gravity, the speed a rocket needed to travel at, what the astronauts would eat, what their clothes had to be made of, how they communicated with Earth. The moon landing was going to be the most thrilling event of her life. The world was waiting to watch it relayed live from thousands of miles away, and as she was driven to Kolonaki, she spotted American flags fluttering from every building and big television screens being put up in the main squares. Unlike her grandparents, few people were wealthy enough to have their own.

When she arrived, her grandmother came out briefly into the hallway to greet her, and then disappeared again into the bedroom. The first thing Helena noticed was how tired she looked. It must be hard to care for an invalid.

The second thing she spotted, as she passed the doorway to the drawing room, was that the television in the drawing room was missing. In the kitchen with Dina, who had made her supper, she plucked up courage to ask the maid if she was going to watch the moon landing.

'I'd like to,' Dina said. 'But the television has been moved to your grandparents' bedroom for now.'

'Oh . . .' said Helena, scarcely able to conceal her disappointment.

'And he doesn't want *anyone* going in there,' Dina added regretfully. 'Just your grandmother. And me with their food.'

When the clock in the hallway struck ten, Helena and Dina were sitting at the kitchen table reading a simple book in Greek together. At that moment, they both knew that the countdown for landing had begun.

Helena glanced at Dina, her eyes full of tears. 'I don't think it's fair,' she said.

'Look,' Dina said, 'I want to see this too. If we're very quiet, we can go down to the square and watch it there.'

'But my grandmother would never agree to you taking me out so late, would she?'

'I don't think she'll know. You'll just have to pretend for the rest of your stay here that you didn't see it.'

Helena threw her arms around Dina and they briefly hugged one another, partners in the crime they were about to commit.

Dina quickly untied her apron, grabbed the key off the hook and took Helena's hand. She opened and closed the door soundlessly, and instead of using the lift, which tended to judder and clank, they padded down the five flights of stairs to the hallway. Dina whispered something to Kýrios Manolis that made him smile. A moment later, they were outside and running down the street. 'Don't worry, Helena. He's my friend. He won't tell anyone,' Dina said.

Before getting to the square, they passed an electrical goods store where people had already taken their positions to watch the TV sets that were on in the window. This was history in so many ways. For Greece, it was the first ever live transmission.

As they approached the square itself, Helena could see that outside every café a small crowd spilled onto the pavement, everyone jostling to see a screen. She and Dina stopped outside the nearest one, packed with old, young and plenty of policemen. People let Helena through to the front, where a band of even smaller children had gathered to witness the moment.

A few minutes later, the blurred image of the moon's surface appeared on the screen above their heads. It was pocked with craters, pitted like the lumpy porridge Helena always had to eat in Scotland. The area they were going to land on was called the Sea of Tranquility, but the faces of the men at Mission Control were anything but calm. It looked cold and treacherous up there, and Helena was certain that she could hear anxiety in the muffled voices of the astronauts.

Then came the euphoria and the relief. They were down safely and everyone in every café and bar around the square and around the world cheered and clapped. 'Bravo! Bravo!' There was no one without a smile on their face and the other children excitedly included Helena in a spontaneous circle that turned round and round until they were all dizzy.

'*Prótos ándras sto fengári! Prótos ándras sto fengári!*' they chanted. 'First man on the moon!'

It was a joyful moment. The café was offering shots of *tsípouro* to the adults and orangeade to the children, and they all raised their glasses:

'To the man on the moon!'

Dina elbowed her way through to Helena, her cheeks flushed from the alcohol.

'Come on, *Elenáki mou*. We should go now.'

'Oh Dina! Please!'

Helena was caught up in the fun of the moment and wanted to stay all night with her new friends. It was the first time she had met

Greek children, and she was bedazzled by the way they had drawn her into their midst.

'*Prépei na fýgoume.*'

Even if she had not spoken a word of Greek, Helena would have known from the tone of the maid's voice what she was saying. They must leave.

As they came out into the street, Helena noticed that the moon was right above them. A perfect half-moon, a bright white semicircle. It was so far away, but up there, somewhere, men had landed. It was a moment of history and she had seen it with her own eyes.

They crept past Kýrios Manolis, who was asleep in his chair. When they were back inside the apartment and the door had been quietly closed, Helena went to bed. She was still shaking with excitement. She and Dina had agreed that very early the following morning they would get up to go and watch the astronauts take their first steps on the moon. It was another moment that neither of them wanted to miss.

Before it was even light, they tiptoed out again and reached the café in time to see Neil Armstrong making his tentative descent down the steps and onto the surface of the moon.

For Helena, it was even more thrilling than the craft itself coming down to land. People all around them were chatting noisily, but she listened intently, at an advantage because the spine-tingling words, the first ever to be spoken on the moon, were in her own language.

'That's one small step for man, one giant leap for mankind,' came the fuzzy sound of Armstrong's voice from more than two hundred thousand miles away.

As they left the café, it was getting light and Helena looked up to see that the moon was no longer visible. Soon she was back in bed while Dina stayed up to begin her chores for the day. The pair of them had shared a great adventure as her grandparents slept.

Later that day, her grandmother asked her if she would like to watch a military parade on the television. She would set up a chair in the bedroom so that she could view it with her grandfather. Helena was incredulous. They had taken no interest in a momentous event in world history the day before and had happily deprived her of seeing it too. And now they wanted her to watch a parade, and a recording of a parade at that.

It was a beautiful sunny day and she could think of nothing worse than sitting in a darkened bedroom to watch a small screen, but knew she had no real choice.

The bedroom curtains were drawn, but a sharp shaft of sunlight gave enough illumination for Helena to see her grandfather lying on the top of the bed, his legs stretched out in front of him. One of them was bandaged up to the thigh, the other was naked, with varicose veins meandering up and down it like big, fat purple worms. His toes were twisted and his yellowing nails were long and cracked. Helena was both repulsed and mesmerised by the sight.

Her grandmother sat on the side of the bed and Helena perched on a chair feeling awkward. Her grandfather appeared to be dozing, so she was too afraid even to ask them whether they had seen the moon landing, the only thing that had been on her mind all day.

Suddenly there was a grunt from Stamatis Papagiannis as he stirred and then opened his eyes. He saw Helena sitting there.

'Your grandmother said you were coming,' he said grumpily, acknowledging her presence but little more. 'You're just in time for the parade.'

Helena managed a smile and then sat there dutifully watching the television. Her grandfather explained who was who, and she nodded occasionally to show she was listening, even though none of it interested her. All the strutting up and down seemed utterly pointless in comparison to a man's first careful steps on the moon.

When the dancing began, her grandmother took her hand and led her round in a circle at the foot of the bed, attempting to teach her some of the steps. Out of the corner of her eye, she watched the *fustanélla*-clad Evzones. At first she was impressed that these tall men could dance with the daintiness of ballerinas, their pompom slippers always landing exactly when and where they should. Soon, though, she realised that the same steps were repeated monotonously, time after time after time.

As soon as the programme ended, she was allowed to leave the room and gratefully went back out into the early-evening light and onto the balcony, where she sat for a while trying to learn some verb constructions to impress the tutor who was scheduled to be coming for the first time the following day. Her concentration was disturbed at one point by the sound of her grandfather's voice gruffly shouting Dina's name. He was silent again after a while, but only after a door had banged several times.

She was curious when the doorbell rang, as they were not expecting any visitors that day. She heard the inner door being opened and the sound of Dina's voice, followed by a man's. Easily distracted from her homework, she went out into the hall, but whoever had come to the house had already disappeared into her grandparents' bedroom. Perhaps it was a doctor.

Dina was in the kitchen preparing something for dinner, and Helena ambled in to talk to her.

'Do you want me to test you?' asked the maid. She sounded like she had a cold.

Helena handed over her exercise book and the two of them sat down at the table.

'*O ánthropos pátise sti selíni*,' Dina said, smiling. 'Man landed on the moon.'

'*Eídame ton ánthropo na patáei sti selíni*,' responded Helena. 'We saw man landing on the moon.'

'*Brávo, Elenáki mou*,' Dina said, praising her for mastering the complex grammatical construction.

At that moment, Helena's grandmother walked in.

'Can you make Arsenis some coffee, Dina.'

'Who is Arsenis?' asked Helena.

32

'He's your grandfather's nephew, *agápi mou*. Your uncle,' said Yiayiá.

Helena had never thought about other relatives she might have in Greece.

'He's come to see your grandfather, but I know he would be happy to meet his young relative.'

Yiayiá left the kitchen, and a few moments later, a slight man, older than her father but younger than her *pappoú* by a long way, with copious greying hair styled into a severe side parting and plastered down with Brylcreem, strode into the room. Helena noted how neatly his moustache was clipped, how crisp were the creases in his trousers, how white his short-sleeved shirt, how polished his brown shoes. For the heat of the day, he seemed too smartly dressed.

From the way Dina greeted him, it was obvious that he was a regular visitor but not one she liked. She knew to make his coffee sweet without asking, and put it on the table, along with a glass of iced water that she clumsily slopped and a piece of *loukoúmi*, a Greek sweet. Helena noticed that he did not say thank you.

'So, this is Helena McCloud,' he said in English, with an accent that Helena had only heard on BBC television. He put out his hand to shake hers, and she looked up at him before taking it. His skin was cold and dry. 'And how do you like Athens, my little redhead?' he asked.

'I like it very much,' Helena answered, blushing to her roots with fury. Uncle Arsenis was still holding her hand tight, and she had to tug it away from him.

'I must take you to some museums,' he said. 'Have you been to the National Archaeological?'

'No,' she said.

'Your uncle would be a good guide,' said her grandmother, walking in. 'He's an expert in ancient things.'

Helena noticed the smile that spread across his face.

'Well, I should go. And perhaps next time we'll go on a little jaunt together.'

He winked at her as he said this, and Helena hoped that she would not have to go on any such jaunt. This uncle gave her the creeps, from the feel of his bristly moustache, which had brushed her face like a garden broom when he bent to kiss her on the cheek, to his audacity in calling her 'redhead'. Just because he was family didn't mean he had any such right to be so familiar.

As he left the apartment, Helena noticed him pick up a small canvas holdall that had been left by the front door.

With her grandmother entirely preoccupied with her bed-bound husband's needs, Helena was left in Dina's company again, and at dusk, the maid asked her if she wanted another adventure.

Except for the early-morning excursion to the square, Helena had been inside all day, and she nodded enthusiastically.

'Will Yiayiá mind?'

'She suggested it, *paidí mou*.'

They walked side by side through Kolonaki Square and down Vasilissis Sofias Avenue. It was one of the grandest streets of the city and led to the parliament building, from where they turned left towards the National Gardens. They passed many groups of soldiers on their way, but Helena was used to that by now.

'Have you been to a cinema before?' asked Dina as they walked.

'Yes,' Helena answered. It seemed a strange question to ask a child. Of course she had. Three times. The film she had loved best of all was *The Sound of Music*, and she had learned the words to all the songs from the record her parents had given her for her birthday.

'This one might be a bit different,' said Dina with a twinkle in her eye.

Soon they arrived at their destination, the Aegli cinema, and Helena saw a group of people standing by a gap in a long wall. Dina purchased tickets from a small kiosk, then they queued at a stall for souvlaki and went inside. Taking seats in the second row, they waited for the film to begin, enjoying a delicious feast of juicy cubes of meat made all the more succulent by a squeeze of lemon juice.

With a fizzy orange drink in her hand, Helena was bursting with excitement even before the programme began. Above them, swallows swooped and dived against the inky sky.

Higher still was the waxing moon, a fraction larger than the night before and even brighter. She was just thinking about the astronauts and whether they were still up there when the lights went down and they were all plunged into darkness.

Operation Apollo had been carefully chosen by Dina, but not because the title was uncannily appropriate for this day in history. The theme itself had no connection with the moon landing. It was about a German prince who falls in love with a ravishing Greek tour guide who is taking a party of tourists around Athens. The light-hearted banter and the singing and dancing were meant to appeal to everyone, old, young and foreign, and it was subtitled, so Dina knew Helena would easily follow the plot. The child did not need to know it was also a film approved by the junta regime, nor that there was nothing much else on offer these days.

For Helena, even the walk home, just after eleven o'clock, was exciting and novel. She noticed that lots of children were still in the streets with their parents or playing in squares with their friends. The previous evening had been the first of her whole life when she'd stayed up until midnight. And now she was doing it again. She was loving Athens more by the day.

'Did you enjoy it?' Dina asked her.

'Yes,' she cried out. 'It's the best film I have ever seen!'

'It's a nice picture of Greece,' agreed Dina. 'But not everywhere is like that.'

Helena was puzzled by the note of criticism in her voice.

To her dismay, Uncle Arsenis turned up again the following day.

'I promised your grandmother that I would show you round the National Archaeological Museum. So here I am,' he said cheerfully.

Helena knew she had no choice. They left the apartment and

crossed to the shady side of the street. It was not a long walk to the museum, but the heat was intense and she began to feel nauseous as she tried to keep up with Arsenis's brisk pace.

The great pillared building came into view, and she was relieved when Arsenis told her that he did not intend to show her every object in every room.

'Just a few highlights,' he said. 'The fewer things you see, the greater the impression each one will make.'

Helena nodded, remembering a school trip to the British Museum when they had visited all the galleries and looked at artefacts from every millennium and every world civilisation. She recalled nothing except confusion about what went with what, and whether the Romans came before or after the Greeks. How had the Egyptians fitted in with them? And what was a massive obelisk actually for? Why was there a statue from Easter Island there, or huge quantities of sculptures from the Parthenon?

'I will show you only beautiful things. Not the most historical, or the most important. Just the most beautiful.'

Her recollection of the British Museum was of monumental objects, perhaps there because of their size or antiquity rather than their beauty, so her interest was immediately piqued.

For the next hour, Arsenis took her from room to room. Occasionally he guided her by the arm, and she flinched, feeling his cold hand on her bare skin. Why could she not simply follow his neat little footsteps?

She soon realised that her uncle's choices were his personal taste. He salivated over anything gold. The Mask of Agamemnon was one of the first things they came to. With its blank, expressionless eyes, it reminded Helena of a creepy Halloween mask. Arsenis seemed to love it for the myths surrounding the man, the all-powerful commander of the Greeks.

'He sacrificed his *daughter*,' he said with bloodthirsty admiration, as if this was the ultimate act of heroism. All Helena could do was nod.

Close to the mask was the fine gold covering made for a baby's dead body, with face, tiny feet and even miniature earrings. She lingered for a moment, remembering a friend in her class losing her little brother, and felt a lump in her throat.

Meanwhile, Arsenis was urging her to come and see a case filled with gold jewellery, in particular the finely wrought rings made for men. He himself wore a signet ring on his little finger, and Helena sensed that he would love to have worn one of these too.

When he moved on to find his next favourite exhibit, Helena paused by a cabinet of simple pottery. Included was a cup from a Mycenaean tomb, delicate with a spiral design and fine handles. She thought it miraculous that it had survived nearly three and a half thousand years. It was exactly the same shape as a favourite mug at home.

'Come on, redhead,' Arsenis called loudly across the gallery, causing other visitors to stare. 'You've got some company here.'

Helena wandered across to the exhibit he was pointing at.

'"Head of a kore. End of the sixth century BC",' he read out to her. 'Look at that hair! You're not the only one, see? And curly, too.'

The evidence of red paint on the bust's hair was indeed still evident. The pigment they used must have been strong to last so many centuries.

As Arsenis spoke, Helena had felt his hand stroking her head, and even when he moved off, she realised that the smell of his cologne still lingered in her hair.

On they went, through the galleries, passing at speed the things that Helena found lovely and pausing only at her uncle's favourites.

'Here's another one you'll like,' he said, entirely oblivious to any of her reactions. 'This is a *stamnos*, a type of urn, with a beautifully painted abduction of your namesake by Theseus. Doesn't look too unhappy, does she, being dragged off by a man? Hardly a rape, really.'

She didn't know what the word 'rape' meant, but the way he was talking made her feel distinctly uncomfortable. This only got worse when he took her arm and marched her to a statue of Aphrodite. The goddess was naked except for a drape that she held with her left hand to cover her pubic area. With her right hand she seemed to touch one nipple, leaving the other breast totally exposed.

'What a naughty little flirt, eh? Quite the seductress. The bosom is one thing, but wait until you see her backside. That's the best part.'

Helena pulled her arm away and walked off. She did not care if he thought her rude. She thought *him* disgusting.

She wanted to return to the previous room. There was something that had caught her eye, something sculpted that could not have been more different from the statue of Aphrodite. It was a young woman, her head modestly inclined, carved in profile on a marble headstone. She appeared to be holding a chest. Helena read the label and understood that this was what was called a stele. Unlike the gravestones in her local churchyard in Suffolk, which were just inscribed with the name of the deceased and their dates, in ancient Greek times these bore a person's likeness. She wished her Aunt Moira, who had died two years before at only forty years old, had a carved portrait of herself on her headstone, rather than just her name in cold capital letters. It would have been a much nicer way to remember her.

She had had enough of this outing and quickly retraced her steps to the Aphrodite room, where Arsenis was looking at another version of the goddess, less voluptuous but this time standing next to Eros.

'I'm really thirsty,' she said boldly. 'And I want to go home.'

'So did you like my selection of beautiful things?' he asked her as they left the museum.

'I think the things *I* think are beautiful are different from the ones *you* think are beautiful.'

'And what is the difference?' sneered her uncle.

Helena hesitated for a moment. Usually there was a right and a wrong answer to a question. How else could school exams work?

'All I know,' she responded with a note of defiance, 'is that they are not the same.'

'It is one of the universe's untouchable truths,' he continued, as if lecturing. 'Beauty exists. And is the most precious thing there is. And yet none of us can truly define it or agree what it actually is. But when you see it, it casts a spell on you.'

Yes, Helena thought. You like seeing women naked or attacked. And gold. I don't.

On the way home, she played a game with herself, putting everything she saw into one of two categories: the beautiful or the un-beautiful. Trees, the colour of the sky, a small dog trotting along behind its owners on a lead. These things seemed beautiful. A lorry, a newly built hotel, two men shouting at each other in the street. These were anything but.

She was still silently playing this game as Arsenis accompanied her up in the lift. The harsh lights were not beautiful, but there was a loveliness to her grandmother's face as she opened the door for them. Her grandfather, who had been helped off the bed and was now in the drawing room, was unsightly in every way. Helena knew that he had once been a proud and handsome man, and the apartment was full of photographs illustrating this, but nothing whatsoever about him suggested beauty. Dina, small and kind, with her soft creased skin and dark hair, seemed as beautiful as anyone she had ever seen. Was it her sparkling hazel eyes? Or the reason that her eyes sparkled in the first place? Her conclusion about Arsenis was that he was the very opposite of beautiful. She found him creepy. She would be happy if she never saw him again.

She did not have to go on another excursion with Arsenis that summer, but he did come to the apartment on several occasions and he usually spent the time in Stamatis Papagiannis's study, sometimes for several hours, or in his bedroom if her grandfather was resting.

A much more welcome guest, for Helena at least, was her tutor, an enthusiastic university graduate called Thomas. He came for two hours each visit and Helena always wished it was for longer. He believed that the most exciting way to extend vocabulary was to learn words *in situ*, so they sometimes went out for a walk: one day to a *laikí agorá*, a street market, where she learned the name of every fruit and herb, another time to a bookstore, where they browsed the shelves and Helena memorised the section titles. They also went to the local hardware store, where she grasped the words for every imaginable tool and household utensil, from *xeskonistíri* (duster) to *gialócharto* (sandpaper). A toyshop was fun as well, and the owner was so enchanted by her grasp of the language that he gave her a Scrabble set in Greek before they left. There was one outing with Thomas, however, that Helena enjoyed less than the others. This was to the National Historical Museum. Her understanding of the country's history was beginning to grow, but there seemed to have been so many wars and conflicts and leaders with long names that it remained a challenge. The only thing she liked was that many captions were only in Greek, and she was now able to read some of them.

Before she knew it, Helena's last day in Athens arrived. The time had passed so happily, with her language tuition and brief outings with Dina, that she was sorry to be leaving.

That morning, her grandmother was in the bedroom with a doctor helping Stamatis in his attempts to walk. Entertaining her granddaughter had not been Eleni Papagiannis's priority this summer. Helena had packed her case and was aimlessly wandering about in the apartment before leaving. Seeing that Dina was polishing some picture frames, she asked her to explain who the other people were in some of the images displayed in the hallway and drawing room.

'That was Andreas, your mother's brother,' explained Dina, pointing out the photograph of a young army recruit whom Helena had assumed was her grandfather as a very young man. 'He was a handsome boy. Four years older than your mother.'

'What happened to him?'

'He died in a battle. The last one at the end of the civil war.'

'That's so sad. My mother never mentioned him . . . or a civil war. Perhaps it's still too painful to talk about.'

'Things can be like that,' said Dina reflectively. 'Civil war is a very terrible thing. Brother fighting brother.'

'Brothers?'

'Sometimes. Yes. Even within the same family there could be a division. But what I really meant was Greeks fighting and killing Greeks.'

'But how did that happen? I thought the Nazis were the enemy.' Helena was struggling with the history.

'You would have thought when we got rid of them that everyone would have been tired of war, wouldn't you? But things only got worse. There were Greek communists who had put up resistance against the Nazis, and afterwards they wanted their share of power. And because of that, fighting broke out between the communists and people who hated them. Both sides wanted to be in charge of Greece.'

'Oh,' said Helena. It did not really make sense to her. Why people would want to carry on fighting when the Nazis had gone was impossible for her to grasp.

On an adjacent shelf, there were several more images of Andreas Papagiannis, at his graduation and in uniform with his regiment. In a low voice, so that there was no chance of being overheard, even from behind the closed door of the bedroom, Dina explained to Helena that her grandparents had been stricken with grief when Andreas was killed. Helena now understood the significance of the little white jug of fresh flowers kept next to the pictures and renewed every other day.

What Dina did not tell her was that Stamatis Papagiannis believed it had been a heroic war, won for God and for Greece, while his wife believed it was a waste of youth and a waste of life.

In the framed wedding picture of her grandparents, her *yiayiá* looked as young and as vulnerable as a child. Dressed in a simple white gown that reached her ankles, a circle of flowers around her head, she resembled a doll. Stamatis Papagiannis, in uniform, towered over her. More than ten years her senior, he looked old enough to be her father. It was an incongruous pairing.

There was also a group photograph taken at the wedding that included a boy of around four years old.

'That's Arsenis,' Dina explained. 'And the man next to him is his father, your grandfather's brother.'

'Arsenis isn't really my uncle, then? He's my mother's cousin?'

'Something like that, I suppose.'

Most striking of all was the sizeable painted portrait of Stamatis Papagiannis hanging over the fireplace in the impressive drawing room. Its sobriety was only brightened by the colourful ribbons of the medals that decorated his uniform. His puffed-out chest gave him an air of extreme self-regard and pomposity. It must be the image of himself he loved most, thought Helena, to hang it in pride of place.

There were many photographs of General Papagiannis too, solo or with his regiment, and also with well-known businessmen and politicians, all of them barrel-chested, severe. In the most recent, he was pictured with the triumvirate of the junta: Papadopoulos, Pattakos and Makarezos.

Of Helena's mother, Mary, there was not a single photograph as teenager or bride. She only appeared as a toddler next to her brother, the pair of them standing stiffly in front of their parents. Her grandmother appeared just twice: in the two wedding photographs. Dina made no comment on this, but Helena was sure she noticed it too.

Helena did not know what to make of this vain collection that she had walked by so many times but had never really studied before.

The driver had arrived to pick her up. She knocked gently on her grandparents' door and Eleni Papagiannis came out to wish her farewell.

'Have a good flight, *Elenáki mou*. I hope your *pappoú* will be on his feet again next year.'

Helena's postcard to Suffolk had been stamped and sent a few days earlier without reference to the moon landing. As she said goodbye to her *yiayiá*, she was still longing to ask why she and her grandfather had been content to deprive her of seeing this historical moment. This summer had revealed that there could be another side to adults. It had unsettled her.

Chapter Three

By the summer of 1970, as his wife had hoped, Stamatis Papagiannis had made a reasonable recovery. He leaned even more heavily on his stick than before, but was able to get about the apartment, and spent a good part of the day in his study, much of it on the telephone. Helena's visit was to take place as planned, and she hoped that Dina would have time to spend with her as she had the previous year.

She soon learned a new word from her Greek tutor: *káfsonas*, literally meaning 'the burning'. The temperature soared. Even by Athens's standards, the days were almost unbearably hot and the nights equally so, with the mercury rarely dropping below forty degrees.

During the whole of the first week, her grandparents insisted that it was perilous to go out, and they sat under the slowly rotating ceiling fans watching dance displays and comedy films on the television. She was grateful that her lessons with her now beloved Thomas continued, taken in the relative cool of the dining room. They were reading a simple version of the Greek myths together.

Helena noticed that there were no allowances made for Dina, who was still expected to keep the apartment clean and run about waiting on Stamatis Papagiannis hand and foot. It was certainly not considered too hot for her to go out shopping, and Helena happily escaped to the outside world to help Dina with her errands. On her return, she had the obligatory siesta in her stuffy bedroom.

In the second week, when the temperature had finally cooled, Eleni Papagiannis told her that they were going to a ceremony. The granddaughter of her closest friend was joining the Youth Legion, known as Álkimoi, and there was to be a big public event. In the late afternoon, the driver took them to the ancient Panathenaic Stadium and Helena watched as ranks of uniformed teenagers, boys and girls, stepped forward to swear an oath of allegiance to the movement. Hundreds of them marched up and down in time to the beating of military drums, all identically clad in navy with wide white belts, the girls in knee-length socks to match.

There were bishops and soldiers present, and the most shocking moment for Helena was when she saw even the very smallest of the recruits raise their right arm in a fascist salute. She had seen such a gesture in her favourite film, *The Sound of Music*, in a scene with Nazi soldiers, but she had never imagined that such a thing still happened.

'Look, look, there's Marianthi!' Eleni Papagiannis cried out, spotting her friend's granddaughter in the crowd, her little hand in the air.

'Marianthi is the youngest *ever* to become a member,' said the child's grandmother to Helena with enormous pride. 'We are very proud of her. Just ten years old. She has been waiting for this moment.'

The whole thing reminded Helena of the Girl Guide movement, which she wanted to join because she heard they went camping and climbing. Her mother was very against her becoming a member, and if it was similarly militaristic, she now understood why.

When it was all over, they collected Marianthi. They were going to celebrate with ice-cream sundaes at Zonars, and the girls were meant to become friends simply on the basis of being girls.

Marianthi, still in her beret, chatted excitedly about what it was like to march like a soldier.

'I shall never, *ever* break my oath,' she pronounced. 'For as long as I live, I will serve my country.'

'Bravo, bravo!' the child's grandmother applauded.

Helena tried not to laugh.

The celebration came to an abrupt end when a large blob of pink ice cream dripped from Marianthi's spoon onto her uniform. For the small blonde-haired child, the afternoon was ruined. Her screams brought waiters hurrying over with paper tissues, damp cloths, towels, anything they could find that might stem the tide of her tears. Another ice cream? Chocolate gateau? Nothing would console her.

With Marianthi's grandmother apologising profusely, the two of them left Helena and her *yiayiá* sitting in the café.

'She must be very overtired,' said Eleni Papagiannis sympathetically. 'Such a long day.'

Helena bit her tongue. They finished their own ice creams, then went outside to where the driver was waiting for them.

Helena happily spent the next day at home learning some new grammar in preparation for Thomas's visit. When he arrived, he announced that he had planned a trip to the Central Market. The Varvakios market, as it was known, turned out to be the most exciting visual experience of Helena's summer. The first giant hall he took her into was packed as far as the eye could see with fish stalls. She could not count how many there were, perhaps one hundred? She scribbled in her vocabulary book as Thomas pointed out all the different fish. Bream, bass, barbounia, mullet, mackerel, she learned all the names. And then the shellfish, most of which she did not even recognise, including the strangely shaped *kolochtýpa*, which looked a bit like a lobster but much friendlier. Squid, octopus, sea urchins . . . by the end, she knew them all, and had vivid images in her mind to help her.

What amazed her most was the lack of smell. Unlike the stink of her local fish shop in Dellbridge, everything here was so freshly caught that the odour was very bearable. The other surprise was the volume of noise. The sellers were all giants, with giant hands and giant voices, each one shouting to be heard above the others to attract the attention of customers. These were housewives and restaurateurs, Thomas told Helena, and they might spend hours comparing prices and quality. Helena found it thrilling: the shapes and colours of the fish, the bustle, the characters, the banter.

Then it was time to go into the equally enormous meat hall. Rows of carcasses swung from hooks, the floor was slippery with blood, and the butchers' blocks were worn and stained by years of chopping. Helena was less enamoured of this part of the market, where the heads of sheep and cows were often still attached to their bodies, tongues lolling out, eyeballs staring.

'We'll just learn all the names for the different cuts,' said Thomas. 'Then we'll go home.' He explained that even parts of an animal that she might find disgusting were not wasted; some of them were delicacies.

The strong smell of raw flesh began to affect Helena, and she quickly noted a few words connected with butchery before asking Thomas if they could leave. It was a relief to find herself outside and breathing in the smell of exhaust fumes once again.

Back in the apartment, they played a game where she was a customer who needed to order a certain quantity of fish, state how much she was prepared to pay and say what she would make with it. Dina walked into the dining room and joined in. She wanted to play a difficult customer. The three of them were laughing so much that Stamatis Papagiannis stormed in and castigated them for making such a noise. He sent Dina from the room, and afterwards Helena could hear him continuing to shout at her.

Before leaving Athens, there was another cultural outing with Arsenis Papagiannis to be endured. This time he took her to a magnificent white mansion just ten minutes' walk from Evdokias. It looked like a private house, but once inside, she discovered it was set out like a museum, with objects, both ancient and modern, displayed in cabinets. Arsenis did not deliver any lectures this time, but instead pressed his nose against the glass and made notes and sketches in a pad. He seemed particularly interested in some ancient vases. Helena felt she had seen enough of those before and made no attempt to hide her boredom.

'I'm going to stay on this floor,' he told her. 'Why don't you go and explore on your own?'

The museum was agreeably air-conditioned, and Helena happily went off to wander through the three floors alone. It felt very grown up, and she was happy to get away from her uncle and the pungent aroma that hung around him.

When she had paced every room, she came down again and found Arsenis perusing a cracked vase. It seemed the two of them were the only visitors in the building, so he was in nobody's way as he sketched it from different angles.

'*Pénte leptá,*' said the guard. 'Five minutes.'

Arsenis snapped his pad shut and slid his silver pencil neatly into his top pocket. 'Your grandmother will be wondering where we are,' he said. 'Let's go.'

Helena recoiled at the feeling of his icy hand on her arm as he led her towards the exit, where he said a polite good evening to the staff on the desk.

'Goodnight, Kýrie Papagiannis,' one of them responded, and she was surprised to learn that they knew his name. He must be a regular visitor.

'What will you do with your drawings?' she asked.

'Nothing . . . nothing,' he answered. 'Just a little hobby of mine.'

As they made their way home, he held her arm as if she were a possession. It was impossible to shrug him off. There was one street with a few shops that displayed what looked like ancient objects in their windows. Arsenis noticed that Helena was interested, and they stopped to look into one of them.

'Why aren't those things in museums?' she asked him.

'Well, they are very valuable but not unique,' he answered. 'So it means that people can buy them for their homes.'

'If they are rich,' Helena said. It seemed strange to her that someone would actually want a statue in their house, unless it was a stately home, of course.

'Yes, Helena. Only the rich. And there's nothing wrong with that.'

He seemed to tighten his grip on her arm as he said this, and only when they got to Evdokias 45 did he release it. As the lift ascended, Helena willed it to speed up, so queasy did she feel from his scent.

Arsenis was at the apartment again the following day. It was her grandfather's *giortí*, St Stamatios's name day, and Stamatis Papagiannis was celebrating.

That morning, Helena had found a gift on her bed from her grandmother. Perhaps everyone had presents on a saint's day, she thought, as she unwrapped the soft package with great excitement. Inside the folds of paper was a dress. Pink. The bodice was made of shiny satin, the skirt comprised alternating layers of taffeta and tulle, all blush-coloured. Even for a fancy dress party it would not have been what she would choose. The colour clashed hideously with her hair, and worst of all, it looked far too short. It might have fitted the previous year, but her grandparents had clearly not noticed that she had grown several inches since then. It would be way above her rather knobbly knees. She hurried into the kitchen to ask Dina what she was supposed to do with this awful costume. As she was holding it up to herself, both she and Dina began to giggle.

Eleni Papagiannis bustled into the room. '*Glykiá mou!* You're going to look lovely in that,' she proclaimed. 'Isn't it pretty?'

Helena mumbled something that her grandmother did not pick up, but the expression on her face revealed enough.

'Well, whether you like it or not,' Eleni snapped, 'your grandfather helped choose it a few weeks ago. So you have to wear it.' With those words, she left the room.

'It's *so* horrible,' said Helena despairingly.

'Treat it like a costume for a role in a play,' advised Dina. 'And you are playing the role of the little granddaughter who makes her grandparents proud. For one night only.'

On Eleni Papagiannis's instruction, Dina brushed Helena's hair and, with plenty of special oil to tame her curls, drew it into a tight bun. By the time she was zipped into the candyfloss frock and had buckled her sandals, she felt uncomfortable from head to toe.

Arsenis arrived half an hour before everyone else and, looking her up and down, told her how charming she looked. Helena stared him out, unsmiling.

At eight in the evening, Yiayiá took her into the drawing room to meet the guests while they had cocktails.

The weighty chandelier at the centre of the ceiling cast a kaleidoscopic pattern on every surface, from the crystal decanters to the diamond jewellery with which many of the women sparkled. With some relief, Helena thought *everyone* looked as if they were in fancy dress.

She politely answered the same banal questions over and over again as she circulated with a bowl of shelled pistachios. How did she like Athens? Did she like the language teacher her grandmother had hired for her? What did she want to do when she grew up? One woman, the wife of a man in military uniform, commented on her 'lovely dress, fit for a princess' and asked her if she wanted to be a ballerina.

'No,' said Helena flatly. 'I want to be an astronaut. I want to be the first woman in space.'

The husband, who wore more medals and ribbons on his chest than her grandfather, roared with laughter. 'She wants to be an *astronaut!*' he repeated to the guests around him, causing titters to ripple around the group.

Helena's grandmother took her to one side.

'Do *not*,' she hissed through her teeth, 'draw attention to yourself. Do you understand?'

Helena nodded and felt her grandmother's hand propelling her towards a small group on the other side of the room. Once this trio had commented on how tall she was for her age and heard her answers to their questions, Helena sensed that they would rather be talking to each other than to her, and was relieved when the dinner bell sounded and she was allowed to leave.

Dina had set her a place at the kitchen table, and while the maid scurried to and from the dining room, Helena enjoyed her meal of fish in lobster sauce.

Dina was an excellent cook. Her family owned a taverna, but she had expanded her very traditional repertoire by using some cookery books that Eleni had bought for her, which were translations of French classics. When visitors came, she showed off her talents to the full. Apart from the odd sprinkling of oregano by her mother, Helena had grown up on a mostly British diet. School dinners comprised fish shaped into fingers, Spam or corned beef, sauce that came out of a bottle, potatoes that had been mashed to a pulp and vegetables that were boiled to bleed them of colour. These summer trips to Athens were an education in flavours as well as much else, and by the time she had finished, her plate was so clean that she could see the delicate pattern of birds at its centre.

'Can I go to my room and read?' she asked Dina. 'I've only got a few chapters of my book to go.' She was racing through Enid Blyton's *Five on a Treasure Island*, enjoying every minute of the adventure.

The maid smiled, unused to being asked permission by anyone for anything, and carried on piping cream onto a five-tiered gateau.

As Helena crossed the hallway, her attention was caught by the sight of the hallway table. It was stacked high with parcels, each one colourfully wrapped and decorated with ribbons and bows. Most were between shoebox and chocolate box in size, and she surveyed the enticing pile.

They looked like presents for a little girl's birthday party, she thought, rather than offerings for her austere grandfather. He was hardly the sort to fiddle with pink bows and tightly fastened ribbons. She picked one of them up and shook it. It was surprisingly heavy for a small package.

On the other side of the tall double doors, she could hear the clinking of glasses and the percussion of cutlery on china. The low drone of male voices and the regular sound of women's laughter told her that the event was in full flow. Dina had not yet been called to collect the plates.

It was a mixture of boredom and curiosity that compelled her to do what she did next. Mischievousness also played a part: she was annoyed at the way her grandmother had told her off, for no reason at all, *and* made her wear this stupid dress.

She went into the kitchen, pulled open a drawer and took out some scissors. Dina did not even glance up. Back out in the hall, she began meticulously snipping the coloured cords, then sliding her finger beneath the tape and peeling away the wrapping paper. The gifts had to be opened at some point, so she was doing her grandfather a favour, wasn't she?

The boxes within were mostly of brown cardboard and of varying shapes. She arranged them in a row with the label bearing the donor's name tucked beneath, and stacked the paper and ribbon in a neat pile behind them. Only one item lacked a box; instead it was well padded in layers of tissue paper.

Helena had helped Dina lay the table and had been in charge of counting knives, side plates, crystal goblets and more, so she knew there were twenty-five guests, and each couple had brought a gift. She could still see Dina hard at work in the kitchen. She flipped open the end of the first box to take a look inside.

In the more square-shaped boxes she found some cups made of reddish-brown pottery with patterns of simple black lines, rather like the one she had admired in the museum. They were unexpectedly light, weighing no more than one of the ivory counters for her grandfather's backgammon board, or *távli*, as she now knew it. They were all similar in shape but with different patterns, and one had two handles. She grouped them together in a set.

In the largest box, she found a vase. Against its terracotta background, men on horseback with spears galloped all the way round. She ran her hand over the smooth shiny surface. It looked perfect, brand new, as though it had never before been taken out of the soft cloth in which it was wrapped.

The layers of tissue paper from the final package floated to the floor to reveal what looked like two stones you might pick up on a beach. They were strangely cold and, in comparison with everything else, heavy, but each fitted neatly into one of her palms. In the low orange glow of the sconces, it was not easy to see what they were or even if they were a single item broken in two. She took them into the kitchen, where a fluorescent strip gave her the light she needed.

She ran her fingernail over the serrated edge of the smaller piece. It was roughly an inch square and scored down the middle. Such a strange object. She turned the other one over. It was more rectangular, and down the centre was a clearly defined ridge. It seemed to Helena very odd indeed to give someone what looked like two bits of rubble.

A bell rang in the kitchen. It connected with the dining room. Dina was reading a newspaper, but sprang to her feet and hurried out and across the hallway.

The double doors were open now, and in the ochre light that flickered from the candelabra along the length of the table, Helena caught sight of flushed and happy faces.

Her grandfather was emerging, perhaps to fetch the wine that he had chosen to go with the dessert, or the drink called *tsípouro*, which looked like water but seemed to make men loud and angry. Twice now when Arsenis had come for dinner, she had been told to leave the table when the bottle was opened. It always marked a new stage of the evening.

53

Helena had a moment of panic in case he was cross about the opened packages. Perhaps she should have asked for permission.

Suddenly, from behind, she felt a firm grip on her shoulders.

'*Éla edó, korítsi mou!* Come with me, my girl!'

He spun her round, pushed her roughly backwards into the kitchen and shut the door firmly behind him with his foot.

'What have you done?' he said, leaning over her so that she could feel his spit on her face. 'How *dare* you touch my possessions? How *dare* you?'

His face was crimson with fury, almost beetroot red in this light. His veins seemed to protrude and pulsate. As he repeated himself, he shook her.

'How *dare* you?'

The rage was exactly how she imagined the eruption of a volcano. It was sudden, and then continued on and on and on.

She wanted to say that she was trying to help, but the words did not come. Being winded, it was impossible to speak.

'How dare you?' he said again, his voice at a higher pitch than she had ever heard from him, his large hands biting into the back of her neck.

On the nearby window ledge, there was a large basil plant, its leaves so profuse that Dina had stuck in a garden cane to support it. In one swift movement, Stamatis Papagiannis drew the stick out like a sword from its sheath and thrashed Helena on the calves. Once, twice, three times, four times, five. She was gasping for breath, so shocked she could not cry. All the while her fists clenched harder and harder round the two small objects that had intrigued her so much. In some strange way, it seemed to help her bear the pain.

With the sound of Dina's steps, she felt the tight grip on her arm release and saw the weapon quickly replaced. The door opened and the maid walked in.

Stamatis Papagiannis calmly walked over to the larder and Helena heard the fridge door being opened. He had a bottle of spirit in each hand when he returned. She stared at the floor, trembling but determined to hold back her tears.

Dina was bustling about with a pile of dirty plates, oblivious to her distress.

Once she had heard the double doors being closed and the sound of conversation was once again inaudible, Helena ran from the kitchen and headed down the corridor to her bedroom. On her way past the table, she noticed that an embroidered cloth now concealed everything she had carefully laid out there.

Throwing herself onto the bed, her face buried in the embroidered pillowcase to muffle any sound, her body began to convulse with sobs.

She had no idea how long she wept, but eventually exhaustion overcame her. She must have slept for an hour or so, because the noise that disturbed her was the sound of the guests gathering in the hallway to leave. While the noise gradually diminished, she lay there in the darkness and held her breath, hoping that her grandmother would not come into her room as she sometimes did.

A while later, she heard the door down the corridor being firmly shut. Her grandparents had gone to bed.

She sat up and put on a side light. Next to her on the bed were the two small stone fragments, and when she looked down, her palms bore their imprints. She must have been gripping them tightly even while sleeping. The protrusion on one had dug into her skin and the serrated edge of the other had made dents in her fingers.

Sliding open the drawer in the bedside cabinet, she put the pieces at the very back and shut it again. Then she went to the sink in the corner of her room, soaked a towel with cold water and dabbed at her burning legs. The cane had left bright criss-cross marks on her skin. It felt like scalding from an iron, but if anyone asked, she would pretend it was sunburn. It was impossible for her to unzip the dress herself, but anger gave her more than enough strength to rip the flimsy fabric from her body.

It was torn to shreds by the time she had finished, and she stuffed it under her bed.

Lying with the icy towel on the sheet beneath her sore skin, Helena stared at the ceiling, gradually feeling calmer. More than anything in the world, she wished to go home. She tried to think of something beautiful, but nothing came to her mind. Everything in this place was ugly.

The following morning, her damp sheets were interpreted as evidence of a fever, and for her two remaining days in Athens, she faked sunstroke so that she could stay in her room. Dina brought her meals on prettily decorated trays, but she ate nothing, and her grandmother popped into her room from time to time to feel her forehead. The old lady was reassured that she displayed no real symptoms of sickness and would be well enough to travel.

Dina was having one of her rare days off and had already said goodbye. Helena got up to pack, and when she heard her grandmother on the telephone in the kitchen, she crept out of her room. All the gifts had disappeared from the hall table, and in their place stood a large vase with a magnificent arrangement of crimson flowers, its size accentuated by its reflection in the ornate gilded mirror behind it.

'Elenaki! You look *much* better this morning,' said her grandmother, choosing that moment to come out into the hallway. 'Still a little pale, but much better than yesterday. Are you all ready to go home? Come and have some fresh pastries. The driver is coming in fifteen minutes, so let's make sure you have eaten something before you leave, *agápi mou.*'

In silence, Helena followed her grandmother into the kitchen so that she would not see the back of her legs. Later, she did the same in the lift.

Downstairs, they gave each other a brief hug, and her grandmother uttered her standard exaggerated endearments.

'It's been so wonderful having you here, *agápi mou*. I'll be counting the days until next summer. I hope you had a lovely time. Your *pappoú* and I so *love* seeing our little Elenaki. And don't forget to give your mother the box of baklava, will you?'

Helena said nothing; her focus was on climbing into the back of the car without displaying her calves either to Kýrios Manolis, to whom she waved goodbye, or to the chauffeur.

Back in Suffolk, the weals on her legs were the first thing her mother noticed. Helena cunningly made up a story about having to walk through some reeds to get to a beach. It was so convincing that Mary believed her, and when her father came in from the surgery that night, he applied some calming antibiotic cream. The marks soon disappeared, but the memory of that evening did not.

A few days later, she found her father reading a postcard at the breakfast table.

On the back of a picture of the ancient Tower of the Winds she had written:

Went to a youth rally and one day to small museum. To church to celebrate the day that the Virgin Mary died. I asked Grandma why we celebrate her death rather than her birth. She explained it's a happy thing if someone goes to heaven, because it's a better place. It's PP's name day soon and there is going to be a party. He says that St Stamatios had his head cut off by the Turks. YY says she will wear a long dress and her best jewellery. Learned conditional tense.

On a very similar card to Jenny, she had added: *Thomas my teacher is TOPS.*

Hamish passed their card over to Mary.

'Sounds like you had a very entertaining time,' he commented with a smile.

'Some of the time. Not all of it, though,' Helena responded.

'That sounds a bit ungrateful,' said her father. 'Perhaps it will be more fun next year. And one day you can say you don't want to go to church.'

Next year . . .

The words buzzed around in Helena's head like a fly. She never wanted to go again.

Mary McCloud did not know which made her angrier: the image of her daughter being taken to church by her grandfather, or being filled with the fanatical patriotism that ran through his veins, or the thought of her being paraded in front of his army friends.

'So how was the big party?' Hamish wanted more detail. 'Were you allowed to stay up? Were there lots of people? Was the food nice?'

More than anything else, Helena did not want to talk about that evening. One day she would pluck up the courage to reveal the real cause of the stripes on her legs. At the same time, she would tell them about the enforced siestas, when she lay sweating in her stuffy bedroom for two hours, how her grandfather was always shouting at the maid, and how uneasy Uncle Arsenis made her feel.

There would not be a 'next year'. She had already made up her mind.

'And how was your grandfather?' asked Hamish. 'Is he walking again?'

'Yes, he was fine,' she answered. 'Everything was fine.'

Chapter Four

One day the following spring, Mary McCloud received a phone call from Dina. Stamatis Papagiannis had died. He had been well into his eighties. There was to be a full military funeral in three days' time.

Mary sent her apologies in a telegram to her mother: *Syllypitíria. Mési examínou, den boró na fýgo.* 'Condolences. I can't leave mid term.'

She told her daughter the news when she returned from school that day, and Helena's response puzzled her a little.

'Poor Yiayiá,' was all she said.

Late that evening, Helena came down from her room to get some water. She had been lying in bed tossing and turning, unable to sleep. Her father had been called out urgently to see a patient and her mother was still up marking Latin translations, giving helpful comments in the margins with a red pen. Helena filled a glass from the tap and sat down opposite Mary at the kitchen table.

'I know I should feel sad,' she said. 'But I don't. He wasn't very nice, was he?'

Mary dropped her pen and took her daughter's hand across the table.

'Did he do something?' she asked anxiously.

'Not really,' lied Helena, not wanting to upset her mother.

'He was very . . . strict, wasn't he?'

'Nothing like Dad.'

'No comparison with your father,' agreed Mary. 'Who is probably the kindest man in England.'

'In the whole wide world,' said Helena. There was a pause before she added: 'Yiayiá is quite kind, though.'

'And she will miss him. Poor thing. They were together for such a long time.'

The conversation was closed. They did not talk about Stamatis Papagiannis again, but as summer approached, Helena asked if she could visit her grandmother. A whole summer in a small Suffolk town was a long and lonely time for an only child. Jenny was going to France for three weeks with her parents, Mary had to teach a holiday classics course, and however much Helena loved her new chemistry set, she could only spend so much time with it. There was much more to do in Athens: outings with Dina, with Thomas, maybe even her grandmother this year. Now that Yiayiá was alone, Helena had no trepidation about going. At eleven years old, she knew her own mind and would have the courage to say that she did not want to go to any museums with Uncle Arsenis.

When she arrived a few weeks later, she was relieved to find that without the heavy presence of her *pappoú* (a word too soft ever to have suited him), the atmosphere in the apartment felt very different.

Although it was only a few months since her husband had died, Eleni was not wearing black. She wore bright floral dresses, and Helena was certain that her hemlines were shorter than they had been in the past. She had no recollection of seeing Yiayiá's dimpled knees before, and now they were on show.

In her grandmother's mood, there was something almost light-hearted. They went on more excursions, out for meals, and on one occasion met some of her friends at the Grande Bretagne, where they all drank cocktails and Helena was allowed Coca-Cola for the first time.

Another change was in the music Yiayiá played. Nowadays it was not just the repetitive folk music that her grandfather had liked, but songs by different composers, and some male singers whose crooning voices she listened to over and over again. Helena's Greek was not fluent enough to understand every line, but there was not a single song without the word *agápi*, love, repeated many times. An accumulation of these new records was spread along the wall by the gramophone, including a few by someone called Giorgos Dalaras. One showed a smiling and very good-looking man, short back and sides, in a cream polo neck. This was the one her grandmother tended to prop up as if she liked to see his soulful eyes looking out at her. The corners of the big square cover were already dog-eared. There were also records by Mikis Theodorakis. One of them was the music from *Zorba the Greek*, and showed the silhouette of a dancing man. Her mother had the same one at home, and when her grandmother put it on, she recognised one of the tunes.

Dina seemed happier too. She looked younger than before, and nowadays took a bus once a fortnight to Kalamata and then a second bus to her village. Her own mother was recently widowed and needed extra help, particularly when the olives were ready to pick or the fruit was ripe and needed to be preserved. This would never have happened before. Stamatis Papagiannis had only allowed her one day off every other month.

Perhaps the most noticeable change was that the photographs of Stamatis Papagiannis were nowhere to be seen. The oil portrait still hung on the wall, but it was the sole remaining image of him. Helena observed that there were two new photos she had not seen before of her mother; one of Mary McCloud alone and one with her brother.

Something else that felt new was that Eleni Papagiannis often went to meet her lawyers. She was very open about the fact that this had something to do with Helena, and one morning she intrigued her by saying: 'I am trying to sort things out for you.'

Eleni Papagiannis's lifestyle was still cushioned by a very comfortable army pension and the use of a chauffeur, who took her wherever she wanted to go in the Rolls-Royce Wraith. Helena enjoyed the latter privilege too, and on her second day in Athens was driven alone to the foot of the Acropolis, where a pre-booked guide met her and took her up to the Parthenon. She was so familiar with it from a distance, and despite the intense heat was excited finally to find herself standing up close and being given the details of its age, its construction, and its various stages of destruction too. Her Greek was now good enough to pick up a hint of bitterness in the guide's voice when she mentioned Lord Elgin's theft of the sculptures, and she felt her skin prickle.

Such was her enthusiasm for this visit that she asked to go to Delphi. Two days later she was on her way, accompanied by Thomas, who was almost as thrilled as she was to be going. As ever, his knowledge was encyclopedic (*egkyklopaidikós*, Helena laughed when she looked the word up that afternoon). He told her all about a priestess who guided people in making decisions back in ancient times, and she thought that sounded very useful. In the museum, he made her learn all the Greek words that might be new to her: chariot, temple, spear, offering and so on.

The visit to Delphi made her curious about revisiting the National Archaeological Museum. To her enormous relief, Arsenis did not seem to turn up these days, so she was certain he would not accompany her this time.

'Can I go with Dina?' she asked her grandmother. 'I am not sure she has ever been.'

Dina was delighted by the idea. She had passed the museum a thousand times but had never been inside.

The two of them set off early the following day so that they would be there for opening time. The temperature was rising by the minute, but they took a winding route through narrow streets that the sun never reached.

Approaching the museum from behind, they passed a plain-looking building, a five-storey block that nobody would have looked at twice. As they went by, both Helena and Dina heard a strange sound from high above. If there had been a car passing at the time, it would probably have been inaudible, but in that momentary silence, a piercing scream cut through the air.

'Did you hear something?' asked Helena, looking up.

Dina glanced at the windows in the building next to them but did not answer.

'There it is again,' pressed Helena. 'It's a woman. I'm sure it's a woman. Do you think she needs help?'

'Let's just keep walking,' said Dina anxiously. 'I don't think there is anything we can do.'

'But . . .'

Another scream was drowned out by the refuse truck trundling down the street.

'We must hurry,' said Dina emphatically. 'We said we wanted to have the museum to ourselves, so we need to get there before the tourist buses arrive.'

Some of the shops were opening now, shutters were being rolled up, and there were people hurrying down the street to get to their offices. Dina set a brisk pace, and they soon rounded the corner, from where they could see the front of the museum. They were five minutes ahead of opening time and sat down on the smooth marble steps to wait.

Helena broke the silence.

'Why didn't we stop?' she said tearfully. 'That person might have needed our help.'

'It's better not to get too involved in these things, *Elenáki mou*,' said Dina gently.

'What things? What do you mean? Tell me, Dina,' Helena entreated. 'Please!'

'Look,' Dina said, unable to resist her, 'you have to *promise* me that you won't tell your grandmother.'

'Won't tell her what?'

'That I have told you anything.'

'I promise.'

Dina looked around as if to make sure that nobody else was listening, then leaned towards Helena.

'Sometimes,' she said in a low voice, 'if someone breaks a rule, they get taken to that building and questioned.'

'But whoever that woman was, it didn't sound like she was being questioned.'

Dina said nothing for a moment.

'Was someone hitting her?'

'I don't know. There are lots of stories about what happens in Bouboulinas Street.'

'And what's my grandmother got to do with it? Why wouldn't she want me to know?'

'It's all to do with the military regime,' Dina replied.

She seemed determined not to share any more information, but what she had said only aroused Helena's curiosity more.

'Military? Like my grandfather?'

Dina's silence was enough to suggest the answer. Helena had so many questions and was determined to ask them. But she could see that nothing further was going to come from Dina's firmly pursed lips.

The big double doors of the museum had swung open, and Dina got to her feet.

'Come on, *paidí mou*, let's go inside. I want you to take me round!'

The two of them stayed longer than Helena had done on her previous visit. Dina wanted to visit every room. Helena pointed out her favourite things, Dina chose her own, and occasionally Helena told her about an object that Arsenis had particularly wanted her to see that first time.

'Oh, you poor girl,' Dina groaned. 'He is so repulsive.'

Helena could laugh about it now, but she recalled that moment in front of the Aphrodite with extreme discomfort.

Dina clapped her hand over her mouth. 'Helena, please don't tell your grandmother that I said that.'

'Of course not,' Helena reassured her. 'Though it is the truth.'

They agreed that every one of Arsenis Papagiannis's choices was typical of him.

Helena was sure that she heard Dina mutter the words, 'All he likes is money and sex.' She giggled until her eyes began to water.

'*S' agapó polý*, Dina,' she said. 'I love you very much, Dina.'

'*Ki egó, s' agapó, Elenáki mou*,' Dina responded. 'I love you too, Helena.'

The rest of Helena's trip passed very happily.

She went again to the Aegli open-air cinema with Dina, to the beach one day, and for short evening strolls out for ice cream with her grandmother. There was a suggestion that she should go and play with the Álkimoi girl, but she declined. She refrained from saying that she had found Marianthi unbearably priggish, but said instead that she must learn her new vocabulary *ap'éxo*, by heart, before her tutor arrived that afternoon. Eleni Papagiannis could hardly object to her granddaughter's desire to study.

Helena formed an even closer relationship with Dina that summer. Once again they had shared some secrets, and the following year when she packed her case for Athens, she admitted to herself that she was more excited about seeing the maid than spending time with her grandmother. She did not, however, admit this to her mother.

Chapter Five

Eleni Papagiannis had become much frailer by the following summer and no longer wanted to venture out so much into the city's streets. She got up a lot later and spent the morning trimming the plants on her balcony and reading the newspaper. Friends occasionally visited her at home in the afternoon, but more often she dozed or watched the television. Helena sat with her a few times to watch one of her favourite comedy series, or played the role of disc jockey, turning over a record when it was needed or suggesting the next one. In this way, she learned the lyrics of many Vassilis Tsitsanis songs.

'Cloudy Sunday,' she sang, 'you resemble my heart . . .'

She noticed from the record covers that Tsitsanis was not as handsome as Dalaras, but his music easily stuck in her memory. Sometimes she looked at her grandmother, who was also singing along, and observed that her widow's heart seemed anything but cloudy.

Thomas came twice a week, and they had started to read simple books that he brought from his own library. He gave Helena lots of encouragement and praise, particularly when she finished one of them on her own. Her favourite was one by Alki Zei: *To Kaplâni tis Vitrínas*, *The Wildcat under Glass*. Thomas told her that the author had written it when she was living in exile in Paris, and confided that he would never have brought the book into the apartment when her grandfather was there. Helena understood that there were all sorts of messages hidden between the lines, and could not wait to tell Jenny that she had been reading something illegal.

They went a few times to the Ancient Agora, once the commercial and social centre of Athens. Amidst the ruins, they looked at some of the ideas of Socrates, Sophocles and Aristotle, translated into modern Greek. Thomas told Helena that it was the ideal place to do this, because these great men had actually spent time there, and had sat perhaps on these very stones. Helena was less interested in the idea that St Paul had also been there, and Thomas let slip that he thought the ancient philosophers were far more important in any case, but she was not to tell her grandmother that this was what he believed.

Each evening at six, before returning to eat dinner, Helena and Dina went for a stroll together. Sometimes they went to the National Gardens, where dense greenery and tall conifers magically transformed hot air into cool.

'It's so fresh in here!' Helena burst out.

'It's nature's magic,' smiled Dina.

Every time they went out together, Dina tested Helena on her verbs. For the first time, the thought entered Helena's head that Dina had no children of her own, which was strange for someone who showed such kindness and ease with her.

When she asked her why, Dina answered cryptically.

'Blessings come to us all in different forms. Some people are blessed with children, some are blessed with long life, some are blessed with work they love.'

'So do you love your work?' asked Helena.

'I am very lucky to have my job and somewhere so nice to live. Your grandparents were very kind to employ me.'

Helena had once walked into Dina's small room at the back of the kitchen. It was just big enough for a single bed and a chair, and there was one small window near the ceiling that opened onto an inner courtyard. Two dresses and a winter coat were hanging from hooks on the wall. The ceiling was stained as if there had once been a leak, and there was a distinct smell of damp. Helena had felt embarrassed that she had gone in without permission and had never told Dina that she had done so. Even more intense was the shame she felt that this kind woman slept in such a claustrophobic space, had zero daylight and such a paucity of clothes. That Dina was expressing gratitude for her living conditions was hard for Helena to understand.

She would ask her about that another time, but for now, she herself was grateful for Dina's kindness to her, the way she took her to places, helped her with the language. There were people in this world who were content with little. This much she now understood.

On the last evening, they went for a long walk. It took them thirty minutes to stroll down from Kolonaki towards Syntagma Square, and then past the National Gardens to the Temple of Zeus, where the guard let them in even though the site had already closed. They wandered, just the two of them, beneath the mighty pillars.

'This is so beautiful,' said Helena.

She looked at Dina and saw that there were tears rolling down her cheeks.

'Dina! Why are you sad?'

'I'm not, *agápi mou:* I live in Athens and yet I have never been so close to something so beautiful.'

'So you're not sad?'

'Not at all, *Elenáki mou,*' she answered. The opposite. I have never had time to come to such a place. *Efcharistó polý*, thank you, *glykiá mou.*'

Helena smiled. It seemed strange to her that she had been the reason for Dina's first visit here.

They sat for a while on a fallen pillar, and left as the sun was disappearing, stopping at the kiosk near home to buy two cold drinks. Dina seemed friendly with the *peripterás,* the man at the kiosk, who smiled and waved at her, holding up four fingers to indicate how much she needed to pay.

'*Efcharistó*, Lefteris,' she said to thank him for the change, and Helena noticed that he did not say anything back. Dina explained that he was deaf.

For the first time, Helena felt truly sorry to be leaving Athens. She would happily have stayed to wander the city with Dina for many more days. The maid had even suggested that the following year they should go to her home village, and Helena loved the idea of travelling somewhere a long way from Athens to explore another part of Greece and its countryside. Having taken the trip to Delphi, she had enjoyed a first glimpse of Greece's spectacular mountains and valleys, and she wanted to see more.

Chapter Six

In the summer of 1973, Helena faced huge disappointment when her mother cancelled the trip to Kolonaki. During the previous few years there had been numerous major attacks by a Palestinian terrorist group, Black September, on Israeli targets in Athens as well as other cities. In addition to several plane hijackings, including one of an Olympic Airways flight, there had been various hostage-takings, and at the Munich Olympics the previous year, eleven Israeli competitors had been murdered, an atrocity that had shocked the world.

On 5 August, just two days before Helena had been due to fly, two Arab gunmen, under orders to attack Israel-bound passengers of any nationality, killed five people in the airport lounge in Athens, using sub-machine guns and grenades. Fifty-five more were wounded.

'If they're killing innocent people, it's out of the question for you to go,' Mary said emphatically. 'Remember those poor athletes, darling? You had been watching them on the television the day before, and then—'

'Sorry, Helena. It's just not safe at the moment,' interrupted Hamish. 'Maybe next year.'

'Will Yiayiá be all right?' Helena asked with real concern.

'Yes, darling. She rarely leaves the apartment. They're not going to harm people like your grandmother. I spoke to her yesterday and she's fine.'

'But she'll be so disappointed that I'm not coming,' Helena pleaded.

'It's just too bad,' her mother said firmly. 'She'll have to understand. Totally innocent people get caught up in terrorist attacks. And I'm not taking the risk of you being one of them.'

The conversation about global instability and the dangers of travelling naturally flowed into a discussion about Greek politics. Mary McCloud followed them obsessively and, as the next few months passed, Helena herself was becoming increasingly curious. Even though her time in Athens had been spent in its most privileged area, she knew that Greece was not a paradise.

One evening that winter, mother and daughter were sitting at the kitchen table, struggling to read by candlelight. Industrial action meant that regular power cuts had become the norm, and they were both wrapped in eiderdowns to stay warm. Helena was wearing fingerless gloves. In the half-light, her homework all finished, she picked up her copy of Dickens's *A Tale of Two Cities*, her set book for the term, a story of the French Revolution. She was wondering if the people currently on strike were staging some kind of revolution themselves.

'Their days are definitely numbered now,' said Mary emphatically.

'Whose?' answered Helena, not even looking up. 'The Conservatives?'

Both her parents hated Edward Heath, and in spite of the inconvenience of sitting in the dark and being cold, they backed the miners, who were striking over wages and restricting supplies of coal to power stations.

'No, darling!' said her mother. 'I'm not talking about this country. I'm talking about the junta! The Colonels! Those tyrants in Greece!'

She passed the newspaper to her daughter, and in the flickering light, Helena read the headline. The letters were large, the words stark: *NINE DEAD IN ATHENS AS TANKS GO ON SHOOTING*.

'Students?' she said. 'That's awful.'

'Yes,' said her mother. 'Kids just a few years older than you. Crushed by an army tank.'

Helena looked up and was startled to see that Mary's eyes were full of tears. They were not tears of sadness but of fury. It was the fiercest display of emotion she had ever seen from her mother.

Squinting in the gloom, she began to scan the article.

'"The forces entrusted with the maintenance of law and order intend to maintain order by all the existing means at their disposal, including the use of arms",' she read out, as her mother simultaneously continued her tirade.

'They're disgusting, all of them. Police. Army. Dictatorship. Barbaric. Hateful . . .'

When she had read as much as she could in the poor light, Helena put the paper on the table.

Her mother had calmed down a little. 'Of course, if there's a big reaction against this, it could bring down the dictatorship. So I hope these young people haven't died in vain.'

They heard the sound of a key in the front door. Hamish McCloud had finished at the surgery. As he walked in, Mary held the paper out towards him.

'Look! They've killed innocent people, Hamish,' she said. 'Young people.'

The newspaper was laid out on the table again and they read it together, Hamish putting his arm across his wife's shoulders.

'It's terrible,' he breathed. 'A massacre.'

'And what's more, they are apparently denying it,' Mary added.

Helena looked at her parents' faces and saw disgust.

That evening, she began to understand how strongly her mother felt about the regime that was in charge of Greece. She had been aware that her own grandfather had been connected with it, but for the first time, the military, the army and the Colonels all came up in conversation in front of her. Her parents were now talking almost as if she was one of the grown-ups. She heard the familiar names of Papadopoulos, Pattakos and Makarezos, and she was aware that Stamatis Papagiannis had known these men. There had been photographs of them in the apartment. One of them had even been there the night of the reception. She had shaken hands with Pattakos.

Helena was now thirteen. She still had long, skinny legs, braces on her teeth, and hair that was as untameable as ever, but she was now officially a teenager. One obvious change to her status was that for the first time, she had been allowed to go on a trip by bus to the county town to celebrate with a few friends. Three of them spent the morning trying on clothes in Top Shop, and then went for lunch at the Wimpy Bar and to a film in the afternoon.

The second change was more subtle, and she had begun to notice it only that evening. Her mother began to speak to her in a more direct way, as if she had been waiting for her daughter's childhood to be over before certain things could be said.

'You understand that my father was part of all that . . . that repression. It's why I left Greece and have never been back. I didn't want to have anything to do with it.'

'But you let me go there?' Helena said hesitantly.

'I wanted you – and still want you – to love and appreciate Greece. It's the most beautiful country on earth, with the greatest culture and language. I haven't rejected any of those things. It's your heritage just as it is mine.'

Helena was glad that the dislike her mother had just expressed for those in charge of Greece had never got in the way of her visits.

'The people who govern the country and the country itself are not one and the same. Like here. I love this country, but I don't like what the Conservative government is doing to it.'

Helena had never heard such bitterness in her mother's voice. The guttering light of the flame in the jam jar had almost plunged them into darkness. She stood up to get a fresh candle from the kitchen drawer and lit the new one from the old.

For a while, she picked up and pretended to study something in her chemistry book for a forthcoming test, but she had already memorised it all and her thoughts were on what her mother had just said. That her grandfather had been part of a murderous regime came as no surprise. She knew all too well the undercurrent of violence that ran through him, something that even now she had not confessed to her mother.

'They say Greece was created by the gods,' Mary told her. 'But it's been ruled by devils for the past few years.'

'But you don't stop me going there? Even with the devils in charge?'

'No, darling. As my mother always tells you, it's a very safe country in many ways. Soldiers on every street corner . . .'

'Anyway, Yiayiá does seem much happier since my grandfather died.' Helena felt a little nervous about expressing such a thought, but she saw something almost like the beginning of a smile on her mother's face and was emboldened. 'And she doesn't even wear black like all her friends.'

'She doesn't wear black?' exclaimed Mary.

'Nope,' Helena replied. 'And I swear she laughs more.'

'That's good to hear.'

'But if he was so horrible all those years, why didn't she leave him?' continued Helena.

'What would she have done? She was totally dependent on him,' said Mary. 'That's how things were in those days.'

'Women haven't burned their bras in Greece yet,' joked Hamish.

'And it's about time they did!' Mary retorted.

Hamish was warming some milk on a camping stove and made Horlicks for them all.

'It's cosy, isn't it?' he said, trying to lighten the mood. 'Like a war, but without any bombs falling.'

Now that her mother had been a little more open about Stamatis Papagiannis, Helena wanted to ask about Andreas. All she knew of him was what Dina had told her, and she was keen to know more. She stirred her hot drink and plucked up the courage.

'Your brother . . .?'

'He didn't really have many choices, rather like my mother. He was bullied into joining the army and eventually was sent off to fight the communists in the mountains. He was not cut out to be a soldier, physically or mentally, and I knew his heart wasn't in it. So did your grandmother,' said Mary. 'His death in that battle was regarded as heroic by my father. And it fuelled his fanatical hatred of the left.'

'I never met your grandfather,' Hamish interjected, addressing his daughter, 'but I understand his views were extreme.'

'For me and my mother, there was *nothing* heroic about Andreas's death,' said Mary. 'It was a tragic loss. And deep inside, I don't think my mother ever forgave that man.'

'So your father forced him to join the army?'

'Without any doubt whatsoever.'

'Poor Andreas,' said Helena. 'And poor Yiayiá.'

'Look, I know she missed seeing you this summer. But it was too dangerous. If everything is more stable next year, I might even come with you.'

'That would be nice, Mum. I think she would like that.'

Listening to his wife and daughter discussing a trip to Athens, Hamish had to interrupt.

'Only if all of this is over,' he said, pointing at the front page of the newspaper. 'For some reason, I doubt it will be.'

'Things happen quickly in Greece, so let's just see what happens, Hamish,' Mary answered. 'Six months' time and everything might have calmed down again. They are promising more liberalisation, so perhaps we should all go. We could have our first Greek holiday together.'

'Oh yes!' Helena cried, spilling her Horlicks across the newspaper in her excitement. 'Please let's do that!'

Mary picked up the paper, the awful front-page news now obliterated, and put it in the bin.

Hamish's scepticism was proved right. The next few months brought anything but stability to Greece. The massacre at the university proved to be the catalyst for further disruption.

Huge demonstrations took place in protest at what had happened when army tanks crushed the gates to the Polytechnic. More than two dozen people had been killed on and around the campus during the days surrounding 17 November, and the deaths of many students and demonstrators had been photographed and filmed. Unlike the countless incidents of clandestine torture that had taken place in the headquarters of the secret police in Bouboulinas Street, island prison camps and numerous other hidden places of detention, the martyrdom of young people demonstrating for democracy was very public. Some of them, Helena realised, were only a few years older than her. This horrifying event had been seen around the world, and she read the newspaper every day now so she could follow what was happening. It must be having an impact on Yiayiá and Dina.

Hardliners blamed Papadopoulos's attempts at liberalisation. Without these, they claimed, a demonstration such as the one that had taken place at the Polytechnic would never have happened. The chief of military police, Dimitrios Ioannides, accused Papadopoulos and his supporters of straying too far from the original principles of the 1967 coup and losing control of the country, and a week later, he staged a counter-coup, put himself in power and organised an internal crackdown.

Helena was determined to follow the complexity of the politics and the machinations of these men. It felt so personal, so close to home. Papadopoulos, the man who had made himself president and was so much admired by Stamatis Papagiannis, was placed under house arrest, and martial law was imposed in Greece. She saw a photograph of a tank in an Athens street and shuddered with fear for Dina and her grandmother.

Chapter Seven

The world was now watching events in Greece. It was soon clear that the new regime was as extreme as the previous one. As well as picking up *The Times* each day, Helena insisted on watching the television news at 9 p.m. every evening, learning for herself that Greece was under a harsher military rule than ever, with an even greater army presence on the streets.

Another action of Dimitrios Ioannides was to try and take over Cyprus. Helena read that one of his ambitions was to force a union of Cyprus with Greece. She looked Cyprus up in the family atlas and was surprised to see how far from Greece it turned out to be. It was actually much nearer Turkey. It looked to her as if some of the Greek islands were almost swimming distance from the Turkish coast too.

Her mother explained to her that there were both Greek Cypriots and Turkish Cypriots living side by side in Cyprus, and that most of the time it was peaceful.

'The island is plenty big enough for all of them,' she said bluntly. 'It's just more aggression that nobody needs in this world right now.'

In the summer of 1974, Ioannides deposed the president of Cyprus, Archbishop Makarios, and installed Nikos Sampson, a notorious and fanatical anti-communist. In doing so, he provoked Turkey, and a day after the coup, Turkish forces landed in the north part of the island.

There was fierce fighting. The Greek Cypriots fled to the south, leaving the north to be occupied by Turkish troops. Refugees poured out by the thousands.

Greek commandos landed on the island, and Greece was put into a state of general mobilisation. Almost overnight, the country found itself on a war footing.

Because Cyprus was a former colony that still had a significant British population and an army base, the press in London covered the situation in great detail. In Suffolk, Helena, Mary and Hamish followed events together, alarmed by how quickly the situation had evolved into what looked like a full-scale war.

'Suppose the Turks invade Greece?' said Mary one night, in despair. 'There are many more of them than us.'

'Would Yiayiá be a prisoner?'

'Who knows, darling? Anything could happen.' She was not trying to hide her anguish from Helena.

'We mustn't be pessimistic,' said Hamish, trying to insert a note of optimism. 'I don't think the British will allow that to happen. Or NATO. Greece is too important.'

'None of us imagined we would be invaded by the Nazis back in 1941,' murmured Mary. 'We thought someone would protect us then, but they didn't. I'll ring my mother tonight.'

Since the death of Stamatis Papagiannis, Mary had rung Yiayiá at least once a week, but the phone call that night brought no real comfort.

'So Dina had to go back to Kalamata?' Helena heard her mother say. 'Are you managing?'

The call was shorter than usual, and Mary came back into the living room grey-faced to report that one of Dina's nephews, a commando with the Greek forces, had been killed in Cyprus. Another nephew, his brother, had been taken prisoner, and there were rumours that he had been shipped off to Turkey. Dina had hurried back to her village for the funeral and to comfort her sister, the mother of both boys. She hoped only to be away for a few days.

The summer continued to bring drama. Within days of the Turkish invasion of Cyprus, Ioannides' military regime collapsed and its leader was pushed out by a group of generals. Political leaders who had been exiled since the junta took over in 1967 began to return to Athens from abroad, including Konstantinos Karamanlis, who was invited back from Paris to take over as prime minister. Despite ongoing peace talks, there was a second invasion of Cyprus by Turkey in mid August.

Although the conflict in Cyprus was continuing, democracy was to return at last, and this was a reason to celebrate in the McCloud family. Mary insisted on a bottle of wine with supper that night, and Hamish poured a little into Helena's glass too.

'Here you are, my little Greek girl, you're fourteen now,' he said.

'We lift our glasses and we say "*Sti dimokratía*",' Mary said. 'To democracy.'

Father and daughter echoed the toast.

'And to the return of the rule of law!'

Helena was about to repeat the words, but her mother had not quite finished.

'And to justice!'

Helena lifted her glass and took a sip. '*Sti dikaiosýni*,' she said. 'To justice.' The wine was cold, pale yellow, slightly sour. Her first ever taste, and she would always associate the flavour with this word.

'I know things are still fragile, and Cyprus is still a mess, but I can't help my optimism,' said Mary. 'It's a new beginning, Helena, so I will come with you next summer.'

'*As to giortásoume!*' smiled Helena. 'Let's celebrate!'

Helena missed Dina, her Greek lessons and swimming in a warm sea that summer, but had accepted that it was far too dangerous to go. Several times over the next few weeks, Mary McCloud passed the phone over to her daughter so that she could have a chat with her grandmother. It was a poor substitute for visiting her, but comforting for them both.

Mary loved hearing Helena's ease with the Greek language. Conversely, it gave Helena a strange feeling when she heard her mother talking fast and fluently in her mother tongue.

'She sounds anxious,' Mary reported to her husband and daughter one evening as the pair of them laid the table for supper. 'Dina is still away. My mother can manage on her own for a while, but I think she feels very vulnerable.'

Vulnerable? thought Helena. Now that she was beginning to grasp more fully what had been happening in Greece over the past decades, she wondered if her grandmother's vulnerability came from the Turks or from her husband's connection with those men who had been running the country all those years and who were now disgraced. Mary told her that most of them would probably spend the rest of their lives in prison.

The fighting continued a while longer in Cyprus, only halted by an agreement that left almost half the island under occupation by Turkish forces. Helena read with grim fascination that tens of thousands of Greek Cypriots had been displaced from their homes in the north, and there were soldiers missing on both sides, their families unable to discover if they had been captured or killed. One of the island's most luxurious and beautiful cities, Famagusta, was abandoned as its inhabitants were forced to flee in terror, leaving behind all their possessions, their meals uneaten on the table. She had no trouble imagining the toys, records and books that were sitting in dark, silent homes waiting for their owners to come back. It made her shudder. The capital city, Nicosia, was now divided down the middle. This reminded her of a place they had just done an essay on. Instead of a wall, as they had in Berlin, though, there was just lots of barbed wire.

Even with a peace agreement, there were still complications and compromises, but eventually the story faded from the screen. Everyone hoped there would be a better settlement for the Greek Cypriots in the future, but the fighting was over for now, and in

Athens at least, there was some kind of fragile normality. Free and democratic elections were planned for November for the first time since the coup in 1967.

Mary and her mother were now speaking on a daily basis, and from her tone of voice, Helena could tell that her mother had softened towards her grandmother. Soon they were making plans for the first three-generation visit to Athens, the following summer.

One winter's evening over dinner, Helena excitedly scribbled a list of all her favourite activities.

'We'll go to Zonars! We'll go to Aegli! Dina's back now and she loves going there. We'll go to the beach! Definitely the National Archaeological. Maybe Delphi?'

As well as being Hamish McCloud's first ever meeting with his *pethará*, his mother-in-law, it would be the first time he had visited Greece, so Helena was determined that he should see the best of everything.

'And,' she said with a huge grin, 'you'll see the *real* Parthenon!'

'Yes,' said Mary. 'And the other marbles too, the ones that Elgin left behind.'

Chapter Eight

One evening in early March, the phone in the hallway rang. Helena raced out to answer it, expecting a call from Jenny. They were going to a fancy dress party in a few days as pirates and needed to discuss their costumes.

She barely recognised Dina's voice. There was no friendly greeting.

'*Boró na milíso me ti mitéra sou?*' she asked immediately. 'Can I speak to your mother?'

Helena put the receiver down on the hall table and raced to the kitchen, shaking slightly. She had guessed from Dina's nasal tone that she had been crying.

'Mum . . . it's for you. Dina. She's on the phone.'

Instinct told them that there could only be one reason for Dina to call.

Eleni Papagiannis had died unexpectedly that afternoon. She had drunk a few sips of her usual cup of camomile tea an hour earlier when she went for her siesta, but when Dina had gone to wake her up, she'd found her lifeless in her bed. She assured Mary that her mother had looked very peaceful. Given her advanced years, 'old age' would be recorded as the cause of death.

Helena was tearful, and a little puzzled that her mother did not seem very upset. She remembered her weeping copiously at the funeral of her sister-in-law, Moira.

'Oh Mum. It's so sad. I think Yiayiá was very excited that we were all going to be together.'

'It's a lovely thought that the prospect of it had made her happy,' said Mary. 'And Dina says she died peacefully, so let's hope that was somewhere in her mind.'

Silently, Mary McCloud admitted to herself that in some ways it was a relief to have avoided the reunion. She would have found it hard to embrace her mother when the pair of them met.

'Are you going to the funeral?' Helena asked.

'Yes,' said Mary. 'I'd better pack immediately. I'll need to catch a plane very early in the morning. It's going to be the day after tomorrow. Give me a shout when Dad gets in.'

She disappeared upstairs, leaving Helena sitting in silence at the kitchen table. She was trying to absorb what had happened. It felt so sudden.

Hamish McCloud came back to eat before starting his home visits and found her still sitting at the table. Mary then appeared, and for a while their shepherd's pie, a family favourite, sat in front of them untouched.

'So who is organising everything?' he asked after they'd told him the news.

'Arsenis,' Mary answered curtly. 'With Dina's help, I suppose, but I think he will do everything that needs to be done for the service.'

'Does he have power of attorney?' asked Hamish.

'I suppose so.'

Helena sat and listened quietly. Power. She could imagine Arsenis Papagiannis enjoying power. 'Attorney' was a word she had only heard in American television dramas. It was something to do with lawyers. As her father put his arm around her, she quietly started to cry again.

'What will happen to Dina?' she asked. 'She is so kind. And she's worked for Yiayiá for so long!'

'Dina?' Her mother looked thoughtful.

'Will she stay in the flat?'

'Darling, I have no idea,' said Mary.

'So if we go to Athens, she won't even be there?'

'Don't worry, sweetheart, I'm sure we won't lose touch with her. I'll find out what her plans are.'

Helena had assumed that there would be many more visits to Athens, and that Yiayiá and Dina would always be there waiting for her. While her grandfather's demise had brought no sorrow, the death of her grandmother awakened thoughts of mortality. Time passes. Change happens. In every corner of life.

This was her adolescent realisation as she lay in bed that night, staring at the ceiling. Even her own body had altered almost beyond recognition since she had last seen her grandmother three years ago. She had shot up by several inches and her feet were now a size four (she had still been a child's size eleven on her last visit). Her copper-coloured hair had got thicker, and she now wore it in two heavy plaits to keep it out of the way. The most unwelcome change had been the arrival of regular migraines that came when her periods had begun.

When Helena got up for school, a taxi had already taken Mary McCloud to the station. It felt very strange to imagine her mother on a plane to Athens without her. She wished they were together.

If it was strange for Helena, it was nothing to match the discomfort Mary felt on arriving at Evdokias 45. It was twenty-five years since she had left. A taxi had brought her from the airport because the chauffeur, Dina explained in a phone call, had been given immediate notice by Arsenis.

The concierge was standing on the outer steps having a cigarette when she arrived.

'*Kóri tis Kyrías Papagianni*? Mrs Papagiannis's daughter?' Kýrios Manolis asked. To Mary, he seemed barely to have changed. '*Syllypitíria.*'

His condolences were sincere, and as he held the door open for her, he asked after Helena. Mary was touched that her daughter had made such a positive impression on the doorman and had evidently always been very polite to him.

Dina was standing at the open apartment door, dressed entirely in the blackest of black dresses with thick black stockings and black shoes. Mary would probably not have recognised her but for her diminutive height. She was completely grey-haired now.

The two women stood and hugged each other for several minutes. Dina was shaking with sobs. Even if Stamatis Papagiannis had often been very harsh to her, her devotion to Eleni had been steadfast for thirty years. Her death so shortly before this longed-for reunion with Mary set off an explosion of emotion.

When the maid had calmed down and dried her tears on the dirty handkerchief pulled from her sleeve, the two women went into the kitchen and sat down.

'So, Dina,' asked Mary gently, 'is everything arranged for tomorrow?'

Dina nodded. 'And then I have to leave,' she said, with tears coursing down her cheeks. 'The next day.'

'So soon?' queried Mary.

'Arsenis . . .'

Mary had to control her reaction. 'But it's not his decision,' she said as quietly as she could.

Dina got up to fetch them water.

'Arsenis has told me that everything is now his and he wants me gone after the funeral. He only gave me another day because I begged him. So I can pack my things up, at least. Then I'll go back to the village.'

Mary felt her face drain of colour. When she finally managed to get some words out, she asked Dina what Arsenis meant.

It was Dina's turn to be surprised. 'You mean you don't know?' she asked incredulously. 'Your father left everything to his nephew. Nothing to your mother. He specified that she could live here until she died, and then *bam*. Everything to that awful man.'

'*Panagía mou!*' Now that she was on Greek soil, it came naturally to Mary to curse in Greek again.

'Your mother was fighting it tooth and nail! She even left a will of her own with her lawyer. She was determined to beat Arsenis at this game. He is a *malákas*. Sorry for the bad language, but he is.'

Mary had no problem with Dina insulting her cousin. She hated him just as much.

'I think I should speak to her lawyer,' she said. 'Right away.' She looked at her watch, which was still on British time. 'It's getting late. Will you find their number for me and I'll see if I can get hold of them now.'

Within a minute, Mary was calling the lawyer's office and explaining. After offering his condolences, the lawyer advised that she should have the locks changed immediately and, when she left the apartment, she should have it sealed so that it would be very obvious if anyone had gone in. With a continuing dispute over a will, this was her best course of action.

'A locksmith, Dina. Is there a local locksmith?'

Dina knew of one in a nearby street that was attached to Pavlidis, the best hardware store in Athens. She often went there to buy cleaning supplies and would ask if they could send someone as soon as possible.

While the maid was gone, Mary wandered about the apartment, opening each door in turn out of simple curiosity.

Everything seemed exactly as it had been on the day she'd left, and she had no appetite to relive even a single memory from the years she had spent there. The last room she came to was her father's study. What a vile, dark space it was, the enormous heavy desk exactly where it had always been.

She could picture him sitting behind it and remembered how he would suddenly get up and thrash her legs with a cane. She slammed the door on it just as Dina returned.

'Someone is coming later this evening,' Dina said triumphantly. 'Bolts, padlocks, mortice locks. They've got the lot.'

'Perfect,' said Mary. 'You were always an angel. I've missed you.'

'I'm not an angel,' Dina said dismissively. 'I've thought plenty of bad thoughts in my time.'

'Everyone does,' said Mary. 'With people like Arsenis in the world, why wouldn't you?'

Dina laughed. 'He is very set on depriving your *Elenáki*.'

'So was that what my mother wanted?' said Mary, mildly surprised. 'For everything to pass straight to my daughter?'

'I thought you would know that, Maria?'

'I didn't. But I'm glad. That's who it would all go to anyway in the end. And I know how much Helena has loved being here. My mother knew what she was doing.'

'I'll make us something to eat from what's in the fridge,' said Dina. 'And then I'll start packing up, I suppose.'

They sat down opposite each other in the kitchen and attempted to catch up on the past quarter of a century. Mary told Dina what it was like arriving in London all those years before, finding her way, starting university, meeting Hamish, becoming a teacher, and then the joy of having Helena. It was her life in brief. They did not reminisce about the years prior to her leaving.

Dina had much more to say. She told Mary about every member of her family, what the village was like now and what she was planning to do there. It was fairly evident that she was excited about returning there to live after all this time.

'It's where I belong,' she said. 'Now that your dear mother has gone, Athens has nothing for me.'

Once Eleni was mentioned, Dina began to cry again.

'Such a kind person,' she continued. 'And I don't know how she bore it. Being married to such a brute. And that Arsenis coming and going like he owned the place. She was so patient. So dutiful. But I think she did suffer a bit. Specially after you left. Things were empty then. No Andreas. No Maria. Just those two awful men. And no way of escaping.'

87

Mary wasn't in the mood to go over the same issues again. She had no regrets about leaving. It had been the right thing to do, and she did not actually believe that if her mother had been determined to get away she could not have found a means to do so. Eleni Papagiannis had made choices, and Mary believed that some small part of her had loved Stamatis Papagiannis enough to stay. It was hard for her to imagine otherwise.

The doorbell was ringing and Dina got up. She pressed the buzzer, and moments later the locksmith walked through the door. He surveyed and measured, had a brief discussion with both Mary and Dina about what he planned to install, and then promised to return the following morning. It was going to take him some hours.

The two women spent the rest of the evening putting spare sheets over the furniture, closing the shutters and curtains. They touched nothing in the rest of the apartment apart from the delicate bone-china cup on Eleni's bedside table. There was a slight stain on the inside, the remains of the camomile tea that Dina had made for her on her very last day.

Dina's possessions fitted into two small suitcases. Mary suggested that she take anything she wanted from Eleni's personal effects, and the maid chose a small powder compact that sat on her employer's dressing table.

'She used it every day for the past thirty years and probably more,' she said. 'It will be a lovely reminder of her.'

'Are you sure that's all you want?' Mary quizzed. She'd been expecting her to take a piece of jewellery.

Dina was adamant. She tucked the compact into her handbag.

There was nothing that Mary wanted. If Arsenis ended up inheriting the place then he could have the task of clearing it.

All Mary had packed was a black skirt and a navy-blue blouse, and the following morning she dressed slowly. She had never imagined herself going to her mother's funeral, but she was glad to have come.

It felt a little strange given the decades that had passed since she had seen her.

The funeral was held in a nearby church in Kolonaki. Mary sat at the back, grateful that there was nobody who recognised her, and nobody she recognised except for Arsenis. It was he who stood by the open coffin and accepted the condolences of friends and acquaintances.

Mary could not bring herself to approach him, even though she knew that he was aware of her presence. She felt like a ghost with these people, a stranger amidst the rituals, chanting and devotion that had become so alien to her. It was supposedly all about her mother, and yet she felt nothing.

Eventually it came to an end and everyone filed out of the church onto the street. Mary slipped away while Dina stayed to talk to people and share out the little plates of *kóllyva,* a mix of wheat, berries, fruit and nuts, the symbolic dinner for the dead that had been supplied for the occasion by Arsenis. Neither Mary nor Dina was going to the interment.

Mary had an eye on her watch. She needed to get back to Evdokias to see how the locks were progressing. The job had to be finished before she left for London that evening.

The locksmith had another hour to go. In the meantime, Dina returned and gathered her bags. Mary helped her down in the lift and the kindly concierge took everything out onto the pavement and hailed a taxi. Dina gave him what seemed to Mary a surprisingly long hug, before turning to her, eyes watering.

'I am not going to weep like the last time I said goodbye to you,' she reassured her. 'Because I know I will see you again.'

Mary stood there until the taxi had turned the corner. On her way back to the lift, she stopped to talk to Kýrios Manolis for a moment and saw him wiping away a tear. Pretending not to notice, she asked him if he would keep a close watch on the apartment now that it was empty.

'No need even to ask, Kyría Maria,' he said sweetly. 'With my life.'

Back upstairs, the locksmith was now testing each of the four very substantial locks.

'Nobody is going to get through here without a battering ram,' he reassured her. 'And if they try that, the world is going to know about it. The concierge, at least. For good measure I am going to add a padlock.'

'Thank you, I'm so grateful,' said Mary, hurrying inside to collect her bag.

'I need another half-hour and then I will tape up the door so if someone goes in, it will be obvious. You'll need to have left before I do that!' he laughed.

Mary took a last wander from room to room. She paused in the drawing room and peered into the display cabinet. Her mother's collection of Meissen figures had grown considerably. Should she take just one? It would be her only inheritance, after all. But no. She wanted no souvenirs of this place or her past.

In the kitchen, she quickly washed the cups she and Dina had used that morning and left them on the draining board.

Taking off her dark clothes, she stuffed them into her overnight bag and put on the linen trousers and jacket she had worn for the journey. Then she went into the bathroom to clean her teeth and apply a smear of lipstick. She was shocked by the face that looked back at her. Pallid and hollow-eyed. This journey had taken more out of her than she had expected.

She turned off all the lights and opened the front door.

'Perfect timing,' said the locksmith. 'All done.'

He snapped the padlock shut and handed her three sets of keys. Then he began to tape the door.

Mary stood watching. The past was finally being sealed off.

Mary dropped into the lawyer's office for a brief meeting. She left all the keys there for safe keeping and then continued to the airport. Her journey home proved arduous. Since the re-establishment of democracy in Greece, many trade unions had begun to use their newly regained freedom to stage industrial action. She called Hamish to let him know that her flight was delayed by three hours and over the crackling telephone line, told her husband the news about the will.

'My mother was disputing it, but she hadn't mentioned anything to me. Now we have to take on the fight. Apparently Arsenis is determined, but we won't let it happen!' she said adamantly. 'Even in the grave, my father manages to be cruel.'

Helena stood quietly on the landing, hoping that the creaky floorboards would not give her away. She could hear her father speaking in a low voice.

'Stay calm, darling. We can't let him do this. And yes, of course we will oppose it.'

Hamish was at Heathrow to meet Mary, and she fell asleep almost as soon as she got into the car.

They arrived back in Dellbridge at two in the morning, and even though they tried to make as little noise as possible, Helena heard the sound of the front door and ran downstairs in her pyjamas.

Mary was very tired, but she sat in the kitchen with her daughter, who had made them both cocoa, and answered her questions about the funeral, how Dina was and who had come.

'Arsenis was there,' she said, 'playing "head of the family".'

'Unbearable man.' Helena chose this moment to admit that 'Uncle' Arsenis had made her feel extremely uncomfortable on several occasions.

'My cousin and I never got on, sweetheart,' Mary reassured her daughter. 'It isn't just you. I disliked him from a very early age. He was creepy. Andreas couldn't stand him either. Arsenis used to boss him around as if he was his older brother. And our father was much nicer to Arsenis than to us,' she added. 'We used to joke that maybe he was his son.'

The following evening, Helena asked her father about the phone call.

'What were you talking about last night? What are you going to oppose?' she asked.

'A new supermarket development,' he said swiftly. 'We've already got plenty in Dellbridge.'

Helena thought no more of it. Besides, more exciting and pressing things got in the way: trials for the county athletics team, end-of-term exams and, now that the holiday in Athens was cancelled, planning for a trip to Ayrshire to see the Scottish side of the family.

Raging inflation was front-page news that summer, and her family had their own unexpected expenses, with the house needing re-roofing and the car replacing. Camping in Scotland was on the agenda for the next few summers, and however much she wished she could, Helena knew not to ask about going to Greece.

Part Two

Chapter Nine

A few weeks after Helena's final school year ended, an almost weightless envelope landed on the mat in Dellbridge. The flimsy scrap of paper inside would determine her future.

She ripped it open and ran her eyes over a row of letters. In her shaking hand, the faint characters danced around the page.

Her father came into the hall, bag in one hand, car keys rattling in the other, ready to go off on his rounds. He paused. It was a moment they had all been anticipating.

'What does it say, Dad? Tell me what it says!' She passed him the letter.

'Congratulations! You clever, clever girl!' He smiled, unable to contain his pride, and passed the paper back to his daughter. 'I think you're in.'

A moment later, his wife appeared at the top of the stairs.

'Has it come? The letter?'

The look on her husband's face told her that the news was good.

With Helena holding her results and her parents looking over her shoulder, her father pointed to each letter, just as he had done when teaching her to read.

'A A A A . . .'

'Oh goodness,' said Mary, gripping the back of the hall chair to support herself. 'Oh my goodness.'

'Home and dry,' said Hamish. 'Chemistry at Oxford!'

'And even more than you needed, sweetheart,' gushed Mary. 'All that hard work. You so deserve it!'

'I think this calls for a big celebration,' said Hamish. 'Will you book, darling? I'm so sorry, I have to rush now, but I'll see you both later.'

He paused a moment before opening the door, then dropped his bag and turned round.

'I am so, so proud of you,' he said, hugging his daughter so tightly she could scarcely breathe.

That evening, Helena, in a long grey velvet skirt and a sea-green tie-dyed T-shirt, was standing in front of the mirror to apply mascara and a smudge of kohl to her eyes. In the past few years, she had started to appreciate her wild hair. It went with the hippy-bohemian look that was currently fashionable, and some of her friends were now curling theirs to get the same style.

Standing sideways on to her reflection, she hoped her breasts would grow a little but that her height would not. Five foot seven in her bare feet seemed tall enough for someone only eight stone in weight. As it was, she had the perfect physique for a runner and had been competing in long-distance events since she began at grammar school, effortlessly breaking school records. Now, for the first time, she allowed herself to wonder if she would make it into the university athletics team.

She slipped on her suede clogs and went downstairs to wait for her mother.

The phone had been ringing all day, as friends phoned to share mostly good news about their grades. Her best friend Jenny, however, had been unreachable. She would give her another try. It was Mrs Slater who answered.

'Sweetheart,' she rasped (Helena could hear the sound of her dragging on a cigarette and the distinctive tinkling of ice in a glass). 'She's so upset, I don't think she'll come to the phone. She totally flunked them. I really don't understand it. I'll say you called. Maybe pop round tomorrow? She might be ready to see you then.'

Helena and Jenny had been inseparable since primary school, and they had both been offered places at Oxford. What Jenny's mother probably didn't know was that her daughter had spent most of her upper-sixth year hanging out in a record shop with a school dropout in his late twenties, the local supplier of anything and everything that a teenager might want.

Jenny's failure dented Helena's pleasure in her own success. She had tried everything to dissuade her friend from wrecking her chances, but Jenny was convinced she was in love with Mike. For the past year she had covered up the smell of marijuana that hung around her by dousing herself with patchouli oil. It had fooled her parents.

Opening the kitchen drawer, Helena dug past a couple of packets of painkillers to find pencil and paper. She would drop a note through Jenny's letter box on the way into town.

What were the right words to write? Encouragement. That was what she would need. She just had to do some retakes, then everything would be back on track. They had shared this dream together: bells chiming for chapel, academic gowns and ball gowns, punting and picnics on the banks of the Isis, candlelit dinners at refectory tables. Lectures and libraries full of leather-bound volumes.

Her mother interrupted her reverie.

'Ready to go, Helena? You look lovely.'

'Yes! Thanks, Mum, so do you!'

Her mother was wearing a pair of bright green trousers that flared from the knee, and a matching satin shirt with billowing sleeves. Although all her clothes were inexpensive, she wore them with a model's elegance and poise. Mary McCloud stood out in Dellbridge. With her shiny deep chestnut hair always held high in a bun and her ebony eyes, she looked very different from all the other mothers Helena knew.

Helena screwed up the piece of paper with the clumsily inadequate note to Jenny. Nothing was quite right. She would try again the following day.

Mother and daughter walked into town and down the high street. At the top was Mrs Greetham's haberdashery, where Helena was doing a summer job. It was the most colourful shop in town, with its shelves of ribbons and trims, tapestry kits and threads, racks of buttons and hooks and eyes and zip fasteners in every shade. Next was the department store, whose windows had displayed the same crimplene skirts and acrylic cardigans for three years now, then Forte, the coffee bar, its windows always opaque with steam, and after that the pub, and then the record shop, with its display of Pink Floyd albums, including *Wish You Were Here*, which she was planning to buy with her first month's wages. There was still a light on inside, and she turned her head away in case Jenny's boyfriend was there.

Towards the end of town was the fishmonger's, which gave off a sour stench even when its shutters were down. 'One, two, three, *now*!' shouted Helena. It was a family joke that they always pinched their noses as they went by. Then came a small branch of Timothy Whites, whose dispensing pharmacist Hamish did not trust, so he sent his patients to the old-fashioned apothecary up the side street by the fish and chip shop. Finally, they came to the railway station, which was flanked by the local pub and the Oxfam shop that kept the teenagers of the town supplied with moth-eaten fur coats and collarless grandad shirts.

Every shopfront looked flimsy. It might have been the aura from a lurking migraine, which often made her feel light-headed, but Helena had the sense that it was all two-dimensional, a cheap film set about to be dismantled. Each building in this familiar street that she had walked more than five thousand times (she had done a rough calculation) was suddenly small and insubstantial and felt as if it already belonged to the past. Eighteen years of her life had passed, and so much already lay behind her.

La Famiglia, the best (and only) trattoria in town, was a few hundred yards beyond the Oxfam shop, just after the parish church and the turning that led up to Helena's school. Hamish was waiting for them outside.

The waiters greeted them like old friends, and her father proudly told them all that his daughter was going to Oxford. Some of them did not know where that was, but they chorused '*Congratulazioni!*' and gave them glasses of Asti Spumante on the house.

The rest was a performance as much as a meal, with a twenty-inch pepper mill flamboyantly wielded by the head waiter to grind over their minestrone soup, and outsize silver domes that were lifted with gusto to reveal meatballs in tomato sauce 'for the *signore*' and osso buco for '*il dottore*'. When the sweet trolley came round, Hamish had profiteroles, because it was a dessert that nobody could make better at home, and Helena had tiramisu.

Conversation flowed, mostly light-hearted except for the news about Jenny, with Helena expressing guilt that she had not done more to keep her friend on the rails.

'Maybe I should have said something to her parents?'

'No, darling, that would have lost you a friend. She'll get over it.'

'Yes, Mum, but I wanted us to be together at Oxford.'

'It will probably mean you'll make more effort to find new friends,' said Hamish, who had never entirely approved of Jenny.

Finally, more for the spectacle than the taste, her parents ordered flaming sambuca. Helena was as amazed now as she had been as a ten-year-old to see the flames licking up from their glasses. She did not want one herself, as her head was beginning to throb after the combination of Asti and half a glass of Chianti, but the spectacle was enough.

When the flames had died down, her father sipped his drink. Her mother did not touch hers.

'We want to celebrate your success,' said Mary.

'I thought that was what we were doing now?' Helena said.

'No, your mother means in another way.'

'We want us all to go on a trip abroad. To Greece. We've booked tickets for the middle of next month, just before you start university.'

Helena was taken aback. She knew it had been her mother's dream that they should go together on such a vacation, but money had not allowed it.

'That's amazing, Mum.' She beamed. 'I'm sure Mrs Greetham can find someone else for a couple of weeks.'

'Specially if you tell her now,' agreed Mary.

'I could suggest Jenny?' said Helena mischievously.

'Helena!' scolded her father.

Chapter Ten

It was dizzyingly hot when they stepped off the plane and onto the tarmac.

Helena observed her father blinking into the sun, adjusting the panama that Mary had bought for him to shield his eyes from the dazzling light. He looked as disorientated now as she remembered feeling on her own first visit.

She felt instantly at home and so happy to be back. How she loved the smell and the hot breeze on her face, the sound of the language as porters shouted to each other in the terminal, the shape of the Greek letters on the signs.

'I hadn't realised how close Athens was to the sea!' said Hamish, surveying the sparkling water close by.

'It's called Athens airport, but we're actually in Glyfada,' said Helena. 'Athens is quite a long drive away. But we're not going there anyway, are we, Mum?'

Mary had planned the route meticulously, and it was her stated desire to avoid Athens on this visit. Although Helena had had a hand in the arrangements, this was not negotiable.

Their first task was to pick up a small rental car, in which they would rattle around on the mainland for a week. It was white, dented on both bumpers and already showing signs of rust.

Hamish had some struggles rising to the challenge of driving on the right, but the greater problem for him was how the Greeks drove. It was not only fast flashy cars that passed him on bends in the road, but battered trucks too and motorbikes.

'Why is everyone in such a hurry?' he snapped.

'They want to get to the beach,' said Helena. 'And life is short.'

'Well, theirs will be even shorter if they crash,' he said.

They were heading for Corinth, where they had booked somewhere to stay for the night before going down to the southernmost part of the Peloponnese. The plan was to visit a few archaeological sites before reaching Kalamata, close to where they hoped to find Dina. Following that they would drive north again to Piraeus to hop on a ferry to the island of Ammos.

Their first small, family-run hotel was basic, just three hard beds in a row and towels with which they could have sanded down the walls for repainting, but it was an adventure. and the three of them shared the same excitement about the coming days.

'I wish we could stop in Athens,' Helena said, for the third time. 'There is so much I'd like Dad to see.'

'Don't nag, sweetheart,' her mother responded. 'Another time.'

Helena knew that blunt tone of voice so well. It was one always applied to the subject of her mother's birthplace. Mary would relent one day, she was sure.

Helena still thought of her grandmother from time to time, but her mother's apparent lack of emotion about the subject generally deterred her from bringing it up. Only now did she mention her again. It seemed unnatural not to.

'Shouldn't we go and put some flowers on Yiayiá's grave?' she asked her father one night, when her mother had already slipped off to bed. 'Couldn't we do it on our way to Piraeus?'

'I don't think your mother will want to do that,' he answered. 'You know it's next to her father's?'

'I didn't know that . . . Well, I wish I could go on my own then,' Helena said crossly. 'I was fond of my grandmother.'

'I think it would be a shame to spoil our holiday.'

Her father's appeal was clear, and the very last thing Helena wanted to do was ruin the harmony of this trip. They all seemed invigorated by the translucence of the light, the warmth in the air that did not drop at night, the wildness of the landscape and the scent of wild thyme and lavender. Everywhere.

They stopped at major sites, and it was not just their antiquity but the enormous scale that astonished Helena. For Hamish McCloud, it was the skill in their construction that impressed him most. At Mycenae, neither of them could understand how any mortal could have lifted the vast stones to create the walls.

'That's why they're known as Cyclopean walls,' said Mary. 'People in the past thought they must have been built by giants.'

Helena and her father did everything that tourists were meant to do. At the archaeological site of Olympia, where the first games were held, they raced around the original running track together even in the heat of the midday sun. Helena ran at half her usual pace so that Hamish could keep up, and slowed at the end so that he could win.

'Gold medal for kindness, Helena!' he said, panting.

They all laughed.

At ancient Epidaurus, father and daughter took turns to stand dead centre of the stage to speak a few lines of Shakespeare while the others climbed to the furthest seat in the amphitheatre to listen. Exactly as the guidebook said, the words were clearly audible even with the noise around them.

For someone with Greek blood, Mary McCloud was strangely intolerant of direct sunlight, and generally sat in the shade reading while her husband and daughter took their time sightseeing. She had visited all these places as a child, but excavation and restoration had progressed in the intervening decades, and she insisted that she was enjoying them again as if for the first time.

On the fifth day, they went to Methoni and Koroni, both sites of splendid Venetian castles, and then spent the night in Kalamata.

Helena was impatient now to see if they could track down Dina. She knew her village was somewhere in the region.

Before leaving after Eleni's funeral, Dina had given Mary the name of her village, scribbled in haste and through tears on a scrap of paper. The word looked not unlike the family name, Papagiannis, and when Hamish looked on a map, there was only one place it could be. Papalianos. Dina's description to Helena of how far it was from the sea, how the houses looked and that it was up in the hills also helped.

'If it's like most villages here,' said Mary as she navigated out of Kalamata, 'it won't have changed very much.'

They drove for about fifteen minutes along the coast road, admiring the sparkling blue sea that stretched to the horizon.

'Can't wait to be in that water,' said Helena.

'We'll swim every day when we get to the islands,' promised her father.

'We need to turn right in around half a mile,' said Mary. 'And then there should be a sharp left.'

After another twenty minutes or more of driving through a landscape dominated by ancient, thick-trunked olive trees, they passed a road sign. Helena had been looking out for it.

'Papalianos!' she cried triumphantly. 'I am sure this is Dina's village.'

They found themselves in a square with a huge plane tree at the centre and two cafés, both of them enjoying its shade. The chairs of one were painted in white, of the other in blue. Like the Greek flag, just as Dina had described. It was around ten in the morning, and only the blue café had any customers, three tables each occupied by a single individual.

'Better start our detective work,' said Hamish, parking the car in a side street.

They all got out and ambled back towards the square.

'Let's sit and have a cold drink,' said Mary, leading them to the blue chairs. 'And we'll ask the owner if we are in the right place. A *kafetzís* in a village like this will know everyone and everything about them.'

Within minutes, they were waiting for Dina to arrive.

'*Échei episképseis!*' the *kafetzís* had told one of his grandchildren excitedly. 'She has visitors! *Pes tis!* Tell her!' The boy was already running up the street to knock on Dina's door.

Helena could not relax. She walked towards the end of the street the child had taken and stood impatiently. It was not a long wait. Moments later, the skinny-legged boy in torn shorts and a Snoopy T-shirt came running back.

'*Érchetai!* She's coming!' he said, brushing past her and dashing towards the café.

Helena could see a familiar figure hurrying down the street towards her. Dina was even wearing the same dress she'd had on when they went to the Temple of Zeus. It was the last time they had been out together, and she could picture her in it.

'*Elenáki mou! Elenáki mou!*'

The two of them hugged each other.

'*Se vríkame!*' cried Helena. 'We found you! I thought I might never see you again.'

'*Elenáki!* You have grown so much! Look at you. A little woman now!'

Helena's Greek came back easily and fluently and the two of them chattered away as they walked towards the café.

'Here's Mum,' she said. 'And my dad, Hamish.'

'Maria,' said Dina warmly. 'It's so lovely to see you again.'

The two women embraced.

Mary's visit for the funeral had given them little opportunity to share memories, but now they had time to sit and talk, which they did at great speed. More than an hour passed, with Helena trying to follow as best she could. Dina looked almost the same as she remembered, except for her grey hair. She and her mother were near contemporaries, and she found herself comparing them. Dina's life had been tough in the past years and her skin was much more lined.

Hamish, not understanding a word, decided to disappear for a while. He walked around the village, visiting the exquisite Byzantine church, and stopped by a memorial in a small fenced garden. He was unable to read the names easily, but he noted that five people with the same family name had died in mid September 1944. He had a vague idea of Dina's surname, and when he transliterated the name on the memorial, which was about all he could do, it spelled out a name that was rather like it: *Sotirópoulos.*

In this, the deadest hour of the afternoon, the silence was broken by the tap-tap-tap of a stick behind him. He turned to see a woman, heavily draped in black despite the afternoon's searing heat. She paused, perhaps to gather energy, and her old crone's face twisted into a grimace.

'*Kommounistés!*' she spat, raising her stick to shake it at the memorial. It was a word that needed no translation. She shrieked it again, this time with more vehemence. '*Kommounistés!*'

Shocked by the sudden presence in this peaceful village of an enraged woman, Hamish did not quite know how to respond. He nodded awkwardly to acknowledge his understanding of the word, though he was baffled by the context. The woman continued on her way, rocking from side to side as she walked, muttering her incomprehensible curses.

Perhaps he could ask Mary to ask Dina. He wanted to understand what was behind this violent outburst.

When he turned the corner, he found himself back in the main square and saw his wife and daughter and their old friend still in a huddle round the table. It was two in the afternoon and the plane tree no longer offered its shade.

'My brother has a taverna nearby,' said Dina. 'Would you like to eat?'

She led the way, and soon they were sitting beneath a densely flowering bougainvillea with many dishes spread on the table in front of them, all of them specialities of the area and freshly cooked:

106

kayianás, scrambled eggs with tomato and sausage; *gourounopoúla*, roast pork; *pastó*, salted pork; chicken with square-cut pasta called *chylopítes*. In addition, there was a salad of black-eyed beans flavoured with oranges, local tomatoes, and a big bowl of olives.

Their appetites had been suppressed by the heat these past days, but soon returned with the aromas of Giorgos's cooking. Until now, they had eaten at places serving only tourist fare, but this meal was of a very different kind.

The dish that delighted Helena most of all was *tsouchtí*, spaghetti pan-fried with soft *mizithra* cheese and topped with a fried egg.

'My favourite things all in one bowl!' she said, enthusiastically tucking in. 'And such a great name! *Tsouchtí!*' The word matched the sound that she made as she sucked the strands of pasta into her mouth.

'Onomatopoeia!' laughed her father.

'See, Dad, you're speaking Greek! I said it was easy! *Ónoma* means name.'

'And *poiein* – to make,' added Mary.

Hamish McCloud was hugely enjoying this new stage of parent-hood, a period of occasional role reversal in which child began to teach father. Inadvertently, of course, she had also reminded him of the name he had seen carved over and over again on that piece of stone.

'Mary,' he said, wiping around his plate with a last piece of doughy bread, the peppery olive oil being too good to waste, 'can you ask Dina something for me?'

'Of course,' she answered.

'There's a monument down that little street, where it bends left onto another small square.' He indicated the direction. 'Like a war memorial. It's for Greeks who died. But I don't think they were killed by the Nazis, because they had mostly left by September 1944, hadn't they? And the date on it is too early for the civil war.'

Dina's English was limited, but she heard the word Nazi, she knew the word memorial, and she recognised the month that he referred to, September being almost the same word in Greek.

Mary had listened as Hamish's thoughts tumbled out. As soon as he finished, she began.

'Yes, the Germans had left. It was Greeks killing Greeks. And there was a massacre not far from here. Meligalas is the name of the place where it happened.'

'We passed a sign to it, didn't we?' he asked.

'More than a thousand people were killed, but I imagine the monument only lists those from this village. Men – and women too – who were executed by their own compatriots. I was fifteen. I actually remember my father talking about it. It was conclusive evidence for him that the communists should be wiped out.'

Dina was looking down into her lap, and Helena saw that she was folding and refolding a paper napkin over and over again.

Dina darted an anxious glance towards Mary. There was a frisson in the air. It passed like a gust of cool wind let in by the opening and shutting of a door, and then was gone.

'Even during the Nazi occupation, Greeks fought against Greeks,' Mary explained to her husband. 'There was regular conflict between the communist partisans who had put up resistance against the invaders, and the right-wingers, Greek government forces, called the Security Battalions, who collaborated with the invaders. And after the Nazis left, there was some vicious fighting between the two groups.'

Helena remembered Dina telling her briefly about this fighting between left and right and how it eventually led to full-scale civil war. It had happened so long ago, but seemed still to lurk in the background.

'Greek against Greeks,' murmured Hamish.

'Yes. This was a kind of practice run,' replied Mary. 'The communists lost in the civil war itself, but in this particular battle in 1944, they were on top. And as I said, they killed hundreds of people. Some even say it could have been two thousand.'

Dina continued to listen intently, trying to follow what Mary was saying.

'There were even more deaths after the battle at Meligalas, due to reprisals. And some of the victims of those revenge killings were innocent women and older people.'

'*Athóoi,*' repeated Dina. 'Innocent.'

Mary said something very rapidly to Dina that Helena did not even attempt to understand. The conversation continued between them for a moment or two before Mary gave Helena and Hamish the gist.

'Dina had a cousin and two brothers who were in the Security Battalions. All three of them died. It was poor enough round here in those days, especially after Nazi occupation. But losing three working male members of the family was a disaster for their economic survival. And there were two other relatives who were also killed.'

'So it *was* her family name that I saw on the plaque,' said Hamish quietly. 'It appeared five times.'

'*Pénte,*' said Mary, turning to Dina. 'Five?'

Dina nodded to confirm.

'After the occupation, Dina heard that there was work for house-keepers in Athens and that preference was given to girls whose families were firmly conservative. The wealthy folk of Athens were not taking in any communists.'

Mary began to reminisce about Dina starting work in the Athens apartment at the beginning of 1945. Life in the city was still in a state of upheaval then, but her arrival had brought some kind of order into the home. The previous maid had disappeared a few months earlier, after the discovery of a left-wing pamphlet in her room. Mary's parents had refused to tell her what had happened to the girl, and for a while there was nobody to cook or clean.

It was only a few months after the deaths of her brothers and cousin, so twenty-year-old Dina had been wearing black when she arrived. As well as being an excellent cook, she got on well with Mary and her brother and soon made the apartment shine again.

Dina spoke rapidly to Mary again, and Helena translated key points for her father. She described how General Papagiannis had given her the job because he knew about her family losses at the hands of the left. He even made sure that Dina's mother was on a programme to receive monthly compensation payments for the death of her sons. Helena reflected on her grandfather's cynical tactic to ensure Dina would not leave, even if she was treated like a slave. She had gathered that this was often the case, and that Arsenis had also been abusive to her on several occasions when Eleni's back was turned.

Giorgos had been coming and going to clear the dishes and plates, and when all was done, he brought a plate piled high with *pastéli*, little sheets of sesame mixed with honey to make a crisp, sweet biscuit.

Dina picked up a piece, but not to eat it. She raised it in the air, and then with a sharp *crack*, snapped it into two.

'*Dexiá . . . Aristerá!*' she said bitterly, holding the pieces up. 'Right . . . left!'

Once again, she took off into a rapid monologue, full of fury. Mary stopped her occasionally, just so she could translate for her family.

'She says she has no time for either side now. These extremes. They destroyed Greece. It has never recovered. The civil war, the junta, the politicians, they broke this country. It is still broken.'

Still holding the two pieces of *pastéli*, Dina spoke her final words on the subject.

'*Elláda*,' she said emphatically. '*Étsi eínai.*'

It was Helena who paraphrased for her father. 'That's Greece, in a nutshell,' she said.

They all sat quietly for a moment, then Dina got up and disappeared into the taverna, indicating that she had nothing more to say.

Mary had lived the painful ambiguity of this country and knew the visceral left–right hatred too well. She did not want her husband and daughter to think badly of Dina's family for being on the right.

For so many people, politics had been a matter of pragmatism, their choice based on how best to survive.

'This country was in a mess then,' she said. 'And working for my parents gave Dina stability, a steady salary, food each day. In this village, things would have been very different. People would have been hungry.'

'We shouldn't make assumptions about people, I suppose,' said Hamish. 'But your father wasn't with the right for reasons of hunger.'

'For him, it was a clear political choice. Yes.'

The cicadas hidden all around them in the trees were now creating a huge wall of sound. Every few minutes, for no reason at all, there would be a crescendo and then sudden silence. And then off they went again.

'Even the insects here have political views,' said Hamish, trying to lighten the mood.

They were the only customers in the restaurant now. The other tables had paid their bills and left, and Giorgos came out to sit with them. He poured little glasses of clear, fiery *tsípouro* and they toasted each other's health. Dina then reappeared with slices of fruit that she had cut up in the kitchen and doused with the juice of an orange.

'*Fáte!*' she cried merrily. '*Froúta apó ton kípo mas!* Eat! Fruit from our garden!'

It was clear that she felt only joy to be back in this village, close to her family, living a simpler life, helping her brother cook and clean and caring for their elderly mother.

'Let's go for a walk,' said Mary. 'I want to see where you live, Dina!'

For the next hour or so, they strolled around the little streets, drank strong coffee in Dina's house, met more family members who lived in other parts of the village, and were shown photographs of the various relatives who were now absent, either because they had emigrated for a better life or were no longer alive. The latter included those whose names were listed on the monument, and the two cousins who had recently been killed in Cyprus.

As the sun was beginning to go down, Hamish looked at his watch for the first time that day.

'It's gone seven! I had no idea. I'm sorry, but we really ought to be going.'

They had a long drive ahead of them that evening, and needed to get to Piraeus to check into their *pension* by midnight at the latest. A ferry was booked for 6.30 the following morning and would be taking them on the second part of their holiday, a trip to the Cyclades.

Before the final fond farewell, there were exclamations of dismay and sorrow, hyperbolic promises, breast-crushing embraces, firm hand-shakes and a few tears. Eventually, the three of them were in the car, waving and hooting as they set off, juddering over the cobbles.

For the early part of the journey, they talked of everything they had heard these past hours. Mary told the others how guilty she felt about Dina's treatment, Helena said she hated Arsenis even more than before, and Hamish observed that you only had to scratch the surface to find stories of conflict in Greece.

'Civil war,' Mary said, 'is almost a constant here, not a period fixed within dates.'

'Did you ever read about the English Civil War, Mum?' Helena said. 'We had to do it at school.'

'No,' Mary admitted.

'Nine years, then it was all over.'

These were the last words Helena said before she dozed off in the back seat.

When she woke up, it was to the sound of a mournful song she dimly recognised. A single cassette tape had been left in the car by the previous hirer and it was whirring round.

'*Tóra pou tha fýgeis . . .*'

Helena stayed horizontal, comfortably spread across the seat, listening to the song and watching the regular flashes of bright light that told her they had reached an urban area. Perhaps they were already close to Piraeus.

'What do the words mean?' her father asked.

'Now that you are leaving . . .' Mary translated the phrase that Giorgos Dalaras was singing.

'Turn it off, Mary. Please. For God's sake. Turn it off *now*, would you?' Helena heard an unfamiliar note of anger in her father's voice.

Mary did what he asked, and the music stopped abruptly.

'My darling, I'm so sorry. I wasn't thinking. It's a song I know and love.'

'Even the melody was unbearably sad,' he said, with a crack in his voice. 'And I can't really manage it at the moment.'

Helena saw her mother reach across the handbrake and grasp her father's hand. She was disturbed by this unusual outburst from her father and sudden affection from her mother. It sounded as if Hamish had been about to cry.

The conversation had finished and the car was slowing down. Helena heard the persistent clicking of the indicator.

'I think you need to take a right just after the next junction. It will say *Liménas*,' said her mother. 'Port. And Hotel Agathi will be somewhere nearby.'

Helena felt her mother's gentle touch on her hip.

'Sweetheart,' she said. 'Time to wake up . . . We're in Piraeus.'

The three of them were sharing a room that night, Helena on a fold-up bed near the window and her parents in a double. She found it hard to sleep, with the sound of her mother's heavy breathing and her father muttering in his sleep.

Chapter Eleven

Helena was grateful when her father's travel alarm went off. At least they all had to get up now and she could stop herself going over and over that strange moment in the car.

Within thirty minutes, they were boarding the ferry. Helena and her mother had to get out and go on foot while Hamish drove up the ramp and tried to interpret the gesticulations and shouts of the young man in charge of packing a hundred cars into a limited space.

Finally they met up again in the lounge, where Helena was already eating a toasted sandwich and a coffee was waiting for Hamish.

Despite their inaccessibility, Mary wanted to visit some of the smallest inhabited islands in the Aegean.

'They'll be the most authentic,' she said. 'Because tourists won't have spoiled them. And they'll have all the best qualities of island life, and none of the worst.'

'And what are the worst?' asked Hamish.

'Burnt Brits,' she laughed. 'The colour of ketchup. And there won't be any of that either.'

'We'd better keep our pasty Celtic skin in the shade then, hadn't we, Helena?'

Having stopped briefly at two larger islands to take on more passengers, they eventually disembarked at the tiny islet of Ammos. It enchanted them instantly.

The majority of inhabitants lived in the buildings clustered around the port, and the place they had booked to stay was right on the seafront. The rest of that afternoon was spent acclimatising to the pace of island life, strolling around the network of narrow streets and walking to one of the little beaches close to the town.

Helena had worn her bikini underneath her shorts and T-shirt and was first into the water. She gasped. Not at the chill of the water, as she had probably done every time she had swum in England or Scotland, but at its warmth.

'Mum! Dad! Come in! It's amazing!'

They watched her from the shore, droplets of water cascading from her arms like diamonds as she waved.

'I think I'll just sit,' Mary said to Hamish. 'You go in.'

Hamish was soon doing an athletic crawl towards his daughter, and the two of them swam round the headland.

'This is bliss,' said Helena, floating on her back for a while. 'Pure and utter bliss.'

'It's very beautiful, isn't it?'

Beneath them were huge shoals of colourful fish.

'It's like being in an aquarium!' Helena cried out with glee. 'It's even nicer than swimming near Athens!'

'Think we'd better get back to Mum,' he said. 'She'll wonder what's happened to us.'

'Race you!' said his daughter.

They splashed through the water, Helena's lithe body fast and efficient but Hamish winning by a few yards.

'You always used to let me win, Dad!' Helena protested.

'Ah, you're too old to be patronised now,' he laughed, trying to catch his breath. 'And you'll beat me again one day.'

Helena lay down on the fine shingle, close to where her mother was sitting under a tree. The sun was still warm enough to dry her skin.

'It was gorgeous, Mum,' she said, gazing up at the cloudless blue sky. 'You should have come in.'

'I was happy here,' Mary replied, closing one of her guidebooks and picking up the other. 'I was just planning our day tomorrow.'

'Please put swimming on the agenda.'

'Of course! But there are some interesting things to see too. If you spend *all* day in the water, you'll shrivel.'

Helena laughed. 'I'll get pretty burnt too,' she said, sitting up. 'Look, my arms have already gone a bit pink, haven't they?'

'They'll be fine if we put some yoghurt on them later.'

'Yoghurt?' Helena frowned.

'It's a wonder cure. Greek yoghurt is the most delicious thing in the world, and the best treatment for sunburn. You'll see!'

'I think I'll need some too,' said Hamish, examining his right shoulder.

That evening, over their plates of *barboúnia* with Greek salad and the best fried potatoes they had ever eaten, Mary showed them the itinerary she had put together. There were a few archaeological sites on the island, and each village had its own small museum, some only open between the hours of five and seven in the evening. The guidebook told them that they would usually have to source a key from a nearby kiosk or *kafeneío*.

They all slept well that night, and got up late the following day. After breakfast in the little café beneath the hotel, they set off on their tour, swimming en route and then taking most of the day to reach their destination, a small village in the north of the island.

Helena expected signs to be in Greek, but the one on the village's museum door was written in a strange cocktail of English and French, with a sprinkling of Greek. The three of them puzzled over it for a few minutes: *Jhon stans perip don klee to episkep.*

'John at the kiosk will give the key to visitors!' Helena cried, with the satisfaction of someone solving a clue in a cryptic crossword.

From the outside, the museum looked uninviting and as if no visitor had bothered to borrow the key from 'Jhon' in a very long time. Helena and her father waited patiently at the door while Mary sauntered off and made conversation with the old man who sat inside the battered wooden kiosk in the square. Eventually she returned, and, after fiddling for a while with a lock that had seized up through lack of use, triumphantly threw open the door. Helena fumbled in the darkness to find a light switch, and suddenly a harsh fluorescent strip illuminated the small space.

There were cabinets on three sides of the room and one in the middle. The walls were nicotine-coloured, there were damp patches on the ceiling, and a single fan began to whir slowly above their heads, stirring the air in the windowless room just a little but doing little to alleviate the heat.

None of the objects looked particularly interesting to Helena. There were no beautiful statues or jewellery, not a single complete item. In her mind, it compared very unfavourably with the big museum in Athens.

'These things are a bit mundane, aren't they?' she said to her mother.

'That's the point, darling. They are *ordinary* things, used by *ordinary* people. Look at the fragments of that cup – it's the same shape as some of ours at home. And that painted bowl? You ate yoghurt out of something similar this morning. Don't you find that interesting? That four thousand years ago, people had the same needs, the same habits, as we do now?'

'But all those random pieces over here,' Helena said, moving to the next cabinet. 'They just look like things Dad might have dug up in his vegetable patch. What makes them important enough to display?'

'Now those pieces are really revealing,' explained Mary, putting her glasses on to better read the labels. 'They're earlier, a different style of decoration. They help us understand a way of life, migration of people, whether they moved from one island to another, whether it was peaceful. So many things . . .' She seemed almost enraptured.

Helena was trying to understand. She thought that objects in such museums were meant to be attempts at beauty. Should they not bear some resemblance to a work of art, or be something more than just bits of broken pottery or simply stones? In the next cabinet, there was a whole shelf of what looked like pebbles.

'And those? They look as if someone picked them up on the beach. What do you think, Dad?'

Hamish McCloud was enjoying his wife's enthusiasm and amused by his daughter's disdain. He was sure that Mary would convert her. As a teacher, his wife had the knack of persuasive explanation.

'I understand what your mother is saying,' he told her. 'It's the information these things give us that is important. We're not in an art gallery, where an artefact is there just because of its appearance.'

'These small bits of marble show that people from here travelled. Because that particular type of marble doesn't exist on this island. So maybe people from Naxos brought it over here. There's plenty of exactly that kind of stone there. Either way, it starts to build a picture. And look, this cabinet has some obsidian blades.'

'Obsidian?' Hamish McCloud interjected. 'The mineral?'

'Mum's giving us a geology lesson now!' Helena teased, impressed by her mother's knowledge. 'I thought classics was your subject.'

'I actually wanted to be an archaeologist when I was your age,' she said. 'Being a teacher wasn't really my plan.'

Helena realised how little she knew of her mother's past, and conjured up an image of her in the echoing spaces of the Archaeological Museum.

'Obsidian comes from volcanic glass,' Mary continued. 'It's extremely hard, and was used for blades to cut and carve marble. And that's another thing that tells us there was travel and commerce between these tiny islands, even five thousand years ago. There's no obsidian found here. They probably got it from Milos, where there is plenty. And suddenly they had something with which they could carve, and cut and shape. It's impossible for us to imagine how significant a change that was back then. They used emery too, for smoothing the marble. Probably also imported from Naxos, like the marble.'

Hamish and Helena listened intently. What had seemed like junk was being transformed by Mary's knowledge and passion.

Helena had pressed her nose against the cracked glass to take a closer look at the cabinet. She tried to decipher the carelessly hand-written labels next to the various pieces. They were also in French, and almost faded to invisibility.

'Why are these in French?' she asked.

'It was probably a French team who did the excavation,' Mary answered.

They moved from cabinet to cabinet. Helena noticed that her mother's short-sleeved cream blouse was sticking to her back, unusually transparent with sweat.

'Are you okay, Mum? Do you want to go?'

'Just a minute more, darling,' Mary replied, her voice hoarse and dry.

They had come to the last cabinet, closest to the door. There were three shelves. Only her father could easily view what was on the top one. Mary could just about see if she stood on tiptoe.

'Some kind of animal?' she asked. 'Maybe a ram or something.'

Helena could see nothing except the edges of some randomly shaped stones.

Mary began to cough.

'I think it's time to leave, don't you?' said Hamish, suddenly and quite brusquely. 'Let's go now before we suffocate. It's impossible to breathe in here.'

When they got outside, Mary sank down onto the step. Helena sat next to her, fanning her with the guidebook while Hamish returned the key to the kiosk, where he bought a small bottle of cold water for his wife.

Mary gulped it down almost in one and her colour began to return.

'I'll be all right in a moment,' she insisted. 'I just felt a bit faint in there.'

'We all need a drink, I think,' said Hamish.

For the next hour or so, the three of them sat beneath a carob tree, reviving themselves with fresh lemonade made from lemons grown in the *kafetzís*'s own orchard, as he was very proud to tell them.

Helena gathered a few of the shiny brown carob pods that had fallen to the ground and made a pile on the little table. It gave the elderly Greek man at the next table the excuse he had been waiting for. He had been dying to show off his English from the moment he heard them speaking.

'Those are magic,' he said. 'When I was a child and we didn't have much to eat, my mother used to grind the little seeds inside into flour to make bread. And if she could spare one, we sucked on the pod and pretended it was chocolate. Try it!'

Helena picked one up and tasted it.

'You're right. It's delicious!'

'They're full of minerals and vitamins and all sorts,' he continued. 'And they were used to feed animals too. Nothing was wasted back then. Nothing at all. Not like today, with all those bins of discarded food in the big town going to waste.'

'So are you from here?' Hamish asked.

'Yes. Born on the island. Left it to study philology in Athens. Went to London to learn English. Came back to be the island teacher. No regrets. This place has everything a man could need. You could live for ever on Ammos, if you didn't have any bad habits.'

He laughed as he lit a cigarette and drew the nicotine deep into his lungs, at the same time raising a glass of firewater to his lips.

'Cheers!' he said. 'Bottoms up!'

The McCloud family lifted their glasses with the dregs of lemonade and chorused, '*Geia mas!*'

'You speak some Greek!' exclaimed their neighbour.

'My wife is Greek,' said Hamish.

'Where from?' asked the man.

'Athens,' Mary said bluntly, sticking to English.

'Ah,' he said. 'Such a frightful city. Filthy, dirty. Nothing to be said for it. So, your family name?'

'Do excuse me,' she said, getting up. 'Just popping to the ladies. And we probably ought to make tracks after that.'

Hamish and the elderly man, who now introduced himself as Dionysus, continued chatting. He was tediously knowledgeable about the economic state of Britain and wanted to engage Hamish in discussion.

Helena followed her mother into the café and found her washing her hands.

'Are you feeling all right?' she asked. 'Just wanted to make sure.'

'I'm fine, sweetheart. Thank you.'

'You didn't seem keen on our new friend.'

'It's a long time since I was in Greece. And I had forgotten the way people like to pinpoint precisely where you're from and what your surname is. Before you know it, you find you're related.'

Mother and daughter were looking at each other in the mirror above the sink. They were so unalike: Mary with her dark hair expertly wound into a bun, her oval face, almond-shaped eyes and neat, straight nose; Helena with her copper-coloured hair – it seemed to vary according to the light – made even more crinkly by salt and sun, her green eyes and a complexion dotted with freckles. Sometimes Helena wished she was more like her mother, so neat, so elegant. Today, though, Mary looked tired.

'And I don't want to share such information with a stranger,' said Mary firmly. 'The Papagiannis name, that is. Maria Papagiannis of Kolonaki, Athens. That's no longer who I am.'

'I get it, Mum,' Helena replied.

'There is a reasonable chance that he would know the name, and apart from anything, he would link me with the junta. For him I would be simply the daughter of a fascist.'

'*And* he was so rude about Athens!' said Helena. 'That really annoyed me. It's a beautiful city!'

'It's typical of a certain kind of islander,' Mary replied. 'To be derogatory about the capital.'

Mary paid for the lemonades inside the café so that they could leave straight away, and rather brusquely told Dionysus that they had to go.

'We have friends waiting for us,' she said. 'And we're already late.'

'Fare thee well, dear travellers in our antique land,' intoned the old man, with a flourish of his hand.

Back in the car, they sang songs, talked about their day and laughed together about the man with the perfect patter.

Chapter Twelve

They were all settling in to a leisurely Greek island pace, enjoying the mix of the sea, the sights and tasty food to punctuate the day.

The three of them were having breakfast by the quayside, watching fishermen mending their nets and others gutting their catch on deck.

'What did you think of the museum yesterday?' Mary asked her daughter, spooning some dark honey onto her yoghurt.

'You made it all really interesting,' Helena replied. 'Even the things that looked like bits of rubble.'

'You don't go into a tiny museum like that for a display of fine sculpture,' Mary said.

'I get that now.'

'I was hoping for a few big statues,' said Hamish with a wry smile.

'They tend to display those in the more important museums,' Mary told him. 'But even in a little museum like that one, you still get glimpses of a much bigger story.'

Hamish got up. 'I want to post these,' he said, waving a sheaf of postcards written the previous day. 'I'll go on a stamp hunt, if you don't mind sitting here a bit longer?'

Mother and daughter continued to chat as he disappeared around the corner.

'How does anyone know anything about most of those objects?'

'Lots of it is scientifically proven through dating methods. But some theories are based on speculation. Like detective work. You have a few clues, and then try and build a picture.'

'It's a mixture of science, then . . .'

'And story-telling. You try to match any evidence you have with a reasonable theory. A story, in other words.'

'So that's what archaeology is,' said Helena. 'Not just digging things up?'

'I would describe it as the place where knowledge meets the imagination.'

'I didn't know you knew so much about it, Mum.'

'When I was a child, we were taught a lot about our ancient past at school.' She smiled. 'It's our heritage. Yours too, of course . . .'

'I never realised you felt so connected with all this.'

'All this? With Greece, you mean?'

The waiter came up at that moment and Mary ordered a second coffee.

'I always wanted us to come on holidays here,' she continued. 'But money, circumstances, time . . .'

Helena seized her moment.

'But Yiayiá's place? We could all have gone there for a few days when she was alive.'

'To Athens? It was lovely for you to have those stays alone, without your parents tagging along.'

'And mostly I had great times. But when were you last there?'

'A long, long time ago.'

'That's so vague, Mum. When exactly?'

Mary looked around her, scanning the little square behind them.

'Do you think your father has got lost? He only went for a few stamps!'

Her discomfort at Helena's question was obvious and only made her daughter more curious.

'Or at least, if you can't remember when you last went, why did you leave in the first place?'

'Everyone wants to leave home at some point, don't they? I wanted to go to university in England. I felt it would be a better place for a female undergraduate. And then I met your father. And stayed. Nobody travelled to and fro like they do now.'

The answer was watertight. And yet it did not fully explain why her mother had essentially broken her connection with her motherland, even changing her name from Maria to Mary. Was it just because of her father's politics?

'But not going back at *all*? Even for a visit?'

'I can see you won't let this one drop,' said Mary defensively.

Helena was tracing a pattern in the condensation on her glass, but if she had been looking more closely at her mother, she would have seen beads of sweat running down her neck.

Though it was rare, tension between them did occasionally explode, and she was not sure it was worth spoiling the mood.

'I'm extremely curious,' she said, staring into her water. 'But you don't have to tell me.' The way she said it carried a hint of challenge.

'I suppose I can tell you why, now that your grandmother has passed away,' Mary began. 'It was more to do with my father than my mother, as I think you know. He was a truly vile man.'

Helena was shocked by the bluntness of her mother's statement, but after the terror of that long-ago encounter with her grandfather, of which she had never breathed a single word to anyone, it was not entirely unexpected. The petite grandmother with her luxurious apartment and gorgeously coiffed Kolonaki friends must have had some dark corners in her life. Helena was old enough to know that most people did.

'I don't want to change your memory of Yiayiá,' said Mary. 'It doesn't seem fair.'

'But maybe it *should* change, if it needs to?'

'She wasn't entirely at fault, I can see that now, but as far as I remember she almost never criticised or challenged him. The first time I was aware that she didn't agree with everything he thought or did was when Andreas died. I always thought she was very cowardly up until then.'

'I told you how she changed when Pappoú died. That she seemed much happier.'

'Yes, so maybe I misread her all that time,' Mary reflected.

A waiter approached with two freshly squeezed orange juices that they had ordered and Helena drank hers down almost in one gulp before resuming her questioning.

'But what were all those medals for on your father's chest? Weren't they for heroic acts?'

'Yes. I suppose you could say that. He was a so-called war hero.'

'Didn't it make you proud to have a father like that?'

'No,' said Mary flatly. 'Not in the least.'

'What did he do exactly, Mum?'

'The men who took over Greece, the junta, were three younger colonels. They got rid of many of the old blood, many of their more experienced superiors, but not my father. He was one of their biggest supporters and saw it as a new opportunity. He had power over the fate of thousands of people, Helena, over a very long period of time, from before the civil war right up until his own death.'

Mary poured this out to her daughter as though it was a relief to confess it.

'He had been in charge of some of the island prisons after the civil war, and then was given the task of overseeing all of them. Thousands of people who opposed the dictatorship were sent to those places. The junta even made him a judge when they got rid of the civil courts so he had the chance to sentence yet more people. And he was considered one of the most extreme anti-communist generals in the army.'

'What made him like that? Was it because of your brother? Dina told me that his death made your father hate the communists more than ever.'

'Yes,' Mary sighed. 'That definitely fuelled his hatred.'

They watched a yacht being expertly steered into the harbour. A crew of three were on deck, tanned and muscular, ready for action, while a woman in a bikini lay stretched out on an upper deck, reading.

'*Eleftheria*,' said Helena, reading the name of the vessel. 'Freedom. You take it for granted until you lose it, I suppose.'

'Your grandfather deprived so many people of it,' said Mary. 'Journalists, poets, musicians, politicians . . . They released fifteen hundred prisoners from those terrible islands, even before the junta fell. My father would have been furious. In my opinion, it's no coincidence that this happened after his death. He would have done anything to prevent it.'

Helena winced. She had been aware from early on that her experience of Athens was a very cloistered one, with a driver, ice creams at Zonars and visits to the cinema and beach. Now it seemed to her that the brutal reality of the dictatorship that had been hidden from her was embodied in one person: her grandfather.

'Where do you think Dad has got to? He can't have got lost, can he?'

At that moment, Hamish McCloud appeared smiling in front of them, waving his postcards in triumph.

'All ready and stamped. Just have to find a postbox now. Apparently the nearest one is on the other side of town.'

'How far is that?' asked Mary.

'It's a very small town,' he said good-naturedly. 'I might as well send these on their way, if you're happy to wait?'

'Do you want me to take them?' asked Helena, hoping for refusal.

'No, it's fine. I could do with the walk.'

Helena was glad for another few minutes alone with her mother.

'But what about Yiayiá? Wasn't she part of it?'

'She was so young when they got married. I don't imagine she really understood what kind of person my father was,' said Mary. 'She was only nineteen and he was in his thirties. I imagine he was very dashing in his army uniform, and young women didn't have the same kind of choices in those days, Helena, you have to remember that.'

'Was it something like an arranged marriage, then?'

'A bit like it, I think,' answered Mary. 'I always assumed that her parents didn't give her a choice. They were very close friends of his family – what they call *kollitoí*, "sticky friends", in Greece.'

'Do you think Yiayiá was unhappy then?'

'Even when I was little, I often saw her crying. I assumed it was because of him. Your grandfather treated everyone badly, not just me and my brother. She was heartbroken when Andreas died, though.'

'That must have been terrible,' said Helena.

'Yes. There's no other word.'

Hamish bounded up to the table, oblivious to the serious conversation they were having.

'Found a box. Rusty old thing, but fingers crossed. In three weeks' time, everyone will have their "wish you were here"! And by then we'll be back home.' He laughed. 'Such a funny tradition, isn't it, sending postcards?'

'Yes.' Mary smiled. 'But you've been so long, I've had time to tell Helena all about my parents.'

Hamish sat down and gulped back his tepid coffee. 'I hope she's not too disillusioned,' he murmured.

'Not even a bit,' said Helena. 'It makes much more sense now that you two didn't visit them yourselves.'

Hamish nodded, and then attracted the waiter's attention to order an iced coffee. He had drunk one for the first time the previous day, and declared the *frappé* the best of all Greek inventions.

'I was telling her what a bully my father was. Anyone who didn't agree with him was an enemy. Even fellow Greeks. In the civil war, he regarded half the country as the enemy. He led campaigns against them, and boasted of his victories. Those were my teenage years,

Helena, the years when you wake up to things. Form your own views.'

'But if you're in the army, aren't you *expected* to kill?'

'Yes. And to give orders for others to kill. But you're not meant to take so much pleasure in it. And in the civil war, he was giving orders to Greeks to kill their fellow countrymen.'

'I never thought about what work he actually did, when I was there.'

'Well, he had a lot of blood on his hands,' said Mary sadly. 'Even if he regarded it as his job.'

With her grandmother, there had never been discussion of anything political, but the old lady's positive comment about the presence of soldiers in the street had always stuck in Helena's mind.

'How did you form your own views then? If your mother seemed to support his?'

'I think it was instinct, sweetheart. For years, it was just a feeling every time he walked in the room. A kind of revulsion. I don't think it bothered him that I tried to avoid being anywhere near him. He always dragged my brother away from our games to teach him about war, and gave him thousands of toy soldiers made of lead, perfectly painted in different uniforms. They were set up on his bedroom floor on a huge piece of green fabric, and he and Andreas re-enacted historic battles whenever our father had an evening at home. They made up their own wars too. It was obsessive. I realised later that he was conditioning my brother.'

'Brainwashing him, you mean?'

'Yes. My brother was kind and gentle, not political at all. But he was forced to follow our father's footsteps into the army. It was as if he didn't have a choice. The other thing was that whenever Andreas made any mistakes in the games they played, my father would slap him round the ear. I don't think he could hear much in his left ear by the time he joined the army.'

Helena felt slightly nauseous even at the thought of her grandfather.

'It was Andreas's terrible misfortune that a civil war was going on and that it was so vicious. He went to the front, fought in a real battle and lasted just a single day.'

After almost thirty years, Helena could see on her mother's face that the memory, if not the grief itself, was still fresh.

'I had to try and support your grandmother as best I could. More than once I caught her outside on one of the big balconies, gazing catatonically downwards. And I know she hid how she felt from my father.'

'Wasn't she allowed to express her grief?'

'The one-year memorial was the limit he gave her. Up until then, he tolerated her tears. But after that, you could see that they just fuelled his anger. From then on, she was expected to entertain his colleagues and fellow generals and go back to normal.'

'Yiayiá was still hosting parties when I used to stay. I would spy on them through a crack in the door, men with shiny buttons and women with masses of jewellery and tinkly voices.'

'That all sounds familiar,' said Mary. 'And did the guests still bring gifts with fancy wrappings and ribbons?'

Helena felt her hair stand on end. This acceptance of gifts had clearly been a habit for a long time. Many decades. She thought of the strange stones once wrapped up as a gift that might still be in that bedroom drawer.

She nodded.

'He sounds quite materialistic for a soldier,' commented Hamish.

'It seemed so,' said Mary.

'But do you think he blamed himself for sending your brother into the army?'

'Definitely,' Mary replied firmly. 'And my mother did too.'

'Poor Yiayiá,' said Helena. 'It's so sad.'

'I can see now how awful her life must have been. But I didn't realise it then. I just saw a woman dedicated to keeping this man's fury contained, at the expense of all else.'

'Anger of that nature, peppered with guilt and grief, is a poisonous mix,' reflected Hamish, who was well used to referring patients for psychological help. He was certain that Stamatis Papagiannis would have benefited from some. 'It has a terrible effect on everyone it touches.'

None of them said anything for a moment. All of them knew it to be true.

'Look, we've got lots to see on this lovely island,' said Mary, picking the guidebook up from the table. It was time to lighten the mood.

Helena had a thousand other questions for her mother, but knew it was high time for her to stop talking about her grandparents. It was not why they had come away together. She leapt up.

'Yes! I want to buy a sunhat, go to that folk museum, visit the monastery and snorkel. All before lunch!'

Hamish laughed.

'Let's get going then, shall we?' smiled Mary, delighted by her daughter's enthusiasm for everything this island had to offer.

They fitted in all the activities on Helena's agenda by four in the afternoon, except for the snorkelling, and were recommended a rocky cove thirty minutes away, overlooked, they were told, by the best fish taverna on the island.

By the time they arrived, the sun was beginning to go down, so Hamish and Helena agreed it was best to swim first and then eat. They spent a contented hour gazing with admiration at the shoals beneath them, striped, mottled, electric blue, yellow with a flash of green, even a parrot fish with its bright red back. Most surprising of all was to see an octopus lurking in the rocks. They were careful to avoid the scores of sea urchins that covered the bottom of the shallows.

'It shows how clean the water is,' said Hamish. 'But if you touch them, I'll spend the rest of the holiday pulling out their spines and tending to your wounds!'

Mary was keeping them a table at the taverna, reading the guide-book and making notes for the following days.

The restaurant more than lived up to expectations. As if the delicate flavour of the fish, the chilled wine and the friendliness of the owner were not enough, the sun set directly opposite. A burst of orange spread across the sea towards them, making their faces and the rocks behind them glow.

Chapter Thirteen

The next day they took an unfamiliar road out of town and before long turned left onto an unsurfaced track that narrowed and became rougher as it began to climb.

'Are you sure this is right?' asked Hamish.

'Completely sure,' said Mary, looking at the map. 'Keep going. I'm sure it's up here.' She was flicking through the guidebook to find the appropriate page. '"The site was only discovered two or three years ago, but is believed to have been an important burial place. Many questions are still to be answered on the findings."'

'Why?'

'It sounds as if there are things that don't really add up.'

Hamish had lost interest in anything other than getting them safely to their destination, wherever that was, but as they progressed, he began to struggle to keep the car on the track. It jolted over the boulder-strewn surface, from time to time losing its grip.

'We'll get a flat tyre at this rate, Mary. This is absolutely *ridiculous*!'

It was now impossible to turn round, so he was obliged to keep climbing, the gears grinding and the exhaust pipe sometimes catching as the already battered hire car lurched up and down, in and out of the ruts in the road. For a few hundred yards, the surface was covered with a layer of fine grit, and from time to time the car slid backwards, the wheels spinning.

'Can we stop and walk?' Helena asked.

'We can't just park in the middle of a road,' said Mary. 'And we must be close now.'

On both sides there was a sudden drop, so even if they did stop it would be virtually impossible to get out of the car. Helena looked anxiously out of the side window, noting the precipitous cliff on one side and a steep slope on the other.

Eventually the track widened a little and ended in a small clearing. With a sigh of relief, Hamish slowed the car and turned off the ignition. He was the first out, and pulled the driver's seat forward to allow Helena to emerge.

The three of them stood in silence, their backs to each other, looking outwards in different directions. They were at the very summit of a hill, higher than anywhere else on the island, with a vast flatness of blue on every side, the line between sea and sky indistinct.

'We're on top of the world,' said Helena, spinning around in a three-hundred-and-sixty-degree circle, her arms held out wide.

'Magnificent,' breathed Mary. 'Really magnificent.'

'Thanks for getting us up here, Dad,' said Helena. 'I think it was worth it.'

Hamish McCloud seemed lost for words, and Helena noticed him take her mother's hand. The view seemed to have moved them both to tears.

She used this moment of mild awkwardness to return to the car. She wanted to get her camera, though quite what the focus of any photograph taken from here would be she was not sure.

As she looked through the lens, she realised that she could never capture the depths of the sea, the void of the sky, of everything and nothing. This was a moment to be felt, not a sight to be recorded.

The only disruption to the view was the appearance of a buzzard, circling high above them, gliding on the thermals.

'He's looking for a hare, I should imagine,' said Mary.

In the distance, as the haze lifted, a few other islands began to emerge, all appearing to float above the misty surface of the sea.

'Beautiful,' said Hamish.

'Let's go over and have a look at the site,' said Mary.

She led them across to an area flimsily fenced off by chicken wire. There was almost nothing to see. Whatever had been dug had been covered over again. There were no markers of any kind. Without the wire, they would have walked straight across the site.

'Do you want to read it out?' Mary said, passing the guidebook to her daughter.

'According to this,' Helena began, 'a French archaeologist discovered some graves up here. "As well as evidence of human remains, there were some marble fragments, pieces of pottery and a golden necklace, all found just below the surface in one area. There has been a suggestion that these were not dug graves, but were possibly caskets left on top of the ground. Possible date given for the "burials" is circa 3000 BC. Evidence of grave-robbing has allowed only sketchy hypotheses around the finds and the importance of the site."'

'Can you imagine a more extraordinary place to spend your afterlife?' said Mary. 'Just you and the sky, the air, the sea breeze? Nowadays someone might build a villa up here, but back then they used it for . . .'

'Eternity?' Hamish suggested.

'Most of us end up below the ground, but these people must have wanted to be close to the surface,' said Helena. 'Presumably so their souls could fly upwards. It does make more sense, doesn't it, given that we always think of heaven as being up there somewhere.' She was pointing up at the sky, where the buzzard continued to circle, still looking for its prey.

Hamish McCloud turned away and started wandering over the brow of the hill, away from the direction in which they had come.

'Where are you going, Dad?' called Helena.

He mumbled an almost audible reply about needing a moment alone.

Helena and her mother strolled for a while around the summit of the hill, but there was little of anything recognisably archaeological.

'Archaeologists always leave a site as they found it,' said her mother. 'So it often doesn't look much when you visit. Unless they've excavated a building or some walls, of course.'

'It was worth coming here, though, wasn't it?' said Helena. 'Just to see this spectacular location.'

'Yes,' Mary said. 'I've never been anywhere quite like it.'

Hamish reappeared. 'It's even steeper on the other side,' he reported.

Helena wanted to capture the moment. She balanced her camera on a rock and activated the timer, making several attempts before it was successful. She wanted a photograph of the three of them, and they lined up in a row against the backdrop of hazy blue: Helena in green-and-white striped T-shirt and denim shorts, Hamish in his panama and linen trousers, and Mary in an azure shift and Jackie O shades.

'Five, four, three, two, one,' she counted. The shutter clicked.

'It's a sensational place,' said Mary, 'but we should start our descent.'

'Hope we don't meet anyone on the way down.' Hamish sounded nervous.

'I shouldn't think many other people bother to come all the way up here,' said Helena.

'Fingers crossed,' added Mary brightly.

Within half an hour they had reached the coast road and were motoring towards another beach with a well-reviewed taverna, the next destination on Mary's itinerary, but the magic of the mountaintop remained in Helena's mind. The mystical place would always live in her memory.

At the taverna, just before their food arrived, Mary went inside to wash her hands. A calendar on the counter with incongruous images of alpine resorts caught her eye and reminded her of the significance of the date. She rushed back outside.

'Hamish! You know what day it is today?'

'Friday?'

'Yes, and . . .?'

'You know I never know what the date is when we're on holiday, Mary. When I haven't got to worry about work, it could be any day of the year as far as I'm concerned.'

'It's the sixteenth of September!'

'Our wedding anniversary!' he cried. 'Of course it is! Happy anniversary, sweetheart!'

'It's twenty-five years!' Mary smiled. 'Twenty-five years today.'

'Happy anniversary, Mum and Dad!'

Helena glanced at her mother's slightly exhausted face and wondered if she was hurt that her father seemed to have forgotten. When she looked back at him, she saw that he had put something on the table. It was a small white box with a blue ribbon.

'I was only teasing,' he said. 'Silver wedding? And you thought I would forget?'

Mary laughed. Both of them knew that he was capable of forgetting important dates. The box bore the name of a jeweller not far from where they were staying. All the while they thought he was looking for stamps, Hamish had also been looking for a gift.

Mary opened the box and smiled, picking up the delicate chain bracelet with one little charm, a blue *máti,* the protecting eye.

'That's absolutely beautiful, Hamish, thank you so much,' she said. 'I love it.'

'It's white gold with a sapphire,' he said. 'At least that's what they told me.'

Helena noticed tears in her mother's eyes.

'Will you put it on for me?' she asked, reaching her slender wrist out towards him.

He fiddled unsuccessfully with the clasp before passing the task to Helena.

'Twenty-five years,' she breathed, shutting the tiny catch for her mother.

'It does feel a long time since that first meeting, doesn't it, Hamish?'
Hamish nodded.

Helena knew that her parents had met when they were both at university in London, but until the previous day, she had never thought about why Mary had left Greece in the first place. It was only when she had been so frank about her father's bullying behaviour and his role in the army that Helena had begun to understand. She could not resist trying to find out more.

'But what made you finally leave home? You had already put up with so much for so long.'

Mary put her fork down. 'A very specific moment crystallised things,' she said. 'I was around your age. Coming home from an afternoon stroll with my best school friend, Despina, who lived close by, right at the lower end of our street.'

'Near the little crossroads?'

'Yes, that's right! Exactly there,' said Mary, gratified that her daughter knew those streets so well. 'The civil war had ended, but leftists were still being persecuted. A group of soldiers, five of them, because I counted, were kicking someone who was lying on the ground.'

She looked down, playing with her new bracelet as she talked, distractedly running her finger along its fine links.

'We couldn't get home without passing them, so we waited out of sight hoping it would come to an end. We loitered in the entrance to some apartments, pretending to be looking for a name on the panel. After five minutes or so, we heard laughter. Then the sound of their boots coming towards us. We didn't dare turn round as they passed, but we could hear them. "Fucking communists", they were saying and laughing.'

'Weren't you afraid?' asked Helena softly.

'They weren't going to pick on us, I knew that, but it made me feel really sick. It wasn't uncommon to see soldiers beating people up then, but this had looked really brutal. And when we emerged to walk up the street, the man was motionless on the ground.'

'You mean he was dead?'

Hamish was listening intently, even though he had heard the story before. A waiter was clearing their plates and another was bringing a dish of melon, pears and grapes.

'Nobody could have survived those injuries,' continued Mary. 'His blood was literally flowing into the gutter. I didn't want to look, but I couldn't help it. And I will never be free of the image. His face was almost unrecognisable, but not quite. Despina fell on top of the body, screaming. Only then did I understand that it was her father. She identified him from his jacket, I think. He was a university professor, Helena. A good man.'

Helena was shocked that her mother had witnessed such a terrible thing, and any words she could think of to say simply dried in her mouth.

'It took no time for a crowd to gather. Suddenly my mother appeared next to me. She had come down from our apartment to bring me home. I wanted to stay with Despina, but she was being comforted by plenty of other people by then, so I watched for the next ten minutes from the balcony as the police came, and an ambulance. There was chaos in the street beneath us. My mother made me come inside, and I suppose I must have been in shock so I did what was I told.'

'Your poor friend,' Helena said, almost inaudibly. 'Did they ever arrest anyone?'

'I wish I could say there had been some kind of justice,' answered Mary. 'That night, things got worse. When my father came home, he knocked on my bedroom door and asked me to come into his study. The man who had died in the street, he said, was a communist ringleader. Such vermin still needed to be weeded out of society, he told me. I remember staring at him. I managed to stop myself from reacting, but I was shaking with anger and disbelief. And the really strange thing for me was that my father was full of anger too. I was gripped by the need to be silent. I said nothing. It felt as if I had turned a key and locked myself in.'

'Did he ever hit you?' asked Helena, who could see that even the memory of her father was a disturbing one for her mother.

'Yes,' replied Mary. 'I was quite often caned.'

'I can't imagine how anyone could ever treat their children in the way your grandfather did, Helena,' said Hamish. He had heard this account before but was still shocked by it.

Mary was impatient to finish telling Helena what had happened and continued at speed.

'Anyway, that night I packed a bag, and when my father had gone to work the following morning, I told my mother I was leaving. She was absolutely distraught, but she couldn't stop me and she knew it. I told her I wanted to go to England and find a university to take me. I could speak the language. The one thing I owe my father is my good education.

'I said that I needed money, which of course she couldn't give me because she had none of her own. But she took me into her bedroom and opened a drawer. She was sobbing, Helena, but I was determined. She piled into my hands tens of thousands of drachmas' worth of jewellery as though it was cheap junk. She didn't care about any of it. A diamond necklace and some earrings, a gold bracelet set with rubies, a couple of rings with huge stones, more earrings, a brooch. I just threw it all into a bag. It was my mother's one act of defiance against my father, and God knows what he did to her when he found out.'

Mary began to weep as she described the moment of leaving.

'My mother couldn't speak,' she continued. 'Dina was there too. She understood why I had to leave. There was no choice. They clung to me and then they clung to each other. And then I left.

'I ran to see Despina, who was about to leave for her father's funeral, and explained what I was doing. She said it was better for me not to come to the church because everyone knew who my father was.

'I learned a lot more later. That her uncle was incarcerated some-where in a prison for leftists, for example. But even Despina had not realised that her family was politically active until that day. It was all so clandestine back then. We kept in touch, writing letters every week, and I understood that she was "branded", so to speak.'

Helena took her mother's hand.

'I had no intention of *ever* coming back.'

'That's so sad,' said Helena.

'It was. I love so much about this country. It is so beautiful and has such a rich heritage, and I never wanted to deprive you of all that,' said Mary.

'And what happened to Despina?' Helena did not feel that she had heard the end of the story.

'She left Greece not long after I did. She went to Australia with her mother to find some relatives. Lots of people had left Greece by then, for a better life.'

'Better in what way?'

'Financially, politically, socially. Her opportunities were going to be limited here with the stigma of a leftist father. We carried on writing for a while, but letters used to take months and we lost touch in the end.'

For Helena, her mother's revelations made sense of everything that she had accepted and yet found strange. The lack of photographs of Mary, for example, explained away by Yiayiá with the words: 'Little Maria always hated having her picture taken.'

Helena could appreciate the complexity of Mary's relationship with her mother. It must have seemed that Eleni Papagiannis always supported her husband at the expense of her children, but Mary acknowledged now that she had tried to protect them as best she could from his explosive temper. Even so, Maria Papagiannis had had good reason to leave and never return.

Hamish felt his role was to lighten the atmosphere today.

'It didn't turn out badly, though, did it?' He smiled. 'More than twenty-five years on!'

'Imagine, if I had stayed in Greece, I wouldn't have met your father!' Mary laughed. 'And I had a head start with classics, because my ancient Greek language was far ahead of everyone else's at university. Nor do I have any regrets about not becoming an archaeologist, which had been my ambition. I don't think I would have survived all those days of sweating it out in the sun. You saw that today. I'm hopeless when it's hot.'

Hamish leaned over and kissed his wife on the forehead. 'And it's pointless to talk about the things in your life that you didn't do,' he emphasised. 'Much more positive to celebrate what you actually achieved.'

In this way, the conversation seemed to be concluded. They needed to get on the road. There was still a waterfall to visit on their way back to the hotel.

Chapter Fourteen

They were all up early the following morning for a day trip to the neighbouring island of Apalos, a place of only seventy-five permanent residents and even further off the tourist map. The passenger ferry went to and fro across the short stretch of water from Ammos only twice a day.

The stillness of the previous evening had been disrupted by a strong Aegean breeze, and a wild, gusty wind whipped through the narrow straits. Waves splashed high enough to spray them on deck as the ferry lurched back and forth.

Gripping the railings very tight, Helena made her way to the front of the boat, leaving her parents sitting at the back. Even from this distance, she could make out the shape of an ancient temple on the horizon, its majestic pillars tall and proud against the blue sky. For millennia, it must have been visible to everyone approaching the island.

As they were coming into the harbour, Helena looked around for her parents. She could see her mother lying flat out across a row of seats, her father kneeling on the deck in front of her fanning her rapidly with his panama. She hurried towards them, lurching side to side. Another couple stood by, the woman kindly offering a cup of water, most of which slopped over Mary's gingham dress.

'What's happened? Dad? Mum, are you okay?'

'She fainted, that's all,' her father said, helping Mary to take a few sips of water.

Helena's mother sat up slowly, her face as white as marble.

'I'll be all right in a minute,' she said feebly. 'I felt very seasick, that's all.'

'She forgot to take one of those pills,' added Hamish. 'They might make you feel drowsy, but they really help.'

'Poor Mum,' said Helena, taking one of her mother's arms while her father supported her with the other.

By now they were alone on the deck and Mary was gradually returning to her normal colour. The ferry docked and they made their way to the nearest café, where shade was provided by a group of scented pines. A waiter brought them iced water.

'Why don't you two go up to the temple and I'll stay here,' Mary suggested.

'But Mum, you said you had always wanted to come here. To see that very temple!'

'I think it might be best if she rests,' affirmed her father. 'We'll take plenty of photos.'

'But we could wait a bit longer. You might feel better soon.'

'I'm fine, darling, really. You go. You can tell me about it afterwards.'

'Let's leave your mother for a while,' said Hamish. 'It's so hot. And the last thing she feels like doing is climbing a hill in the heat.'

It was unusual for her father to speak on her mother's behalf, but Helena had noticed him doing it several times on this holiday.

'Mum?'

'Your father's right,' Mary said, thirstily taking down a whole glass of water. 'I'll read my book and wait for you.'

Father and daughter began the steep climb out of the village and up to the top of the hill. It took them more than thirty minutes with the sun beating down on their shoulders.

The temple was spectacular for a small island that seemed to have so little significance now, but the site felt abandoned. Helena and her father found themselves there alone.

The ten surviving pillars were of a golden stone, each perfectly fluted, with a circular pediment and carved capital. Helena looked up towards the blinding sun to marvel at their height, colour and sharply rendered carving. From the balcony of her grandmother's Kolonaki flat, she had looked so often at the Parthenon, and still remembered her guided tour of the Acropolis. On several occasions since then she had visited the British Museum. She thought now of its dirty neoclassical façade, which attempted to echo elements of a Greek temple but failed miserably in the grey London light.

Some huge broken fragments were spread across the ground and the guidebook told them this had happened during an earthquake in the nineteenth century. From these sections, it was clearer that the columns were tapered.

'How did they even carry the stone here? Let alone build them to that height and make them so strong and appear so straight? It's incredible, isn't it?' asked Helena, touching a pillar to feel its smooth, warm surface.

'Unless you have a human figure in a photo,' Hamish said, 'you get no idea at all of the scale.'

Helena, squinting against the sun, patiently posed for her father.

'I promised to take photos for your mother!' he called out to her. 'Just a couple more!'

On the way down the hill, they saw a small sign that they had missed going the other way: *Kouros*.

They followed some arrows painted onto the rocks that lined the path and soon found themselves in a clearing. Lying on its back, half buried in the ground, was a colossal stone figure. The head, body, legs and arms were all roughly formed, but as they approached, they could see that the features were yet to be carved. He was inchoate. Nascent.

'A fallen giant,' breathed Helena.

She leafed through the guidebook to find an explanation. If it had ever been completed, it would have been a monumental statue, twice life-size, but during the process of being carved it had cracked, and from that moment it had served no purpose. There was something inestimably sad about the sight of this abandoned man, left in the ground.

'Born and died in a grave,' Helena commented ruefully.

Her father turned away. 'Let's go and find your mother,' he said snappily. 'She'll be wondering what's happened to us.'

Helena felt his change of mood as he set a fast pace back to the port, though it was true that they had been gone for more than an hour and a half.

Mary was still sitting at the café table where they had left her.

'How was it?' she asked cheerfully. 'They say it's really wonderful!'

'It is,' Helena answered, happy to see that colour had returned to her mother's cheeks. 'Dad took lots of pictures. And there was a huge statue up there, just lying in the ground.'

'The waiter told me that there's a museum. Just over there behind the church. It's open for another half an hour,' Mary said, looking at her watch. 'Shall we go and see it?'

Both father and daughter were eager for a cold drink, but they could wait. Helena drained what was left in her mother's water glass and the three of them walked towards the church.

Helena was deep in thought. The beauty of the temple and the pathos of the uncompleted Kouros had profoundly stirred her.

'Dad, I want to take a picture of you and Mum here,' she said, stopping outside the church. 'It's such a lovely doorway and you should have an anniversary photo. Like your wedding, but twenty-five years on.'

'We didn't get married in church, Helena. You know that.'

'And even if we had, it wouldn't have been as picturesque as this one,' Hamish added.

They both posed, smiling, Mary making sure that her new bracelet was on show.

The museum had a guard, an elderly man who sat at a desk, took a few drachmas from each visitor and laboriously wrote out a receipt, his arthritis making the task slow and the result illegible.

The building followed the same model as the museum they had visited the previous day: a single room with dark-framed cabinets and dusty glass, some of it cracked.

'Some of these dates are very precise,' Helena commented. 'How can they be so sure?'

'Usually by scientific analysis of bones,' said Mary.

'These aren't bones, though.'

'But they were probably found close to some bones. Many of these things were discovered in graves. People were buried with possessions back then, perhaps to take with them to the afterlife. Like those people who were buried at the top of the hill we went to yesterday.'

'The Egyptians did that too, didn't they?' said Helena.

'So you did learn something in history lessons?' said Hamish, laughing. 'Your mother despaired when you gave it up before O level.'

'I know. I think I did it to annoy you, Mum . . . sorry,' Helena responded, smiling.

'That's all right. I forgive you,' said her mother, squeezing her arm.

'Daughters are always keener to please their fathers,' Hamish chipped in.

'Dad, don't be so competitive!' Helena laughed. 'I was always better at the sciences, that's all.'

'But you see how there are bridges between different subjects?' said Mary. 'History needs science and vice versa.'

Helena was peering closely into one of the cabinets, her breath clouding the glass, when the geriatric guard called out.

'*Sygnómi!* Excuse me!' He hobbled towards her. '*Nicht* so close! You too close!'

'So sorry,' said Helena, stepping away.

She carried on looking, but at a greater distance.

'So what were people doing in Britain when people here were decorating this beautiful pottery?' she asked.

'Just struggling to survive, weren't they?' Hamish asked, consulting his wife.

'Yes. I think everybody had to fight for survival at that time. There were stone circles – Stonehenge was built around that time – but there was no art.'

'I think Greece was way ahead of Britain for a long time,' said Hamish. 'They were building temples and palaces, discussing philosophy, inventing democracy, performing plays long before we were civilised.'

'Hamish!' smiled Mary. 'You sound quite the philhellene!'

Something had caught Helena's eye on the top shelf of an adjacent cabinet, and she stood on tiptoe to take a closer look.

'What's that?' she asked, pointing.

'It's a little bowl,' Mary replied, 'shaped like a pig.'

'It's even got a snout,' Helena pointed out. 'And a curly tail!'

'And it's five thousand years old,' Mary said. 'Miraculous, isn't it?'

From his desk, the museum guard called out again.

'Close! Close!'

Helena stood back. Perhaps they had stepped too near the cabinets again, but without doing so, it seemed impossible to see anything properly.

The guard was approaching them.

'*Close!*' he repeated; then, seeing that they were not getting the point, he tapped his watch.

'He means "closed"!' said Hamish. 'But I think it's time to go now anyway.' He had noticed his wife's breathlessness and pallor.

'Goodness,' said Mary, as they emerged into the dazzling sunshine. Hamish was supporting her. 'I felt a bit dizzy in there. Not even a fan.'

'We ought to eat something,' said Hamish. 'It's a long time since breakfast.'

They sat down at a simple taverna, one of two in the village, and Helena ordered the things that had become their favourites: stuffed vine leaves, mountain greens, tzatziki, fava. She noticed that her mother did not eat. It must be the heat.

They chatted for a while about the business of dating objects, and Helena was impressed by Mary's knowledge of how techniques were developing and becoming more accurate. For almost her whole life she had been aware of a journal, *From Ancient to Archaic*, landing on the mat in a brown envelope, the title printed on the outside. The unopened envelope used to lie on the hall table for a few days before disappearing. Perhaps her mother had been reading it after all.

'So why do we no longer take things to the grave?' Helena asked abstractly. 'You see things on children's graves, don't you? Like teddy bears or footballs. But that's on top.' She was ravenous and aware that she was talking with her mouth full. Usually her father would point that out. Enthusiastically devouring her plate of meze, she continued, 'It would be quite comforting to take a few of your favourite things with you, wouldn't it? Even if you didn't have a strong belief in the afterlife? What would you two take with you? Just so I know!'

She looked up and noticed her parents exchange a glance. It was nothing more than that, but it was a look of recognition between two people who did not want this conversation.

For a moment there was silence.

'I don't know,' her mother responded eventually.

'Perhaps people will start to do it again,' said Helena. 'That would puzzle archaeologists in a few thousand years' time, wouldn't it? Plastic toys that never rot. A favourite mug? A holiday souvenir?'

Her father had left the table. When he returned, he looked almost as ashen-faced as her mother and sat down silently, his eyes downcast to avoid his daughter's gaze.

'What's wrong, Dad?'

'Helena,' interjected her mother. 'There is something we need to tell you.'

Helena swallowed, remembering her father's reaction to the song in the car, a moment she had gone over in her mind but eventually dismissed.

'What? What's happened?'

Her mother's tone brought back the morning after her first ever night away from home. She was six years old and had been staying with Jenny, who lived in the next street. It had felt like the other side of the planet, and so grown up to sleep in a strange bed. On her return, her mother had sat her down and told her gently that her cat had been killed on the main road. It was the moment her world changed. The end of innocence, and the first time she understood that random disasters could take place, catastrophes created by no fault of the victim, and that however loudly you shouted 'Why?' there might not be an answer. Nothing could stop her sobs. Even the suggestion that there was some kind of feline afterlife did nothing to assuage her grief. Since then, she had not felt such anguish, even over the death of her grandmother.

Now she braced herself, her guts knotted with dread. Her legs felt as if they would not support her had she wanted to stand.

'Tell me.'

She looked from one parent to the other. Both appeared colourless in the bright light of this Greek afternoon.

Her father leaned forward. 'Your mother's not well.'

Helena turned to her mother, urgently seeking an explanation. 'The heat's too much, is that what it is?'

Her mother said nothing for a moment, but Helena was impatient.

'Tell me, Mum,' she demanded, almost in a whisper. 'Please.'

'I'm really sorry,' Mary said.

'*What* are you sorry for?' urged Helena, panicking now. 'Tell me.'

She turned back to her father. Perhaps he would satisfy her urgent need to know. But Hamish couldn't meet her eye. Both he and his wife had procrastinated so long about telling their daughter a simple, unalterable truth that he now felt incapable.

'Cancer. Lung,' said her mother.

There was silence as Helena took it in.

'But surely they can do something?' she said at last.

'It seems they can't,' Mary replied.

Helena looked at her father pleadingly, but he had tears in his eyes and one of them began to roll down his cheek.

'But you've never even smoked!' Helena said with indignation to Mary. 'It's not fair!'

Mary put her arms around her daughter, who fought to hold back her tears, and for a few minutes they sat locked in silent embrace. Carefree holidaymakers (a moment before, Helena would have counted herself as one of them) continued with their meals, oblivious of what was happening at the neighbouring table.

Hamish slipped away to pay the bill. The ferry would be arriving in fifteen minutes and it was the last one of the day.

They gathered their bags and walked in silence to the quayside to watch the steady approach of the rusting vessel, every moment heavy with the sense of passing time. Helena glanced at her mother. How many months, weeks, even days did she have left? She tried to control her rising panic, told herself not to let her parents down and to behave like an adult. But the child in her longed to go back in time, to the happy moments they had spent in the museum, last night in the taverna, the days driving between ancient monuments. Now even those memories seemed tainted.

They finally boarded and found a space in the lounge. Hamish said he would stay on deck for a while.

Helena lay down in her mother's lap and closed her eyes. Her head had begun to throb and her vision to blur. Mary stroked her forehead and began to talk gently to her.

'It's a very rare type. So I have to live as well as I can, for as long as I can,' she said. 'Spending time together as we are doing is really important to me.'

'There must be *something* they can do?' Helena said, her tears dampening her mother's dress. 'Dad's a doctor, for heaven's sake!'

'Believe me, he has investigated everything,' Mary told her. 'And we have to accept it.'

'How long have you known?'

'Six months or so.'

'Why didn't you tell me before? You knew at Easter, and we just carried on as normal. Like everything was fine. All this time, you were hiding it from me.'

Helena sat up now. Her father had come down into the lounge.

'We wanted you to get through your exams without worrying, and we hoped we would be able to tell you some good news, even if there was bad news too. Everyone hopes for treatment. But they haven't cracked the cure for all cancers yet, have they, Hamish?'

'No, they haven't,' he mumbled. 'Perhaps one day. But we have to be realistic. It won't be in time to help your mother.'

The rational, scientific side of Helena spurred her to ply her parents with questions. What was going to happen? What were the stages? The timescale? They gave her all the answers they could. Much about the next few months was unknown, but the specialist had been truthful – it was pointless to be otherwise. The prognosis was bad.

The boat journey lasted only twenty-five minutes, but it seemed to Helena that it would never end.

When she looked at her mother, she realised that her slim figure was actually on the edge of being thin, and now understood why she had decided not to put her costume on when Helena went swimming. Other things made sense too: her lack of energy, and a mild cough that had become a more persistent one, even in these past days.

As they disembarked, Helena instinctively took her mother's hand. It was something she had not done since childhood. Her hand had once fitted neatly into her mother's, but now the roles were reversed. Her mother's fingers felt small, her knuckles bony. Helena told herself she must be strong. Not just for herself, but for her parents too.

Chapter Fifteen

The next seventy-two hours were suffused with a surreal normality. For as long as they were on Ammos, their routine gave them a sense that nothing had changed: warm cheese pies from the local bakery for breakfast, dips for Hamish and Helena in clear seas and drying off in the steady warmth of the September days, eating every night in the same taverna. Helena tried to shake off the constantly nagging thought that she would one day be looking back at these times. She must live in the here and now and, as her mother had asked her to do, savour each moment.

There was another small site to visit on the other side of the island, and according to the guidebook, it had an adjacent museum. Helena appreciated even more than before her mother's pleasure in being their guide.

Hamish drove them carefully along the potholed roads in the shabby hire car. They sang favourite songs to pass the time, and perhaps to avoid conversation. Eventually they reached a village where a sign led them down a narrow dirt track. When they could go no further, they stopped and got out. The almost deafening sound of cicadas encircled them.

'If there was no barbed wire, you wouldn't even know there was anything here,' said Helena.

'True,' agreed Hamish. 'Looks like any field, full of stones.'

'I think that's what the farmer must have thought. Until he started digging up something more interesting than a few rocks.'

Mary was holding the guidebook in one hand and pointing out lines of stones, the remains of walls of long-vanished houses.

'You can see their thresholds in a few places. They've obviously fenced it off to stop people walking over them.'

Helena nodded, pretending that she could make out everything her mother was showing them. She knew her father was probably doing the same.

'According to this,' Mary read, 'the farmer came across some small figures in another field. And human remains too. It turned out to be a burial site.'

Helena noticed her father's expression. Even the reference to an ancient grave seemed to upset him.

'All the archaeologists' findings from this area are now on display in the town's museum,' she concluded triumphantly. 'Shall we go and see them?'

Helena inwardly marvelled at her mother's enthusiasm. Whether or not it was an act, it kept their spirits buoyed.

Twenty minutes later, they were inside a small stone building hidden away in a side street. A party of schoolchildren was ahead of them, and the noise of thirty or so teenagers filled the echoey building.

They were gathered in a circle in the central space of the museum around the larger-than-life statue of a woman, the goddess of beauty, Aphrodite. Bright white marble, she stood high on a plinth, which heightened the impression of her imposing size. Her generous breasts were exposed and the rest of her was scarcely concealed by a fine piece of diaphanous fabric, which the artist had masterfully sculpted to evoke transparency. Those among the group who had stopped giggling over her nudity were attempting to capture her likeness on big sheets of paper.

Helena glanced at their work as she passed. Some of them were skilled, and one of the girls had sketched a face that was even more beautiful than the original.

'Aphrodite was also the goddess of love,' Mary whispered in her daughter's ear. 'The Romans called her Venus.'

'Love . . .' Helena pondered. 'Do you think the sculptor was in love with his model?'

'There's something very bold about her nakedness, isn't there?' said Mary. 'But I quite like that. In her way she's a powerful representation of womanhood. She isn't a victim. She's in charge.'

'It is powerful,' agreed Helena. 'But I wouldn't want to live with a statue like that in my home, however big my house was!'

She recalled how Arsenis had salivated over a similar statue in the Athens museum, years before.

They edged past the group and went into a side room, where the guidebook had suggested the findings from Ano Ammos, the upper part of the island, could be seen.

The museum was much newer than most they had visited on this trip, and the cabinets had not yet had time to become smeared with dust and fingerprints. There was a smell of new paint, and some of the special objects of interest had spotlights trained on them.

'More pots,' Helena said, pleased by the terracotta cups in the first case. 'And pieces of pot.'

'Not over here.'

She turned around and went to stand next to her mother, and was immediately arrested by the contents of the case in front of them.

Illuminated from above was an erect figure of such simplicity and contemporaneity it could have passed for modernist art. Less than a foot in height, the sculpture had a long, elegant neck, small breasts, and arms folded across her belly. She seemed demure, shy even, compared with the bold, shapely Venus in the other room.

She was pale ochre in colour, slightly rough in texture, and her head was flat at the top, almost harp-shaped, and angled so that she seemed to gaze at the sky.

'She is so beautiful,' whispered Helena, surveying the interior of the cabinet for a label. She was stunned to see that the figure was dated 2700 BC, pre-dating Aphrodite by many centuries. 'Who is she?'

'Nobody knows,' her mother whispered reverently. 'Very little is known about her. Each figurine is unique, but they tend to follow certain patterns – the way their arms are folded, for example. And they are very rarely found in one piece.'

'She's like a doll.'

'Exactly,' said Mary.

'So they were playing with dolls all those years ago?'

The feet pointed downwards like a ballerina *en pointe*, and Helena remembered how her Barbie had the same anatomical quirk, her plastic feet moulded to make it impossible for her to stand. The vision of a child holding this doll gave her an unexpected sense of connection with the past.

'Nobody is sure what they were for, darling,' said Mary. 'Maybe worship, maybe a doll, as you say. But it's one of the earliest attempts at creating human likeness. These figurines pre-date writing, so they'll probably always keep their mystery.'

The figure was symmetrical, except for her folded arms, left above right. How natural her stance seemed, reminding Helena of the way people stood when they gossiped. In real life, people rarely left their arms hanging loose at their sides, and whoever had carved her had observed this.

Hamish was studying something on the wall next to the cabinet. It was a photograph of a skeleton, not stretched out, but almost folded, and next to its skull lay the little sculpted figure that was displayed in the cabinet.

'It was obviously found in a grave,' he said sombrely, then turned for the door. 'I'll see you outside.'

'Your poor father,' said Mary. 'I feel terrible making him go through all of this.'

'It's not your fault, Mum,' Helena said, sounding brave but not feeling it. 'We've all just got to make the best of things.'

The two of them turned their gaze back to the figurine, transfixed by her for a moment.

'The thing about archaeology,' Mary said with a wry smile, 'is that a lot of it is to do with spiritual beliefs.'

'I suppose it is,' agreed Helena, tears pricking her eyes.

However hard she battled with them, she could not keep her thoughts from straying to the subject of death. She considered all the objects someone acquired over their life, and how none of them really mattered in the end. And what about the travesty that all the knowledge stored inside a person went to waste when they died? Everyone had a collection of ideas, memories, theories and certainties gathered over a lifetime, but all of them went with them to the grave.

She told herself to think positively. Mary McCloud had imparted plenty of what she knew to her and to her pupils; she had shared her love and understanding of ancient languages. But Helena now realised that there was so much more: within her mother was a well of information, from which she wanted to drink. Before it was too late.

'It's almost ironic that the most important things we have learned about this civilisation are from their burial habits,' Mary continued. 'So from death, we can try to work out how they lived.'

'And we can bring them alive again, maybe. In our imaginations, at least.'

'Well, that's what I think, darling.'

'This object does seem very alive . . .'

'And yet she's almost five thousand years old.'

For the first time that afternoon, Helena's mood lightened just a little. For a moment she could embrace the thought that her own life, her mother's, her father's were but the blink of an eye in history's timeline.

'She's so lovely. Perfection.'

'Yes. And if you look from the side, you'll see that her belly is slightly rounded.'

'As if she's pregnant?'

'Possibly,' Mary responded. 'But even if not, it suggests fertility.'

Mother and daughter stared through the glass at the elegant figurine. Her only facial feature was a long aquiline nose, but even without eyes, she seemed to watch them with a knowing expression.

'I've only seen figures like these in photographs. But in real life she is even more beautiful. I can honestly say that she is the most exquisite things I have *ever* seen.' Mary spoke these words as if she was coming to a final conclusion. 'Except my gorgeous girl, of course!'

She hugged Helena, and the two of them laughed. Such a moment of levity seemed almost impossible.

It was time to leave the museum. Hamish would be waiting for them.

As she followed her mother, tall and slim in her sand-coloured T-shirt and slacks, Helena was struck by the resemblance between Mary McCloud and the elegant representation of womanhood that had so entranced them both. A swan-like neck, slender hips and the legs of a mannequin. Both the marble figure and her mother were the quintessence of femininity.

She took a last glimpse at the enigmatic idol with her contentedly folded arms, perhaps with child, perhaps not. Serene, strong and mysterious.

When she turned round, her mother had gone.

Part Three

Chapter Sixteen

Midsummer's night, and a golden glow from the vanishing sun was still visible in the sky. The pillars of a ruined temple cast their long shadows in the dying light of the day. Even the leaves on the trees were silent and still.

Jason stood before his wife, who was kneeling, the small corpses of their two sons laid out in her arms. Medea's white robe was stained with fresh blood, her waxen face twisted in a hideous grimace of both grief and triumph.

Fists clenched, paralysed by horror and fury, Jason looked at the sky and addressed the unseen king of the gods, Zeus. Then he turned to the woman who had brutally murdered their children as an act of revenge and masterminded the death of his new bride. What scale of anger was appropriate for such evil? How could the victim of these heinous actions express his grief?

Jason, just a few feet away from the audience, allowed them to enter into his pain, as surely as if Medea was slowly driving knives into all their hearts.

The sight of the two small, still bodies was a powerful one. The murderess stood up and proudly admitted all her crimes.

'Let me touch my children's skin,' Jason pleaded.

'Never,' rebuked Medea. 'Don't waste your words.'

Jason was aware of a thousand eyes on him and felt the thrill of it. He was particularly conscious of the gaze of a girl at the centre of the front row.

Helena's chest was so tight, she could scarcely catch her breath. Was it the stifling heat of the night, or the intensity of his eyes, which stared out across the crowd and finally, as his words tailed away, seemed to lock with hers? Her top stuck to her back and tears ran unchecked down her face. On a hard wooden bench in twentieth-century Oxford, she felt the irresistible pull of time and place like a rip tide dragging a powerless body.

On such a stifling night, the hottest of the century they said, the words written millennia before retained their power, intensified all the more for Helena by her memory of visiting the ancient town of Corinth with her parents. It was the setting for the play.

Jason stood there for a full five minutes, receiving the rapturous applause from the audience. The actor had brought the ancient world before them and laid bare its losses and its violence. It was for him that most had come. He already had a reputation as the new Peter O'Toole, not just for his mop of blond hair and his blue eyes, but for his talent on stage. His name was on everyone's lips. They were not just family and friends easily won over by a student performance. Members of the public had queued for spare tickets, even tutors and fellows, and there were rumours that a critic from a national newspaper was somewhere in the audience.

Like a human wave, from the front row to the back, people began to stand. There were calls of 'Bravo! Bravo!' and wolf whistles of appreciation pierced the air. All the other actors reappeared to take their bows, holding hands, stepping forward and bending low, a movement as perfectly timed and well rehearsed as the play itself.

The audience was seated in a semicircle to emulate a fourth-century BC theatre, and the stage extended outwards so that those in the first few rows were drawn into the heart of the action. Helena's friend Sally had been part of the chorus, so Helena had volunteered to hand out flyers and pin up posters around the city. All three nights of the play had sold out, and the cast and the producer were happy and relieved. They had spent more on scenery than they could afford (the pillars were solid plaster, not merely painted on a backdrop), and the costumes had been hired from Angels in London.

The spell cast by the tragic story was broken when the lights went up, but still something lingered that made Helena's heart leaden. She felt the sudden return of the deep grief that she had experienced when her mother had died. The extreme pallor of Medea's skin was just like Mary's on those last terrible days in the hospital, the white shrouds in which the children were wrapped evoked memories of her mother's deathbed sheets, and the despair of knowing that someone had gone and could never return was painfully conveyed by Jason.

She had learned that this was how bereavement worked. Even eighteen months after Mary McCloud's death, powerful emotions as fresh as they were at the moment of her passing could suddenly rise to the surface, triggered by an association.

It took a while for the audience to disperse, partly because many were loath to leave. Vacating their seats would mean admitting that this traumatic but magical evening was over. The space would no longer be ancient Corinth, but once again the pretty quad of an Oxford college, scented by roses climbing across its golden façades.

Helena lingered in her seat, reading the cast list that had been handed out as people entered. Her eyes ran down the list of names and the colleges to which they belonged. The only name she recognised was Sally's. The rest mostly went to the colleges favoured by public school boys. She and Sally were at St Hugh's, an all-girls college, a choice Helena had never regretted. Some of the female students at co-educational colleges told stories of being made to feel inferior by both dons and their peers. This university could be a hostile environment for women, and Helena was glad that behind the gates of her college was a place where she felt secure.

During her second and third years, following her mother's death, she had had neither the will nor the energy to socialise. All she could manage during those terms was to meet the demands of her studies and go to meetings of the athletics club. Running a few laps of the university track three times a week helped to keep her sane. Fellow students still invited her to parties and plays, but did not expect her to attend, and her handful of close friends all knew her circumstances and never pressured her to come. They teasingly called her Helena the Hermit. In any toss-up between accepting a party invitation and staying in to study, the latter always won. Helena's desire for security was satisfied by meeting friends in their rooms for endless cups of Maxwell House and Coffee Mate. Such things got her through those endless terms, along with many packets of digestive biscuits.

Nicholas Hayes-Jones. Her eyes rested on the name of the boy who had played Jason. He had unsettled her. Christ Church. That was no surprise. A college for those already certain about their place in the world, and somewhere she had only visited once for a concert in its magnificent cathedral. She folded up the sheet and put it in a pocket.

Suddenly aware that she was alone, Helena looked up. Sally was hurrying towards her from the improvised green room, a small marquee that had been erected in a corner of the quad. Helena noticed that her friend still had her hair wound up in theatrical ancient Greek style and had not removed her costume. She managed to look voluptuous even in a toga, making Helena only more aware of her own boyish figure.

'Hels! What did you think?' Sally asked breathlessly. Without waiting for an answer, she gushed, 'Wasn't it great? Wasn't the girl who played Medea amazing? Everyone is so happy! Sad that it's over, but happy too. Nobody forgot a single word. We didn't even need Freddie sitting there all night as prompt – not for a moment. Everyone is saying we could take it to the Edinburgh Festival. And someone's dad said he saw the critic from the *Daily Telegraph*. That old bloke with glasses in the third row? Just behind you? If it's true, that could really change things for some of us. Two of them have applied to RADA for the postgrad course anyway. But seriously, what did you think?'

'It was very moving,' said Helena. '*Really* moving.' She meant it. She had never before been so affected by a play.

'We've got the after party now,' babbled Sally obliviously, tugging her friend's hand. 'The drinks are only free for a couple of hours, so we'd better hurry.'

'But I won't know anyone!' protested Helena. 'And all I did was put up a few posters.'

'That doesn't matter. There are loads of people going – make-up, props, lighting. Boyfriends, girlfriends – everybody is invited! Do come. It's the end of term. No more essays! No more anything! School's out for *ever*!'

'Not for all of us,' smiled Helena. She was one of the few amongst their friends who would be returning in October. Chemistry was a four-year course.

Sally, by contrast, was all set for a job in public relations, and was excited about getting started on her career. For her, Oxford had been a three-year degree in acting and partying, so she was already well qualified when she was signed up during the 'milk round', the process whereby London recruiters came to seek out their graduate intake. She had bluffed her way through the English course, persuading her tutors that she had digested the whole of Dickens and Shakespeare when all she had done was read study notes for A level students. It had been obvious to the human resources director who had recruited her that she had all the requisite skills for an entry-level position as account executive at Bell and Bell PR.

The two girls could not have been more different, Sally always centre stage, Helena content backstage, but their friendship worked.

Helena would miss Sally, but they had agreed they would flat-share once Helena graduated.

'*If* I come to London,' she said.

'But of course you'll be in London!' Sally had insisted. 'Where else would you go? Where else does *any*body go?'

Tonight, Helena would happily have sloped back to her own college to lie on the grass and gaze up at the stars. She could imagine the party: hundreds of bright young things, many of them the thespian types who had starred in the play, like Sally still wearing their diaphanous costumes and make-up, all of them oozing the same confidence they had arrived with in this city three years before. Helena had never been like them.

'Pleeeeease come with me,' entreated Sally. 'It might be ages until we see each other again. And there's someone I really want you to meet.'

'Ah! So that's why you want me there,' joked Helena. It was typical of her friend to be hiding the real agenda. 'Who is it?'

'You see! You're interested now. Well, if you want to find out, you have to come!'

The girls laughed, linked their arms together and made for the porters' lodge. Outside in the lane, there was a tangle of bikes leaning against the wall, and having extracted their own, they wheeled them along side by side. Sally was worried about her dress getting caught up in the chain.

'So, what's his name?' enquired Helena.

'He's an ancient Greek.'

'Stop being such a tease, Sally. I knew there was a reason you were so enthusiastic about rehearsals. Go on, tell me!'

'You'll meet him in a moment,' Sally replied coyly. 'I've had a huge crush on him from the first day of the first read-through.'

'And has anything happened?'

'Well, just a kiss . . . a couple of times.'

'You dark horse. You never breathed a word. So—'

'I know what you're going to say! That there's not much time. I know, I know. Tonight's the night. Tomorrow it's all over. Bye-bye, Oxford.'

'I'm sure you'll be back, racing up the M40 in your company car to take penniless undergraduates like me out to lunch.'

'I'm beginning to feel sad, you know? It all went by so quickly. Feels like yesterday that we arrived, naïve, fresh-faced . . .'

'Yep. Freshers. And that's how we felt. Brand new. Three years of chemistry and I don't feel so fresh any more. Stale is more accurate.'

'Come on, Hels. It's a means to an end. You know it will pay off when you're earning millions in a big drug company. It's you who'll have the red Ferrari.'

'Not quite my style,' Helena laughed. 'And I'm going to miss everyone when I come back next year.'

'There'll be nothing to distract you. Goggles on, head down in that lab from nine till midnight, exploding test tubes, new discoveries!'

'You make it sound almost exciting.'

For three years now, Sally had been making Helena laugh with her version of what science was about. Helena had given up trying to explain what her day in the faculty really comprised. Sally's English course seemed much less arduous, and there had been many times when she had envied the sight of her lying on her bed reading poetry to prepare for an essay, or seeing her curtains still closed as she came back from a morning at the science faculty.

They had arrived at their destination. Helena already regretted agreeing to come. As she'd suspected, everyone else pouring through the archway and onto the grassy quad behind was dressed in costume or party clothes. The evening was still warm, and she felt hot in a patchwork maxi skirt and scoop-neck top. She would feel out of place next to the other partygoers, who all seemed ready for a Roman Bacchanalia.

Sally grabbed her friend's hand and strode across towards the drinks table, where a member of the cast ladled punch from a huge silver bowl while two others poured in bottle after bottle of vodka, fizzy wine and gallons of cheap pineapple juice.

Helena took one of the overfilled half-pint glasses and immediately slopped it down her top.

'Damn,' she muttered, dabbing vainly at the fabric.

'Don't worry about it,' Sally reassured her. 'It's almost dark. Nobody is going to notice anything much after a few of these.'

Helena took a long swig to quench her thirst and felt the alcohol have an immediate and dizzying effect.

Across the quad, a crowd had gathered round an imposing figure in a striped jacket. His outfit and his voice were as loud as each other. Helena followed Sally towards this character, who was gesticulating theatrically and addressing an audience who hung on every word.

'That's Charles Smythson, the director,' explained Sally behind her hand. 'He's a postgrad. Old Etonian.'

'It's going to be a big deal if we get that review,' Smythson was saying. 'And if it's a good one, it's Edinburgh in six weeks. Rehearsals for two, and then three weeks of performances, matinees and evenings. Is everyone in?'

Everybody in the circle raised an affirmative hand, including Sally.

'But you're starting work mid August, aren't you?' protested Helena in a whisper that only her friend could hear.

'Helena! They'll wait for me. I wouldn't miss this chance for anything. And it will give me more time to spend with . . .'

Sally scanned the group. The person she was looking for was not there.

'But the whole thing is hypothetical,' she laughed, 'if our leading man has vanished.'

Helena realised that her friend's crush must be the same boy who had mesmerised her during these past few hours. It was no surprise. It was unlikely that she was the first to be struck by such charisma.

Cast members gathered excitedly together in a clique, hugging each other and reminiscing about favourite moments in the play. As

Sally joined them, Helena wandered off. She could still hear shrieks of laughter even when she was strolling around the walled garden adjacent to the quad, where the party was now in full swing.

The borders were carefully planted and dense with colourful flowering shrubs. Along the walls on all four sides, honeysuckle intertwined with the second blooming of an ancient wisteria, both sending out their heady scent.

She sat down on one of the lichen-covered benches, took another long draught of the potent drink and closed her eyes. Images of the play, lines, phrases, words, came back to her. They had excavated so much from its text, and her memory of Jason's grief would last well beyond tonight.

Soft saxophone notes, a chromatic scale, rose into the air. Some friends of Sally's with a jazz band had said they might play. It did not match Helena's mood, but she kept her eyes shut just a while longer and enjoyed the aromas around her.

Suddenly she felt something on her cheek. A mosquito? Given the humidity of the night, it was hardly surprising, especially with a small circular pond sitting at the centre of this garden. She brushed it away without opening her eyes. Another one began to tickle the back of her neck beneath her hair. She shook her head with annoyance and opened her eyes.

Jason was kneeling at her feet, still dressed in full costume and holding a stem from the end of which dangled some feathery fronds. He must have been using this long grass to tickle her.

Her irritation instantly evaporated. 'I thought I was being attacked by gnats!' She laughed shyly.

'Sorry, I couldn't resist. You looked so lost in your thoughts, I wanted to bring you back. Were you meditating?'

'Meditating? Gosh, no!'

After a glass of the strong punch, she felt almost bold enough to follow this with the words: 'I was thinking about you,' but stopped herself.

He got up from his knees, and Helena moved over so that he could sit next to her on the bench.

'So why are you sitting here when there's a party going on a few yards away?'

'I could ask you the same,' said Helena. 'And you were the leading man.'

'I was,' he said. 'And you were in the audience. I noticed you. You were crying.'

She looked at him with confusion.

'Why?' he persisted.

His question seemed almost ridiculous to her.

'Because I was moved! You . . . the play . . . the grief . . . they affected me. Enormously.'

There was much more she could have said, or even asked, but Jason was no longer Jason. She had believed in him so profoundly, and it almost seemed a pity that he had now separated illusion from reality.

The jazz band was louder now, and a trumpet solo rose in the air.

'I'm Nick, by the way,' he said, grabbing her hand. 'Come on, let's go and join the fray. They'll be wondering where we are.'

'But I don't really know anyone at the party except my friend Sally. She was in the chorus. I helped with advertising and stuff. Putting up posters, that kind of thing. That's the only reason I got a seat.'

'Oh,' he said, with apparent lack of recognition at Sally's name, which was strange given that they had kissed. 'You have no idea how beautiful you looked just now. Sitting there on a bench, so still, just breathing. You looked like a painting. Your auburn hair.'

Helena was totally taken aback. No one had ever said anything like this to her before.

'You look like Jane Morris,' persisted Nick.

'Who?'

'William Morris's wife. The woman that Rossetti was madly in love with.'

Helena did not recognise a single one of this string of names.

'They were all part of the same group, the Pre-Raphaelites. And she modelled for Rossetti.'

Helena was still lost but did not dare to admit it. Modelled what? Clothes?

'"Afar from mine own self I seem, and wing. Strange ways in thought, and listen for a sign . . ."' He stepped away from the bench, pulling a rose off a bush and striking a pose with the flower in his right hand and his neck wistfully tilted.

'There's a very famous painting of her,' he continued. 'And that's the poem written by Rossetti on the back of the frame. She was very much *not* a plain Jane. Long auburn hair, beautiful mouth, dark eyes . . . ravishing. He was madly in love with her but she married someone else. But you can tell his passion from the painting. It leaps out at you from the canvas.'

'I must go and see it,' said Helena, intrigued but doubtful that she could bear any resemblance to such a woman. She had always been insecure about her looks, from her thick, untameable hair to her over-generous lips and porcelain skin. She had always yearned for blue eyes, blonde hair, skin that tanned golden brown in summer and brows that did not bush out like caterpillars. Her mother had constantly reassured her she was lovely 'in her own way', but she was wise enough to know that parents were never objective about their own children.

'I haven't read much poetry,' she admitted. 'And I only know one by heart. By Keats.'

'That's sad,' he reflected. 'But maybe you were related to Jane.'

'I doubt it,' Helena smiled. 'Greek mother, and Scottish blood on my father's side.'

'Greek, eh? And do you speak the language?'

'Modern, yes, but not ancient.'

She found him looking at her once again with an appreciation she was unused to, and changed the subject.

'All those lines in the play? How does so much stay in your head?'

'Acting!' he intoned theatrically. 'That's what acting is. Memorising and then making someone else's words your own.'

'Mmm,' responded Helena thoughtfully. 'I suppose it is.'

'What are you reading? Let me guess. Not English, otherwise you would know about learning chunks of text by heart.'

Sweeping his cloak theatrically behind him, Nick stood back, took Helena's left hand and pulled her up from the bench.

'Let me take a closer look . . .'

Their faces were nose to nose. For the third time that evening, Helena felt her chest tighten. The deep blue eyes of Nick Hayes-Jones now gazed into hers.

'It must be one of the sciences,' he said, his lips just brushing hers.

Then he abruptly stepped away.

'Am I right?'

'Yes! Chemistry,' she answered, aware of how dull that sounded. 'And you? English, I think?'

'Of course! Otherwise known as a degree in acting and loafing about,' he said. 'But alas, poor Yorick, it's over.'

Helena saw a look of almost genuine sadness on his face.

'Well, I have another joyful year in the science faculty while all my friends are living it up in London,' she laughed. 'Which would you rather?'

Nick did not answer.

'Did you get scooped up on the milk round?' she enquired. 'Advertising? Accountancy?'

'Not really my kind of thing,' he answered. 'I'm planning a year off now.'

The strains of Gershwin's 'Summertime' rose in the air. The mood of the music created an irresistibly romantic moment.

Nick stepped towards Helena and enfolded her in his arms, the voluminous sleeves of his costume wrapping around them both like wings.

'May I kiss you?' he asked, with impeccable politeness.

Helena answered by tilting her face upwards.

For a moment, she felt clumsy, self-consciously out of practice, afraid even. She had spent the past few years avoiding anyone who might have kissed her. Each day had been spent shoulder to shoulder in lectures and laboratories with boys who were more like brothers. Most were studious types in anoraks and Crimplene slacks.

She had lost her virginity to Jenny's cousin when she was seventeen. This clumsy, drunken encounter behind the village community centre with someone she never saw again had served its purpose: to rid herself of the burden of being a virgin and also to end the childish accusations of frigidity that both boys and girls had aimed at her.

For all the years of her undergraduate life, anyone who asked Helena out on a date was turned down. She had no desire to hold anyone's hand or be pecked on the mouth. The next time someone touched her, there must be romance and desire. As she felt Nick's generous lips on hers and a tongue that gently searched for hers, she felt as if she was melting inside.

'My room is in this quad,' he said, gently moving her hair aside to whisper close to her ear. 'We can be alone there.'

They were the only people in the garden, but anyone could wander through, so she willingly took his hand. He led her towards the small archway that led to his staircase.

Without turning on a light, he lit two candles that stood on his coffee table. They were stuck into old champagne bottles encrusted with wax. Three coffee mugs sat next to them, and an empty whisky bottle. The only other things Helena noticed in the gloaming were a single book on the desk and an evening suit lying across a chair.

They fell onto his already crumpled sheets. For the first time since her mother's death, Helena was freed from the emotional vacuum in which she had been suspended, and everything she had guarded herself against was forgotten. Her fear of losing control was replaced by a desire to do exactly that.

For a brief while afterwards, their slim, naked limbs remained entwined. The sound of the jazz band floated through the open window.

'Don't you think you should be at the party?' Helena said.

'Probably.'

He sat up and looked at her, her vibrant hair spread dramatically across the pillows.

'How can I leave your side?' he asked. 'The side of Venus?'

Helena giggled. What new hyperbole was this?

'Venus, goddess of love,' he smiled. 'Specifically, Botticelli's version, with her flowing red hair.'

Helena felt herself blush. Nick's frame of reference and his flow of compliments were both as unfamiliar as each other.

'You're right, though. I should put in an appearance,' he said. 'I'll have a quick shower.'

While he disappeared to a shared bathroom somewhere on the staircase, Helena washed in the tiny sink in the corner of the room. Even in the cracked mirror, she could see that her cheeks were still flushed. With difficulty, she ran her fingers through her now matted hair and attempted to rub the stains of smudged mascara from beneath her eyes. She dressed again, straightened the sheets and sat on the edge of the bed.

Nick reappeared wrapped in a towel, his golden hair glistening with dampness. Despite what had just happened, she felt self-conscious as she watched him dry and dress himself in jeans and a logoed T-shirt.

'Your favourite band?' she asked him. 'The Rolling Stones?'

'Of course.' He smiled. 'Legends.'

He looked very different now, still handsome, but no longer Jason. His arms were tanned and muscular, the T-shirt showing off a well-defined torso.

'Come on, Jane, let's go and party!' he said, taking both her hands. Before they went through the archway, she slipped her hand out of his, suddenly conscious of what Sally had said to her. It was something she would need to manage carefully.

'If you don't mind, I won't come,' she said. 'It's your night.'

Once they were in the main quad, where the gathering of more than two hundred people was taking place, he turned to her and kissed her on the lips.

'It was lovely to meet you, Jane,' he said. 'Please let it not be for the last time.'

With that, he walked away, and was soon lost in the great throng around the drinks table. Helena heard whoops of joy as people welcomed him into their midst, and for a moment saw him lifted above the crowd.

Nobody was looking in her direction, so she slipped out of the quad, retrieved her bike and pedalled slowly back to college. For a while, the sound of a saxophone followed her home.

All night, the face of Jason and the memory of his eyes stayed with her.

He had not even asked her name.

Chapter Seventeen

Helena slept in late the following day. Even that small amount of punch had given her a headache, but her father was coming at two and she needed to get organised.

There was no sound from Sally's room, so at ten o'clock, Helena knocked gently. She knew that her friend's parents were arriving at around the same time, and that Sally had not even begun to pack.

'Sally?'

She tried again. With the constant slamming of doors up and down the corridor, it was surprising that her friend could sleep.

There was plenty of activity, but little conversation, as girls scurried about with cardboard boxes. For some, if not for Helena, it was a morning tinged with huge sadness as they left the university for the very last time. Mugs, vinyl records, rolled-up posters, half-used bags of sugar were all chucked into boxes. Lever-arch files of essays that had seemed so world-altering at the time now had ink running down their pages from kettles carelessly thrown on top. In their new homes, they might display a few framed photographs, one of matriculation, the other of graduation and, if they had any, perhaps one of a memorable night at a Commemorative ball, or college sports team. All the rest of these student possessions, apart from a few books intended for re-reading, would never see the light again. The precious and the sentimental along with the valueless archives of scholarly work would be stored in attics until the remains, nibbled by vermin, would one day be thrown out by another generation.

Helena finished her own packing, borrowed a trolley from one of the caretakers, and wheeled her boxes to a storage place. Fourth-year students were given permission to leave belongings there until the following term. As she returned to her room, Sally appeared blearily at her door in a man-sized Pink Floyd T-shirt with mascara smudged around her eyes.

'Hels . . .' she said croakily. 'Coffee?'

'Mine's all packed away. Shall I come to you?'

Sally's room was in chaos. Clothes were strewn about, books were spread across the grubby carpet and dirty cups were piled up in the corner sink. It was in its normal state.

Helena picked her way across the floor, switched the kettle on and rinsed a couple of mugs under the cold tap.

'So how was the party?' she asked over her shoulder.

Sally was sitting slumped on the bed, her head in her hands.

A cup of instant coffee, black with two sugars, revived her, and Helena sat on the floor to listen to her account of the celebrations.

'Okay, I suppose. I drank too much. Nicholas Hayes-Jones ignored me, but I don't care. I really don't care. It was stupid of me to like him in the first place.'

'Mmm.' Helena gave a non-committal response. Nicholas. Nick. Whatever he liked to be called. Perhaps this was a pattern for him. She sat with half an ear on what Sally was saying, but her mind was elsewhere. She told herself that what had happened with Nick must remain a pleasurable memory, that was all. Sooner or later he would vanish from her mind. It would help if she could stop herself thinking about him, though.

'And then *Charles* – you know, the director of the play,' Sally was saying. 'He came up to me and declared his undying love. I hadn't even realised he had noticed me, and anyway, I thought he was gay. Everyone does. With those exaggerated mannerisms and that boating blazer.'

Nothing more was required of Helena than to nod occasionally, which she duly did.

'And I knew that Pierre, the guy from the Ruskin who painted the sets, had a massive crush on him. He kept asking me what he should do, how he could get Charles to notice him. And last night I had him crying on my shoulder because he said he'll probably never see him ever again and he had missed his chance with the love of his life, etc., etc. . . . Everyone was really sloshed by the end. Nobody was talking any sense. God knows what was going into the punch.' She paused to draw breath, and took a long sip from her mug. 'Aah, this coffee is nice. Thank you, Helena. What will I do without you?'

'So what happened with Charles?' Helena was interested in that part of the story, though Sally was already going off on a tangent.

'Charles? Oh yes, Charles! Well, I think I could quite like him. Once I get used to the idea. He's handsome. Clever. And most important, he's rich. Like *Emma*!'

'Emma? Was she in the play too?'

'Oh Helena, too many hours in the lab. *Emma*. Jane Austen's *Emma*. We have to get you reading more literature. Anyway, Charles owns a house in London, and he asked me if I wanted to rent a room. Can you believe it? He's already got friends coming to live there, but he says it's big and he has a couple of bedrooms left. And I thought, why not? Especially after he had hugged me and whispered nice things in my ear. All he wants is a share of the bills. And it's such a nice part of London. And when you come up to town you can live there too!'

'Sounds like you might be sharing a room with the landlord by then!' Helena giggled.

'Dunno,' Sally said coyly. 'But after last night, maybe yes. That nerdy but nice guy Simon, who did the music for the play, had an amazing record collection and he was doing the disco. Charles just threw out names of songs and he put them on. Bee Gees, Stones, Olivia Newton-John . . . everything! And *then* Eric Clapton.'

Helena smiled. Sally seemed to have recovered from her hangover and was now skipping around the room in her bare feet, dodging pairs of her own pants, a hairbrush, album covers and everything else that littered the floor.

'"Lay down, Sally . . ." So, these lines, over and over again, and I suddenly realised that Charles was addressing them to *me*, and not just because of my name.'

'Mmm . . .' Helena murmured, gathering things off the floor to move them out of her friend's way, but also aware of the time ticking away. 'That's so—'

'And he's such a great dancer too. Slow. Smoochy. And he held onto me all the way through. So close . . .'

Sally began to sing again. She had a sweet voice, and Helena, who was now sitting on the bed to keep out of her way, watched her dancing with an imaginary partner, her arms wrapped seductively around her own shoulders so that from behind it looked as if someone was hugging her tight.

'"Just the way you are . . ."' she crooned, eyes closed.

When she had sung the whole of the Billy Joel hit, with barely a pause for breath, Sally plonked herself down on the bed with Helena.

'And he could actually waltz! Properly. All those classes we did in our first year – you remember those ballroom dancing lessons? – came back to me, and we were waltzing round the common room like a pair of professionals on *Come Dancing*! And everyone else had stopped to watch.'

'It sounds romantic, really romantic.'

'And that was it. The horrid Bulldogs raided. They turned the lights on. Pulled Simon's plugs out of the sockets. Ordered us to clear up the glasses and leave. There was no arguing with them.'

'Killjoys!'

'I think we'd kept the whole college awake, though. And it was two in the morning.'

'But who would have thought that on the very last night of your time here, you would meet someone? Someone nice?'

Sally had spent three years chasing after boys who played in Blues teams, having one-night stands and getting her heart broken. She had always vowed that she would not leave Oxford without finding a husband. 'Out in the big wide world, there's no chance,' she had said to Helena in their second year.

'It's sad to be leaving,' she reflected. 'But somehow not so sad now.'

'Well, you *are* leaving,' said Helena, looking at her watch, 'And very shortly, your mum and dad will be here. I'll help you. You get dressed and I'll go and grab some boxes.'

'What a friend you are,' said Sally, rummaging in the corner cupboard. She pulled on a revealing red dress with gold embroidery around the hem. 'Don't be cross if I'm not here when you get back with the boxes. I'm just nipping out to see Charles. I promised him that I would drop by before I left.'

She was hurriedly brushing her luxuriant blonde waves, and in less than a minute had transformed herself.

'You're the only person I know who can still look fabulous even after a late night,' Helena laughed. 'But don't forget your parents!'

'I won't, Hels,' said Sally running out the door, still fastening some earrings. 'I promise not to be long.'

Sally could be maddening, but Helena loved her, for all her flaws. She was never sure if her spontaneity was one of them, but she admired it just the same. Without her friend's gaiety, she would not have made it through these past three years.

Even in the weeks running up to exams, Sally had been there for her. On a break from the nearby science faculty, Helena had gone to sit in the University Parks for solitude and silence. It was late May, and she made for an area where there were several different kinds of magnolia tree. The *stellata* was in full bloom, its fragrant, creamy flowers covering the tree and carpeting the grass beneath. It had a small identifying label next to it, as did many species in the Parks, and she saw that it had been planted in 1929, the year of her mother's birth. She was overwhelmed by melancholy and tears.

More than an hour later, she was still sitting beneath the tree. Suddenly looking at her watch, she realised she was going to be late for a tutorial. She jumped on her bike and pedalled off, unaware that her precious bracelet with the sapphire *máti* had dropped from her wrist.

Later that day, having searched high and low, she returned to her room almost hysterical. Sally found her there and took her to the police station, a sandstone building next to Christ Church that had been built with similar grandeur and elegance to many of the colleges.

Their enquiry was met with kind concern at the front desk, and after a two-minute wait, a young constable handed Helena a small brown envelope. She tipped the contents out into her palm and thanked him profusely and tearfully.

'You see,' said Sally. 'Nothing is ever lost. It just might not be where you thought it was.'

Helena would miss her friend in her remaining three terms.

Dragging in some spare boxes that had been abandoned in the corridor, she began to pack up Sally's things. As she worked, she found herself humming the same Billy Joel song that Sally had danced to, and pictured Nick's face. The lyrics seemed trite compared with anything he had said on stage, and yet they were both talking about the same thing, it seemed. Helena was painfully aware that she had little experience of love. A crush was a different thing, and while she had experienced those since childhood, she knew they were naïve, superficial even, and left no scars. Her mind wandered to Sally, who seemed to have forgotten her adoration of Nick as soon as Charles declared an interest. Had Nick forgotten her in the same way?

What did love look like? Her friends who had studied English seemed to be experts. Sally had so often burst into her room with excitement to read a passage from a novel, a play, a poem. And was the theme ever anything but love? To Helena, it seemed as if they had spent their nine terms immersed in a single topic. From Shakespeare, to Wordsworth, to the Brontë sisters, each time Sally had enthused, it was always the same. Love, love, love, with the occasional detour into religion, which often turned out to be a metaphor for love after all. And Helena, meanwhile, had been staring into a lens, at microscopic particles. No wonder she felt so green.

Nick had quoted love poetry at her the previous evening and she had had nothing to offer in response. As she picked her way around Sally's room, she found her mind returning to him time and time again. The idea of never seeing him again filled her with deepening dismay. Was that just a crush? On the first day of her vacation, she would go to the local public library and look up the Pre-Raphaelites to find their paintings and poems. Then she would also discover whether there really was any resemblance between herself and Jane Morris.

She looked at the stack of invitations pinned one on top of each other on Sally's noticeboard. They were just a single term's worth of parties. Sally had asked her to come to every one of them, but she always made an excuse of a deadline or an assignment.

She moved on to the bookcase. Sally's books fitted into one box, as she had borrowed most of those she needed from the library, and her essay files slotted on top. On the bottom shelf there were copies of *Isis* magazine and piles of the weekly student newspaper, *Cherwell*. Sally had written articles for them both. Helena put them into another box. On the desk, next to a jumble of other books, there was a Penguin Classic: the text of *Medea*. She sat down on the worn swivel chair and leafed through it, flicking to the end to reread Jason's final speech. Next to the text were Sally's annotations and a row of childlike hearts in red biro. Helena felt a hot pang of jealousy. She shut the book and dropped it on top of the others.

At that moment, Sally burst in through the door with her parents behind her.

'Just in time,' she said breathlessly. 'Look who I found downstairs!'

Sally's mother, pretty, fair-haired and sweet-faced like her daughter, and her father, in navy jacket with gold buttons and golf club tie, came into the room and greeted Helena warmly. They had met many times over the years, and had even gone out to lunch when Mr and Mrs Pearson visited.

'You have been such a good friend to Sally,' said Mrs Pearson, as her husband picked up the last of the boxes. 'I know she's going to miss you.'

'I don't know what I would have done without her,' Helena responded. 'I was ready to leave after Mum died. Sally kept me here.'

'That's what friendship is about, isn't it? Helping each other?'

'Yes,' interrupted Sally. 'And Hels has been my rock, every day of every term.'

The two girls hugged each other tightly, both in tears.

'Promise me you'll come to London,' sniffed Sally.

Helena nodded.

'We should get going soon,' said Mr Pearson gruffly. 'I'm on a double yellow.'

The girls reluctantly let go of one another.

Back in her own room, Helena had everything she needed for the long summer holiday packed into a single suitcase, with her bigger books in a box. She lay on the bare mattress and closed her eyes. There was still a hammering in her head from the alcohol the night before.

A gentle knock on the door roused her.

Her father was slightly more stooped than when she had seen him at Easter. He was neatly shaved, but his hair could definitely do with a visit to the barber and his linen jacket was in need of an iron.

'Dad!' she said, throwing her arms around him. 'It's so nice to see you.'

'Hello, sweetheart,' he replied. 'Everything all right?'

'Yes. Busy term. I'm so sorry I didn't manage a visit.'

'Don't worry, darling. I understand. Exams? How were they?'

'Tough, to be honest. I'm trying not to think about them, but we'll have the results soon. And they can't throw me out now!'

They both laughed. Hamish McCloud picked up the suitcase and Helena the box. On top of it she balanced the cheese plant that she had lovingly tended since her first term, and then grabbed her shoulder bag from the desk.

'I think that's it,' she said, taking a last look around.

'Aren't you taking that?' asked her father, indicating a dying spider plant on the window ledge.

'No, that can be my welcome gift to the next lucky winner of this room,' she smiled. 'I'll be in that new building in the back quad next year. Hot and cold water! Even radiators that actually work.'

'It hasn't been that bad, has it, darling?' he asked sympathetically. 'Compared with my university accommodation, it's luxury in here. We had no heating, lead-framed windows that didn't close, a cold shower we had to queue up for . . .'

'Ah yes, the bad old days . . . and how many thousands of miles to the nearest toilet?'

'The closest one was up three flights of stairs!'

Helena laughed. It was a ritual for her father to list the hardships of post-war university and to tease his daughter about the cushy life she led.

'Your mum's digs at Royal Holloway were just as bad. Maybe worse. She didn't even have a shower in the same building. Imagine trekking across the snow in a towel?'

'You're right, Dad. We do have it easy,' Helena said, holding open the door for her father.

They stopped chatting and teasing each other for a few minutes and started the struggle down three flights of stairs. Mention of Helena's mother always subdued them both for a while.

Hamish's battered Cortina estate was parked close to the college gates, and soon they were pulling out into the Woodstock Road.

Even eighteen months on, it felt strange to occupy the front seat next to her father. She would always think of it as her mother's place.

All her things had fitted into the boot, but she nursed her plant between her knees to protect its growing shoots. Mary McCloud had given it to her daughter on her first day of college, and Helena was determined to keep it alive. It represented some kind of immortality.

They chatted throughout the journey. The motion of the car made her sleepy, but she forced herself to stay awake, making noises in the right places about a new development in their Suffolk town, the retirement of one of the other GPs at the practice, what was ready in the vegetable garden, and a walking weekend her father had been on in Norfolk.

She yearned to put some music on, but for most of the drive, the car radio had little signal. The only other option was a Dave Brubeck tape, which was trapped inside the cassette player and played on a loop. It had been her mother's favourite. When her father's news was exhausted, Helena told him about her ideas for her Part II thesis, an inter-college athletics meet, and the various careers that her friends were going into, including Sally's job in PR.

'What exactly is PR?' quizzed her father.

'It's . . . er, public relations. And press relations too. The art of persuading people. A bit like advertising,' answered Helena. 'It's being really positive about something in order to sell it.'

'I see. Do you think she'll be good at that?'

'Yes,' said Helena. 'Very.'

'Do *you* have ideas for after?'

She paused and looked out of the passenger window for a few seconds, considering her response. She didn't want to disappoint her father.

'Some pharmaceutical companies came to the careers fair, but to be honest, Dad, I can't face working for one of them.'

'They pay well, presumably?' questioned her father.

'A lot. And I did get an offer from one of them.'

'That's exciting, darling,' he responded proudly.

'But I've been stuck in a lab for my whole life . . .'

'That's an exaggeration, isn't it?'

'It feels like it sometimes, day in day out, when my friends are all lounging around on the college lawn reading books.'

They sat in silence for a while, observing the landscape, rolling fields of pastureland at the peak of lush midsummer. After a while, Helena no longer saw the green hills. Her mind drifted to the previous evening, travelling in time and space to ancient Greece. Jason. Nick. His body and hers briefly one. The memory was vivid and sweet.

'Our Little Chef comes up at the next roundabout,' said Hamish.

'Perfect,' said Helena, snapping out of her reverie. 'I'm starving. Bacon, egg and beans?'

Stopping at this particular café had become a tradition on the journey from Oxford to Dellbridge. It was one of the rituals they had created together over these past few years that might have seemed trivial to others but was important to them.

As he drew into the car park, Helena watched her father politely allow other cars to pass in front of him, then get out to direct an elderly couple who were having difficulty vacating their parking space. Putting others before himself was something Dr Hamish McCloud did without a second thought. It was a tendency that she admired. A child falling off a swing, a pregnant woman fainting in a restaurant, a cyclist being knocked off his bike: whatever the emergency, Hamish volunteered his services.

As they sat at a Formica table enjoying the indulgence of breakfast eaten mid afternoon, Hamish asked the question that Helena always expected.

'And what about medicine? Have you considered it?'

She had an idea that this was her father's hidden dream.

'I just don't think I'm altruistic enough,' she answered. 'Maybe if I was more of a saint, Dad, more like you, but I'm not.'

'I don't think it's altruism exactly, but it has to be a vocation,' he said, deflecting the compliment. 'But you have grown up understanding the reality of it.'

Since the death of his wife, Hamish had always been careful to ensure that he did not live through his daughter. The temptation had been there, but he knew that undue pressure on the only child of a widower could be a crushing burden.

It had been his ambition to be a GP from the day that a young doctor had been summoned by his parents for a house visit. He strode into the boy's bedroom, bicycle clips still in place and Brylcreemed hair sparkling with droplets from the misty night outside. For many years afterwards, Hamish could picture the anxious faces of his parents in the shadows. They seemed like powerless mortals next to this god-like man. The doctor set down a polished leather bag, as shiny as a fresh conker, on the bedside table, snapped open the catch, and one by one drew out a set of gleaming instruments, confidently listening to young Hamish's heartbeat through chest and back, taking his temperature, examining his ears and then his throat with a special torch.

'Say aah!'

Hamish's response had been muted, his throat too painful to emit the smallest sound.

The young doctor shone a bright light into one eye and then the other.

'Now give me a little cough, please,'

The oddly shaped objects were replaced one by one, all fitting precisely into their spaces: stethoscope, thermometer, torch. Then the bag was snapped shut.

At that point, the doctor had sat at the end of the bed and taken one of Hamish's hands. Correctly as it turned out, he suspected tuberculosis, so the boy was taken to an isolation hospital and nursed for many weeks. Hamish recalled little of that time except being cared for by angelic women and regularly visited by the same young doctor, who went out of his way to keep a check on his progress. Hamish's impression was that kindness itself was a cure, and one that was as powerful as any drug. Many years later, when he went to study medicine himself, he was happy to discover that the science proved fascinating too.

'I know you want someone to pass your stethoscope on to,' Helena laughed. 'But I wouldn't be any good at using it.'

'Don't worry, darling, the way you used to care for your dolls gave me a clue.' Hamish smiled. 'They were more mummified than bandaged.'

They strolled to the car and were soon back on the road, talking about what some of Helena's group were planning to do after their chemistry degrees.

Traffic was fairly heavy, but they had passed the county sign for Suffolk when Hamish was suddenly forced to swerve almost into the ditch to let a yellow Ford Capri roar past.

'What an idiotic thing to do on a bend!' Helena shrieked.

'Why are people in such a hurry?' said Hamish. Impatience was one of the things that he least understood.

Moments later, the cars in front of them stopped. Nothing was coming in the other direction, and with the curve in the road it was impossible to see what was happening up ahead.

'Perhaps it's cows. It is milking time, isn't it?' Helena said, checking her watch.

They were not far from home, and it was quite common in their part of Suffolk to be held up like this, so they sat patiently for several minutes chatting. Then they heard the sound of sirens from behind them. A blinding convoy of flashing blue lights sped past: police car, fire engine and ambulance.

In a single movement, Hamish removed his seat belt and retrieved a small bag from the glove compartment.

'Stay there,' he instructed his daughter, before getting out and hastening away.

It had not entered Helena's head to do anything else, and she knew that there was no point in protesting. She had admired her father's commitment to the Hippocratic oath since she was a child. He had a framed print of it on his study wall, and for him, saving lives was his priority: *Into whatsoever houses I enter, I will enter to help the sick.*

She wound down her window and sat for a while breathing in the fragrance of cow parsley and wild honeysuckle that was growing in a nearby hedgerow. There were no further sirens, and it was almost uncannily quiet with all the engines turned off. Traffic had built up behind, and after a while people began to get out of their cars to go and investigate.

Ten minutes or so passed before a few of them returned, anguish etched on their faces. One woman was crying and shaking her head. A broad-shouldered man in a singlet who had been driving the truck immediately behind Hamish and Helena had walked to the front of the jam and was leaning down into open car windows to report on the situation.

'It's a mess down there,' Helena heard him say. 'Three cars. Can't tell one from another. I'd turn around if I were you.'

Two more ambulances were arriving, which held up the exodus from the queue behind her, but eventually the road was clear enough for everyone to make the awkward manoeuvre on the narrow country road and leave in the other direction. Except for Helena. Her father had not returned. And she did not want to go looking for him.

After a while, another police car appeared, and she could hear the incomprehensible crackle of the radio as it slowed down.

'No point sitting here, love,' the driver called across to her. 'You won't get through. Could be hours. They're waiting for a rescue truck. Got to cut someone out.'

'Oh, right. I see.'

Still Helena waited. Nothing would have induced her to go and see what was happening for herself. She imagined her father there, comforting people, treating anyone in shock, holding the hands of the dying to try and sustain their consciousness. Perhaps he was giving a statement as a witness to the reckless driving by the owner of the Capri that had no doubt been involved.

Her mouth felt dry, so she rummaged for some chewing gum in the depths of the leather satchel that she had carried through school days and that still served as her shoulder bag. No gum, but she did find the folded cast sheet from the play. That evening under the stars already seemed a lifetime ago. The tragedy of Medea, the grief of Jason. She perused the list of names. Nicholas Hayes-Jones. His name was imprinted on her mind.

She slipped the paper back into her bag, then got out of the car to stretch her legs. The sun was beginning to go down, and over the hedge she could see a flock of sheep mindlessly grazing on clover. The road had obviously been blocked both ways, so there was just birdsong and the occasional bleat from a lamb.

She took one of her books out of the boot and spread herself across the back seat to read. Peter Atkins' *Physical Chemistry*, the bible on the subject. It fell open at a page on 'The entropy of a monatomic gas'. It would be useful to memorise some of the formulae.

$$U_m - U_m(0) = (2.567 \ kJ \ mol^{-1}) \ x \ (.0355) \ x \ (1.550) = 1.413 \ kJ \ mol^{-1}$$

Soon, though, the letters and symbols were swimming in front of her eyes, and she nodded off.

She woke with a start at the sound of her father's voice.

'Helena! I'm back.' He sounded slightly breathless.

'Oh . . . hi, Dad. Are you okay?' She sat up, rubbing her neck, which was slightly cricked from the awkward position in which she had been sleeping. 'What time is it?'

'Just after nine. I'm sorry I was gone for so long.' He spoke as if he had just returned from shopping or the library. 'Let's get home. They'll be opening the road again any moment.'

Helena had a feeling that her father's inability to save the woman he had loved, the most important patient of his life, had left him with a deep sense of failure, one that could only be assuaged by working harder, caring more, spending unlimited time at the bedside of the sick or at the roadside with the dying.

A few moments later, they passed the scene of the crash. The mangled wrecks of three cars, one of them yellow, had been moved to a lay-by. There were still a few policemen standing about, making notes, speaking into their walkie-talkies.

Helena knew when not to ask questions, and did not want to hear details of the horror in any case. Her heart almost ached with admiration for her father, and for now, the thought of his courage was the only one she wanted in her head.

The accident was only half an hour from the outskirts of Dellbridge. Helena and her father remained silent all the way home.

Chapter Eighteen

The house looked as it always had done, and Hamish McCloud had gone to great efforts to keep it that way. It was tidy, almost too tidy. There was no crockery on the draining board, no old newspapers lying around; everything was in its place.

Helena smiled at the sight of the fruit bowl rather formally positioned in the middle of the dining table: Granny Smiths polished to a gleam, bananas still tipped with a trace of green, a bunch of grapes carefully draped over the top.

'I got you some fruit,' he said. 'And that wholewheat bread you like from the farm shop.'

Helena put her cheese plant down next to the fruit and gave her father a hug. She could see he was drained: the hours by the roadside, the driving to and from Oxford. It must have exhausted him.

'Do you mind if I go straight to bed?' he asked. 'We can unload the car tomorrow.'

'Of course, Dad.'

There was a moment's pause.

'Was it awful?' Helena asked.

'Yes, darling, it was. Two children. The worst.'

'Oh my God.'

'Yes, and they were so little,' he added. Helena could see that he was holding back tears. 'Every death makes the world smaller, doesn't it?'

As she watched her father trudge upstairs, she realised that every death also reminded him of losing his wife.

As the bedroom door closed behind him, the phone on the hall table rang. She answered it quickly. If it was someone asking for a house call, she would say her father was unavailable.

'Dellbridge 2026,' she answered crisply, ready to field the request.

'Oh, hello. I wanted to speak to a girl who looks like Jane Morris,' said a voice.

'Jane Morris? I think you've got the wrong . . .'

Then suddenly she remembered the comment from the previous evening, about how she looked like someone in a painting. Yes. Someone called Jane Morris.

'Nick?'

His name had been on her mind so many times since they parted, and his voice on stage had become familiar to her even before he'd found her in the garden.

'Yes, it's me. Your friend Sally gave me your number. I had to describe you, but she knew who I meant. The amazing hair. The poster girl.'

'Poster girl?'

'The girl who put up posters for us,' he laughed.

'Oh.' She was lost for words.

'You didn't come to the party. It was so dull without you.'

Helena's heart was pounding. She could think of no response to these statements. It would have helped if he asked a question, but none came.

'Are you still in Oxford?' she asked finally, and immediately realised that her question was banal. What did it matter?

'Sort of. Planning some travel and stuff.'

'Oh. Right.'

'I was wondering if you would like to come,' he suggested, as casually as though he was inviting her out for a meal.

Before she even had time to react, he continued.

195

'Greece, probably. In the footsteps of Jason, maybe. I think he'd like that. And you said you speak a little Greek.'

Helena laughed, even though dark images of dead children came to her mind: her father's sad words just a few moments ago, the memory of the limp bodies in the play with little shoes dangling from their feet, an image of small still bodies in a crumpled car.

'I'd love to,' she said. 'But . . .'

'That's a shame, Jane. I thought you might like to.'

There it was again. Another statement.

She had become so used to keeping her fragile emotions intact by avoiding all but friendship with men that the abruptness of his invitation was difficult to respond to. And not only that. As well as her natural caution about people she hardly knew, there was her father to consider. He was alone so much of the time, and for her to arrive home and then leave again would be hard on him.

Weighed up against all of this, though, was a yearning of a kind she had never experienced before. The urge to see Nick again, to be with him, to lie in his arms was an irresistibly powerful one. And Greece itself exerted an immense pull. It was her mother's country, the place where the three of them had spent their final holiday, a place where she herself had such strong connections.

'Think about it,' said Nick.

He gave her no time to reconsider, and with that blunt version of a farewell, the line went dead.

She held the receiver in her hand for a moment before putting it down. The last twenty-four hours had been extremely strange. Love, death, sorrow, regret, grief, nostalgia, separation, doubt, desire, confusion, all of these and more, present and intense in such a short space of time, both in reality and imagination.

Someone wanted to go on a journey with her. Just like that. Someone whom she had known for less than a day.

With her legs still slightly shaking, she went into the living room and sank down into the old chintz-covered sofa, feeling its springs pushing up into her thighs. The side table next to her was crowded with framed photographs. There were several of her holding up county athletics trophies: Under 13, Under 15, Under 18. Her parents had been so proud. There were also some of them all with the Scottish cousins. Then, grouped together, were the pictures taken on their Greek holiday.

In one of them, she was dwarfed by a row of temple pillars. She picked up another and examined it more closely. It was an image of her parents, arms linked, by the church near the Apalos museum. It was a beautiful shot of Mary McCloud, her smile capturing the happiness of the moment. Her pleasure during those sunny days had been palpable, despite her knowledge that her remaining months might be few.

Now that she scrutinised this picture, perhaps more than before Helena could see a woman who was living in the moment. However hard she studied her mother's expression, she could not detect even the slightest hint of what she must have known. There was no shadow of it, no foreboding.

In another photo of the three of them, the one Helena had set up with a self-timer at the top of the hill against the bluest of blue skies, a gust of wind had blown Helena's hair across her face but Mary McCloud in her azure shift had a beaming smile and radiated unmistakable joy. What was obvious now was that her father's happiness was fake. He was not a good actor.

She tried to replace the frames in the exact places they had been, and in her mind had an imaginary conversation with her mother. If she had still been alive, Helena would have asked her straight away: 'What do you think? Shall I go? Is it mad?'

She tried to imagine what her mother's answer would have been, but could not.

Absent-mindedly, she turned on the television. It was the evening news, covering the latest IRA story. A gun battle somewhere in Ireland and an image of dark stains on the pavement, presumably the blood of victims. The McCloud household had never upgraded to colour, but Helena had no appetite for violence, even in mono-chrome, so she switched it off.

The gentle ticking of the carriage clock on the mantelpiece was audible now. All it did was remind her of time passing, inexorably, relentlessly. Even after a few optional classes with a physics professor in her first year, her understanding of theories relating to time, such as movement at the speed of light, were no clearer. She was not convinced that anyone or anything could go backwards in time. If it was possible, surely humankind would be making more effort to make it happen. She could not be the only person who longed to see someone from her past.

Behind the small gold clock, which had lived on the mantelpiece for her entire life, her mother had stacked the postcards Helena had sent her parents from her summer trips to Athens. Mary McCloud had not been a hoarder, but she was very particular about the few things she did keep. If she wanted the cards there, that was where they must stay, Hamish had insisted.

Helena took them down and curled up in a chair to reread them, amused at her neat, childish handwriting and how much she had managed to cram into the space: it read like notes from a diary, written in minuscule lettering, some of which had been obliterated by the postmark. As well as being a perfunctory version of events, the postcards only ever described the first few days, because as her grandmother told her, unless they got them in the post quickly, Helena would get home before they did. When she had finished, she carefully replaced them, making sure they were in chronological order.

As a child, she used to be fascinated by the movements of the clock's intricate mechanism, visible through the glass at the back. Her feelings towards this wedding gift to her mother from Eleni and Stamatis Papagiannis had changed a little since she had learned more about them, but the inscription on the back seemed as important as ever: '*Pánta ekkalýpton o chrónos eis to phos ágei*' – 'Time sees and hears all things and discloses all.' Presumably Sophocles was right, and time itself would make things clear and give the answers.

She sat contemplating other things that her mother had been eager for her to learn. Many of them were expressed in Latin phrases that she used to write on little pieces of paper. Sometimes she left them on Helena's bedside table, and there were still a few stuck to the fridge door, their edges curled with time, the ink almost faded to invisibility. It had begun when Helena had chosen needlework instead of a language in the third form, a small and futile act of rebellion against her academic parents.

'*Amor vincit omnia*' ('Love conquers all'), '*Sapientia potentia est*' ('Wisdom is power'), '*Bono malum superate*' ('Overcome evil with good') were some that remained with her, but her mother's favourite had been '*Carpe diem*' ('Seize the day'). And she thought of that one now. They had been moments away from a fatal accident and the victims could easily have been her and her father.

Nick's invitation to go travelling began to nag at her. Conflicting voices inside her head offered one opinion and then another. A vision of herself on the road with someone she hardly knew was alien, of course, and yet if she turned the chance down, it would haunt her. Surely if time flew, then she must grab at such an opportunity when it came? But was it safe? Was it wise?

The clock seemed to taunt her. Life is short, she thought to herself. How many times do I need to be reminded?

She went to bed in a state of excited confusion. Her night was filled with vivid dreams: ancient pillars collapsing behind her as she ran to escape something unknown, perhaps a fire or the burning sun; her mother calling her, then her father's voice somewhere far away. She was alone, choked with dust, fleeing, afraid . . .

'Helena. Helena!'

She felt a hand on her shoulder. Whatever had been in pursuit had caught up with her. She woke, gasping.

'Helena, darling. You're all right.'

Her screams had penetrated the bedroom wall. Her father was sitting on the edge of her bed, stroking her shoulder.

'Water . . . can I have some water?'

He reached for the glass on her bedside table and handed it to her.

'Such a bad dream, Dad. Really bad.'

'You used to have night terrors when you were little,' he reminded her. 'I thought they had stopped.'

'They have on the whole. Still the occasional nightmare, though.'

'It's not surprising. Today was a bit strange, wasn't it?'

'Yes.'

'Try and think of something nice before you go back to sleep.'

'I will, Dad. And sorry I woke you.'

Into her mind she summoned the tranquil interior of a little haberdashery. There was a box of odd buttons, and it was these that Helena always imagined herself counting, rather than sheep. Within a few moments, it invariably led to a dreamless sleep.

She slept well and woke with Nick on her mind. She could, of course, see if Sally had his number. But if he really had meant the invitation, he would call back, wouldn't he?

Meanwhile, she would earn some money so that if he did, she would be able to go. The following morning, she would call in on Mrs Greetham to ask if she needed help.

'What a lovely thought, dear,' smiled the elderly woman. 'I only open three days a week now, and I know that some of my customers would appreciate it if you could do the other three. I've a few ladies who collect their weekly pension and then come straight in here to get their knitting wool. I keep it by for them and they get upset when they see the "Closed" sign.'

'Of course,' said Helena sympathetically. 'They can't go without for too many days, can they?'

She looked around her at the shelves that rose from floor to ceiling.

They were a tangled mess of ribbons, tapes, tapestry silk and skeins of wool.

'And I could have a bit of a tidy-up, couldn't I?' She could now reach many of the upper shelves that Mrs Greetham could not, and the elderly lady was reluctant to climb a ladder these days.

'That would be wonderful, dear. And I'm not far away if you need me.'

Dorothy Greetham lived above her shop, as she had done for decades. She still held on to the hope that her daughter would take over one day, even though she had moved to Melbourne ten years earlier along with her husband and two boys. Now, at the age of seventy, her hands were getting too arthritic to rewind ribbons onto their spools at the end of each day, and she had little energy to ensure that paper patterns had been filed correctly. Helena would be more than happy to do those things for her.

A three-day-a-week routine left Helena plenty of time to start planning what she would do for her fourth-year dissertation. Her supervisor had suggested 'Organometallic reagents in selective carbon–carbon bond formation'. She would need to do some background reading on it before going back in October and must make sure she was well enough prepared in case she went travelling with Nick. On days when she studied, she went to the local library, where she found it much easier to concentrate than at home, mostly because she was not reminded of her mother.

She took the opportunity to ask the librarian if there was a book on the Pre-Raphaelites, and was directed to the small art section, where there was a single volume with black-and-white plates. Jane Morris was not hard to find. There were many paintings of her, and Helena studied them closely. Jane's bold features, porcelain skin and copious quantities of hair were very idiosyncratic, her face one that her mother would have described as *jolie laide*.

Every night for several weeks she was on edge, yearning for the phone to come to life. On all the occasions that it did, the voice at the other end asked for her father, but she did not give up hope that the next call would be for her and she would hear Nick's sonorous thespian voice.

One evening she joined some of her old school friends in the local pub to catch up on their lives. Several of her contemporaries already had children, one had married the day after they left school and was already divorced, one was with an older wealthy man and spent most of the day at her health club. A few had started jobs straight after sixth form and already climbed up several rungs of the company ladder. One was an air stewardess and had been round the world twice, another was a swimmer training for the next Olympics. The most entrepreneurial of them had opened a shop, making handmade cards and painting house signs. Jenny had gone to live with an aunt in London after her disastrous A level results and got herself a job as a dogsbody at the BBC. She was now an assistant on *Top of the Pops* and going out with the drummer of a new band that had just burst onto the scene.

As one of the few students in the group, Helena felt that her life lacked adventure. All these girls had packed much more into the past three years than she had, and she found something enviable in each of their lives.

When she got home that evening, three Cinzanos and two glasses of wine later (far more than enough, she had realised as she ambled haphazardly along the road, arm in arm with Jenny), her father was in the living room, reading. Some gentle jazz piano was playing in the background. A thimble measure of whisky was balanced on the arm of his chair.

'Dad, you didn't need to wait up for me!' she told him, dropping her bag onto the sofa. 'I have my own key! Do you want a cup of tea? I'm going to have one – and some toast, I think.'

'No thanks, darling. Did you have a nice evening?'

'Yes. Sorry. Had too much to drink, I think. But it was fun. Tried to make chemistry sound interesting. But people's eyes glaze over.

Don't blame them really. Unless it's the cure for a disease, or space travel, nobody really cares about science.'

Her father laughed. 'You do exaggerate, sweetheart. I'm sure they're fascinated really.'

A few minutes later, Helena returned with her mug, slopping a few drops onto the rug as she sat down.

'God, sorry, Dad. I'm so clumsy.'

'Mind the photos,' he told her, as she put the mug down on the side table.

'Yes, yes.'

Both of them caught sight of the framed photo taken on the Greek hilltop, very aware of how precious it was. It was the last picture ever taken of the three of them, Hamish, Mary and Helena McCloud. Hamish leaned forward to rescue it and nursed it in his lap.

'I'm on call early tomorrow, sweetheart, so I will probably miss you in the morning.'

'You work so hard, Dad. You really care about your patients, don't you?'

'I do,' he said.

'Don't suppose anybody rang for me?' she asked casually.

'For once the phone didn't ring at all,' he said, gently kissing the top of his daughter's head. He left the room with his book tucked under his arm.

It was midnight now, and a little drunkenly, Helena dialled Sally's number. Perhaps her new boyfriend, Charles, might have heard from Nick. They had seemed like great friends, after all.

Sally answered almost immediately.

'Sally! It's me.'

'Hels! How are you?'

'Hope it's not too late to ring.'

'Of course not, parents are at a do at the golf club anyway. And I'm packing.'

'For Edinburgh? Are you taking the play?'

'No, half the cast didn't want to go. Medea is trying for drama school in LA. Jason vanished somewhere. Even Charles, who he was supposed to be moving in with, doesn't have a clue where he is. So it's London for me! I'm taking the room in Charles's house. I've been staying there already. With him. And the induction course for the job starts soon. I'm excited. About everything. It all seems to be opening up. Love, life, London, Ladbroke Grove . . . How about you?'

The incorrigible Sally. As self-absorbed as ever, but redeeming herself at the end. Helena was still hearing the words 'Jason vanished somewhere', though. What did Sally mean? She was desperate to ask where to, but if someone had 'vanished', the question was in vain.

'I'm fine,' she said instead. 'Selling knitting wool. Cooking for Dad. Trying to decide on some options for next year. You know, the usual.' She made her life sound dull and decided not to mention the call from Nick. 'It will sound silly, but I was trying to remember those last lines in *Medea*. The ones you had to say at the very end. We don't have a bookshop in the town and our library here doesn't have a copy, so I couldn't look them up.'

Sally didn't miss a beat. It was like pressing a button on a talking doll:

> Olympic Zeus controls our fate,
> And the gods allow the unexpected to happen
> And things we thought would happen don't.

'Say them again, slowly,' Helena said, scribbling the words down as Sally delivered them again, this time with more drama.

'He's good, isn't he, Euripides? But simultaneously cruel.' Beneath the gaiety of her manner and the party-girl exterior, Helena knew Sally had true depth and empathy, as she had shown in those weeks after Mary's death. 'I'd love to hear what it sounds like in the original.'

'Me too,' said Helena, not meaning it at all.

'Look, I'd better go. I promised to collect the sozzled parents from the golf club. Talk soon? Come to London to see the house before term starts. Promise?' Sally assumed an answer and the line clicked.

Helena sat for a while mulling over the speech that closed *Medea*. More than two millennia later, the words had as much resonance as when they were first written. Time after time it had been confirmed to her that *things we thought would happen don't*. It was better to expect the unexpected. Or maybe she should drink less the next time she went out with her girlfriends, she smiled to herself.

Taking her confused thoughts to bed, she dreamed of being in the Kolonaki apartment. Nick and her grandfather were sitting at the kitchen table smoking and drinking. Arsenis was cooking something. She was scrubbing the floor, unnoticed by any of them. Neither her grandmother nor Dina was there. Suddenly her father was kneeling down next to her and helping her up off the floor and back into bed.

The following morning, she had to be at the shop early to help Mrs Greetham with stocktaking. Over the next few days, as she wound spools of ribbon and colour-coded all the buttons, she kept thinking about returning to Greece. Nick was in her mind every second of her day as she served customers, counting out quantities of hooks or change and cutting lengths of trim or pieces of felt. He was always present in her imagination, walking across Peloponnesian hillsides or climbing a mountain in Attica. She was furious with herself for letting the chance to see him slip by.

A fortnight later, Helena had saved plenty of money, but it had begun to seem a little pointless.

They were in front of the TV one evening, watching *Moonraker* – Bond films were her father's favourites – when the phone rang.

Watching the red-headed female star, Helena recalled how meanly her grandfather's friends had laughed at her when she told them she wanted to be an astronaut. There had been so many moments of humiliation on those visits.

Hamish was expecting a call from a patient and went out to the hall to answer.

She turned the sound down so that the patient would not hear the noise of gunshots and explosions.

'Yes. Of course. Who shall I say is calling?' she heard her father asking.

A moment later, he was back in the room.

'Darling, it's for you . . . Jason?'

She leapt off the sofa and ran into the hall.

'Jane.'

It was that same rich voice she had tried to reimagine for all these weeks, immediately summoning images of their night together.

'Nick! How are you?'

The line was breaking up.

'I'm well!'

'Did you go travelling?'

'Of course I did. I'm on an island now. A Greek island. It's beautiful.'

'Lucky you! Wish I'd come,' she answered.

'Well, why don't you? That's why I rang. I'm staying on a while. And I'm helping on a dig.'

'That sounds interesting.'

'Look – they need a few more people before they have to stop for the winter. And I was wondering if you fancied coming as a volunteer?'

'But I'm not an archaeologist.'

'Neither am I,' said Nick. 'You don't have to be. They need willing hands, that's all.'

'Oh,' she said. This was exactly the kind of adventure she had told herself she needed, the kind of risk that was worth taking.

'They put us up in a hostel, give us food, as much wine as anyone could drink. All you have to do is get here.'

Us. This sweet word was enough.

'Yes,' she said. 'I would love to come. Where? How?'

After giving her some scant details, he said he would be waiting for her. The ferry always arrived on the island around ten in the evening.

'I'm counting the hours, my beautiful Helena-Jane,' he purred. 'See you in two days, my gorgeous girl.'

Then the coins dropped through and the line went dead.

She had earned enough to fly herself to Greece and back, and the travel agent she visited the next day said that she could buy her ferry ticket once she got to Rafina. Nick had told her she didn't need to bring much; just some shorts, loose trousers with pockets, and plenty of long-sleeved T-shirts. She would need spare trousers for the evening because the midges came out then, a hat, and a bikini. It all seemed wildly adventurous, perhaps the most spontaneous thing she had ever done. All summer she had been waiting and hoping, and while she had wanted to ask why he had not contacted her earlier, she told herself it did not matter.

She felt the urge to let Sally know what she was going to do. It was a while since they had spoken, and Sally was now living happily with Charles. As Helena had anticipated, they were already sharing a room.

'That sounds fabulous,' squealed her friend. 'Exactly what you *should* be doing. I'm so envious! The working life isn't all it's cracked up to be. I have plenty of money now but no time to spend it. If it wasn't for Charles, I'd be going mad. I have to be in the office at eight thirty, and rarely leave before eight in the evening. But we have lots of fun at weekends, long weekends in the country, seeing all the old gang.'

Sally did not pause for breath, and Helena was happy that her friend had not given Nick a second thought since the final performance of the play.

'If I find a phone box somewhere,' she promised her, 'I'll ring you.'

'Don't worry about doing that!' Sally said ecstatically. 'Just enjoy the moment, enjoy the place. Find some treasure. Have a great time. *Carpe diem!'*

Chapter Nineteen

The plane journey was a reminder of her last trip out, when she had sat squeezed between her parents, excited about her first holiday here with them, oblivious of what was to come. She knew her mother would have been pleased that she was returning to Greece, but Helena was glad that the destination was somewhere fresh and new.

The airport at Glyfada had not changed, but after that, everything was different. A bus took her to Rafina, and within an hour or so the ferry had departed, visiting two other islands on the way. Nick had told her that there was only one main town on Nisos, which was also the port, and that she would find him and the team in the big taverna, Marina's, on the seafront. If the ferry docked on schedule, they would all be there having dinner.

It had sounded impossibly simple, but as the anchor chain dropped, Helena realised everything had gone to plan, exactly. It was ten on the dot when she disembarked, and as the boat headed out to its next destination, she stood there slightly uncertainly, her rucksack on the ground at her feet.

Even from a distance, she could identify the taverna. A long table that stretched all the way across the front of the building was filled with a party of diners. There was singing at one end, and from the other came shrieks of laughter. Someone had just delivered the punchline of a joke, perhaps. She approached slightly gingerly, looking for

Nick in the crowd. She could see nobody who even resembled him. Perhaps all of this had been a terrible mistake.

'Jane!'

She heard her nickname almost squealed above the noise, and a boy she now realised was Nick was heading her way, his arms wide open to embrace her. He had changed. She should have expected him to be a little tanned after a summer here, but his skin was deep bronze and his eyes seemed even bluer. His hair had grown almost to his shoulders and was white-blond. He wore a straw hat slightly cocked to one side.

'Jane, you're here! *Kalós órises!* Welcome!'

He kissed her on the mouth, took her hand and led her to the table. When he tapped a wine glass, the whole party immediately fell silent. Helena realised that it was Nick who had been telling the joke that had ended in an eruption of laughter.

'Introductions! This is Helena, aka Jane. Doesn't she look like Jane Morris, everyone? We were at Oxford together and she's come out for our last weeks.'

He then proceeded to name everyone at the table and they each gave a little wave. Helena stood, very self-conscious of being the pale neophyte, as he began with Professor Carver, the distinguished archaeologist who was leading the dig, and worked his way down the hierarchy, tactfully naming all the academics by descending order of rank, followed by the students and helpers. They were a mix of various European nationalities and a handful of Americans.

A chair was squeezed in next to Nick, or Nikos as he was called here.

A waiter approached her with a plate and asked her if she was hungry.

'*Óchi efcharistó*,' she said, politely declining the stodgy-looking moussaka. 'No thanks. *Mípos écheis mia Fanta lemóni?*'

Her fluent request for a soft drink provoked a long discussion with the man. He wanted to know how someone who was clearly not Greek spoke his language so perfectly. She explained in brief, and the people sitting close by who overheard the conversation were equally curious and impressed.

'I love hearing you speak,' Nick whispered close to her ear. 'Will you teach me?'

Helena smiled in response. Nick was caressing her thigh beneath the table.

They all remained sitting there for another hour, eating platters of fruit and bowls of ice cream. More drinks came around and Helena listened to the conversation even though her mind was elsewhere, distracted. Mostly the group shared anecdotes of other archaeological digs, precious objects discovered and then accidentally dropped; vases found on a rubbish tip that were put in a local museum before being claimed by a local woman who said that she had made them herself; the Victorian coin that one of the young students had found in his garden as a ten-year-old that had set him on a life quest to be an archaeologist. It turned out that his father had put it there as a trick, only telling him the truth many years later.

Many of the other girls were as tanned as Nick, their hair blonde and crinkly from the sea. Helena looked at them slightly enviously, knowing that her skin would never go that colour and her hair would remain stubbornly *kókkina*.

Just before midnight, Nick stood up. The professor tapped his glass with a knife and everyone fell silent. Helena was intrigued. She saw Nick pull a book out of his back pocket, and then he began to declaim:

> The isles of Greece! The isles of Greece
> Where burning Sappho loved and sung,
> Where grew the arts of war and peace,
> Where Delos rose, and Phoebus sprung!
> Eternal summer gilds them yet,
> But all, except their sun, is set . . .

The sound of his voice reminded her of how she had fallen under his spell in Oxford. She looked around to see everyone, men and women alike, gazing at him with adoration. There was whooping and cheering as soon as the poem ended.

Nick bowed, soaking up the ecstatic response, then bent to whisper in Helena's ear. 'Everyone here worships Byron.'

When the noise had died down, one of the academics stood up and clapped his hands.

'The bus leaves at five thirty. Breakfast at the dig. Anyone who misses it has a two-hour walk.' He paused for a moment to push his glasses up his nose. 'Those staying here to sort the finds – that's Harriet, Samantha, Timothy, Jâcques, Anne-Marie and Francis – have a half-hour lie-in, but no more. I want you to make the most of the day. And we need the light. We found a lot today. Thank you, everyone. Bedtime.'

There was a general scraping of chairs as everyone got up.

Helena picked up her rucksack, which she had left leaning against a tree, and followed Nick along the road by the sea and then up a sandy track. Soon they reached a pair of single-storey, prefabricated buildings that resembled army barracks.

The accommodation was more spartan than she had expected. There were ten girls sleeping in dormitory-style single beds, five on each side of a room, and a similar arrangement for the boys, though there were twelve of them sharing the same space. Toilets were male and female, while a row of shower rooms was communal, each one divided only by a plastic curtain. In a separate building, the academics had a room each with bathroom en suite.

'Sorry it's all a bit basic,' said Nick. 'Elpida will show you the ropes.' He grabbed the arm of a plump woman with long greying hair who was passing. 'Elpida, Helena. Helena, Elpida,' he said. 'Can you be Helena's guide?'

'Of course, Nikos,' the woman answered with a heavy Greek accent. '*Éla*, Eleni! Come!'

Nick gave Helena a lingering kiss before disappearing into the men's dormitory, and she followed Elpida, dragging her rucksack behind her and trying to contain her disappointment at how they were going to live. It was not in the least what she had expected.

Lying on her camp bed, the rough sheet pulled over her face to escape from the high-pitched whine of a mosquito, she briefly questioned her decision to come before telling herself it was going to be worth it simply to be here with Nick. His warmth and the attention he had given her more than justified the discomfort of the struts that were digging into her back and the bites she already had on her neck.

It felt to Helena that scarcely a few minutes passed before she heard the sound of a bell clanging outside.

'Rise and shine! Rise and shine!' came a cheery call. It was not yet light.

A bleary-eyed group, hastily dressed in dirty sweatshirts, loose linen trousers in shades of fawn, and wide-brimmed hats, filed onto a battered old bus. Each of them had an army kitbag slung over one shoulder and a large metal water flask over the other. Helena was acutely aware that she did not have the right gear, but Nick had not given her much of a brief. She glimpsed him at the back, the seat next to him already taken, as Elpida shepherded her to a vacant place near the front.

A moment later, she felt something touching her hair, unbrushed since her arrival here. Turning round, she realised it was Nick, stroking the top of her head.

'*Kaliméra*, beautiful Jane. *Ti káneis?*'

Helena answered cheerfully in Greek. '*Kaliméra, Níko. Kalá eímai.*'

The noisy vibration of the engine and the grunts and rattles as the bus constantly changed gear and negotiated bends in the narrow road precluded any conversation. Most of the passengers dozed or gazed wearily out of the window, lost in their own thoughts.

'Do you mind swapping?' Nick asked Helena's neighbour, who gave him a gleaming smile and walked to the back of the bus.

He took Helena's hand as he sat down.

'I hope you're going to have a good time,' he whispered, his lips touching her ear. 'It's hard work, but you'll get into it. And we'll be together every evening.'

With his head tilted slightly to one side as he stroked her fingers, his smile was enough to dispel any doubts she had. She gazed into his eyes for a moment, as though she might able to read something in them, and resisted the desire to kiss him.

The bus was now making its way up an unsurfaced track, and the clouds of dust stirred into the air obscured any views of the journey. Those closest to the windows slid them shut.

'Here we are,' said Nick, as they eventually jolted to a halt. 'The site.'

They gathered into five groups and set off towards a fenced area fifty yards away. Helena was directed away from Nick, into Elpida's group. She bit back her frustration at being separated all day as well, wondering if she would be able to swap into his group later.

The professor strode ahead of them all. It was he who held the key to the padlock that loosely protected the site. Once through the gate, Helena lost sight of Nick. Elpida took her arm and led her to an area marked out by blue string. Two men, locals, were carrying a heavy chest full of larger tools in case they were needed. The site bore no resemblance to the magnificent place she had visited with her mother and father, where birds soared above and sea and sky stretched to infinity. This area looked like a dry, abandoned field with a few trees and bushes sticking out of the surface.

She spent the day under instruction from one of the junior academics, Spiros, who was in charge of the team. She would not be digging, but instead was helping to brush away the soil around any items that had been semi-excavated and were not quite loose enough to be removed from the ground. It was painstaking work.

Even small fragments of pottery, known as 'sherds', had to be carefully removed and examined.

Nothing of excitement happened for her first few days on any part of the dig, but Nick told her that sometimes weeks might pass with little of any note being found. One afternoon, though, when the sun was beginning to go down and others were packing up their tools, Spiros gathered a few of them round so that they could focus on one area of the pit.

'We have an hour to get this out of the ground,' he said, pointing to an area where there was a sizeable piece of exposed ceramic.

'Why the hurry?' asked Helena. She was weary that day and her back had got burnt even through her shirt.

'Looters,' replied Elpida. 'We can't take the risk. As soon as they get wind of anything, they find a way.'

'With the gate? The fence?' Helena queried. 'Even with the guard?'

'Especially with the guard,' Elpida said under her breath.

As the professor had told them every evening so far, there was a problem with theft of these antiquities. Demand for them was burgeoning. Items regularly came onto the international market and sold for tens of thousands of pounds in London.

Helena was surprised by the insinuation. Surely it would be impossible for someone to remove something and dispose of it on this small island?

They all gathered around and with their miniature picks carefully loosened the impacted earth that held what was a significant section of a pot, slightly curved and more than six inches square. Once it had been freed from its thousands of years of darkness it was lifted by one of the academics on the team.

Professor Carver joined them, and seemed thrilled with the find, inspecting it closely along with the other pieces they had gathered that day, all of them held in a rubber basket on the ground.

'Well done, everyone. It's been a very good day. It's clear now that we have something important beneath us. Everything you have in here points to that. The style of painting even on this sherd indicates the Bronze Age. And look at the curvature of this piece!'

He held the pottery fragment aloft for them to observe the edge. It was easy to calculate that the pot from which it came might have been more than two feet in diameter.

'I believe that this was an immense pithos. The rest will be down there.' He picked out a non-descript piece of pottery no bigger than a thumbnail that to Helena looked no different from any other rubble on the ground. 'And see here, perhaps the rim of a vase?'

At the nightly review of the day's work given by one of the trained archaeologists, it seemed that the findings from her group, along with similar pieces found by others some distance away, had been the conclusive proof that they were on the edge of an extensive settlement.

That evening at dinner, everyone remained in their working groups to discuss the day. Helena broke the unspoken rule. For four nights running she had watched Nick flirting and laughing with the same two American girls who had bagged the seats on either side of him. Tonight she planted herself next to him to be sure of his attention, and as the director gave the day's update, they discreetly held hands.

'So, we now know that we are working on a sizeable site. This will mean commitment from some of you for perhaps several years.'

The mood was high. There were cheers from the other end of the table and glasses were clinked.

'Now, we all know what every settlement has – and generally not far away . . .'

The professor left a pause, always aware of his role as teacher of the next generation of younger archaeologists.

One of the Californian girls, denied her place next to Nick, had sat under the professor's nose. She raised her hand in the air.

'A ceme-taaaary, sir.'

'Yes. Exactly. Thank you, Ashley. So please be on the lookout. The cemetery is often the source of the most valuable and exciting discoveries. People took their wealth with them to the next life. Some of the finds might be smaller than these sherds with which you have already filled your buckets, but even the tiniest pieces can be of vital importance to us, so don't discount them. And remember,' he concluded, 'eyes wide open, mouths tight shut. Goodnight, all.'

Leaning on his stick, he got up and left the table, leaving the rest to finish the raki and wine.

Nick turned to speak to the girls around him, and Helena could hear shrieks of laughter from the clique that had gathered to his right. She glanced over, saw him refill Ashley's glass and felt a stab of resentment.

Elpida was sitting not far away, so Helena leaned across to speak to her.

'Mouths shut tight?' she queried. 'Does he prefer us not to talk during the dig?'

'Of course not,' smiled Elpida. 'He means that we shouldn't share information with any outsiders about our finds.'

'I don't really know any outsiders.'

'Some people here do, though. They go to different bars and end up drinking with the locals.'

'Something wrong with that?'

'So far, no. But in the past, there have been huge problems with looting. Even when there is a guard. All kinds of things happen. I was on a dig a few years ago, on another part of Nisos with Professor Carver. We finished in the autumn, and when we came back in spring, a huge area next to the site had been dug up. We will never know what was taken, but the loss of every single item, whether it is one hundred or one thousand years old, means the loss of knowledge. It's like losing half the pieces of a jigsaw. You can never complete the picture. It becomes literally pointless.'

'What happened to the finds?'

'Nobody really knows, but there was a woman who gave us a

few clues. She was old and blind, so not perhaps the best witness, but she told the prof she had overheard some looters.'

Helena felt Nick's hand on her shoulder.

'We're going to have another drink in the bar,' he said. 'Coming?'

'I'll see you there,' she smiled. 'In two minutes.' She was absorbed by what Elpida was telling her and wanted to hear the rest.

'According to the sister of the blind one, a man from Athens had come to stay that previous winter. He had a very flashy car, so he really stood out. This is such a small community once the summer and autumn are over that everyone noticed him. He wanted to buy land for a hotel and drove about all over the island with a real-estate agent.

'About a week later, the sister went down to the quayside to buy some fish and saw the red car waiting in the queue to board the ferry. This time it had a big trunk strapped to the roof. It looked odd on top of this sports car, so she went closer and saw a second trunk squeezed onto the back seat. It seemed strange to her for someone who had come on a business trip to have so much luggage, and she was sure he'd had less when he arrived.'

'And?' Helena was expecting an ending to the story.

'That was all we ever found out,' said Elpida. 'The professor and his team made a few enquiries, but nobody else had anything to offer. No one had seen anything else out of the ordinary. Or at least they didn't tell us if they had. The so-called real-estate agent was based in Athens too, and he apparently left two days after the guy with the sports car. All we knew for certain was that the site had been looted sometime between when we had left in the autumn and when we returned.'

'Even though it was presumably all fenced off?'

'That's rarely enough of an obstacle,' answered Elpida.

Most people had drifted away, leaving Helena and Elpida at the long table with a couple of the qualified archaeologists, who had been listening in to their conversation.

'It's becoming harder and harder to unmask,' said one. 'In Italy, where I used to be based, they call the perpetrators *tombaroli*. There was such extensive theft down in Calabria, you wouldn't believe it. And when I say extensive, I mean highly organised and on an industrial scale.'

'And what makes it such a difficult crime to stamp out is that you might not even know it's happened,' exclaimed the other. 'It's often theft of treasures that people didn't know existed in the first place. And the people who do it don't care about anything except money. They'll even break something that's whole to make it easier to smuggle.'

Helena remembered her mother explaining in the museums on Ammos and Apalos that every object, however broken or small, could provide a clue to the understanding of civilisation. But to break things deliberately and sell them was criminal.

'*Archaiokápiloi* is what they're called in this country,' said Elpida. 'Tomb raiders . . . thieves.'

This was a new word for Helena, and she repeated it over and over to herself as she made her way towards the bar where Nick had said to meet. *Archaiokápiloi*. Like arch-villains, she thought to herself.

Even from a distance, she could hear the beat of the music, and when she turned the corner, a crowd was dancing in a circle with a row of musicians behind them: two bouzouki players, a drummer and an electric guitar. The circle was made up of Nick and ten women. He had already mastered the steps by copying the wife of the café owner, and now the girls around him were trying to keep up, collapsing with laughter as they tripped, carried away by the pure fun of it all. Ashley was clamped to his side, dancing perfectly in time, her head held high, her laughter displaying teeth that gleamed even whiter than Nick's.

Helena watched for a while, but one dance led straight into another without a breath in between, and the minutes ticked by. When the church clock announced that it was midnight, she turned away.

She walked slowly up the hill towards the hostel, telling herself to accept that Nick's popularity was not something she would ever want to change. His magnetism was part of him. Suddenly she heard the crunch of loose stones behind her and turned.

'Helena!' Nick panted. 'You should have joined in the dancing. The steps were so easy. You could do it!'

'Don't worry,' she answered. 'There'll be another time, I'm sure.'

There was a pause as they stood and looked at each other. Nick moved forward to kiss her, but she stepped away.

'You should go back,' she said. 'It looked like fun.'

'Not as much fun as if you were there,' he said. 'I'd had enough anyway. Early start tomorrow.'

As they walked, Nick held Helena's hand tightly, at the same time stroking the inside of her wrist. Halfway up the hill, he led her along the path into the olive grove. The night air was still soft and balmy, and around the well-watered roots of the olive trees lush vegetation had grown. The ground made a much softer bed than the mattress in his Oxford room, but her burnt shoulders were rubbed raw even through her shirt.

When she finally got to the dormitory that night, she slept soundly and had sweet dreams. When she spotted Ashley leaning so closely towards Nick the next morning that it looked as if they might kiss, she managed to control her jealousy. She, Helena, was his girlfriend. From then on, the eight hours of back-breaking work, crouched down under a cruel sun, were spent in the haze of a daydream, waiting for that single hour beneath the silvery-leafed trees. Though they saw little of each other in the day, the nights made up for it. When they were together and alone, Nick's ardour was overwhelming, and left her in a state of intoxication that carried her into the following day.

Throughout the long, hot mornings, Elpida was the perfect companion and teacher. She was a volunteer, several years older than most people on the dig, but dedicated to her hobby, and she had picked up immense knowledge over the past fifteen years. Her parents had not been able to afford for her to go to university, but she had found another way to pursue her dream. Each summer she worked on a dig, and in the winter returned to Thessaloniki to take care of her mother and do part-time jobs. She lived for the thrill of the find, of knowing that she was playing a part in expanding man's understanding of the world, however modestly. Her knowledge of how the work was done and how the evidence was pieced together was as extensive as that of any archaeologist.

Like Elpida, Nick seemed to know more than most volunteers. It was not only because he stuck close to the professor and seemed to be in a group where most pieces were found, but also because he had been appointed as the team member who went to and from the *apothíki*, the storeroom, with finds. He had plenty of opportunity to loiter at the benches, observing how things were sorted, labelled and meticulously recorded.

He was clearly the professor's favourite. The elderly man always joshed with him at dinner, and often encouraged Nick to give a recital of Byron's poems. On the nights when he sat up late, he offered Nick one of his cigars to smoke as they sat looking at the midnight stars. He was encouraging Nick to do a master's in archaeology and had agreed for him to bypass certain papers, promising to fast-track him to the next stage.

Each day, when the groups stopped to take their lunch break, Helena made for the shade of a few pine trees perched on the top of a mound some distance from their trench. In weary silence, the few others who gathered there too nibbled on their meagre picnic of bread and hard *graviéra* cheese. She sometimes closed her eyes and recalled the hilltop with the infinite seascape below that had so enchanted her and her parents.

The recollection of their happiness on that last holiday was so strong that she felt her mother close by, kneeling next to her on the stony ground.

Sometimes, though, grief would catch her unawares. A sudden vivid memory – the fragrance of the Greek coffee her mother had loved so much, or the whiff of oregano, which she had often used in her cooking (and only now did Helena appreciate the Greekness of it) – could be the catalyst for an unexpected lump in her throat or tightness in her chest. She held back from showing any sadness in front of Nick, but on the evening of what would have been her mother's birthday, he noticed her tears. His sympathy was like a warm blanket, and made her weep all the more. It was an opportunity to ask him about his own parents, something she had never done before, and he confided that he had also lost his mother but was so young at the time that he had no recollection of her. Helena was aghast. At least she had enjoyed a close relationship with her mother, whereas poor Nick had been mostly brought up by a nanny.

'And your mother was able to teach you her beautiful language,' he said, winding a lengthy frond of Helena's hair round and round his finger. 'You know, I would love you to teach me some more Greek. It would be really useful if I am going to be coming back to this dig.'

Nick had an actor's talent for picking up language and intonation and already knew a reasonable amount of vocabulary, but he wanted to progress. He said that technical words to do with archaeology and antiquities would be very helpful.

There was nothing that would please Helena more, and that evening, his lessons began.

Chapter Twenty

Helena's remaining days on Nisos, which had seemed to stretch out into eternity when she first arrived, could now be counted on one hand.

One night she woke from a dream in which she and her mother were working together on a dig. They were trying to loosen something from the ground. It was marble, pale and smooth, and when they brushed away the dirt, Helena saw that it was a face. It resembled her mother: beautiful, with a kind expression and an elegant nose. But when she looked round, her mother had gone and the face itself had disappeared too. She lay on her lumpy mattress, listening to the breathing and snores of the other women, and felt herself on the edge of sobbing. Some of the others were also light sleepers and she was afraid of disturbing them, so she gathered up her shorts and T-shirt from the end of the bed and quietly left the stuffy dormitory.

It was mid September now, so the nights were cooling a little, and she took some deep, refreshing breaths. The full moon was so bright that she could have sat outside and read. There was no possibility of getting to sleep again, at least not for a while, so she decided to walk down to the sea. From where she stood, high above the shore, she could see the reflection of the moon on the glassy surface of the water. It was dramatic and she wanted to be closer, perhaps even to take a night-time dip if nobody was around. One of the other girls had swum late the night before and had described a spectral phosphorescence in the shallows. Helena was hoping to see it herself.

Barefoot, she walked down the path. Her plimsolls were still under her bed, but it was not far to the junction with the main road, and the path was sandy enough. Turning left would take her to the town and the port, and right to a small sandy beach where some of them often went for a swim after their long days in their trenches. For a moment she stood simply gazing at the shimmer on the water. Most of the lights in the village had been turned out now, so there was a pleasing inkiness in the sky and sea, where the ripples of water were painted with streaks of white moonshine.

The path to the beach itself was just after a bend in the road, and it was quite easy to miss even in the light. Pine trees lined the road, their branches as motionless as the sea, and Helena enjoyed their sweet scent as she walked. Suddenly, just before the road curved, she heard voices, and her heart began to pound against her chest. She had not expected to meet anyone here and suddenly felt vulnerable and afraid. The moonlight had given her too much confidence – what had she been thinking of coming out like this?

Instinctively she stepped back into the trees and ducked down, pine needles pricking the soles of her feet. Whoever it was, they were speaking quietly. With the brilliant light of the moon illuminating everything in the landscape, she knew her light-coloured clothes would stand out if they looked her way, so she crouched behind a bush and out of sight.

A few minutes later, the voices drew closer. Men's voices, speaking in Greek but not loudly enough to be fully audible. They were walking as they talked, and once Helena was confident that they had passed her hiding place, she stood up to watch their receding backs. She could clearly see the outlines of two men walking away down the road towards the port, each of them carrying something. A third had taken the path up to the hostel.

Hanging back until the pair were out of sight, she abandoned her plan to swim and followed the third person at a safe distance as he walked casually up towards one of the dormitories. He was long-legged, skinny, shaggy-haired, wearing shorts, a straw hat balanced at an angle. She told herself it could be any one of the team. Even with moonlight, it was impossible to identify someone with certainty from such a distance. Halfway up the path, he halted. There was no reason for him to turn round, but Helena froze with fear. In the flash of a flame she saw the silhouette of tousled hair and could just make out the shape of some lips on the back of his T-shirt: the distinctive Rolling Stones logo. A moment later, she understood why he had stopped. A great billow of smoke rose into the air, and even from fifty or so yards away, the smell was distinctive. There was only one person on the dig who had a supply of cigars, and that was the professor, but this was not an old man she was following. It was the only person he often shared them with. Nick.

Her heart pounded even more violently now. What had Nick been doing out at this time of night? The other figures she had seen were definitely male, but why was he with them?

He quickened his stride, took a final few puffs on the cigar and moments later had disappeared inside his dormitory.

Helena made her way back to bed, anxious and bemused, and spent the rest of the night in a state of troubled wakefulness.

She caught a glimpse of Nick on the morning bus. Unlike most others, who were monosyllabic at that time of day, he was locked in animated conversation with the deputy of the dig. They were sitting at the front and Helena passed them as she looked for a seat. He looked up at her and smiled, then turned back to his travel companion.

When everyone piled off the bus, Nick was first off, and had disappeared by the time Helena had descended the steps.

Elpida took her arm. 'Only two more days to go,' she said.

'I'm feeling a mixture of sadness and relief, to be honest. I need a break. How about you?'

That morning, Helena did not really know what she felt but had to say something.

'I'll miss being in Greece,' she said, yawning. 'And being with my boyfriend.'

'I don't think my old body could do another week. You're still young.'

'I have to go back for my final year of university,' said Helena. 'Term starts next week and I think it's going to be challenging.'

'Well, let's make the best of these days,' said Elpida. 'I'll definitely be back next year if they'll have me. Will you come?'

'If I can, but I might have to start a proper job straight after my degree. I don't know yet.'

Helena had allowed herself to fantasise about a future with Nick, even though he never mentioned his own plans.

That day was mostly spent tidying up, covering up some exposed areas to prevent looting and helping to fence in the site. Helena was not really thinking about what she was doing. It was mechanical. What occupied her mind that day was whether she would mention to Nick her night-time stroll.

When they arrived back at the hostel that evening, she grabbed his arm as he got off the bus. Everyone else was scurrying off to queue for a shower after a dusty, sweaty day.

'Nick . . . I went for a walk last night. Couldn't sleep. I was going to have a swim.' She hesitated, almost losing the courage to confront him.

'Poor you, not sleeping. You should have snuck in to get me . . . we could have swum together. We should do that tonight. In the dark.'

'I couldn't come into the men's dorm!' she laughed.

'We could have had a midnight tryst.' He smiled, taking her hand.

'Anyway, I saw you and two other men. On the road. What were you all doing?'

He threw his arms around her and gave her a hug. 'Darling Helena,

226

I should have told you,' he said, kissing her on the neck. 'The dig director asked me to hand over the money we owed to the locals who've helped us. Everything has to be done in cash, so it probably did look a bit clandestine. And they wanted to have a drink first, so it was pretty late at night . . .'

Helena was relieved to hear his explanation.

'But I wish I had known you were up,' he continued. 'I would have loved a night swim. Next time, tell me, okay?'

'It'll be next year now,' she said. It was the closest she had ever come to any reference to the future, and it felt bold.

'Yes, we pack up tomorrow,' Nick said, almost sorrowfully. 'And there's so much more waiting to be found here.'

'It's all been lying there for thousands of years,' responded Helena. 'So there's no urgency, is there?'

There was a pause.

'Let's go and get cleaned up. We'll be partying tonight!'

After so many weeks in the same baggy trousers and dusty T-shirts, she felt very feminine in a deep red wraparound skirt and an embroidered cheesecloth shirt that was clean and unworn. The sunshine had given her skin a warm glow, and even in her resolutely red hair there were some blonde streaks. There was only a small mirror in the hostel, but she was happy for once with her appearance.

She was surprised to find Nick waiting for her when she emerged to walk to the taverna.

'You look amazing!' he said. 'Come here. I want to kiss you.'

For the first time, he pulled her towards him and gave her a long kiss in front of the others.

'You are so beautiful,' he whispered in her ear.

Helena felt herself flush and her legs went weak.

'I want you to come and stay with me at Charles's,' he said. 'As often as possible.'

'Of course, I will,' Helena whispered, overcome with affection for him.

'Actually, talking of Charles,' Nick said, 'I got him a souvenir for the house. Do you mind taking it? I only brought a small rucksack.'

'No problem,' said Helena. 'Give it to me later.'

A few hours later, everyone was down at Marina's.

The mood was high. However much anyone usually drank, tonight they consumed double. There were speeches and toasts to everyone: the professor, the archaeologists, the students, the volunteers, the locals, the taverna owner who fed them every night, the baker who made their bread – anyone who had provided any kind of service or kindness on the dig.

On a cue from Professor Carver, who was at the head of the table, everyone rose to their feet and raised a glass.

'To the past. And to the future of finding the past.'

'*To the past. And to the future of finding the past.*' They all echoed the words as if chanting the creed.

'May it always shed light on the present!'

'*May it always shed light on the present!*'

There were three cheers from everyone, and then to the delight of the crowd, Nick drew out his volume of Byron's poetry and waved it in the air. Everyone sat down, and there was a hush as he began to declaim:

'"Through cloudless skies, in silvery sheen . . ."'

When he came to the end of the poem, a band struck up and the dancing began. The Greek members of the team led the way, with Nick close behind and the rest copying the steps as well as they could.

Helena boldly broke the ring of dancers to be next to him, ignoring the furious look from Ashley, who withdrew and sat down next to her friend. Each time the circle turned so that she was facing in their direction, Helena saw them both glaring at her.

They did not ruin her night. Nothing could deny her this euphoria. The music, the movement, her passion for the man next to her, the touch of his hand, the memories of his kisses, all of them combined.

Not only was she in love with Nick, she was also grateful to him. Without him she would never have come on an excavation. Even as a volunteer, she had learned so many things in these past weeks. One of them was that every detail mattered. Even the smallest sherd, the tiniest fragment of bone or sliver of stone was part of a bigger picture, providing clues to how her ancestors had lived. Those people had been here so many years before, but each day the gap between then and now seemed to have narrowed.

The next morning, as the ferry chugged towards the mainland, Helena stood on deck gazing at the horizon, excited for the future.

Chapter Twenty-One

When they arrived at Charles Smythson's grand but shabby west London home, the door was on the latch. Helena was going to spend a few nights there with Nick, and she was excited about seeing Sally. Both their lives had changed so much since they had parted in June.

Term would begin in four days' time, and Hamish had already delivered a box of books and a suitcase to her new college accommodation. Helena was determined to make the most of her time before the lab walls hemmed her in for a final year, and she knew her father understood why she wanted to spend the remaining days of the long vacation in London.

Charles had inherited the house from his uncle, who had died suddenly as Charles was starting his finals. According to Sally, who had shared the information with Helena on a phone call to Greece, other nephews and nieces had been left a few thousand pounds each, but Charles became the sole owner of the substantial four-bedroom house, along with a battered Morris Minor. He had been Uncle Norman's favourite nephew. It was as simple as that, even if this fact came as a surprise to his cousins.

'Such a shame he never met Mrs Right,' Charles's mother used to say with unthinking regularity. 'He would have made *such* a lovely father.'

Charles had understood more about Uncle Norman than Norman's own sister did. As a teenager, he had often been taken for lunch by his uncle at his club in Pall Mall, and on several occasions they had been joined by a young man. It was a different one each time, and never much older than Charles himself. It was self-evident what his uncle's status as a confirmed bachelor really meant.

During most university vacations, Charles had stayed for a few days in the shambolic Victorian house, studying in the book-lined library, which included a shelf with ten volumes on Renaissance portraitists compiled by Norman himself. Charles would sleep in a small spare room darkened by extravagantly draped curtains and adorned with a series of sixteenth-century drawings. These were not his only treasures. He had some Renaissance oil paintings, the majority of which had been picked up 'for a song' in Florence. He had even managed to spot a Piero della Francesca in a London gallery that had been wrongly identified and bought it for a tenth of what it was worth. Norman had instilled in his nephew a great love of art and taught him how to spot trends and sell at the height of the market. Stocks and shares operated on the same basis, he told him, but you could not enjoy them on your walls. Charles himself decided to deal in both, and was already enjoying effortless success with a taste for twentieth-century naïve.

When they walked into the house, they were confronted by an enormous painting of a nude woman reclining on a chaise longue.

'Good old Charles,' said Nick. 'He's been shopping again.' Leaving Helena to contemplate the voluptuous creature, he bounded up the stairs with their luggage.

Drawn by the sound of Sally's laughter and the smell of cooking, she gingerly pushed open the kitchen door.

Sally saw her first and leapt up from the kitchen table to embrace her friend.

'Hels! I didn't even hear you come in. Amazing! It's so lovely to see you!' she said.

Charles was at the Aga stirring gravy, but he threw the wooden spoon down to give her a crushing hug. Since that first sighting in the Oxford quad, Helena noted that he had adopted a different and very traditional look, with his hair swept back, red corduroy trousers, and a girth that had considerably increased. His job in the City meant that four-course lunches were a daily event, and his blue-and-white-striped chef's apron only just reached around his middle.

'Darling!' he roared, as if she was a long-lost friend, 'I wasn't sure what time you'd arrive, but I've done a full Sunday roast. Chicken, bread sauce, stuffing, all the trimmings.'

Sally went back to the kitchen table and continued chopping apples into a dish.

'And apple crumble. We decided you needed a proper welcome home! How many plates of moussaka have you eaten in the past few weeks?'

Helena smiled, touched by their thoughtfulness, and put a bottle of retsina they had brought back from Greece on the sideboard.

'Countless. Every other day for six weeks.'

'So that's as if you had eaten a moussaka as big as this *whole* table,' said Sally.

'I think that's about right,' Helena nodded, surveying the kitchen table that comfortably (and regularly) accommodated ten. 'And I never want to eat it ever again.'

She meant it. Hours of manual labour had always worked up an appetite for the generous portions of aubergine and mince, but the indigestible mix then sat in her stomach like a brick. The catering on the dig had kept them all alive, but that was its only function.

The door opened and in strolled a lanky man in a checked shirt, his face buried in *The Times*.

'Six down, Tory takes horse's home for English painter, nine letters, fourth letter *s*,' he said.

He glanced up to see if anyone had an answer and noticed Helena sitting there.

'I'm so sorry! I'm Edward,' he said warmly, holding out his hand. 'You must be Helena. My room's across the landing from Nick's.'

'Constable,' Charles called out.

'Nice to meet you,' said Helena. 'Are you an old college friend too?'

'Yes,' he replied. 'And same house at Eton.'

'Where's the old rogue then?' asked Charles, glancing at the Greek wine, knowing he would use it later in a casserole.

'Just taking our things upstairs,' Helena answered.

Edward began to lay the table and Charles uncorked a bottle.

'Château Margaux 1959,' he announced, sniffing the cork with approval. 'One of Uncle Norm's favourites.'

Nick walked in not long after, looking fresh in a crisp white shirt. He had already managed to shower and change.

'Nothing like the sound of a cork popping, is there?' he said. 'Better than a dinner gong.'

'Nick!' cried Charles. The two men enveloped each other in a bear hug. 'You must have so much to tell us. Dinner will be ready in two. You pour the wine, old man.'

Nick filled five glasses generously.

'Put a splash in the gravy, would you?' Charles joked, and then stood aside while his friend poured a generous helping of the vintage claret into his saucepan.

'Charles, that's mad,' reprimanded Sally. 'Your uncle would turn in his grave. It's one of the best wines in the cellar.'

'I know, darling. But there are at least ten crates of it. And plenty more from the same château. We won't run out yet.'

Sally laughed, accepting a glass from Charles and raising it.

'To Helena and Nick,' she said. 'Welcome home.'

'Ah, thank you, Sally. It's lovely to see you all again.'

Each glass touched all the others, then all five of them simultaneously took a sip.

'Dear God,' cried Charles. 'It's corked!'

The others laughed.

'It's fine,' declared Sally.

'Well, it's *not* fine by me.' He took their glasses and emptied them down the sink. 'I hope it didn't ruin the gravy.'

Helena had definitely drunk rougher wines in Greece, but there was no dissuading him from vanishing down into the cellar to find something else. There was no suggestion that they should open the bottle freshly imported from their trip.

When the door opened again, it was a petite brunette with heavy horn-rimmed spectacles, who introduced herself as Edward's girl-friend, Caroline.

'We met each other in our first week at college,' she said apologetically. 'Both studying law. We're the dull couple.'

'No,' contradicted Helena. 'You were lucky.'

A moment later, Charles was back, holding a bottle high in the air like a trophy.

'A Côtes du Rhône,' he said triumphantly. 'Actually, a much better companion for chicken.'

Nobody else in the house shared Charles's knowledge of expensive wine, but they drank it with enthusiasm to humour him.

Five minutes later, he put a large oval platter on the table: a plump chicken roasted to perfection and surrounded by crisp golden pota-toes. He lowered a gleaming silver dome onto it to keep it warm, and then brought across a set of matching vegetable dishes. Thanks to his uncle, the crockery was Limoges, the glasses crystal and the cutlery solid silver. Whenever anyone took the time to polish the knives and forks, a simple meal resembled a banquet.

Charles placed a tarnished candelabra in the middle of the table, Edward lit the candles and turned out the overhead lights, and Nick replenished the glasses. In the flickering candlelight, the room took on a golden glow. Everyone sat down.

'*Benedictus benedicat . . .*'

Charles often said Latin grace. Memories of dining in formal hall at Oxford were sweet ones, and he still missed the rarefied environment of their college years. His time studying philosophy and theology had been a joyous experience, a world away from the job in finance that he mildly despised.

'Amen,' echoed Helena.

'It's Charles I want to thank for this food,' said Sally. 'Not God.'

'Typical Sally,' murmured Charles affectionately.

'You're the one that's been slaving away in the kitchen, aren't you?'

Helena was happy to see how sweet Charles and Sally were with each other. Their relationship seemed to have developed quickly into one of domesticity and trust, and yet there was clearly romance too. She wondered if she and Nick would ever be like that. The other two, Edward and Caroline, already seemed like a married couple.

Nick did most of the talking that night, describing the island of Nisos, the professor, the other academics, the landscape, the finds, the swimming, the accommodation, the food, the dancing, the wild nights of drinking with the locals. He made caricatures of everyone, to the point that Helena wondered if she had been on the same excavation, so little did she recognise them.

When dinner was finished, Edward and Caroline went off to bed. Both had 6 a.m. starts with their law firms. Sally and Helena got up to do the dishes.

Nick presented Charles with the gift Helena had carried back from Nisos in her rucksack. He had already taken it out of its newspaper wrapping. It was an ashtray in the shape of a donkey, a cigarette hanging out of its mouth. Charles roared with laughter.

'We have to christen it,' he said. 'Montecristo?'

He always had a ready supply of good cigars, and the two men were soon lost in a cloud of smoke.

Helena and Sally were at the sink.

'Did you enjoy your time out there?' Sally asked, carefully rinsing one of the gold-edged plates.

'Apart from the searing heat and the terrible bed, it was great. I loved what we were doing, or rather *why* we were doing it. Ultimately, it's like detective work. With many, many clues. And discovering that humankind doesn't really change so much is somehow fascinating.'

'You look incredibly well,' said Sally. 'I think those tresses might have got lighter.'

They laughed, both knowing that Helena would happily swap her hair for almost anybody else's.

'What about you, Sally? I can see things are going well on one front at least.' Helena smiled.

'We've had an incredible summer. Charles is so caring and generous, and actually quite laid-back. There's never any jealousy if I talk to other people,' said a Sally that Helena hardly recognised. 'I think I'm in love with him. It's so unexpected, really, for us both to have got serious so quickly.' She glanced over her shoulder and then back to the bowl of suds. 'And what about you and Nick?'

Helena paused in her drying-up. 'It's going well.' She smiled coyly. 'He's very popular with other women, though. But I'll have to get used to that, won't I?'

Sally held out the last plate for her to dry. The sound of the water gurgling down the plughole drowned a rather non-committal answer.

The next few evenings were spent in a similarly convivial fashion, with long dinners, dark wines and candlelight. For a while they could imagine that they had not entirely left behind their Oxford days. Flowering jasmine rambling over the brick wall in the garden was reminiscent enough of a college façade, and Bach from a nearby open window served as a reminder of madrigals in chapel. On Helena's last night, other old university friends dropped by, and the dining table was crammed with most of the cast of *Medea*, its leading man again taking centre stage. She told herself not to be annoyed by Nick's apparent intimacy with the girl who had played the leading role. She was about to leave for a drama course in Los Angeles in any case.

The next morning, Helena packed her bags and left reluctantly to catch a train.

Nick had already gone out to his temporary job as a porter at White's, the major auction house, something Charles had arranged with the chairman, Hugo White, grandson of the founder. The family were friends of his late uncle. Nick had told Charles that he was saving to rejoin the dig the following spring and would begin a master's at Cambridge after that.

Helena had more Oxford days to come. Soon she was back to the laboratory and the library. For the first week, she was very disciplined: Monday to Friday, punctilious about her routine, outside the science building a minute before it opened and there until five in the afternoon. But the summer with Nick, perhaps Nick himself, had thrown her off course. In the second week, she left early on Friday afternoon and stayed in London with Nick until Monday morning.

With this pattern, it meant that she only had three whole days without him. Always at the back of her mind was that if she was not a presence in the house, her place would be filled by someone else. She once asked him if he would come to Oxford for a weekend just so she could put in a few more hours of study on the Friday, but he refused quite brusquely.

'I've done with that place,' he said.

One Friday afternoon when she arrived at the house, a heated conversation was going on in the kitchen. She kept hearing Nick's name, and when she walked in to greet everyone there was an embarrassed silence and a moment of palpable awkwardness. Charles, Sally, Edward and Caroline all stopped talking. Nick did not come back until much later that evening.

On a few other occasions, Nick himself seemed distant and Helena had to remind herself constantly that everything was worth it just for the good times.

As the Michaelmas term came to an end, she knew she was losing the thread of her studies and her marks were dropping. Organometallic reagents no longer seemed that interesting. Nick was talking constantly about resuming work at the excavation in the spring, and encouraging her to join him the day that the summer term ended, or perhaps even earlier.

'I know it's irrational, Sally,' she confided to her friend, 'but I don't care about anything except being with him.'

'You should think of your future as well,' Sally warned her gently.

'But maybe he *is* my future,' Helena protested, annoyed by her friend's note of caution.

Sally gave her a quizzical look.

'I know what I'm doing,' Helena said stubbornly.

'I hope so, Helena,' said Sally. 'I really do.'

Helena was furious. How dare her friend put any doubt in her mind? For the first time, she wondered if Sally might be jealous of her, despite being with the charming Charles. She stormed out of the room and went to lie on Nick's bed, her mind crowded with resentful thoughts about his housemates. She allowed herself to dwell on the froideur that she had also noticed of late between Edward and her boyfriend. Perhaps it was natural for other men to be envious of Nick, with all his charisma.

She fell asleep long before he slid into bed next to her.

The next day, he told her that there was a sale scheduled in two days' time, so everyone had been asked to work late. This was his reason for not returning until the early hours.

Chapter Twenty-Two

Throughout the winter and into the following spring, Helena spent as much time as possible in London. At weekends, she and Nick would stroll in Kensington Gardens, get cheap seats at the theatre and drink in their favourite wine bar, Julie's. On the Saturdays when Nick was working, Charles took both Sally and Helena to the National Gallery and the Tate, determined to give them both a crash course in art. Helena had also realised that she needed to expand her knowledge of literature, and Sally lent her books by her favourite poets and novelists. She started with Keats and Shelley, then went on to the Brontës and Austen, plus some du Maurier for light relief.

On Sunday evenings, the whole house would cook together and the doorbell would chime five, six, seven times as new and old friends piled in, bottles of wine and boxes of after-dinner mints in hand.

Helena loved to watch Nick perform. He lit up the room when he read poetry or quoted great chunks of Shakespeare. He could make people laugh; he could equally well move them to tears.

Apart from two days at Christmas, she returned to Suffolk only once before her final term, for a weekend in March. Nick had promised he would come, but cancelled at the last minute because White's had asked him to do overtime.

She was relieved to find her father well and cheerful. Hamish was now playing bridge once a week and going on regular walking trips with a local group, so her guilt at neglecting him was assuaged. They talked mostly of her mother and of Helena's embryonic plans for the following year. Hamish assumed that the reason for her long absence was that she had been studying hard, and Helena did not disabuse him.

Even though it was still weeks away from the beginning of the dig, Nick suddenly announced that he had stopped working at White's. Helena found herself paying for them both whenever they went out, and was growing anxious that her student grant would not see her through to the end of her studies.

When the summer term began and the date for handing in her thesis was only a few weeks away, she had a slight regret that she had spent the Easter vacation in London rather than in her college room. This should have been her final push, but she couldn't bear to miss those weeks with Nick before he returned to Nisos.

When the deadline for her thesis arrived, what she handed in was desultory. She felt wretched and full of self-recrimination. Her supervisor had been asking to see a draft for some time, and had always accepted her excuses. She knew that the diligence with which she had studied during the first three years would save her from abject failure, as she already had a reasonable degree, but a decent thesis had also been expected. She was aware that what she had produced deserved little more than a tick.

She would drop her things back in Ladbroke Grove and then go to see her father to tell him the news.

She made dinner and was waiting in the kitchen when Hamish came home from evening surgery.

'Darling! It's so lovely to see you. And I'm sorry I wasn't there to collect you at the station.'

'Don't worry, Dad, I picked up some food on the way home.'

Over shepherd's pie, which she had made in her mother's favourite floral Pyrex dish, Helena told him about her final thesis.

Her father took a moment to respond.

'I know how difficult things were at the beginning,' he said, spearing a pea with his fork. 'But I still don't really understand. It's like you lost interest in the subject.'

Seeing the disappointment in his eyes when he finally looked up was the moment that she cried.

'I'm really sorry, Dad. I've let you down. And Mum.'

Hamish McCloud, warm and forgiving as ever, leaned over and took his daughter's hand.

'But look, you've got a degree,' he said gently. 'And it's not the end of the world, is it? Lots of people don't even have A levels, and they do well enough in life.'

'Yes, but . . .'

'Tell me about Nick. If you're so mad keen on him, I hope he's worth it.'

Helena was taken aback. She had scarcely told her father anything about Nick, but he had obviously surmised enough.

'Children always underestimate their parents' understanding,' he said with a smile. 'You've changed. Blossomed like a flower.'

She smiled with relief. Her father did not seem remotely angry with her.

'Well, yes. Life is more exciting than it might have been. As well as Nick, I have made lots of new friends, stayed in a house full of great people and have a love for archaeology that's surprised even me.'

'I hope I'll meet him soon,' said Hamish. 'He's obviously had a big impact on your life.'

As they ate, Helena talked about her experience on the excavation, the people she had met and what had been found.

'I'm planning to go back to the dig for a while this summer,' she said. 'They need volunteers again, and they're moving into a new phase – a new area of the site.'

'You have to fly to Athens to get there?' asked Hamish.

'Yes. And then take a boat.'

'Would you have time to spend a few days in Athens before you go to the dig?' he asked.

'Why would I? There's no reason for me to go there now,' she said wistfully. 'No Yiayiá, no Dina. Maybe Thomas, my language tutor. But he probably wouldn't remember me.'

Hamish got up. Tucked between a teapot and a jug on the kitchen dresser was a long brown envelope, which he slid out and put face downwards on the table.

'Something came in the post while you were away.'

'What is it?' Helena leaned forward. 'You're being mysterious.'

'It's something good! Something very, very good. It's to do with your grandmother's flat.'

Helena had not given the Kolonaki apartment a thought since her grandmother had died. She'd assumed her connection with it was over and that her visits had ended for good.

'I didn't tell you what was going on, because I didn't want you to get too bound up with it,' Hamish said. 'Greek law is so complicated. The word "labyrinthine" doesn't get close.'

'What's happened?' She felt a tiny stirring of excitement, but her father was being slow to get to the point.

'When your grandfather died, your grandmother discovered that he had left nothing to her. She could live in the apartment until she died, and that was it.'

'He left her nothing? That's unbelievable!'

'She had his pension. Which was quite a big one, I'm told.'

'It must have been, because she never seemed short of money.'

'In any case, it wasn't your grandmother he wanted to deprive. It was your mother.'

'Mum did hate him, I suppose.'

'Well, your grandmother did nothing about this will at first. But when you continued to visit, she apparently decided to contest it. She wanted everything to be left to you.'

'Me?' Helena was trying to take this in. 'And who did my grand-father name as heir?'

'Some nephew of his.'

'Arsenis,' Helena said with certainty. 'It makes sense. He was always there sucking up to him.'

'Your grandmother was still contesting the will when she died. And she left a will of her own. It's taken ten years, but last week, the judge decided in favour of your late grandmother – and you. The letter came today. It needs translation, but the lawyer in Athens called me, and I understand that the principle is settled. They will deliver the keys to the apartment whenever you want.'

Hamish turned the envelope over and slid it across to Helena. She noted the rows of stamps, at least a dozen, which almost covered the surface. The address was handwritten, and with so many errors ('Dollbritch'), it was a miracle it had reached them at all.

Her father had already slit it open with a knife, so she pulled the official-looking document out and unfolded it.

'I suppose I'll have to learn Greek legalese,' she laughed. 'It looks impenetrable.'

'However complicated they have made it look, the simple fact is that you now own a flat in Kolonaki and everything in it.'

Helena was scanning the covering letter, her brow creased with concentration.

'You don't look very pleased, darling. I know it's a bit of a surprise, but it does show how fond your grandmother was of you, doesn't it? And if your mother had inherited things as she should, it would have passed to you in any case.'

'Yes. It's fantastic news. I'm just trying to take it in. It's so out of the blue.'

Hamish began to clear the dishes from the table and stacked the plates in the sink. He put the kettle on, humming to himself.

'The best thing might be just to clear it, and then sell,' he said over his shoulder. 'It would give you a lovely nest egg, wouldn't it?'

'To buy something here, you mean?'

'In London, perhaps. If you end up there. We can talk more about it tomorrow. Shall we go to La Famiglia? It is something to celebrate, isn't it?'

'Oh Dad, no. I'm happy to cook again. I'll do something with all those peas and broad beans from the garden. And I'll get some lamb chops, maybe?'

It would have been the first time they had revisited the restaurant without her mother, and Helena was not ready.

The phone rang, and Hamish hastened out into the hall to answer it. Helena heard him giving some advice, and then those very familiar words, 'I'm on my way.'

'Sorry, darling,' he said, coming back into the kitchen. 'It was Mrs Greetham. She's had a fall.'

'Oh Dad! I'm so sorry! I hope she's okay.'

Hamish McCloud kissed the top of his daughter's head and left.

Helena sat for a while longer reading through the documents she had been sent. Some of them would require her signature. She was thinking how excited Nick would be by her news and could hardly wait to share it with him. He seemed to love Greece as much as she did these days. It was impossible for her to call him, but when he had time, he sometimes used the phone in the village bar. She found herself willing him to ring.

She gave up on trying to translate the document and idled the rest of the evening away watching *The Pink Panther* on VHS. Peter Sellers' mannerisms made her ache with laughter, and when her father came home, he sat down and watched the end of it with her. It had been Mary's favourite film, after all.

The following afternoon, Helena went to the new flower shop, next to the haberdashery. It made Helena sad to see the 'Closed' sign. She bought some fragrant pink stocks and took them to the cottage hospital to visit Mrs Greetham, who had broken her hip and was likely to be in for some time.

That evening, after several calls for her father, the phone finally rang for Helena.

'Nick? . . . Hello! Hello!'

There was so much background noise that it was hard to make out if he was even on the line at all.

'I'll be there soon,' said Helena. 'But I've had some exciting news. My grandmother left me the flat. In Athens.'

'Sorry, Helena! I can't really hear you! When are you coming?'

'I'll be there in seven days' time. I have to stop in Athens on the way!'

Both of them were having to raise their voices.

'Eleven days, did you say?'

'No! *Seven!*'

At that moment, the line went dead. Even if Nick had not grasped when she would arrive, she was already counting the days.

Before that, though, the Kolonaki flat was waiting for her. It was almost fifteen years since her first visit, and with the same excitement and trepidation that she had felt as an eight-year-old, Helena boarded a plane.

Chapter Twenty-Three

Athens seemed a very different place. On all her previous visits to the city, Helena had been met and chauffeured to her grandmother's apartment by a polite, besuited man. Now she had to negotiate with a taxi driver, stubbled and in a dirty shirt undone to reveal the gold medallion on a grotesquely hairy chest. Even before she asked him to extinguish his cigarette he was hostile, but from then on, he was even worse. Holding the wheel and changing gears with the same hand, he weaved his way through the rush-hour traffic. Engulfed by smoke, Helena wound the window down, only to find herself taking the fumes of the city into her lungs instead.

The parched streets, the scruffy concrete apartment buildings, some with tinted windows, the impatient drivers, nose to tail, all blasting their horns and angrily gesturing at each other. It was not as she remembered it. It seemed noisier, more anarchic, more confusing.

Eventually, after a journey that was a good deal longer than she recalled, Helena began to recognise some of the streets. They passed the parliament building and several museums, then the driver took a left and a right and a moment later drew up next to a kiosk. There was the ratcheting sound of the handbrake, and then he swung open his door, retrieved her rucksack from the boot and dropped it on the pavement.

'*Oktakósia*,' he growled, dragging on a fresh cigarette. Eight hundred.

The meter had stopped working halfway to her destination, so she had no choice but to hand over a thousand-drachma note, hoping that she might be owed some change. The driver stuffed the money into the top pocket of his shirt, then slumped back into his seat and slammed the door. His final gesture of contempt was to put his foot hard down on the accelerator to asphyxiate Helena with exhaust fumes.

She stood alone in the empty street, the sun beating down on her head, feeling very alone and bewildered, uncertain that she was even in the right place. New buildings had gone up since her last visit to Evdokias 45, and the shops all looked different. Nothing was familiar. Until she turned round.

'*Sygnómi*,' she asked politely at the small window of the kiosk, holding out a scrap of paper with the address on. 'Excuse me.'

The old man inside did not acknowledge her, and she suddenly remembered that this was the deaf *peripterás*, Lefteris. Perhaps she needed to buy something to get his attention. She picked out a small bar of chocolate from the display, then fished inside her purse and put a note down on the counter.

'*Sygnómi*,' she repeated, holding out the address again and pointing at the words. '*Pou*? Where?'

This time, the man emerged through a small door at the side, took her firmly by the shoulders and spun her round through one hundred and eighty degrees. It seemed a gesture of impatience, and yet it solved her problem. Following his pointing finger to where the street rose towards Lycabettus Hill, she suddenly recognised where she was. The awning of the smart café had changed colour, but it was otherwise familiar. Up and to the right, she would find the apartment. She picked up her rucksack and set off.

Seconds later, the kiosk owner was next to her, pressing both the chocolate and the hundred-drachma note into her hand. A slightly muffled sound came from his mouth. He did not want her money.

'*Efcharistó! Efcharistó polý!*' she cried, patting her heart to show her gratitude. 'Thank you! Thank you so much!'

On the way, she had to put the rucksack down several times. She knew already that she had been overly optimistic about the number of books she would get through during the summer. Finally she reached the apartment building. There was a polished brass panel with a row of bells, just as she remembered, and the Papagiannis name was still there. It was more faded than the rest, so perhaps the other owners were more recent to the building. It only now struck her as strange that she had never seen any of the residents who lived below.

Peering inside, she could see that the art deco hallway, with its marble floor and fan-shaped wall lights was gleamingly clean as always. She rang the bell for the concierge, and a moment later saw Kýrios Manolis approaching to open the heavy glass door. They greeted each other warmly, Helena commenting that he had not changed at all in the intervening years.

'And Miss Helena,' he said, wanting to show off his English as he always had. 'Still with her *kókkina* hair! And I happy to hear the news. Man coming today with . . . this.' He walked across to his desk and picked up a small package.

As soon as her father had revealed the news of her inheritance, Helena had called the lawyers in Athens and requested to have the services switched back on. She had also asked them to deliver the keys to the concierge. When she opened the package, she expected to find the familiar set of keys that her grandmother had kept on a green ribbon. Instead, there were three sets of four very substantial keys for mortice locks and three slightly smaller ones for a padlock.

Manolis carried her bag to the lift and she squeezed into the small space with her luggage. The door banged shut and the lift juddered up to the penthouse.

The landing was pitch dark until she felt her way along the wall and found the button to press for a light. Without it she would not even have been able to find her grandmother's door. Not her grand-mother's now, but hers, she kept telling herself. The lawyers had mentioned the substantial tape that securely sealed the property, a precaution that they had regularly checked up on. Helena was glad to see that it was unbroken, and began to try and pull it off. Even after all this time, however, it was stubborn, and she ran down the stairs to see if Manolis had a penknife.

He came back up with her, and after five minutes of scoring it through with some scissors, they were able to strip the tape away from the door frame.

'I need go,' Manolis said, in a hurry to get back to his post, a place he rarely left except to go outside for a smoke.

The locks themselves opened smoothly. The weighty padlock was the first, then the four mortices that ran from the top of the door, luckily within her reach, to the bottom. The keys had to be rotated several times, and made a satisfying *clunk* on the final turn. Finally the solid wooden door swung open.

She was almost overpowered by the musty smell. She had seen many derelict houses on the islands she had visited, from small village homes to mansions. It was incomprehensible to her that somewhere could simply be abandoned and left to rot, but it sounded as if this flat might have met the same fate. Her mother had explained that it often happened in Greece, because a home might be left to three children, who then each had three children, and each of those had three as well. In less than half a century, nearly thirty people might own a single house that none of them could agree either to sell or inhabit, and as the years went by the situation only worsened. In the case of Evdokias 45, the story had been different. Only one other person had a claim, and now that she thought of it, it made her nervous.

The heavy door slammed behind her, and for a moment she stood in the silent, windowless hallway, before turning round and locking herself in with just one of the keys, aware of how much Arsenis must have wanted to be standing here. She was grateful for the presence of the concierge downstairs.

All four doors that led off the hallway were shut, and for a moment she could not remember what lay behind each one. She opened the one to the right and groped for the light switch. The kitchen. Next to it was the cloakroom, ahead of her was the drawing room, then the dining room, and close by her grandfather's study. Down the corridor past the dining room were five bedrooms and three bathrooms. The dust sheets on the furniture created whole rooms of strange, spectral shapes. The only recognisable objects were the crystal chandeliers, their sparkle dulled with dust. Gone was the pervasive beeswax smell from her childhood. It was fusty now, and spiders had been busy in every corner of the ceiling. The place felt smaller through her adult eyes.

She felt compelled to open some windows. It was three in the afternoon and the flat would immediately heat up, but it would be better than enduring the smell of dust and decay. She turned on several lights in order to see her way through the gloom. The heavy damask curtains in every room were tightly shut, the windows locked, and then, the third hurdle, the shutters were fastened.

She hoped that the floral porcelain jug was still on the kitchen shelf. It was where her grandmother used to keep all her keys. Reassured to find it, and to hear a metallic rattle inside, she proceeded to try and match them to the appropriate locks. She gave up after the drawing room and the dining room, with their huge floor-to-ceiling windows and balconies outside. The breeze that now blew through the place disturbed the air a little, so surely the smell would dissipate sooner or later.

She stood for a while leaning against the balustrade to gaze towards the golden stones of the Parthenon. Lining the edge of the balcony were numerous ornamental urns, with the plants they had contained now just dry twigs poking up from the soil.

Going back inside, she carefully removed the dust sheet from one of the ghostly shapes, folding it to contain the cloud of particles that rose into the air. Then she sat down in the worn comfort of her grandmother's favourite chair, where, despite the growing hum of rush-hour traffic, punctuated by the cacophony of car horns, she succumbed to the fatigue of the journey.

Helena woke in the darkness, her throat parched, her stomach moaning with hunger and her neck cricked by her awkward sleeping position. It took her a moment to recognise her surroundings; all those menacing shapes around her seemed to have grown. Once all the lights were on, side lights, table lamps and the hefty chandelier in the middle, the place seemed marginally less threatening.

Out on the balcony again, she stood and enjoyed the soft night air. There was a spectacular canopy of bright stars above her, and a sliver of new moon now hung over the Parthenon.

Water. That was what she needed, more than anything. Wandering into the kitchen, the only room without dust sheets, she went to the cupboard for a glass. They were lined up in perfect rows, just as they had always been, heavy cut-glass tumblers and matching sets of wine glasses, all now opaque with dust. She took one down to rinse it. The tap juddered and spewed out a spray of brown liquid, with streaks of green. She remembered that even on previous visits, her grandmother had told her to clean her teeth with bottled or boiled water.

It was late, but she hoped the kiosk would still be open.

The pavements were busy now and the cafes in the square were full. Waiters, smartly dressed in black trousers and white waistcoats, just as she remembered them, bustled tirelessly between the bar and the tables bearing large round trays crowded with glasses. She envied the groups of friends, huddled close to hear one another in the din of noisy chatter, and for a moment felt intensely lonely. She did not know a soul in this city. Had it been rash to turn up here alone? Perhaps the flat should have gone to her uncle after all. All the tables were taken, so there was no chance of sitting down at one of them, even had she had the heart to do so.

It was gone ten in the evening, but the lights of the kiosk were still on and Lefteris was sitting inside. He had plenty of business. A few young men loitered in a queue to buy cigarettes, matches, chocolate and fizzy drinks, and Helena stood behind them. One of them turned to smile at her and said something that made all the others laugh. When he touched her arm, she stepped away. Feeling vulnerable and hungry, she reached into the fridge for a small carton of juice and a large bottle of water, and took a packet of plain biscuits from a rack.

'*Kalispéra*. Good evening,' she said to Lefteris. He nodded vigorously as he handed over her change and then passed her a packet of caramels. She understood from his gesture that this was a gift and thanked him profusely. Perhaps he remembered her from her childhood visits.

The juice quenched her thirst and gave her the energy to take a short detour on the way home. She was in no hurry to get back to the isolation of the apartment, and slowed her pace to study some of the shop windows. Many had displays of high-class ladies' fashions, much more glamorous than the cheap boutiques in her own town. Likewise the two jewellery shops. Diamonds, emeralds and sapphires set in intricate settings of gold and platinum sparkled in the artificial light: necklaces, drop earrings and bracelets so elaborate she wondered if they were even real. Dellbridge boasted a small shop that sold cheap engagement rings and mended watches for a pound.

Two couples walked by, the women's heels clicking almost in unison on the marble pavement. Helena had not studied them closely, but underneath their long, thick hair, she imagined they would be wearing similar gems. Their husbands were smoking, and the aroma of cigars clung to the air around them, reminding her of Nick.

She paused to look into an unlit shop window, where she could make out pieces of furniture not dissimilar from some in the flat.

There were side tables that would have been at home in a French château, a chaise longue that was decorative rather than functional, and some chairs embellished with gilt that glinted even in the darkness.

Retracing her steps, she saw that the kiosk lights were off now, and hastened her pace. It must be past midnight. The cafés were still full, and music was coming out of a nearby bar. The temperature seemed to have risen again.

Back in the flat, and out on the balcony again, she tore open the packet of biscuits and ate half a dozen, one after the other. As she leaned forward, observing the odd passer-by beneath her, something occurred to her: there had not been a single soldier in the street. Nor a policeman. Back in the days when she stayed with her grandmother, both had been a feature on every corner. This was a clear sign that the positive changes in Athens she had read about were real.

She retrieved a toothbrush from her rucksack that still stood in the hall, filled a glass with bottled water and cleaned her teeth.

It was certain that nobody had been inside this place since the day after her grandmother's funeral, and if there were sheets on the beds, she dreaded to imagine their condition after so long. She would sleep the night on one of the sofas in the drawing room and start the task of clearing the place the following day. Everything looked better in daylight, she told herself.

The bulky wooden cabinet that housed the large black-and-white television still stood in the corner. It also held her grandmother's radio and record player. Helena was not ready to sleep yet, so she switched on the TV and was happily surprised when it sprang to life. She turned the dial beneath the screen. There were only two channels. One displayed a blank screen with a logo; the other was showing a film. The plot was easy to follow: a woman (middle-aged and plump) believes that her husband (portly and rich) is cheating on her. She suspects a relationship with the maid (naïve, ravishing, blonde) and sets traps for them both, only to discover that their apparent collusion is over the preparation of a surprise party for her. At the party, the couple's son reveals that he has fallen helplessly in love with the maid, and proposes to her. The event becomes a combined birthday/engagement celebration.

This simple farce, with cases of mistaken identity, doors that opened and shut every few minutes, and a happy ending (with a little sting in the tail when the audience is given a glimpse of the father's jealousy of his son), took Helena's mind off the ghosts that seemed to hover around her. Every performance was exaggerated or improbable. How different from the gloom of Greek tragedy. More than a year on, she was still haunted by the image of Medea's lifeless infants, the fury of a mother, the anguish of a father.

Her head on one of the soft satin-covered cushions, she dozed off with thoughts of Jason. She pictured him at the dig site, his hair turning gold at the ends, his arms bronzed. In her mind's eye, he was a god. She fell asleep with the curtains still wide open.

The sun rose early.

'You have inherited a beautiful flat in the centre of a vibrant city.'

Whether it was in her dream or her subconscious, Helena felt as if someone had spoken these words in her ear. Her mother, perhaps, who was a regular presence in her dreams. She sat up with a start and looked around the room. It might have been a place of bad memories for Mary, but she herself must see it as a blessing, not a burden. At the very least it was a responsibility.

Swinging her legs off the sofa, she got up and faced the mantelpiece. The hideous portrait of her grandfather was still there.

She gulped back what was left of the water straight from the bottle and then went methodically from room to room, heaving open the bulky curtains in the gloomy bedrooms. The sun, rather than being worshipped, must have been considered the enemy, to be kept out at all costs. The combination of heavy drapes and dark wooden flooring was mood-lowering. The greens and golds of the walls and curtains seemed to absorb most of the light, and the dark brown of the furniture and floors sucked out the rest. The absence of light did have one advantage, however. The furniture had never faded, and the colours in the rugs were as bright as the day they had been woven.

In each room there were fine antique pieces: mahogany wardrobes with elaborate marquetry, bow-fronted chests of drawers with ornately turned legs, dressing tables with mirrors inlaid with mother-of-pearl. She had never much liked these things when she visited as a child, but now realised she had an overwhelming desire to get rid of them. They represented the conservatism and ostentation with which her mother had grown up, and which she had hated for good reason.

A quick look inside one of the cabinets confirmed that the fine dinner service, even fussier than the one that Charles had inherited, was still inside.

As she padded from room to room in her battered espadrilles, she envisaged the apartment decorated in a restful, modern fashion: plain, fresh and above all, light. Only then would it be possible to allay some of the darkness of its past, the bitterness of a father–daughter relationship that had driven her mother into a form of exile, the ghosts of the fascistic and uniformed, the polished buttons. She wanted to bring the rays of the sun into every room.

She made a call to Dellbridge and left a message with the receptionist at the surgery to let her father know she had arrived safely. Then she opened all the windows, leaving the rooms to air, and started to remove the acres of dirty sheeting.

That done, she looked around for cleaning products. The small, windowless room off the kitchen where Dina had lived housed some, but over the years, everything had hardened or decomposed. She made a list and set out into the sunshine.

She soon found a sizeable hardware shop, Pavlídis, in a side street, and when she pushed open the door, she suddenly recalled being there with Thomas. A gangly young man in a white coat and large square-framed glasses watched with amusement as she mimed various actions such as removing limescale and cleaning down inside a plughole, the vocabulary for some of which she could not remember. He then produced what she needed for every task. The other customers applauded and Helena took an embarrassed bow.

'That was an excellent performance,' the assistant said in immaculate English, packing the goods into a paper bag.

Helena took a step back. 'I don't believe it!' she said with disbelief. 'You made me do all of that?'

'It was so funny,' he said, smiling broadly. 'I couldn't help it.'

Both of them began to laugh. He turned briefly to the rest of the customers to serve them, while Helena sorted out a confusion of tatty drachma notes, baffled by how many zeros were required. When she glanced up, the shop was empty again and she handed over the money.

'I hope you didn't really mind?' the young man said, removing his spectacles.

'I just had no idea. I do feel a bit embarrassed, though,' she said, looking up shyly. 'I made an assumption. But how . . .?'

'I just finished a master's in international politics. London School of Economics.'

Helena shook her head from side to side. 'Did you like London?' she asked for want of something to say.

'I did. But not as much as Athens. I love my home town. So where are you planning to do all this cleaning?'

'In a flat up there,' she answered, pointing vaguely in the direction of Lycabettus.

'So you're a housekeeper?' There was a distinct note of irony in his voice.

Helena smiled. 'In a way.'

She hesitated, in no hurry to leave. The busy city already felt like a lonely place for someone on their own, and once she had bought some food and returned home, she would probably not have another conversation that day.

'I'm Mihalis,' he said. 'And if you need any more refuse sacks or dusters, I'll be here. Or a coffee, even.'

'Thanks, Mihalis. I'm sure I'll run out of something. It's a big enough place.'

'Must be a rich boss,' he responded, evidently wanting to prolong the conversation too. 'We had a one-room flat above this shop when I was born, but for the same money, my father bought one hundred and fifty square metres in Patissia.'

'Mmm,' she said, without any idea where that was.

Other customers had come into the shop now.

'Maybe see you again, then,' Helena said, picking up the bag and tucking a mop under her arm.

'Definitely. I would love to have some English practice,' said Mihalis, 'otherwise it will get rusty.'

'We could do half and half,' Helena laughed. 'I definitely have some gaps in my vocabulary.'

She went out into the sunshine, and headed back to the apartment. Even having made a single acquaintance, she felt more at ease. Once she had dropped off her purchases, she wandered out again and found a small grocery shop, the pavement outside it a display of shiny crimson tomatoes and extravagant bunches of fresh herbs, their leaves ornate enough to put in a vase.

Afterwards, she was led by its alluring scent to the bakery around the corner. She remembered it from her previous visits, and nothing had changed.

'*Agápi mou!*' cried the lady behind the counter. '*Elenáki! Elenáki!*' She had immediately recognised Helena from her distinctive hair. '*I yiayiá péthane, lypámai, lypámai,*' she said with sorrow. '*Syllypitíria.* My condolences.'

'Yes, yes, my grandma died, that's right.' Helena acknowledged her expression of sympathy by placing her palm across her heart. She knew that this was the standard gesture of appreciation. The elderly lady, probably the same age as her grandmother had been, was diminutive in height, and as warm and plump as her well-risen bread. Her widow's weeds were dusted with flour.

Once they had got the issue of death out of the way, Helena pointed to one of the honey-coloured loaves, which was swiftly wrapped in tissue and put on the counter, and then indicated that she would like a slice of the spinach pie that sat temptingly in the cabinet.

Along with her purchases, she left with several warm apple pastries, a gift from the baker.

Her final stop was for water at the kiosk, and the owner greeted her with his usual voiceless enthusiasm. Helena smiled at him. He felt like an old friend.

Chapter Twenty-Four

Back at home, she unloaded all the cleaning materials onto the kitchen table. With her days here limited, the task needed organisation, so she strode from room to room with a pad of paper, making a list of what there was: twenty-five matching dining chairs and a long dining table, three sideboards, two bureaux, several dressing tables, three formal settees and a number of upholstered chairs, countless occasional tables, four wardrobes large enough to hide several adults, four elaborate beds with side tables, five chests of drawers and numerous fussy footstools, some bookshelves (mostly empty of books), various display cabinets, magazine racks, free-standing mirrors and other items. Before selling the flat, she wanted to get rid of the furniture, so it all needed to shine as brightly as the pieces she had seen in the shop window the previous evening.

Knowing that everything about this place had been anathema to Mary McCloud, it felt like a favour to her to strip it of its heavy history. If she found something small that reminded her of her grandmother, she would keep it.

The master bedroom was first on her list, and here the smell of the past was burdensome. Everything from the curtains to the counterpane to the rug reeked of decay.

There were two wardrobes in this room. The one in the corner was slimmer, so she would start with that. She pulled the handles so that both doors swung open together, and immediately clapped a hand over her mouth.

'Oh my God!' she shrieked with a mixture of shock and disgust.

Hanging directly in front of her was Stamatis Papagiannis's army uniform, the medals still in place, the hat on a shelf above it, his polished shoes on the floor, their toecaps peeking out from beneath the trousers. The jacket had swayed slightly as she pulled open the doors, and a shiver ran down her back. How often had her grandmother opened this wardrobe to admire the uniform? To imagine he was still there with her?

She slammed the doors shut and put a chair in front of them. She knew what she was going to do, but could not bring herself to touch it for now. She had inadvertently released the stink of stale nicotine into the room, but it felt like more than that. It was as if she had released his ghost to wander the apartment.

She could not get rid of the feeling that he was watching her.

The other wardrobe was enormous but was not going to be a challenging task, she told herself. There was no question of keeping anything and no decisions to be made. It was a matter of taking things off hangers and dropping them into plastic sacks.

This second closet was packed full of clothes, some that she remembered her grandmother wearing: expensive silk blouses, dozens of shapeless floral button-through dresses, coats in different shades of dark green and maroon, all in heavy wool for the chilly Athenian winters, and many jackets and cardigans, everything quite petite. There were some more elegant clothes from her younger days – a few stylish suits and some evening dresses that must have been too beautiful for her to part with. Helena had a flash of sadness for her grandmother and how much she might have wanted to hold on to parts of her glamorous past. Among the suits was a black one, very slim cut. Perhaps Eleni Papagiannis had worn this to her son's funeral.

There were several items that would have been displayed on the vintage rack in her local Oxfam and fetched good money, and for a moment she was tempted to keep them. She held a couple of blouses against herself in the mirror, but they were far too short in the arm. She suddenly had a vivid memory of Dina's reaction when she had told her that one of her skirts was from a charity shop. Even to the maid, the idea of wearing something second-hand was un-acceptable, an affront to her pride, so Helena was sure there was nowhere in Athens that would take these clothes.

There were various chests of drawers, all homes to colonies of moths who had worked hard to leave every woollen item in tatters. Scarves, vests, socks, were all now turned to lace.

From those years of summer visits, she could picture her grand-mother plodding around the apartment in one of her simple shirt dresses, or rolling up the sleeves of her cardigan to water her favourite plants. Throwing away old cardigans was not to discard memories, she told herself, gathering things from the rail by the armful and deciding that even the hangers must go.

She was working faster now, shoving everything into bags, piling items unceremoniously one on top of another. By the time she had finished, there were eleven misshapen sacks. She knotted the tops tightly so that the smell could not escape.

There was a beautiful dove-grey cashmere shawl on the back of the door. Helena put it round her shoulders. Should she keep it? Just one item? She glanced at herself in the hall mirror, which had clouded over with time, and knew the answer: shrouding herself in a dead woman's clothes was macabre. She dropped it onto the pile to be discarded.

Clearing out the shoes was a different ordeal. A dozen pairs of well-worn brown leather brogues, the shape of her grandmother's twisted feet, were lined up in a row on the floor of the wardrobe. A nutmeg-sized bump protruded from the side of each shoe, moulded by her grandmother's bunions, and the deep creases in the leather made her think of walnuts, the pattern of twisted lines as unique as a fingerprint. Helena herself rarely wore anything but plimsolls or espadrilles, and she turned one of the shoes over in her hand, marvelling at the amount of care and polishing that had clearly gone into making it last. She recalled seeing Dina at the task. It was typical of her grandmother. It did not matter how much time had passed since the years of occupation and rationing, nor how wealthy this family had seemed; Yiayiá had often reminded Helena how important it was to look after your possessions.

Just for a second, she imagined that the shoe felt warm from her grandmother's foot, and quickly dropped it into a nearby refuse sack. She grabbed the rest of the shoes with no regard for pairing and hurriedly disposed of them too.

Finally she went back to her grandfather's uniform. She bundled it into a bin liner, knotted the top, and then spent five minutes washing her hands until they were almost raw. Eleni Papagiannis had always carried a scent of sweetness around her that was somewhere between sugar and roses, and when Helena sniffed the talcum powder on the bathroom shelf, it was as if her grandmother was in the room. She liberally sprinkled her own hands with it.

Making several journeys, she struggled down to the end of the street, four bags at a time, and threw everything into a bin. As the last one went in, she sighed with relief.

It was time for her mother's childhood bedroom. The skirting boards were thick with dust, and she pulled out a chest to clean behind it. Here she found two small books, both with the initials MP, Maria Papagiannis, pencilled on the title page.

The fatter of the two was *O Teleftaíos Peirasmós* by Nikos Kazantzakis. *The Last Temptation of Christ.* Helena remembered her mother telling her that it had been banned by the Greek Orthodox Church for portraying Jesus as a normal man who married Mary Magdalene, and that the author had been excommunicated. When she flicked through, there were many passages underlined, and she paused for a moment to try and read them.

The other book was *Kaváfi Poiémata*, the poems of Cavafy. Mary McCloud had often quoted lines from this poet, and Helena knew how much he meant to her. There were many poems marked with faint vertical lines, exclamation marks and asterisks, and on some there were more detailed notes. One poem, 'Ithaka', was almost obscured by annotations, and a particular line had been heavily underscored: '*Na éfchesai na 'nai makrýs o drómos.* May your journey be a long one.' At this moment, Helena could not bear the poignancy of these words, and she snapped the book shut.

The clever boy she had met earlier that day came to her mind. She was friendless in this big city, and asking Mihalis to help her decipher a few of her mother's scribbles would be a good excuse to see him again. She put the worn cloth-bound volumes into her shoulder bag.

The temperature soared higher than the previous day, and through the wide-open windows drifted the hum of city life: snatches of music from the cafés in the square, car horns sounding with such regularity they made their own melodies, the buzz of mopeds. Helena suddenly felt that the whole of Athens was keeping her company.

The kitchen took little time. As well as having sentimental value, many things crammed in the drawers and stacked in the cupboards still served their purpose. She remembered Dina using some of the old kitchen knives and the cracked lemon squeezer. The sense of the maid's presence would be comforting. The sink was going to need scouring, as a dripping tap had built a stalactite of limescale, and rust had taken hold of both fridge and oven.

The two bureaux in the drawing room needed keys, easily found in the floral jug. She remembered asking her grandmother what was in them when she was younger. Yiayiá told her it was *yliká*, just 'stuff'. This miscellany turned out to be paperwork.

Her grandmother had been fastidious about clean surfaces, and always fussed about the appearance of her home, but as Helena had already discovered in the kitchen, in every drawer and cupboard lurked the mess of life. When she opened the larger of the two bureaux, stacks of papers cascaded out. She piled everything onto the kitchen table, making several journeys until the dresser was empty. Several pages floated to the floor, but as nothing was in chronological order, it did not matter.

Most of the sheets were historic bills, easily discarded. But just in case there was anything important, she began the task of scanning every page. After two hours, the table was still covered with paper, not a square inch of the polished wood visible. The sound of an ornate ticking clock began to taunt her. The noise from outside had obscured it, but its steady metronome beat and the chiming on the quarter-hour now irritated her. She recalled the message on her parents' clock, but needed no reminder that time was flying. It puzzled her that this one had kept going all this time without being wound up. She hoped it would gradually wind down, but meanwhile put it on her list of things to sell.

For now, music would help drown it out. She wandered into the drawing room, where a pile of vinyl records was stacked high on a small table next to the gramophone. She began to look through them. On the top were the few dozen that she remembered her grandmother playing: Giorgos Dalaras, Dimitris Mitropanos, Vassilis Tsitsanis and Mikis Theodorakis, the latter both songs and orchestral works.

The slightly yellow-tinted images of her grandmother's favourite singers were almost life-size, and Helena recalled how Yiayiá used to prop their smiling faces on top of the gramophone as she listened. 'It's almost as good as having them in the room,' she used to say, as the turntable whirred around noisily, audible beneath the crackle and hiss of the worn-out records. Helena removed one of the Dalaras discs from its sleeve and carefully lowered it onto the turntable, lifting the arm to activate the mechanism and letting the stylus slowly descend to the edge.

With the volume turned up as high as it could go, the sound of Dalaras's sweet voice filled the entire room with sound and Helena with sadness. It was rarely words that sent a wave of emotion running through her. It was always music, a run of notes or a pairing of chords that suddenly reminded her of the Pie Jesu played at her mother's funeral. She remembered sitting in church, her eyes fixed on the words of *Ode on a Grecian Urn* printed in the order of service, knowing that when the last notes of the Fauré died away, she would have to get up and read it. She had been squeezed so close to her father that she could feel his breathing, the two of them struggling to give each other strength while the grief they felt inside threatened to overwhelm them. Some less soulful music was needed for a moment.

Many of the records showed images of women dressed for folk dancing, some with men as well. Helena tolerated the jingoistic sound for a while before she was ready to revert to her grandmother's favourite, who stirred so much depth of feeling in her heart.

She lined up all the records with Dalaras's name on the outside and made a plan to listen to them one by one.

Her decision on whether a record should stay or go was simple. Those she was sure had been purchased by her grandmother were to be kept. The ones collected and enjoyed by her grandfather were to be disposed of.

Every twenty minutes, she got up to flip a record over or to choose a new one. Time went by more enjoyably now as she ruthlessly ditched decades of utility, tax and house repair invoices. Some of the bills went back to the early 1960s, and many had the word 'paid' scrawled in her grandfather's handwriting across the drachma sum. While Giorgos Dalaras crooned on, the contents of an entire dresser disappeared into refuse sacks, leaving just a few papers that fitted easily into a single manila envelope.

Now it was time to tackle the smaller of the two elegant bureaux in the drawing room. Inside this one, things seemed to have been more carefully sorted, tied into bundles or even packed into small cartons. At the very back were a number of shoeboxes. It seemed as if they had been concealed.

Helena moved these onto the dining room table, then wandered back to the drawing room to put on another record. The Dalaras collection was exhausted, so she picked the next in the pile, songs composed by Mikis Theodorakis. There were at least a dozen of these, which would last her well into the afternoon. The mood was different, less romantic. Some of the music was dark, with insistent rhythms that lowered her mood. Many of the songs had an air of pain about them, and love was clearly not the theme. Occasionally she understood a line or two, and found it hard to imagine her grandmother choosing to listen to such melancholy.

'I can see you in a narrow cell.'

The strong voices of powerful women filled the apartment. No, this was not romance they referred to. It was a song of protest, not a song of love. A song of suffering, a song of resistance.

Helena put on another record and went to sort the contents of the shoeboxes. They all came from the same place, and the graceful signature logo of the shop-owner adorned the lids: *Ypodímata Galanákis*. Galanakis Footwear. A label on the side illustrated the original contents in colour. Helena would never have guessed that there had once been a time when her grandmother had worn such elegant footwear: pointy-toed court shoes in green satin, strappy sandals with a platform in cherry red. It had been another age, a phase of Eleni Papagiannis's life that Helena hadn't witnessed. Another epoch.

She could tell from the weight of the boxes that the shoes were no longer inside.

The first one held several pieces of embroidered linen, wrapped in tissue, some baby clothes (a baptism robe, perhaps) and a lace bonnet. They were carefully pressed and lovingly folded, not as you would store simple keepsakes, but as if the baby who had worn them had died. There were also some soft shoes, the style a child would wear in the pram before they could walk. The embroidery and the smocking on the little robe were exquisite. There were three layers to the dress; the final layer was fine linen, the two on top were tulle. Some tiny hand-laced knickerbockers were tucked inside. She could not even imagine how adult hands could have created such stitching.

She took another look inside the box and picked up a small scalloped-edged photograph. On the back, in her grandmother's writing, were the words *Maria Papagiánnis, Gennithike 10 Septemvríou 1929, Baptístike 8 Noemvríou 1929*. They were the dates of her mother's birth and baptism. An image showed her grandparents – the baby in her mother's arms – flanked by another couple, presumably the godparents. Her grandfather looked haughty and unsmiling as usual. There was also an envelope, inside which there was a formal, printed invitation to the baptism, and a lock of dark hair. Finally, in a green velvet box was a diamond-set gold cross, the symbol of the religion her mother had rejected, along with so much else in her homeland. There was also a fine chain bracelet, with a minuscule *máti*. So like the one she kept safely in her jewellery box in Dellbridge.

Helena laid the tissue out on the table, placed all the clothes on top and put the jewellery next to them. Though she had mostly cleared out her grandmother's possessions without emotion, when she found herself looking at this tableau of her mother as an infant, her tears fell. It was the shape of innocence: the newborn hair, the suggestion of soft-soled feet that had never felt the ground, the pristine, still-boxed jewellery.

She packed the garments away again, folding them exactly as before to avoid making new creases. For a moment, she contemplated taking the cross and wearing it, but knew that her mother would have disapproved.

She imagined the love and hope with which her grandmother had originally packed all this away, and was almost certain that the box had not been opened since then. She understood that her grandfather had wanted everything to do with his daughter disposed of when she left. Would he have made an exception for these mementoes of her innocence, or was their concealment an act of rebellion by her grandmother?

Another box was labelled 'Bank Certificates', which confirmed her notion that this was a clandestine store of memorabilia. It was full of school reports for her mother in chronological order, with a few missing for the years when the Nazis had occupied Greece and schools were shut. The young Maria Papagiannis's academic ability was impressive. She had full marks in every subject, with only a single 7 out of 10 during the whole decade of her education.

Two more boxes were packed with photographs. All of them were of her mother, or had her mother at the centre of the image, and all were annotated on the reverse. Many bore indentations that showed they had once been in frames, displayed with pride. Once again, Helena found herself saddened, not just by all these souvenirs of her mother but by the evidence that she had been written out of history by Stamatis Papagiannis. Mary McCloud had effectively died twice. Despite the heat of the day, Helena shuddered. Her grandmother had loved her daughter, that much was very clear, but she had loved her husband too and perhaps had never stood up to him.

Equally sad was a box of memorabilia for Andreas Papagiannis, Helena's uncle. There was a birth certificate and a death certificate. There was a photograph of his baptism, and the outfit he had worn that day. His school reports were noticeably less impressive than his sister's. There were documents relating to his army enrolment and a small envelope with a few medals. None of these things could be disposed of. They were all that was left of him.

She spent the rest of the day clearing out the other pieces of furniture in the bedrooms, getting rid of old bed linen and bottles of medication, along with rusted tins from the kitchen store cupboards and jars of herbs that had turned to dust.

For Helena, a home with so few books was an empty place. In her father's house, they were piled high even on the floor. Here, there was just one small bookcase, in the corner of the drawing room. It was occupied by military histories, studies of war, analyses of battles, titles such as: *From Ancient Times to Modern: The Strategy of Conflict, Great Army Victories Around the World, Coups and Counter-Coups, The Case for Discipline in the Internment Camp, The Communist Crisis, The Red Rebellion.* She questioned why her grandmother had kept these, until she looked into the indexes and saw her grandfather's name listed with several entries. Most of the copies had a dedication to him from the author. One of them was a gift on St Stamatios's Day from Papadopoulos himself.

In the master bedroom was a shelf of trashy romantic novels that she remembered her grandmother reading, but only after her grandfather's death. She threw every one of these into the same box as her grandfather's grisly collection, ready to carry them out to the bin, then sat down on the upholstered stool at Yiayiá's dressing table. To the left of the mirror was a wooden chest, its lid prettily inlaid with mother-of-pearl. It was packed with jewellery, and Helena remembered each piece: the brooches that her grandmother had pinned to her coats, strings of beads, a row of rings slotted into a specially made grooved section. As a child, she had never given much thought to any of it, but now she examined everything with more curiosity. The scarlet stones in one of the brooches, were they rubies? Were these beads pure jet? What about the stones in those rings? Were they just glass, or diamonds and emeralds? What was valuable? What was imitation?

She dropped the lid down. Given what her mother had taken to England to sell, she guessed that all of this was real. She would never wear any of it herself and would probably sell it in due course.

The latest record had come to an end and the apartment was silent again. The past had buried her these past hours and she suddenly felt that she had paid enough homage to her grandmother's favourite composers. Even Theodorakis had begun to get on her nerves.

Going out onto the balcony to draw some fresh air into her lungs, she was met by the sound of birds massing in the trees. Swallows were roosting for the night. She looked up into a clear sky, daylight still, but dusk too. It was the magic hour. With a need to be in the streets that felt almost urgent, she swept up a bunch of keys from the hall table, grabbed her bag and left. It did not matter to her that she was filthy, with the debris of decades beneath her fingernails.

Chapter Twenty-Five

Kolonaki was full of smart men and women sitting outside the cafés, and as Helena strolled across the square, she observed that their interest was only stirred by those who were similarly well dressed. In her long denim skirt and *Dark Side of the Moon* T-shirt, she was invisible to the people-watchers, except for a brief moment when her bright hair caught their attention. Then they looked away. Her flaming curls were enough, however, to get the attention of one of the younger waiters in a café that she used to visit with her grandmother. He stood across her path, as he often did with tourists, to tempt her in with a menu.

'*Éla korítsi. Éla na kátseis!*' he said. 'Come in, miss. Come in and have a seat!'

Won over by his smile, and the idea of chilled wine on a hot night, Helena followed him to a free table. As she sipped her drink and ate the nuts that accompanied it, it was her turn to survey the crowd. They were younger than she remembered from the morning coffee times with her grandmother, and mostly businessmen in suits, a few with their wives.

Then she suddenly saw a face she recognised. It was Mihalis, the boy from the hardware store. He had dispensed with the sack-coloured cotton coat he had been wearing in the shop, and was sporting a fitted blue shirt and pale flares.

Helena waved, her reaction instinctive, perhaps overexcited to see

271

someone familiar in a city of strangers. She immediately felt embarrassed, realising that he probably had dozens of customers every day. To her great relief, however, he waved back with enthusiasm and crossed the street to speak to her.

'*Kalispéra!*' He greeted her like an old friend. 'How did the cleaning go, Mrs Danvers?'

'Mrs Danvers?' Helena laughed.

'Well, you didn't tell me your name. So I've given you one.'

'You mean the housekeeper in *Rebecca*?'

'Of course! I *adore* Daphne du Maurier. More than Dickens, more than Jane Austen. More than anyone, except Shakespeare of course.'

'You're so funny,' she said. 'When did you discover all these English authors?'

'While I was in London. They're such great storytellers. I was meant to be studying politics, but when I had spare time, that's what I did. I read Daphne.'

'You're a true Anglophile,' said Helena. 'I loved *Rebecca* too, but I never saw myself as Mrs Danvers.'

'You're not really like her,' said Mihalis. 'Except for the mop. But unless you tell me your name, that's what I shall keep calling you.'

'I'm Helena,' she laughed.

'So, Helena, why are you sitting here all on your own?'

Before she had time to give an answer, the waiter had put a bill down on the table and was hovering for payment.

'Would you like a drink?' she asked Mihalis, putting a note on top of the bill.

'Not here,' he said decisively. 'Not my kind of place.' Helena noticed him throw a hostile glance at the waiter, who was counting out some coins before sprinkling them dismissively on the table. One of them spun away onto the pavement. The tension was palpable.

'I'm going to meet some friends,' said Mihalis, picking up the stray five-drachma piece. 'Why don't you come with me?'

'But . . .' She felt confused by the distinctly chilly behaviour from the waiter, who had served her with such friendliness only minutes before. 'Yes, why not?'

She got up, and they set off, away from the square.

'What was that about?' she asked, struggling to keep pace with Mihalis's long strides. 'He was so rude, that waiter. I hadn't even finished my wine!'

'Let's put it this way,' he answered. 'It's a very conservative area. Politically and in every other way.'

'Oh,' she said. 'But did I do something wrong? Was it how I'm dressed?'

'No, it was nothing to do with you,' he replied. 'It was me.'

As they walked, Helena mulled over his words.

'Have you got comfortable shoes on?' Mihalis asked.

She looked down at her shabby espadrilles. 'Very,' she answered. 'They're scruffy, but they can take me anywhere. So where are we going?'

'Just to a bar. A place where people hang out.'

The pavements were packed with people, so it was hard to walk side by side. Eventually Helena spoke again.

'So what *exactly* happened in the café?'

'Very simple, really. That waiter and I grew up in the same neighbourhood. Patissia. The area I told you about where my family moved to. We were at the same school. What can I tell you? He was a bully. And he knew I was gay. That was enough really.' His tone, so light-hearted until now, had changed. 'It was more like persecution than bullying. And often physical.'

'That's awful,' Helena said.

'There's a deep undercurrent of homophobia in this city, Helena. It's been legal for longer to be gay in Greece, but somehow in London I felt freer.'

'I don't know London that well, but even when I was at Oxford, there were people in the closet. There's still a taboo in plenty of places, I promise you.'

'But we have to do military service here. And that's no fun if you're gay.'

'I can imagine. If people have such an attitude . . . I won't be going to that café again!'

'It's not only him. All the waiters are like that in there. They may as well have a sign up: *No Gays Allowed* . . . Anyway, I know it was much worse under the Colonels. My friends were always being victimised in those years.'

A bitter memory had been stirred. It was hard to place in a precise moment in time, but it was a word she recalled coming from her grandfather's mouth: *omofylófilos*. It was more spat than spoken. She had asked Dina what it meant, and initially the maid would not tell her.

The word had a pleasing rhythm, so she had chanted it to herself over and over again like a jingle: *o-mo-fy-ló-fi-los*. Later that day, her grandfather heard her doing this and smacked her hand hard.

'*Óchi!*' he had screamed. 'No!'

She remembered thinking it must be a swear word, but Dina had explained to her later that it meant a man loving a man. All she knew was that she must not say it in front of her grandfather.

'So, there are certain places we go these days. I'll take you to my favourite before we meet the rest of my *paréa*, the gang.'

The waiter had been forgotten now, Mihalis's mood had lightened, and Helena felt the flower of an unexpected friendship beginning to open.

'Gianni's was one of the first gay bars in Athens. I think you'll like it. You don't have to be *omofylófilos* to go there!'

They were winding their way through narrow side streets. Helena had no idea how Mihalis kept track of where he was going: left, left, right, left, right and right again as the streets narrowed. It was quieter now as they entered an area where only pedestrians were permitted.

'These are some of the oldest paved streets in the world,' he said proudly.

'I've been to Plaka before,' Helena told him, 'but never along these little roads.'

Soon they reached a small doorway and went inside. It was Gianni's. At the back was a shady courtyard, and they sat for an hour over cold beer. Helena found herself telling Mihalis about her childhood trips to Athens, and how she had now inherited the large, gloomy apartment that had belonged to her grandparents.

'Sorry, I'm talking far too much,' she said. 'I've been locked away on my own for a few days.'

'Keep talking!' he encouraged her. They were speaking in English for now. 'You have a slight accent. It's lovely to listen to.'

'Suffolk, probably. But enough of me. Tell me more about your family, Mihalis. You said you were born above the shop and then you went to LSE. It seems a big leap.'

'My great-grandfather was a travelling salesman. He went from village to village up in north Greece, with a cart laden with brushes and brooms and buckets. All sorts. And he would literally bed down for the night on some straw, wherever he could find somewhere to stable his horse. He earned money but never spent any. After a few years of living a gypsy life, suddenly *Keravnovólos érotas*!' He spoke these words with a great flourish.

'What happened?' asked Helena eagerly.

'A thunderclap! Love at first sight! A young widow came out of her house to buy something from him and they fell into each other's arms. That's the story, anyhow.'

'It's a nice one. I'm sure it can happen,' Helena said, remembering her first sight of Nick.

'So Melina, that was her name, wasn't interested in living on the road. She wanted to move to Athens. She was a clever woman, found a place they could afford and they opened a shop together. I never met them, but my father says they were the happiest people he ever knew, perfect equals. And the place they bought was a good investment. The shop still makes plenty of money. People don't expect to find a hardware shop in such a smart area, but every home, wherever it is, needs the things we sell, so we do well. And when my parents sold the upper floor, they were able to buy somewhere much bigger, as I told you.'

'What a success story. From sleeping rough to a feather bed in Kolonaki.'

'It happened a lot in those days. Opportunities were huge if you worked hard. And after a while, they didn't really fit in around Kolonaki.'

'What do you mean?'

'The type of people who moved in there . . .'

'Wealthy people like my grandparents, I suppose,' she said.

They finished their beers and strolled out again. Between two tumbledown buildings, Helena noticed the outline of the Temple of Zeus, its tall pillars silhouetted against the darkening sky, and thought of Dina.

'I do envy you being Athenian,' she said to Mihalis. 'Growing up with all of this so close by.'

'Pros and cons,' Mihalis answered non-committally.

A few minutes later, they turned a corner. Leading upwards from where they stood was a long flight of broad stone steps. It reminded Helena of an amphitheatre, but without a stage. Crowds of young-sters divided into various groups lounged on the stairs all the way up to the top of the hill. Mihalis surveyed the throng and spotted his friends. He caught their attention, and one of them made his way down towards them, greeting Mihalis with a kiss on the cheek.

'Páno, échoume mia kainoúrgia fíli,' Mihalis told him. 'We have a new friend, Eleni.'

The old friend shook hands with the new, and Helena was taken up to meet the rest of the gang. Mihalis's friends looked beautiful, their skin uniformly golden from the long Greek summer, at ease with their bodies and themselves. There were two girls in the group, who parted so that Helena could squeeze between them on the step.

Everyone had to shout above the hubbub, and waiters weaved their way between them with huge trays of drinks that magically reached their destinations.

The charismatic Panos was clearly the group leader. Helena had noticed how everyone seemed to hang on his every word, especially Mihalis, who sat next to him, his arm linked through his. They were, she realised, a couple.

Initially the sound of nine people speaking at once in Greek was a challenge, even though she was fluent. Sentences collided with each other and even agreement felt like argument. The frequent *nai, nai, nai* sounded negative, and Helena constantly had to remind herself it meant yes. She concentrated hard, trying to catch the gist of the various conversations. She was grateful whenever someone broke off to explain the context of a debate, which was inevitably a political one.

Mihalis's friends adopted Helena into their group without question, and gradually she picked up what they all did. A couple were postgraduate students, one a lawyer, two were teachers, Panos was an architect. Another had taken on his parents' shop as Mihalis had done.

A fresh drink appeared in her hand whenever her glass was empty, and each time there was a new round, they all clinked glasses one by one, looking directly into each other's eyes: '*Stin ygeiá mas!* Cheers!' Each toast felt like a pact of friendship.

At some point after midnight, a boy sitting at the top of the steps began to strum a tune on his guitar and everyone started to sing. The sound spread from top to bottom, like a gentle wave, and between the lines, Mihalis spoke the translation into Helena's ear:

'"Our songs have bitter words . . . We live injustice from our birth."'

'It's beautiful. But why does everyone know the words?'

'It would be the same if you were in a big crowd in London and everyone started singing a Beatles song. Or the Rolling Stones. You'd join in, wouldn't you?'

'Yes, but this feels a bit more emotional to me.'

'You're right to have sensed that,' Mihalis said appreciatively. 'It was originally sung by Giorgos Dalaras.'

'Dalaras! I've been listening to him all afternoon! He was one of my grandmother's pin-ups. I've probably even heard this song before.'

'It's a very special one. Like an anthem for us. The junta banned Dalaras's first release and he's a hero for all of us here, not just for your grandma.'

The crowd launched into another song, quietly at first, and then gradually the swell of sound grew.

'That's a *baglamás*,' Mihalis said, identifying a miniature bouzouki-shaped instrument now being plucked by one of their own group. 'And this song is another favourite. I'll tell you what the words mean later.' He began singing.

As far as Helena could tell, there was no rousing chorus that she could join in with, and no verses seemed to be repeated. She was mesmerised by the expressions on people's faces; some had their eyes rapturously closed, and all of them sang every syllable of the lengthy song without hesitation. Everyone was word perfect.

'However often I hear it, it moves me,' said Panos, brushing a hand over his face. Helena noticed the gesture and realised that he had tears in his eyes.

Mihalis, who was on the other side of Panos, leaned in. 'He's a softie,' he said, stroking Panos's hair. 'It's another cheery one that got banned for mentioning the dictatorship.'

'Mihalis, you *know* why it moves me,' Panos responded, smiling at the gentle ribbing.

'Of course, I do, *agápi mou*. I just don't want to depress our new friend. We might never see her again.'

'Apart from anything, our history is hers too,' Panos retorted defensively. 'She's *misí-misí*, half and half.'

'So why did it move you especially?' asked Helena.

'It's called "*Malamaténia Lógia*", "Gilded Words",' explained Mihalis. 'It's iconic for lots of reasons. And for Panos, it's personal.'

'It talks about the persecution of resistance fighters during the Nazi occupation,' said Panos. 'My uncle was executed in Kaisariani, not so far from here. I didn't even know him. But the thought of it makes me angry.'

'That's terrible,' murmured Helena.

'I had another uncle who was a communist. He died in a camp after the civil war.' Panos looked at Helena, and she wondered for a moment if he knew something about her family background. She felt suddenly uncomfortable.

'I would say that in a group like this, almost everyone has some kind of story to tell,' he continued. 'Mihalis's Uncle Petros was exiled to Makronisos and tortured under the junta for so-called subversive activities. He's never recovered. We visit him in this depressing psychiatric hospital every week.'

Helena was conscious of the inadequacy of words. She wanted to ask a thousand questions, but this was not the time and place. More than ever, she felt the stain of her grandfather on her.

'But look at us now!' continued Panos. 'Life is good, Helena. We have no dictatorship! No censorship! No ridiculous royal family! We have democracy! We can *live*!'

'It seems pretty perfect to me,' Helena said with total sincerity. 'Right now, I can't imagine a more beautiful place to be.'

It was the early hours of the morning, and they were sitting under a starry sky, caressed by a warm breeze. Another guitarist had appeared; there were more songs to be sung and no sign that this happy time was yet drawing to an end. Someone in the group wandered off and returned with a generous package of souvlaki sticks, more than enough for their group. Panos squeezed several lemon segments over the fragrant pile of meat and it was shared around.

Helena had never tasted such succulent pork, which was all the more delicious for her ravenous hunger. Her diet over the past few days had comprised mostly bread and tomatoes.

Everything about the evening had bewitched her. From the way she had been welcomed to the sense of spontaneity. There were more drinks, more toasts, more music, and then around three o'clock, people began to drift away.

'Four hours of sleep are more than enough at this time of year!' said Eftasia, who was training to be a doctor. 'That's all I'll have when I'm qualified, so I might as well get used to it.'

Helena was grateful that all she had to get up for was to clear a few dusty knick-knacks.

Mihalis and Panos took her with them in their taxi home, dropping her off in Kolonaki.

'Call on me in the shop, Helena,' said Mihalis, holding her hand before she got out. 'I mean it. And come out with us again at the weekend.'

'Saturday night is the best for music!' confirmed Panos.

'And we'll make sure it's cheerful this time,' Mihalis chipped in.

'He's lying,' said Panos. 'Even if Greek music is upbeat for a few songs, you're always going to get the songs of suffering thrown in. That's just how it is.'

'Well, I loved it all tonight. Happy, sad, the two sometimes all at once. It was wonderful.'

'It's a complex culture, this,' Panos laughed. 'Melancholy is usually in the mix somewhere, even in a moment of joy.'

His words echoed in her ears as she went up in the lift and into the empty apartment. As soon as she was done with clearing it out, she would be on a ferry to see Nick. It seemed an age since she had even heard his voice.

Chapter Twenty-Six

Her desire to get the flat finished before she left for Nisos spurred Helena to work even harder. She put in long hours over the next two days boxing up crockery and going to and from the rubbish bins with bags of mouldy linen and more papers.

Early evening, at around the time of day that her father sometimes called her, the phone on the sideboard rang. She picked it up, ready to update him on her new group of friends.

'*Egó eímai, o Níkos!*'

Helena felt herself weaken at the sound of his voice.

'Nick,' she laughed. 'It's so lovely to hear you. Your Greek is coming on!'

'*Nai, agápi mou,*' he confirmed.

'How did you get this number?'

'Your lovely father gave it to me!'

'Oh! Great. Look, I'm nearly done here. I'll be with you very soon,' she told him.

'I have a surprise for you,' he replied. 'I've got a couple of days off and I was thinking of coming to Athens for a change of scene. I'll be there tomorrow morning and I'll leave the following day.'

'Really? That's wonderful!' Helena responded with enthusiasm. 'Though I might not be able to come back to Nisos with you yet.'

'Don't worry, *pouláki mou,*' he responded, delighting her with a Greek term of endearment. 'I'll be waiting for you.'

Just before the pips began, Helena quickly gave him her address. She was excited that she would have him all to herself, even if it was just for one day. Life on the dig was convivial, but communal too, and she knew she would have to share him.

Distracted by the anticipation of Nick's visit, she suddenly realised that she only had five minutes before Mihalis and Panos were coming to collect her. They had promised to show her more of their Athens.

That evening, they went to a packed open-air cinema and sat beneath the stars, cold drinks in hand, swallows swooping above them. Helena's new friends had a taste for the political films of Theo Angelopoulos, and she sat patiently through one of his darkest but most popular films, O Thíasos, The Travelling Players, banned, Mihalis told her, until the fall of the junta.

It was already 11 p.m. when they came out, but the streets still thronged with people and the cafés and bars were packed with customers.

'Let's have a drink,' said Panos. 'Exarchia Square?'

Mihalis nodded, and they set off to a café where Panos decoded the film for Helena. Although set in another repressive period, between 1932 and 1954, it was pointedly critical of the Colonels, and Helena realised that whether or not something was conveyed through metaphor, almost everything she saw and heard in this city was a response to the turmoil of past decades: famine, occupation, civil war, dictatorship.

Panos confirmed this. 'Everything here is politics,' he said.

'And if it doesn't appear so on the surface, it's all buried in there somewhere,' Mihalis added.

Helena looked around the square. Although so close, it seemed a world away from the cafés in Kolonaki, which attracted an after-work crowd of the networking wealthy, along with men from various nearby government ministries. Here there were big groups, earnest talk but laughter too, debates and voices raised, but not in anger. Anyone who sat down was drawn into a conversation, and there were no strangers, only friends. Most here had long hair, both girls and boys, and in every other café someone strummed a guitar. Each played a different tune, but there seemed no lack of harmony between them.

The spirit was relaxed and yet febrile. Defiance and the heady scent of marijuana mingled.

'The police don't come anywhere near here,' Mihalis told Helena over their drinks. 'The students at the London School of Economics think they're militant, but they're mild compared with the ones who hang out here. The smallest spark can set things off in this area.'

As they were leaving, Panos and Mihalis were greeted by people at a nearby table. There were embraces and introductions and promises of a future rendezvous.

It would be too hot to sleep much tonight, so they agreed to stroll, and their route took them past a place that Helena realised she recognised.

'That's where I did my first degree,' said Mihalis.

'My God,' she said very quietly, holding the railings and looking through. 'It's the Polytechnic.'

The twisted gates stoved in by army tanks on that night in November 1973 still lay on the ground, left as a sombre memorial to those who had died from being crushed or shot.

'I know plenty of people who witnessed it,' said Panos. 'There were thousands who saw it happening from outside and many behind the gates who stared straight down the barrels of those guns. Think what it was like to realise that those monster tanks were actually moving towards you, and the shock that they were about to do the unthinkable. Can you even imagine what the noise was like as they crushed the gates?'

Helena had no trouble imagining the fear.

'I remember seeing it on the front page in England,' she said. 'And I remember being shocked. But seeing those gates in real life brings it home . . . It must have been totally horrifying.'

She shared the blood of someone who had probably given similarly brutal orders, and felt a knot in her stomach. Even though her grandfather had died before this terrible act had been perpetrated, he would probably have endorsed it. At some point soon, she must tell Mihalis and Panos about him. It was beginning to feel like a weighty secret.

She took a last look through the railings, glad that the debris had not been cleared away, hoping it would remain there for ever.

As they made their way up Patision Avenue, the complexion of the neighbourhood changed. The streets to left and right were crowded with five-storey apartment blocks, art deco, art nouveau and Bauhaus. Panos pointed out the different styles, proud of this era when architects in his city had thrived and experimented.

'It's an architect's dream,' he said. 'Most of that neoclassical stuff in the centre is such awful pastiche.'

Mihalis was pushing open the door of a tiny establishment. 'Au Revoir,' he said, turning to Helena. 'Welcome to the oldest bar in Athens.'

It was smaller than the drawing room in Kolonaki, with just half a dozen tables, only one of which was free.

The barman was so enamoured of Helena's hair that he insisted on treating them all to large balloons of his best brandy.

'Is same colour as Metaxa!' he cried out so loudly that everyone looked. 'Coral! Burnt orange! Fire! She has hair of mermaid!'

Amid the continued chatter about Angelopoulos and a short interlude when Helena produced her mother's *Kaváfi Poiémata* and asked Mihalis to decipher something in the margin, she knew that the moment was coming when she had to confess her blood connection to a leading member of the right.

'He was pretty brave to start making that film under the junta,' Mihalis was saying to Panos. 'You would think they would have had an eye on him. My Uncle Petros did less than that to get thrown onto Makronisos.'

Surely this was her cue. Be brave, she urged herself. Easier said than done when both of them had family members who had been damaged by the hard right, possibly even by Stamatis Papagiannis himself.

One more sip, and she had the courage she needed.

'Mihalis,' she began. 'Panos. I hope it doesn't change our friendship, but I need to tell you both something.'

Panos leaned forward. 'What's happened?'

'My grandfather,' she said. 'He was in the island camps.'

'I didn't realise . . .' There was concern in his voice.

'Not as a prisoner, Panos. He was an army general. He was in charge.'

Panos was evidently shocked, and appeared to be struggling to take it in. Mihalis had not yet spoken.

'You can't imagine how ashamed I am to be so closely related to such a person. Even though he is dead, I feel stained.'

Mihalis put his hand on her arm. 'Look, I have a confession too. While we were waiting outside for you tonight, I saw the name Papagiannis on the nameplate. I wondered . . .'

'You didn't say anything!'

'That was cowardly of me,' he admitted. 'He was infamous and I wanted to ask you, but I didn't have the nerve. And anyway, what does it matter? You and he are not the same person. You can't carry the crimes of the past on your shoulders.'

'It changes nothing for us,' said Panos. 'It must have been awful for you to find out who he was.'

'I hated him even before I knew what he did,' said Helena, with immense relief at their reaction. 'My mother actually left Greece and didn't return for twenty-five years, she loathed him so much. And I knew nothing about any of it until a few years ago.'

By now, it was well into the early hours of the morning.

'If we don't leave soon,' she said, 'it'll be light.'

'And we need to walk you home.'

Taking her on the final detour of the day, they walked down one of the main side streets, all of them named after Greek islands, and found themselves in a small grassy square overlooked by apartment blocks. On some of the balconies, people were still sitting out.

'This is my square,' said Mihalis proudly. 'I wanted you to see it.'

He identified the rocky outcrops in the distance above them as the *Tourkovoúnia*, the Turkish Mountains. Helena asked why they were called that.

'Let's leave that for another day. It's a bit late for five hundred years of Greek history.'

'True. I'm shattered.'

They marched back down Patision Avenue and eventually reached Kolonaki. The *períptero* in the square still had its lights on and was doing brisk business.

'Just need some tobacco,' said Mihalis.

He put some coins down on the plastic ledge and Helena gave the owner a friendly wave before they continued walking.

'You know he's deaf?' she said quizzically.

'Of course I do,' replied Mihalis. 'But he can lip-read perfectly. I've known Lefteris my whole life. He used to give me free sweets when I was little, and for a few familiar customers like me, he scribbles things on a pad.'

'He gave me some chocolate when I first got here,' Helena recalled. 'How does he make any money?'

'Ah, there's plenty around here. I saw him in the bank once. Bags and bags of cash. Just a day's takings. My parents told me that he used to sing in a nightclub before he took over the kiosk. Apparently he had a very rich voice.'

'But it seems like he can hardly speak!'

'He lost the ability when he lost his hearing.'

'That's tragic. How did it happen?'

'Helena, I'll have put you off this country by the time you go back to London . . .'

'Tell me,' she insisted.

'He spent five years in the prison camp on Makronisos. They used to torture the inmates, and he was beaten so badly round the head it destroyed his hearing.'

Helena felt queasy. She had not expected such a blunt answer. It was not beyond possibility that her grandfather had been involved. Whatever Mihalis and Panos said, the guilt was hard to shift.

'He was there at the same time as Mikis Theodorakis. They became friends and used to sing together. Lefteris is really proud of that. Last year he published a small pamphlet about it – he sells copies in the kiosk. I've seen Mikis buying cigarettes there more than once.'

'Really?' said Helena. When she had been listening to Theodorakis's music, it had seemed a window onto another age, but here he was, the great composer himself, apparently still wandering about in Athens, part of history but of the present too. The two were inextricably intertwined in this city.

'He's seen it all really, hasn't he?'

'He probably has. And he just scribbled a note to me saying that anyone with your beautiful hair must have beautiful politics.'

'Oh, that's good,' said Helena. 'Because if he has connected me with my grandfather, I would hate him to think I was anything like him.'

'Don't worry,' smiled Mihalis. 'He knows.'

Chapter Twenty-Seven

Helena slept late the following morning, only stirring with the sound of the doorbell. It was 9.30.

Throwing on a T-shirt, she raced to the door and stood by the lift, impatient for its arrival. When Nick emerged, she threw herself into his arms.

'*Elenáki mou, Elenáki mou . . .*' he murmured in her ear.

'I've missed you, *Nikoláki mou*,' she said.

As they went into the apartment, he looked around him.

'It's such a mess,' Helena apologised. 'There's been a lot of clearing to do.'

'It's an impressive place,' he said, taking in the gilt mirrors, the marble fireplaces, the antique furniture, the portrait.

'It's all going,' she said. 'I have to get rid of everything. And then sell the flat.'

'You'll be a very rich woman,' he said, stroking her arm.

'Not after all the taxes that have to be paid. But it might get me enough for a flat of my own one day. We can't live with Charles for ever . . .'

She thought she saw a momentary look of surprise, discomfort perhaps, on Nick's face, but the moment passed. Perhaps she had been presumptuous.

He kissed her hair and her neck, and soon they were on the

narrow bed where she was sleeping, making love as the morning sunshine streamed in through a gap between the shutters. It was dreamlike for Helena. She had never imagined Nick being in this place with her.

For a while they dozed, his legs carelessly thrown across her. The weight of his limbs meant that she could not move, but she lay there enjoying the feel of his skin on hers.

'Do you have anything in the fridge?' he asked, suddenly stirring.

'Just some milk,' Helena replied. 'But there are a thousand cafés in this city, about thirty just in this neighbourhood.'

Half an hour later, they were strolling through Kolonaki.

'Here,' she said decisively, 'this one.'

'Why this one, out of all the ones we could have picked?' Nick said, with unexpected scorn. 'The others look much nicer.'

'It's where I saw the moon landing,' Helena replied. 'And not one tiny detail has changed. Same television on the wall, same tables, same owner, same waiter, probably even the same coffee machine.'

'Seems a good reason to avoid it,' he snapped. But the waiter was already welcoming them and showing them to a table, so it was too late to go elsewhere. It was the first time Helena had felt such obvious friction between them, and the frostiness seemed at odds with the warm day.

'The coffee . . .' complained Nick. 'It's so bitter.'

Helena said nothing. She was distracted. Coming towards them was somebody she had hoped never to see again. Arsenis Papagiannis. He was smiling, the toothy grin exactly as she remembered.

'My little redhead!' he announced rather proprietorially. 'So many years, but so unchanged!'

For the thousandth time in her life, Helena cursed her hair.

'Nick, this is my Uncle Arsenis,' she said stiffly.

There was a third seat at the table, which Arsenis took without invitation, immediately waving the waiter over.

'I wouldn't order coffee if I were you,' Nick said. 'It's terrible.'

'Can't imagine why you came to this place anyway,' Arsenis said under his breath.

'An iced tea for me,' he instructed the waiter. 'So, little niece, what are you doing back in Athens?'

Helena had no doubt that he knew exactly why she was there. His sarcasm had a bitter edge to it. Was he going to confront her about the inheritance?

'I'm on the way to a dig with Nick,' she said bluntly.

Arsenis shifted his focus to Nick, and it was evident to Helena that Nick was impressed by him. His dapper suit, mother-of-pearl cufflinks, neat hair, the glimpse of an expensive watch, a signet ring on his little finger.

'So, Nick,' he said. 'You're an archaeologist, are you?'

'In that world,' Nick said enigmatically. 'Our dig's down in Nisos. I've introduced Helena to archaeology.'

'Ah, yes. The face that launched a thousand ships. Or just a ferry in your case,' smirked Arsenis, nudging Helena's arm.

'She's sorting out this flat before she joins me.'

'And how's that going?' Arsenis asked her. It was a loaded question, she knew.

'Look,' she said, 'we ought to be going. We wanted to catch a museum before it closes.'

He turned back to Nick. 'I'm an expert in *objets d'art*, as Helena knows,' he said. 'Would you like me to accompany you?'

'I would like that very much,' said Nick. 'Always better to go somewhere with a guide.'

Helena had to hide her fury. From the moment he had sat down, Arsenis had clearly sensed the gap between her and Nick and sought to widen it, simply to spite her. In just a few moments he had built a masculine camaraderie that excluded her.

'Let's go in two minutes, then,' said Arsenis bossily. 'National Archaeological?'

'Spot on,' said Nick.

Helena made the decision not to accompany them. She did not want to spend even half an hour with Arsenis and had no wish to repeat a visit to that museum with him. Let him take Nick, and she would use the time to continue clearing the flat. Nick did not seem to mind at all that they would be apart for a few hours, and given his mood, neither did she.

In a few days' time, she would be with him in Nisos. And there would be no Uncle Arsenis there.

'I'll have him back at your grandparents' flat by five,' Arsenis said. She saw Nick's eyes flit to the gold Rolex as he checked the time.

It annoyed her that Arsenis had pointedly refused to acknowledge the property's new ownership.

The two men got up and left, leaving Helena to pay the bill. On her way back to the flat, Arsenis's flashy red car roared past. She caught a glimpse of Nick's smiling face.

She felt disgruntled, stung that Nick had been rude about her favourite café and had then chosen not to spend the afternoon with her, but she resolved to go home and tackle the room she had been dreading: her grandfather's study.

Bracing herself against the smell when she walked in, she was almost relieved when the desk drawers would not budge, however hard she pulled them. There had been plenty of random keys in the jug, but none of them were the right size for this piece of furniture, which gave her the excuse to put off the task until another time. She began to dispose of more bed linen instead.

Nick returned on the stroke of five. His hours with Arsenis seemed to have brought back his good humour. He waxed lyrical about the museum, all the things that had been explained to him by his expert guide, and the hour they had spent drinking whisky in an elegant hotel bar.

'He's such an interesting, cultured man,' he told her. 'Showed me some great treasures – he has exquisite taste. All that Mycenaean gold.'

Helena said nothing. Her irritation over Arsenis hijacking Nick had subsided. She had spent the time productively, but one day, when the moment was right, she would tell Nick more about Arsenis Papagiannis. For now, sensing that the alcohol might make him volatile, she smiled and listened. He was leaving the next day on the early ferry, so they only had a short time together.

He strolled about the flat, asking her questions about her grandparents, and what she was going to do with the valuables. Clocks? Paintings? Mirrors?

'Everything is going,' she said flatly. His interest in how much it was all worth was starting to annoy her. 'I don't want to keep a single thing.'

Nick nodded and changed the subject, but his questions had left her with a feeling of ill ease.

Chapter Twenty-Eight

Helena was woken at seven in the morning by the touch of Nick's lips on hers.

'I'll see you very soon, *agápi mou*,' he said, stroking her hair, which was spread across the pillow.

'*S' agapó*,' Helena said sleepily. 'I love you.'

She dozed for another half an hour, then got up and left the apartment. The night they had spent together had wiped out any irritation she had felt with Nick. Everything seemed heightened, beautiful and fresh, even the cracked paving stones and some littered sweet wrappers picked up by the breeze. Her footsteps were light.

The only other people in the streets at that time were the refuse collectors, a man sweeping the square, and a couple of café owners wearily rolling up their shutters. She wondered if it showed on her face that she might burst with elation.

Her mission was to note down any shops that might buy some of her grandmother's furniture, and she pressed her nose against the plate glass of one to see what lay beyond the metal grille. There were several pieces similar to hers, and even some oil paintings for sale. She would happily get rid of that grim-faced portrait of her grandfather. She would not even want money for it. So close to the window was she that it began to steam up, and when she suddenly saw movement inside, she felt a little embarrassed. A young man, slim and dark, was making his way towards the door and unlocking it. She had no choice but to wait for him to emerge.

'Can I help you?'

Immaculate in a pressed white shirt and navy trousers, he spoke English without a trace of an accent, obviously assuming from Helena's colouring that she didn't speak Greek.

She mumbled her way through an explanation of having some antiques to sell, and he handed her a card from his wallet with the shop's name and details.

'My sister does the valuations,' he said, clearly wanting to get back to whatever he had been doing. 'I will tell her to expect your call. Your name is?'

'Helena.'

'Helena,' he repeated. 'Irish?'

'No, half Scottish.' She smiled, impressed by his knowledge of Celtic looks.

'Anyway, I'll tell Anna you might call,' he said.

He went back inside, and Helena continued along the road, tucking the card into the pocket of her jeans. At the crossroads, she turned left into a narrower street and saw a bigger shop, also selling antiques but with rather grander items in the window and some Roman statuary on display.

The words *Internationally Renowned Dealers in Objets d'Art and Antiquities* were painted on the window in gold, along with a phone number, which she scribbled down.

She returned to the apartment, eager to get on with clearing it out so that she could leave for Nisos. As she returned from taking more bin liners downstairs, she realised she had forgotten to do anything with her grandmother's Meissen collection, which was still housed in the walnut display cabinet in the drawing room. Tugging in vain at the little crystal doorknobs, she realised that it needed a key, and a search at the bottom of the floral jug soon produced the solution. There was a tiny one, distinctively different from the rest. It turned with a satisfying click and the doors flew open.

Helena knelt on the floor and carefully took out a woman in eighteenth-century costume. She remembered being allowed to hold it when she was a child, but only when she was sitting down with her grandmother hovering around. The only other time she had seen them close to was when Dina cleaned them.

One by one she took the pieces out and placed them carefully on various side tables. They were not really to her taste, but she recalled how much Eleni Papagiannis had loved them. Yiayiá had once told her that each of them had been a gift from her husband, one for every anniversary of their marriage. Helena counted. Fifty-three. How had she tolerated him even for one?

She went out onto the balcony and gazed down at the street below. There was a Friday-lunchtime atmosphere, a palpable sense of anticipation in their air, people already tuning out from work and excited about the hedonism that the weekend would bring.

She called the number on the business card first. The phone was answered by a woman. She was polite and sweetly sympathetic when Helena explained that she was selling her late grandmother's effects.

'I'll happily call in to see them,' she said politely. 'You're not far away. I could come later?'

The second call was picked up by a man. His English was not quite as good as the woman's, but it was adequate. Helena was deterred by his offhand manner, but she wanted at least a second opinion on the value of the things she was selling, so she kept her patience.

'Tell me where you are then,' he said brusquely, 'and I'll see when I can fit this in.'

Helena gave him the address. She was aware of a pause and thought the line had gone dead.

'Hello . . . hello? Are you still there?' she enquired.

'*Nai, nai*. I'm still here. *Sygnómi*. My apologies. Just someone coming into the shop.' He had gone from disinterest to obsequious politeness in the space of a moment. 'In an hour or so, if that suits you.'

It gave Helena a deadline to make sure that the smarter pieces were all polished. She flicked at the surfaces with a duster and paused over the more attractive items of furniture. The swirled patterns made by woodgrain and inlay were works of art in themselves.

At precisely two minutes past two, the buzzer rang. Helena could hear that Manolis had opened the door five floors below, and soon a portly middle-aged man in a pale grey suit emerged from the lift and turned towards her, his hand out. She automatically offered hers, and felt the squeeze of his fingers. He wore a bulky signet ring on one of his pudgy fingers, and his handshake was self-consciously firm, as if to say 'Trust me, I am sincere.'

'Giannis Ligakis,' he said.

He followed her into the apartment and Helena could feel him walking close behind her, almost as if his toes might touch her heels. His aftershave was pungent.

'So, there is a chaise longue, a dining table, chairs, sideboards, occasional tables, various cabinets and cupboards. And in the bedrooms, some ornate bedsteads and side tables. I haven't quite finished emptying things out, but almost.'

'Do you mind if I take some pictures?' he said, interrupting her.

'Feel free,' Helena replied. 'I hope there is enough light. My grandmother liked to keep it quite dark in here.'

She showed him the drawing room first, pointing out the various pieces of furniture, and he jotted down details in a small notebook and then painstakingly took photos from all angles.

He paused by the portrait and stared at it without making notes or taking a photograph.

'That picture is definitely for sale,' she said emphatically.

'I see,' he said, cold eyes meeting hers.

Helena noted very white teeth that were emphasised by his tan, and his slicked-back hair was suspiciously dark. An otherwise dapper appearance was spoiled by the dark patches of sweat that spread beneath his armpits, and she noted that he seemed a little out of breath even walking room to room, his extra weight made it an effort.

She followed him from the drawing room into the bedrooms, and for a moment it felt to Helena as though he was showing her the apartment rather than the other way around. Perhaps most apartments had a similar layout. He must have been to many of them in order to do valuations, she thought.

Without invitation, he marched into her grandfather's study and paused in front of the desk.

'Lovely piece,' he said, pulling at one of the drawers.

'I haven't cleared it yet,' Helena said, standing in the doorway. 'It's a good size, though, isn't it?'

Ligakis smiled, stroking the wood. Helena could not help noticing that he had tiny hands.

Once he had finished in the study, they returned to the drawing room.

'The chaise longue?' she enquired, expecting him to be more interested in that than the ugly desk.

'No one really wants such things now, but I am sure I can get you a price. Even if it's a modest one.'

She could already tell that his comments were part of an act. If he expressed an interest in something, he would be obliged to offer a better price. It was a canny dealer's tactic.

'And what about this bric-a-brac?' he asked, pointing at the porcelain figures with some disdain.

Despite the dismissive nature of his tone and gesture, there was a glint in his eye. He knew as well as she did that the Meissen was valuable. They were not cheap copies.

'Well, I am sure someone might have a collection they'd like to add to, so I'd be happy to have a valuation,' she said.

Ligakis got out a monocle and fixed it into his left eye, then picked up the shepherd and shepherdess to look for the Meissen mark.

'Give me a moment, would you? I'll do some quick calculations,' he said. He took a seat, folded back the spine of his notebook and began to jot down some figures on a blank page.

'Coffee?' Helena said. 'Would you like some coffee while you're doing that?'

He refused her offer with a slight movement of his head.

'I'll just get you some water then,' she said, not waiting for a reply. Even though she did not want him to stay any longer than necessary, she needed an excuse to leave the room in order to escape both the smell of cologne and his patronising manner.

When she went back in, she could see that he had already scribbled down a list. There was a price against each item.

'There are some quite nice things here,' he said. 'I'll be honest with you, though, fashions have changed a bit, so there isn't the market for them that there used to be.'

Helena knew that when people claimed to be honest, they were usually anything but.

'But there are still people in certain parts of Athens who want something a little "presidential", if you see what I mean. What I call embassy-style furniture.'

He slid the paper towards her and she ran her eyes down the prices.

'Those are the best I can do.'

The total for the furniture was one million drachmas. It sounded an enormous sum but was only around ten thousand pounds. It was considerably less than she had expected, and almost seemed an insult to her grandmother, who had loved her elegant home. The highest price was for the walnut display cabinet. As she had already realised, it was the best piece there was.

'That,' he said, 'is a treasure. French. Nineteenth century. I wouldn't be surprised if it had a really good pedigree. Made at the height of the Napoleonic period. An *objet d'art* in itself.'

For the first time, he sounded as if he actually liked antiques. If he didn't, then why was he a dealer?

'And the very ornate clock. I will need to do some research on that. Might need to pop back and have another look.'

Almost as an afterthought, he pointed out the row of Meissen figures.

'I could give you twenty thousand drachmas for those miscellaneous bits and pieces.'

To describe them as 'bits and pieces' insulted her intelligence, and the offer was risible.

'The only thing that would be easy to sell on is that desk. It's a very fine piece of mahogany and everyone needs one. I could have it out of here and sold in the shop by tomorrow. How about a separate price for that? Two hundred thousand? Two fifty? Even in cash if you want?'

Helena found this sudden gush of enthusiasm for the desk as off-putting as his disdain for everything else.

'Well, let me think about it,' she responded. 'I'll call you.'

'Please do,' he said, carefully placing a glossy business card on the dining table.

Just before pressing the button for the lift, he hesitated and then turned around.

'For the bric-a-brac,' he said, 'I could give a little more.'

'Thanks,' said Helena, not giving him the opportunity to say what that 'little more' might be. 'I'll be in touch.'

Wanting the last word to be hers, she shut the door.

Even if the next valuation was half what this man had offered, she would take it. He was so unlikeable and seemed not to realise it. There was nothing about his appearance or manner that suggested he was to be trusted in any way. Apart from anything, he reminded her too much of Uncle Arsenis.

Helena returned to the drawing room to clear away the water glass, and stopped to contemplate the three Meissen ladies who stood as if waiting for an invitation to dance. These beautiful objects had been slighted by that ghastly man and did not deserve to be delivered into his hands.

A while later, the bell went again and she hastened to the door. A very chic woman emerged from the lift.

'Anna Morakis,' she said briskly. 'You met my brother Haris this morning. Thank you for inviting me.'

Helena felt instantly at ease with this woman. She was so unlike the previous dealer. Much younger for a start, in her mid thirties, perhaps, and clearly well educated. Her almost black glossy hair, not one out of place, just touched the shoulder pads of a simple turquoise shift dress, and she had deep brown eyes and thick lashes. Helena silently admired the gold bracelet that spiralled from wrist to elbow like a snake, and noticed that she wore an expensive watch on the other hand. Caramel-coloured court shoes matched the bag that hung from her shoulder. Anna Morakis exuded success in the same measure that Giannis Ligakis had exuded sleaze.

Helena repeated the tour of the apartment, and Anna too made notes. Back in the drawing room, her eyes flickered over the business card that was still lying on the coffee table. The two shops were presumably rivals.

'That's another dealer,' Helena said, trying to cover her embarrassment. 'He came earlier. I thought I should get a second opinion.'

'Of course, Kyría McCloud. That's the sensible thing to do,' Anna responded kindly. 'I suppose you know that Ligakis and General Papagiannis were friends, or at least acquaintances? I couldn't help noticing that portrait of him. Am I right in thinking that he was your grandfather?'

Helena nodded. This woman was both smart and honest.

Ligakis must have known exactly whose apartment he was in but had said nothing.

'He acted as if he had never set foot here before,' she said.

'That doesn't really surprise me,' said Anna Morakis, smiling.

'Why? Why would he do that?'

'I can't say exactly. Your grandfather never came into our shop, but he was such a distinctive figure. Everyone knew who he was.'

The word 'distinctive' was surely a euphemism.

Helena liked this woman, who had visibly admired the pieces she was here to value. She wanted to keep her talking, and delaying her with coffee might be the way to do this.

'Can I make you a drink, Kyría Morakis?'

'That would be so kind, thank you. Nescafé is fine. No sugar,' she said. 'And please call me Anna.'

'And I'm Helena.'

'May I sit?'

Helena was touched by her good manners.

'Please,' she said, drawing out a chair for her visitor. 'I'll be back in a moment.'

Over their coffee, the two women began to chat.

'Didn't your grandfather have a nephew?' Anna asked.

'Yes. Arsenis Papagiannis. He was often here when I used to come and stay as a child.'

'For some while, my father bought things from him,' said Anna. 'It was when I was still at school, and my brother and I used to do our homework in a little back office that had a window onto the shop. We lived above it, but we preferred to be downstairs, because there was always something going on.'

She blew for a second on her coffee to cool it down and then took a sip.

'A bell rang every time someone came in and we always peered through the glass to see who it was. It was impossible not to because the clanging made such a loud noise. We knew all the customers and some of the stranger characters who used to come in to sell things. Sometimes you only saw somebody once and never again, but there were others who were regulars and came in several times a month or even more.'

'Was Arsenis one of those?'

'Yes.'

Helena shifted in her seat. The thought of that man made her feel uncomfortable even now.

'I can't say that any of that helped me to concentrate on my school work,' said Anna. 'But it's how we learned everything about this business. We saw what people brought in. Most of the sellers didn't want to show their possessions, or whatever you call them, in the main part of the shop. They came into the back office where we were sitting. They must have imagined that we were quietly minding our own business, but in reality we were all eyes and ears.'

'Much more interesting than just doing homework!' interjected Helena.

'Yes. And it's funny how invisible you can be as children. Anyway, my father had to assess risk. He had to weigh up the person who was bringing something in, the object they were trying to sell and whether there would be a customer for it.'

'What was the risk?'

Anna smiled. 'Every object, whether it's old, new, beautiful or even ugly, has a life. A starting point, a journey, a story. Whatever you want to call it. Some have places where they really belong, which is different from the location where they find themselves.'

Helena understood what she meant. She recalled the parcels that her grandfather's guests had brought to the apartment. Most of them in inappropriate wrapping. There was always something that had not felt quite right about that.

'The point is,' said Anna, doodling in her notebook, 'there is often something illegal going on with antiques. The object itself is innocent, but the person bringing it in may not be – and you can make much more money if you are prepared to take a risk. I know my father had to make difficult decisions. Perhaps it's the same in any business.

'My father bought a few things that turned out to be stolen goods. He was afraid of naming the source and told the police that he had purchased them from foreigners who hadn't given an address. So obviously it meant the sellers were untraceable. But it meant that my father got stung himself because he had to hand over objects he had paid good money for to the police. I have no doubt that some of the things he bought from Arsenis Papagiannis were not acquired in the way your relative claimed.'

'I'm certain they weren't,' interjected Helena. It was yet another reason to be ashamed of her family.

'Am I speaking out of turn here?' Anna asked, apparently concerned. She was implying that Helena's relative was dishonest, after all.

'No, not at all,' Helena reassured her. 'There was . . . is . . . no love lost between us.'

'As well as using my father to sell on a few things that I am sure were illegal in some way, Arsenis Papagiannis also protected him sometimes. On one occasion when something in the shop came under suspicion, he managed to smooth things over. He persuaded the police to leave my father alone.'

'Sounds a bit mafioso,' Helena commented.

'Shades of it,' Anna agreed. 'And then one day, our father decided that enough was enough. The stress of uncertainty was too much. At heart, he was an honest man, and he had reached the point where he wanted to feel safe, even if he was bringing in less of an income. It meant deciding that he longer wanted to have anything to do with Arsenis Papagiannis and his illegal sources of *objets d'art*. After that, I'm told that Arsenis began to sell everything through Giannis Ligakis' – she motioned to the card on the table – 'and they formed some kind of partnership.'

There was a brief pause.

'All of that was in the past,' said Anna. 'I have told you more than I should have, probably. But my father died some time ago. He made the decision that he was only going to buy and sell very securely provenanced pieces and we have continued with that. We only deal in things that are beyond suspicion. The world of antiquities is full of grey areas, Helena, but we like to stay in the black-and-white zones.'

In a world that was clearly full of shady dealings, Anna seemed to shine with honesty.

'I love my business. I love handling beautiful things. Not the obvious type of beauty, like a perfectly symmetrical vase or a pretty statue. I mean things that tell a story, that tell us who we are. "Beauty is truth",' she added.

'I know that poem so well!' exclaimed Helena. 'It was my mother's favourite. *Ode on a Grecian Urn.*'

In unison, the two women recited the final lines:

> Beauty is truth, truth beauty, That is all
> Ye know on earth, and all ye need to know.

They smiled at one another.

'It's more than just a poem, isn't it?' reflected Helena. 'It feels like something to live by.'

'Definitely,' agreed Anna. 'And I think of those words every day. Even more so when someone brings in a badly faked urn.'

Helena laughed. 'Keats wrote it specially for you!'

'I think he helped me learn how to spot the difference. The genuine article has a beauty that can't be forged.'

Helena got up to fetch some cold water for them both. The windows were wide open and welcoming in an uncomfortably hot breeze.

'*Káfsona!*' said Anna, fanning herself with her hand. 'We have a heatwave.'

She stood up, her attention caught by the rows of Meissen close by.

'This is such a beautiful collection!' she declared with real appreciation.

Helena watched her turn one of the pieces to look at the underside, knowing that she was looking for the crossed sword symbol.

'Magnificent!' she declared. 'And worth a fortune.'

'I didn't get that impression from Ligakis,' Helena told her.

Anna shot her a glance, and Helena laughed.

'I think I've already realised that I should take everything he said with a pinch of salt.'

The moment they had recited the lines of Mary McCloud's favourite poem together, Helena knew that she could trust this woman. How someone defined beauty said so much about them. It was as true of Arsenis Papagiannis as anyone.

Anna went back into the dining room and sat down at the table.

'I've done a few estimates for the furniture,' she said. 'And the clocks. Those in particular are worth a lot. Your grandparents had very expensive taste.' She glanced at her notebook. 'Two million drachma for the furniture. Five hundred thousand drachmas for the clocks.' She looked up. 'Are you certain you want to sell everything?'

'Absolutely. Including the Meissen.'

Helena was adamant. She felt more determined than ever to rid the apartment of these antiques. French, Italian, rococo, baroque, real or fake. She did not care. They had belonged to Stamatis Papagiannis. It occurred to her that she should even give the proceeds away.

'Each Meissen piece will need an individual valuation. But I do want you to think about it for a day or two,' said Anna, who knew that her clients often had a change of heart.

'I'm leaving in a few days,' said Helena, her thoughts flitting to Nick. 'It's a bit soon to get things collected, but I know I won't change my mind.'

She ran her eyes down the numbers, gut instinct allowing her to trust this young woman. In any case, these prices were considerably more than Ligakis had offered.

'Well, whenever you are ready to decide, we can make arrange—'

'I nearly forgot,' Helena interrupted. 'There's something else, a big mahogany desk. Have you got time to take a quick look?'

Anna followed her into the study.

'What a gloomy room,' she commented.

'Ligakis reckoned this was extremely valuable,' Helena told her.

'Really?' Anna responded. 'It's reasonable wood, but there's absolutely no market for huge desks like this any longer. Nobody wants a thing like this in their home, and offices prefer modern designs. If you don't mind me saying, it's hideous. I wouldn't give you two thousand drachmas for it.'

'Oh,' said Helena, calculating that this was about twenty pounds. 'That's odd. He was willing to pay a quarter of a million.'

'What!' Anna was incredulous.

'I don't even have the keys to the drawers,' said Helena.

'Perhaps you should sell it to him, then,' laughed Anna. 'But I really don't understand it. It's not even in good condition.'

As ever when she was in her grandfather's study, Helena could not wait to get out of the room. She led Anna into the hallway.

'Well, it was lovely to meet you.'

'Likewise. And even if you decide not to part with anything at all, it would be nice to have a coffee whenever you are in Athens.'

'I'd love that,' replied Helena, giving Anna a wave as she disappeared into the lift.

Helena's anticipation was building. Soon she would be with Nick. She was aching to be out of this flat and was counting the hours till she could leave.

She selected one of her grandmother's records, noting that it had been released in 1975. It must have been the last one Eleni Papagiannis ever bought: *50 Chronia Rebetiko Tragoudi, 50 Years of Rebetiko Songs.* She put it on at maximum volume so that she could hear Dalaras's voice in the bedroom, and started packing. Then she had a long shower, watching the dust of the day gathering around her feet as she lathered her mass of hair.

In the briefest moment of silence between songs, she heard the phone ringing. Her father, perhaps, or even Nick. She wrapped herself in a towel and stepped carefully across the tiled floor towards the hallway.

'Helena! What are you doing?'

It was Mihalis. She could just about hear him over the loud music.

'Showering. Packing,' she shouted.

'You can't spend your last night in Athens doing that. You're coming out. Get dressed. We're picking you up in fifteen minutes.'

'Mihalis! I can't!'

He had gone. Helena had heard a note of real excitement in his voice.

The social life of this city was irresistibly spontaneous, and she was lucky to have been adopted into it by such a welcoming crowd. Mihalis was right. It was her last evening here, and how was she going to spend it? Sitting under her grandfather's portrait?

She hastily rinsed her hair and put on a flowing purple cheesecloth dress with bright emerald trim. It was slightly bohemian in style and she knew it suited her. She felt right. Everything that was about to come seemed thrilling and desirable. Anticipation was sweet.

Chapter Twenty-Nine

As planned, Mihalis rang on her bell at six to let her know he was waiting outside, and with her hair still damp, Helena tore down the stairs.

'*Geia sou, Elenáki!*'

Mihalis kissed her on one cheek, Panos pecked her on the other.

'We've got a surprise for you,' said Panos cryptically.

'What is it? Tell me!'

'You have to wait. We promise you won't be disappointed.'

The three of them walked down towards Hermou. They were meeting a few more of their *paréa* in Plateia Agias Irinis before the surprise and detoured through nearby Monastiraki.

In the back streets of the area, a few stallholders had laid out their wares. It was a flea market where everything from surgical instruments from the 1920s to military buttons and old radios could be found. All of these things had been the discarded junk of someone clearing a home, just like her, and every object evoked a feeling – fear, sorrow, romance, nostalgia or simply curiosity.

Mihalis and Panos were looking for art deco lamps to decorate the home they were planning to set up together, but were currently rifling through an old chest full of antique keys.

'Look at this one,' Mihalis called out. 'In a dark and haunted castle . . .'

'. . . a maiden screamed as the door to the dungeon slammed behind her,' Panos finished.

Helena laughed, picking up an old photo album packed with small scalloped-edged photographs from another age. Carefully turning its pages, she saw dozens of unnamed people who were just ghosts now, their faces mingled with discarded crockery and candlesticks. Chipped coffee pots and tarnished fire irons were their only friends.

'*Éla, Elenáki!*' said Panos. 'I can see you dreaming!'

'We've got things to do, places to go tonight,' coaxed Mihalis, taking Helena's hand and jolting her back to reality.

'To be honest, I've had more than enough of old stuff today,' she said.

As they walked, they passed a bar where somebody was belting out a song of love and rejection.

'*Skyládika!*' said Panos scornfully, using the slang name given to popular singers with voices no better than dogs.

'He loves it really,' Mihalis explained to Helena. 'That music is as much part of his psyche as a film by Angelopoulos.'

'It's true. They're both quintessentially Greek, that's why. Culturally equal,' declared Panos.

Helena enjoyed the idea that these opposites truly belonged to the same whole.

It was a short walk to where they were meeting the others. They were mostly the same crowd from the other night, so no introductions were needed this time. Helena already felt like one of them.

In the heat, her hair had dried into a mass of ringlets, each one as tight as a corkscrew. Against the pallor of her skin and the purple dress, she invited compliments from everyone, friends and strangers. She could not remember this ever happening in her entire life. Perhaps she should abandon all attempts to try and tame her locks.

'We need to be off,' said Mihalis. 'We're going to a football stadium.'

'Football?' Helena laughed. 'I hate football!'

'Shame! No choice. Are you okay to go with Eftasia in her car? She can take six.'

Helena nodded, increasingly intrigued.

While most of the group paired up to go on scooters or hailed taxis, Helena and a few others wound their way through the back streets until Eftasia found the place where she had parked. Helena was surprised to see that the car was a shiny three-wheeled vehicle. It hardly looked big enough to take two people, but they all piled in: two on the front passenger seat, four in the back. The engine choked to a start, and Eftasia pulled away from the kerb and crunched into second gear, steering confidently round corners, all the while talking over her shoulder, even holding hands at times with her boyfriend.

'Do you like my car, Helena?' she shouted over the noise. 'It's my father's old Alta 200! Ten years old and still goes like a dream.'

For its size and the number of passengers, the car could move surprisingly fast, but Eftasia's insistence on being nose to tail with the vehicle in front terrified Helena.

They arrived after all the others, who were already gathered outside the stadium. People were streaming through the gates. Thousands of them. Then Helena saw a face she knew well. Giorgos Dalaras. There were huge posters of him at the entrance.

'Dalaras! *Den to pistévo*,' she murmured. 'I don't believe it.'

She was completely overwhelmed. She had never imagined this, and immediately thought of her grandmother. It would have been her dream to see Dalaras live.

One of their group collected their tickets from a booth, and then they all filed into the stadium. The enormous space was packed. Helena followed the others to a reserved section, where they had seats with a clear view of the stage. It turned out that Eftasia's cousin was a friend of one of the backing musicians. A couple of their group went to find drinks, and soon they were all making toasts: for someone's saint's day, congratulations for a new job, a book of poetry just published, a belated birthday.

Around her Helena saw people of every age, not only bohemian youths like them, denim clad with long hair (both boys and girls), but also older people dressed up for a special occasion, men in jackets and women in chiffon blouses and their baptism best. They were all united by the same objective: to share the thrill of seeing a legend.

Half an hour or more passed. On the stage, men were coming and going, carrying equipment, unravelling wires, setting down various instruments, plugging in microphones and lights, arranging chairs. By the time they had finished, it was dark.

All the stage lights were suddenly lowered, and immediately the noisy chatter of eighty thousand people ceased. A ripple of excitement ran through the stadium, followed by silence. The hush seemed impossible for such a closely packed mass of humanity.

Then, out of the darkness, came the sound of a lone violin.

When a shaft of light fell on a slim figure simply dressed in slacks and shirt, the crowd went wild. His mouth close to the microphone, he began to sing in a voice of honey sweetness that filled the air. There was no comparison between this and the crackly version Helena had been listening to in the apartment. The sound was pure and melodious.

After the first song, the crowd were on their feet and Dalaras had to wait many minutes to acknowledge the applause, cheers and whistles of appreciation. With humility, he expressed his disbelief and thanks that so many people had come.

Helena was so grateful to be one of them and to be so close that she could see the creases round his eyes when he smiled.

Then he raised his arms in the air.

'Like a V for victory,' Helena said into Mihalis's ear.

'Or a «v» for νίκη in Greek,' he smiled.

Lights now went up across the stage to reveal a bank of musicians behind the singer, whose mane of glossy hair shone under their glare as he began a more melancholic tune. Hit after hit followed. The crowd knew every number and gave each one a more ecstatic reception than the one before. In most, Dalaras accompanied himself on one of the many stringed instruments he could play. He was tireless, and the quality and clarity of his voice never wavered.

Helena found herself singing along to the choruses and swaying in time to the music along with the others, entering wholeheartedly into the spirit of the night. Mihalis threaded his arm through hers, and if any doubt had remained, she now knew for certain that her friends placed no blame on her for the sins of her grandfather.

'*Anatrichiázeis?*' he asked, enquiring if her hairs were standing on end.

Helena did not need to answer.

An hour or so in, Dalaras took a short break and the backing musicians played alone. Against the noise of excited chatter, Panos explained each instrument in turn to Helena. Apart from a guitar, there was the *bouzoúki*, a long-necked *laoúto*; the *tzourás* and the *baglamás*, smaller versions of the *bouzoúki*; and the *oud*, another plucked stringed instrument but notoriously harder to play as it was without frets. Other instruments included the occasionally harsh-sounding *klaríno*, a kind of clarinet, and a *santoúri*, which was similar to a zither but with delicate sticks to hit the strings. Helena tried to take it all in, but her head was spinning with music, alcohol and heat.

When Dalaras returned to the stage, she immediately recognised the opening chords of '*Malamaténia Lógia*', and was able to sing along to parts she remembered. With Mihalis on one side and Eftasia on the other, they swayed as they sang. It was a sombre moment, a moment of memorial.

From then on, the mood lightened. Guest stars now entered from the wings and duetted with Dalaras. The crowd recognised all of them, and cheered and applauded each time a new one appeared. It was an evening they wanted to last for ever, a party they would never forget.

Music, sentiment and nostalgia mingled with the trauma stamped on the population by the brutal politics of previous decades. Several hours later, as fireworks exploded and flowered in the sky above them, they knew it was coming to an end.

A few people had brought flowers to toss onto the stage. Red and white carnations flew through the air.

Blood and peace, thought Helena. This country seemed to oscillate between the two.

It took some time to exit, but eventually they all spilled out onto the street. Helena saw somebody in the crowd she could not place at first. With neat facial features and a stature not unlike Dalaras's, he was walking with a strikingly beautiful woman who had glossy, well-behaved hair that reached her waist. She suddenly realised it was the brother of Anna, the woman from the shop. The couple disappeared into the mêlée.

Helena held on to Mihalis's sleeve to avoid being separated and found herself being led to a stall selling souvlaki. Only then did she realise it was daylight. In her whole life she had not seen anything like it. The Greek dawn arrived with a misty, ghostly light. Nothing was familiar. Everything was beautiful, she thought, tearing cubes of succulent meat off a stick with her teeth.

'What a night,' she mumbled, juice running down her chin. She could think of no other words.

Mihalis and Panos were next to her. This pair, who never seemed to tire of debate, wanted to know what Helena thought. 'For some people here, he is just a handsome singer,' said Panos. 'For others he's a hero.'

'Can't he be both?' asked Helena. 'Art and politics seem totally wrapped up with each other here, so why not?'

She struggled to think of even one popular British singer with any kind of political message. There was punk, but it was relatively limited in appeal. It might have been angry, but would her aunt in Scotland be listening to it? Then there was 'Another Brick in the Wall', definitely a protest song, but even Pink Floyd did not have the broad appeal of Dalaras, across every generation and back into the past. Perhaps there had simply not been enough suffering or risk to life in Britain. It seemed to Helena that it was this that had inspired the range and depth of music that existed here.

It was 6 a.m. by the time she reached Kolonaki. Mihalis and Panos had brought her back in a taxi, and they wearily said their goodbyes and made promises about meeting again soon. Helena would be back after the dig.

She only had a little time before leaving for the ferry. Her hair and clothes stank of smoke, so she had a speedy shower and went to bed for a couple of hours.

A line from one of her favourite songs of the night circled hypnotically in her head: 'I think of nothing, only you.'

Very soon, she was asleep.

Chapter Thirty

Helena's arrival on Nisos felt similar to the previous time. It was like coming late and as a stranger to a party where everyone else was old friends.

When she got off the ferry, she went straight to the taverna, where the group were just finishing their evening meal.

She was happy that some of them remembered her from the year before and she was warmly greeted by Professor Carver, who seemed to have aged considerably. Nick took her round to meet the people she didn't recognise. The only person to whom he did not introduce her was a girl with fairy blonde hair and pale blue eyes. Helena picked up her name in any case: Brigitte. She was French.

'Elpida?' she asked. 'Isn't she here this time?'

'No, sadly she couldn't make it. But you're in a group with some cool people. And our quarters are different this time,' said Nick triumphantly. 'I was given one of the rooms in the guest house. Promotion. And it's a double.'

Helena smiled. It was typical of Nick to have charmed his way into better accommodation, and she had to admit that she had not enjoyed sleeping in a dormitory, not least because she wanted to share his bed. The romanticism of sex in the olive grove had worn thin.

'It was worth sharing cigars with the professor,' he said with a grin.

'So it wasn't for your archaeological expertise?' she joshed.

Nick effortlessly slung Helena's rucksack over one shoulder, took her hand and led her towards the other side of the village, where his room was situated.

As they walked, she told him about her last couple of days in Athens.

'Do you have to sell the flat?'

'I love Athens,' she said. 'But that place is full of my grandfather's spectre. Maybe when it's cleared of everything he ever touched, I'll feel different.'

He was interested only in how much it was worth. Had the furniture been valued? She gave vague answers, because she really did not know.

In the first few weeks, they went for night swims, sometimes with other people, sometimes just the two of them. The water was as warm as a bath, and Nick and Helena swam out as far as they dared in the darkness. Nick often held her and kissed her passionately in the depths before they returned to shore.

For the first time in her life, Helena experienced the phenomenon of phosphorescence. Bright flashes of light seemed to jump up from the sea as they splashed through the waves. It seemed supernatural, but as they dried off on the beach and watched it happening in front of them, she explained that it was created when the atoms on the surface absorbed light energy and then emitted some of it as a different colour of light.

'My beautiful scientist,' said Nick, kissing her wet shoulder. '*S' agapó.*'

As in the previous year, Helena was allocated to a team working in a different area of the dig, so she did not see Nick from morning until dinner. At least sharing a room meant that they could be close for a few hours, and most nights they made love.

Helena noticed that the great sense of optimism with which they had departed the summer before had waned. Now she heard several of the archaeologists complaining that the number of finds was disappointing. They had hoped for more from an ancient cemetery, but all they had uncovered were some pottery fragments and pyxes, lidded vessels, plus many practical items such as knives and tweezers.

Nick had confirmed this to Helena on her first day. 'Everyone's pretty disillusioned with the excavation,' he said. 'Might as well not be here.'

Maybe it was boredom that had driven him to visit Athens, she thought.

There were different theories for the lack of finds. Some people were saying that the island must have been poorer than they had at first thought; others suggested that someone had already looted these graves and done a good job of covering up their crime.

One night during her third week, they had just fallen asleep when there was a rumbling. Helena and Nick clung to each other as the earth shook. There were several progressively more extreme tremors. Helena sat up.

'Come on, Nick! We have to get outside,' she said. 'My grand-mother always told me that. In case the ceiling falls in.'

As she got up, the floor was vibrating and she fell back onto the bed.

'Look, before the next big one we have to be out of that door.'

A picture of a fishing boat was now hanging at an angle on the wall, and a glass on the small table in the corner smashed onto the floor.

They both staggered towards the door, clutching on to furniture as they went.

There were many others outside, everyone similarly dressed in underclothes and T-shirts, looking vulnerable and uncertain. About thirty of them had gathered in an open space just beyond the build-ings, and Helena noticed that Nick went straight to Brigitte to comfort her. She seemed to have been particularly scared, and he did not leave her side for some time.

After a few hours in which some of them tried to doze and others spent the night talking, morning came. The tremors seemed to have stopped, so everyone hurried into their accommodation to get dressed, and re-emerged ready for the day.

News circulated that the earthquake had measured just over a five on the Richter scale and had caused considerable damage to one of the villages on Nisos. Fortunately nobody had been badly injured, but when they reached the excavation site, the archaeologists could see that the ground had been significantly disturbed by the earth movement. This could set them back many days.

Helena admitted to herself that she did not share the disappointment at the loss of time. The reason she was here was to be near the man she loved, and each day seemed to bring them closer in every way.

Soon afterwards, her team moved into a new area of the excavation site. Professor Carver had noticed with his watery but sharp eyes that the earthquake had created a fissure in one stretch of ground, and he wanted them to work close to it. Under his watchful gaze, they began their work. The professor had recently celebrated his ninetieth birthday, so nobody objected to the fact that he was not bent double in the sunshine. Even in the shade, his wisps of silver hair were stuck to his face with perspiration.

They began carefully and meticulously to dust away the layers in their allocated patch of ground. A few hours later, one of the more experienced archaeologists among them had made good progress down to a level of nine inches or so from the surface. This was when he saw something that aroused his interest. He stopped and went to find the professor, who was sitting under a tree, ready to inspect and comment on anything that was found, however small or insignificant.

Along with all the others, Helena paused to watch as the old man made his way across the uneven ground to the place under scrutiny. Even though he used a stick, he was very agile for his age. Many others downed tools and gathered around.

Words were exchanged between a small group of them, and then the professor watched as some additional layers were smoothed away and something distinctly paler than the reddish earth began to emerge. For a while they used the smallest of brushes to sweep away the final traces of soil. One of the students then stepped aside to allow the professor space to come into the pit, where he eased himself down onto his knees. He reached into the cavity and with both hands lifted something out. All heads leaned in, while those behind formed a circle and craned their necks to see what the fuss was about.

They had all seen fragments of the small human figures that had been found on other islands, either in museums or books, and it was everyone's dream to find something similar here. A whole *eidólio*, as Helena had seen when she was with her mother, was in their wildest dreams.

Whatever the object was, it was still covered in soil, and the old man used his big, clumsy fingers to wipe some of it away. One of the students passed him a brush so that he could clean it more efficiently, and soon he was ready to display it. With the flourish of an actor triumphantly raising an Academy Award, he held it aloft for all to see.

Helena tried not to be disappointed. Even from a few yards away, it did not look very thrilling. He had found the middle section, from breasts to pubic bone, of a Cycladic figurine, very chipped and eroded. The whole piece was no more than five inches long.

The news quickly circulated, and the archaeologists from every area of the site put down their tools and gathered to see what had happened. Helena spotted Nick and made her way towards him. She wanted to be by his side, but so, it seemed, did Brigitte. The French girl was beginning to feel ever present, Helena noticed.

The professor's rheumy old eyes seemed more watery than ever. Though his face was mostly concealed in the shadow of a brimmed hat, Helena could see droplets of water rolling down his cheeks.

Nick insisted later that it was sweat, but she was certain he was wrong.

That night, over dinner, the professor delivered a short speech.

'I will happily confess to you all that the piece of figurine we found today gives the past few years of this excavation new meaning. This is not to belittle all the other discoveries we have made. All the bone fragments, seeds, fossils and sherds contribute to the bigger picture. But even a section of one of these iconic figures is what I have hoped for and suggests that there might be much more to come. Every one of you here has contributed to its discovery. Thank you all, so much.'

Once more his cheeks were damp. When Helena looked around, she could see that there were many others who felt equally emotional. To find a piece of something, a fragment, however small, was always uplifting.

The next few days confirmed that the new area had been a burial place of some importance. Microscopic fragments of more figures, some feet and a nose (how did they know? Helena wondered), were put into baskets and taken away for analysis and photography, but as the weeks passed, nothing bigger was found. There was, though, a constant flow of other prized objects and fragments: some carved marble doves, a lidded marble pot, and painted vases. Compared with the previous weeks, discoveries came thick and fast.

In spite of the excitement, Helena was always happy when the midday break came. She needed to stretch her aching back for ten minutes and yearned to be out of the sun's glare for a while. Even with constant application of suncream, her pale legs and hands were burnt.

In the final week of their stay, she could not help noticing that Nick always arrived at the refreshment area with Brigitte. They were in the same group, and their heads seemed constantly close in intimate conversation, provoking jealousy that Helena found hard to control. For this single reason, she would be glad when the dig was over. Nick's camaraderie with the professor gave him an excuse for coming late to their room, but she noticed that he did not always bring a whiff of cigars with him. One night as he climbed into bed and took her in his arms, she was aware of a floral scent. Helena did not even own any perfume. The following night, pretending to be asleep when he returned, she observed him through half-closed eyes. This time, she could see there was dirt all over his T-shirt.

On the very last evening, there was a huge celebration, with wine and *tsípouro* flowing like water, and towards the end of the meal, someone began a chant that soon caught alight:

'Byron! Nikos! Byron! Nikos!'

With a convincing display of modesty, Nick rose from his seat and pulled out his battered copy of Byron.

> Daughter of Jove! in Britain's injured name,
> A true-born Briton may the deed disclaim.
> Frown not on England; England owns him not:
> Athena, no! thy plunderer was a Scot.

He did not read all two hundred lines of *The Curse of Minerva*, but enough to fire the audience and to remind them of Elgin's removal of the sculptures from the Parthenon. As far as Helena remembered, Elgin's life had ended in relative penury and misery, so perhaps a curse did have this power.

That night, the dancing and drinking went on into the early hours. Helena tried to ignore Nick's behaviour with some of the other girls, telling herself it was harmless flirtation with people he would never see again, girls who lived in the US, France, Holland, Germany and several other countries. Every so often, he came across to where she sat with her digging group, to check she was having a good time, and she was reassured. In little more than a day's time, they would be back in London, living together in Charles's house, and she would have him to herself.

On the final morning, just as they were about to leave for the ferry, he popped out to buy cigarettes from the kiosk. Helena did a last-minute check of the room, looking under the bed and pulling out drawers to make sure that nothing was left behind. She noticed that one of her favourite T-shirts was still on the drying rack in the bathroom and rolled it up. It was still damp, so she stuffed it down the side of her rucksack. Her hand encountered something solid. All her books were in her leather satchel, so she was puzzled.

One item at a time, she pulled out her towel, some long-sleeved shirts, her patchwork wraparound skirt and her underwear. Then came a T-shirt that seemed to be wrapped around something hard. When she unrolled it, a dirty object fell into her hands.

'Oh my God. No . . .' She was almost too shocked to breathe.

Trembling, she held it with both hands.

It was a figurine. Complete, perfect. At least fourteen inches in height, much taller and slimmer than the one she had seen in Ammos with her mother, the neck longer and the head slightly tilted, as if lifted to the sky. Biscuit-coloured, the marble felt warm, almost alive, and Helena was spellbound by it, for a moment simply staring at the beauty that lay in her hands.

She had read that when they were first made, various features on these figurines had been painted. Where the paint had eroded, the surface of the marble had been left smooth and pale. Now the ghosts of these sightless eyes seemed to stare back into hers.

'What am I going to do with you?' she whispered.

Just for a fraction of a second, she imagined possessing her, living with her, keeping her on a shelf by her side. Though she was utterly horrified at what Nick had done, confronting something of such antiquity in close proximity was intoxicating. She was horrified, and yet mesmerised.

Suddenly, reality returned with the sound of the door latch behind her. It was Nick. He immediately noticed that her things were strewn across the bed.

'Helena! Come on! Why have you unpacked?' he said snappily,

grabbling his own holdall. 'The ferry is only ten minutes from docking and everyone else is down there waiting.'

Then she turned around.

He saw what she was holding and froze.

'Why?' she said quietly, looking at him. It was the only word that came into her head.

Nick's face crumpled. It was the expression of a child caught red-handed scrumping an apple. He looked ready to cry.

'I did it for us. I wanted us to be able to afford a place of our own to live. Somewhere for just the two of us.'

At first he made attempts to win her over. He was gentle, conciliatory, logical even. The idea, though, that this theft was motivated by a desire to buy a home for them was unconvincing, especially as he knew she would soon have the proceeds from Kolonaki.

'Forgive me, *pouláki mou.*'

He had so often won her round with similarly sweet terms of endearment. But not this time. His entreaties were empty. They deserved no more than the blank expression she gave him in return.

'Don't be angry!' he pleaded. 'You must try and understand . . .'

She shook her head in admonition and saw his mood change instantaneously. He leaned back by just an inch or two, no longer on the defensive, and then attacked.

'What do you want me to do with it, then?' he shouted into her face. 'Put it back?' As he said this, he snatched the figurine from her hands and waved it around in the air. 'Can you steal something when nobody even knows it exists in the first place?' he demanded. 'Nobody saw it. Just me. *I* found it. Is that really theft?'

Helena did not answer. She felt a preternatural calm descend on her and turned her back on him. Slowly she began putting her belongings back in her rucksack.

This gesture of defiance, along with her silence, seemed to drive Nick to even greater anger, and when she eventually turned around, he thrust the figurine towards her chest, viciously digging it into her ribs.

'You put it back then! Go on, *you* take it! Go and rebury it and let someone else dig it up,' he screamed at her.

'Nick,' she implored, fearful of this Mr Hyde that she had never known existed.

'Someone else can put it in their pocket instead. But you won't care about that, will you? You won't give a damn! It's fine for you, you're an heiress now, but I'm just a lodger in a friend's house! I want my share of privilege! I want some kind of respect in this world!'

His anger and bitterness were not the only things this outburst revealed. Another was how much he was driven by money. Helena's shock was deepening.

'Go on! Take it! Take it! Put it back!' he ranted. 'You go and put it back!'

In an attempt to stop him jabbing at her chest, Helena grabbed the figurine, and for a moment she held the head and he the feet. They were like two children with a doll, ready to tear it apart rather than let the other one take possession.

Then suddenly Nick released his grip.

Helena was unprepared, and toppled backwards, bashing her temple on the bed and landing hard on the stone tiles. Her head and the figurine's simultaneously met the floor.

There was a moment of darkness before the light returned and she struggled to get up. Dazed, it took her a second to notice the parts of the statue lying scattered all around her. There were uneven breaks between the feet, legs and torso, but the head looked as if it had been guillotined, so neatly was it split from the rest.

Nick's anger was fully directed against her now. He pointed at the pieces.

'Look what you've done!' he shrieked. 'Christ, Helena! Look what you've *done*!'

Quaking at this renewed attack, Helena managed to get up, rubbing at the side of her head. For a few seconds she could only hear a ringing in her ears.

She looked again at the lumps of marble lying on the floor.

'Oh my God . . .' she said, dry-mouthed.

'You stupid, stupid cow!' screamed Nick. 'You stupid fucking *bitch*!'

Helena felt as if she had murdered something. It was *she* who had dropped it. It was *her* fault. She had never seen anything more beautiful, or broken, and worst of all, it was almost five thousand years old, created before the Parthenon, before the Pyramids, before almost anything else considered as art.

The two of them stood, as still as statues themselves, staring down at the floor. Any passing thought of reburying this looted object had gone. Both of them knew that even if it had been a possibility before, the freshness of such breaks in the marble would be instantly detected if it was rediscovered.

It was Nick who broke the silence.

'Are you going to take her back now!' he screamed into her face, his angry spittle splashing onto her lips.

Helena's guilt vanished. She felt only scorn as she looked him in the eyes. She no longer saw Nicholas or Nick or Nikos, or even Jason, for that matter. She simply saw a man she hated.

She watched him scrambling about on his knees, collecting the pieces. He looked like a miser picking up small coins he had dropped in the street, pathetic and desperate.

She had no idea whether he was going to bury them somewhere new, sell them, or hand them over to an island local. The worst scenario was that he might throw them into the sea and they would be lost for ever.

Through the open window, they both heard the sound of the ferry's horn, signalling that it was leaving the port. It was too late to run for it now, and the next one would not be until the following day. It seemed to Helena like the least of her problems.

Saying nothing, Nick threw the fragments into his bag, then opened the door and strode out, slamming it behind him.

Feeling hot and sick, Helena went into the shower room to splash herself with cold water. She had to lean on the sink to steady herself, and stared at her face in the mirror above it. There was a crack down the middle of the glass that distorted her features and made her look ghoulish and lopsided. A few moments later, nausea overcame her, and she vomited copiously, retching again and again.

A while later, she got herself back to the bed to lie down. She ran her fingers over her face. An egg-sized lump had formed above her temple.

Eventually, as the pain subsided, she fell asleep.

The following morning, she woke full of rage. It was an emotion she had never felt before. It was even stronger than love.

Chapter Thirty-One

Helena went alone to the port, her head still throbbing from the fall.

She spotted a few of the senior archaeologists who had stayed on an extra day to plan their schedule for publishing the excavation reports. She kept her distance. She did not want to be seen with this swelling on her head and a graze down the side of her face. They would ask questions. In any case, she wanted solitude more than company. She needed space to think. There was no doubt that her relationship with Nick had ended. She felt she had experienced the shock of a sudden death, even if everything seemed hazy today through the aura of a worsening migraine and mild concussion.

Pulling her cap down as low as she could, she hung back, allowing the other foot passengers to board ahead of her. Before planting her rucksack in a rack, she removed a few things from the side pocket. She wanted her notebooks for the journey.

Spotting more faces she recognised in the lounge, she chose a seat on deck as far away from anyone she knew as possible. After an hour or so, needing to stretch her legs, she saw through the window that Nick had joined the group. She felt sick.

He had a canvas bag casually slung over his shoulder and the air of someone without a care in the world. Now that she had seen beneath the mask, how fake seemed his smiles and laughter. She wondered if the figurine fragments were inside the bag, just a few inches from the professor's face. For a moment she imagined herself running over, grabbing it and tipping the contents out onto the table in front of the unsuspecting academics.

She sat down again. Not only had this love ended without warning, but she was leaving the translucent Aegean light behind, that glorious canopy of blue under which they had been living. The first hour of the journey was on a calm sea, but as they headed out into open waters, the size of the waves increased and the dizzier she became. Fumes and fury were a perfect recipe for nausea.

She sat on deck in a plastic chair, her head in her hands, and several times clung to the railings before throwing up over the side. She was both ashamed and embarrassed, but even more so when a father and his young son pointedly moved away.

Even the water she sipped at tasted of metal, and each time the ferry lurched forward, she heaved. It was a journey that seemed to last for ever. On the way out it had taken three hours, but they pitched and rocked for many more on the return journey. More than five hours after embarking, Rafina came into view.

As the giant anchor chains were dropped and the ferry docked, Helena's relief from nausea was instant. Only a sense that a stone sat in her belly remained, and the sea could not be blamed for that. For a short while, she remained in her seat. Cleaners had already boarded and were sweeping the debris on the deck, picking up plastic cups and hosing cigarette butts into a corner. One of them stopped in front of her and leaned on her broom. She muttered something and pointed at a clock. There was no mistaking the message. Before long, the boat would be leaving again.

Helena got to her feet and went to retrieve her rucksack. It was the only one still on the rack. Before going down the stairs to the exit, she looked over the railings at the back and saw the merging of two crowds, those leaving and those waiting to board.

As everyone shuffled forward to get off the boat, she spotted the top of Nick's head. His distinctive blond hair caught the light in the throng of passengers spreading out on the quayside, greeting relatives, hugging friends and hurrying for various buses that were drawing up, and she saw that he was with a young couple.

It was no surprise to see him climb into the same taxi. She knew he would have spent the journey working out how he could get a free ride to the airport, and befriending strangers came naturally to him. Her vision was blurred by her migraine, so she told herself it was in her imagination, but she was sure another blonde had joined the trio, one who reminded her of Brigitte. Two days ago, she would not have had such a cynical thought. But when the figurine smashed, so did the spell of infatuation. In the space of a moment, all his charms had become his flaws.

Safe in the knowledge that she would not bump into him, she hoisted her bag onto her shoulders, checked her wallet for some drachmas and felt the reassuring shape of her passport. All she wanted now was to be home. Missing the ferry the previous day had scuppered her plan to spend a final night in Athens.

Confronted by chaos and confusion at the nearby bus station, she sat for a moment on a bench as buses came and went in every direction, belching out diesel fumes in clouds of black smoke. She was desperately thirsty, and a solitary Polo mint in the pocket of her shorts was a welcome find now that her flask of water was empty.

Many travellers were at a complete loss trying to find buses to their destinations, and she was happy that her Greek allowed her to help them, translating the place names on the front. Eventually she found one marked *Aeroliménas*. If she didn't catch this one, there was every chance she would miss the plane.

There was only one seat free. It was right at the back and her nausea soon returned, exacerbated by the cigarette smoke that enveloped her. An old man opened the window a little to let it escape, but still it hung heavily in the air.

It was early October. Even though she shut her eyes, a sharp blaze of sunlight flared through the window and penetrated her eyelids like a razor. She badly needed an aspirin.

There was still one obstacle to face. Nick would be on the plane. They had booked together, and their seats would be adjacent.

The girl at the Olympic desk was helpful when she asked if she could change to a different row. Her English was beautiful. Just shy of perfect. Shakespearean almost.

'Of course. If you are happy to accept a seat in the area designated for smokers, we can welcome you in row twenty-nine. To give you accommodation there would afford us great pleasure.'

There would be more fumes, but Helena gratefully accepted. It was at least fifteen rows away from where Nick would be sitting, and for a four-and-a-half-hour flight, she would happily pay the price of asphyxiation rather than sit anywhere close to him.

The immaculate mask of the check-in girl did not drop even when Helena handed over her filthy rucksack to be weighed. The young woman handed back her ticket with a smile.

'Is there anything more I can do for you?'

'I don't suppose,' said Helena, shyly, 'you have any painkillers?'

'Let me see, madam,' she said, bending down to rummage in her own bag.

A moment later, she was holding her hand out, two white pills on her palm.

'*Kaló taxídi*,' she said. 'Bon voyage. And I hope you will choose Olympic again in the future.'

Helena nodded with gratitude. She had badly needed this small gesture of kindness.

Once through passport control, she realised that passengers were already queuing to board the flight. Her heart beat furiously as she looked anxiously about her. Any taxi was likely to have arrived an hour or more before the bus. Nick must be here somewhere.

Her legs were shaking with anxiety, so she took a vacant seat, concluding that he must be trying to keep out of her sight. The antipathy was surely mutual, and she hoped there would be no continuation of the violent argument that had already finished their relationship.

With the childlike hope that if she did not see Nick then he would not see her either, she kept her eyes lowered and the brim of her cap down.

Finally she took her place in the queue and was soon settling into her seat. She was only a couple of rows from the toilet and was surrounded by smokers, who were listening to the announcement to extinguish cigarettes for take-off. Many were taking their final puffs. Reluctantly her neighbour stubbed his out, and Helena watched a thin line of smoke curl out of the ashtray. In twenty minutes' time, he would be able to light up again.

As soon as they were in the air, Helena unfastened her seat belt and stood. From the back of the plane she could see the top of every passenger's head. The familiar mop of blond hair was not visible. Most people on this aircraft were dark, and now that she thought about it, she had not heard a single English voice as they queued to get on. The majority of the passengers looked Greek.

She could not relax, and kept a watchful eye throughout the flight. If he was on board, surely, at some point in the journey, he would have to visit the toilet, of which there were only two, both of them at the back of the plane. A few hours into the journey, though, she wondered if he had talked his way into the first-class cabin, an act that was well within his capabilities.

Whatever the truth, she remained on edge. After a meal (processed cheese between triangles of white bread curled at the edges) had been served and cleared, her neighbour, a silver-haired octogenarian in a smart but well-worn suit, lolled over and slept on her shoulder. Only when her arm went dead did she feel the need to stir him.

Meanwhile, his warmth, the scent of his fresh shirt and the faint sound of his breathing were strangely soothing.

As the plane came in to land, dense cloud and strong winds made for a bumpy landing. Helena looked out of the window at the grey skies that hung over equally grey terminal buildings. *Welcome to Heathrow* read a sign. After the bright sunshine of Nisos and its diminutive whitewashed buildings, she had never felt less welcome anywhere.

Would Nick be at the carousel? She hung back to survey the crowd gathering to collect their baggage. Her dirty rucksack had already circled a few times, noticeably scruffier than the smart, carefully labelled suitcases either side of it.

Hurriedly throwing it over her shoulder, she made for the exit, ensuring that the wounded side of her face was obscured.

She was happy and surprised to see Charles and Sally waiting at arrivals. Nick was not with them.

'Welcome home!' they chorused, hugging her in turn.

'We've missed you!' said Sally, holding out a bunch of flowers.

'Hasn't Nick's bag come through?' asked Charles.

'Even his luggage likes to make an entrance!' joked Sally.

'How did it go?'

'Tell us your news!'

'You look so well!'

'What did you find?'

'Was it hard work?'

'So lovely you're home!'

Their questions and exclamations came thick and fast, leaving Helena without the smallest opportunity to respond to any of them.

'Where the hell is the old rogue?' said Charles eventually. 'We'll get a parking ticket.'

'Can we just go?' urged Helena.

'What? Without Nick?' protested Sally.

'Seems a bit harsh,' Charles agreed.

He would have been out of the arrivals area before her if he had been on the plane. Helena was certain now.

'I think he must have missed the flight,' she said, as breezily as she could.

Both her friends looked puzzled.

'You weren't together, then?' asked Charles. 'Had a tiff?'

'Look, please can we go? It's so nice of you to collect me, it really is. And I am sure he'll be on a plane tomorrow.'

Charles sensed that it was not the moment to ask questions. His eyes met Helena's pleading look and he saw lines of tiredness on her face.

She willingly allowed him to lift the bag from her shoulders.

His Morris Minor was parked close by, and Helena slipped into the back seat. Sally was watching her in the rear-view mirror.

'Are you okay?' she asked.

'I'm fine,' Helena answered curtly. 'Really.'

Sally turned to speak to her. Helena's face was mostly obscured by her cap, but it was obvious that she was crying. Sally fished in her pocket for some tissues and handed them to her silently.

Charles was too busy negotiating roundabouts and giving a running commentary on the drivers around him to notice Helena's unhappiness.

'That bloody lorry driver. If he thinks I'm moving over to let him pass, he can bugger off . . . What an arse! Just stop flashing me, you fool!'

Sally, on the other hand, was fully aware of her friend's distress, but when she turned around again a moment later to comfort her, Helena had fallen asleep.

She touched Charles on the arm, her finger to her lips. Charles lit a cigarette and wound down the window. They continued the journey in silence.

Within an hour, the car was pulling up outside the house off Ladbroke Grove. Despite the noisy ratcheting of the handbrake, Helena did not stir.

'Come on, Helena!' called Charles cheerfully over his shoulder. 'Wakey-wakey!'

'Charles! Can't you see the poor girl is exhausted?'

He had already removed the key from the ignition and was opening the boot to remove Helena's rucksack.

'I'll wait here with her for a few minutes. I'm sure she'll wake up soon.'

'Up to you,' said Charles, shutting the boot clumsily. 'I'll put the kettle on.'

Sally contemplated Helena's face. She must have been travelling for twelve hours, so it was not surprising that her skin was dusty, and she noticed that a tear had left a trail. It felt wrong to be scrutinising someone when they were asleep, so she turned to look out the windscreen, and watched some teenagers cycling up and down the road, riding without hands, performing tricks and showing off to each other with wheelies.

Perhaps ten minutes later, Helena stirred.

'Gosh . . . have we arrived? So sorry. Are we here?'

'Yes. We're home,' Sally answered. 'Charles is inside making you some tea.'

'Better go in, then,' said Helena with false cheer. 'Haven't had a decent cuppa for weeks!'

Sally hopped out of the front seat and opened the rear door, offering her hand.

'My leg is completely dead!' Helena moaned.

'You were fast asleep,' Sally told her.

'I'm exhausted,' Helena said quietly. Her head was throbbing. 'It's been a long couple of days.'

She took Sally's arm and, as life came back to her leg, hobbled towards the house. Caroline was waiting at the front door.

'You're so tanned! Look at you! And your hair!' she cried. 'You look wonderful!'

Helena managed a feeble thank you. She felt anything but

wonderful and knew that the fragrance of stale sun lotion hung around her. It felt like days since she had showered. She kept her cap jammed on, not just to hide her dirty hair but mostly to conceal her bruise.

Charles was already at the top of the stairs with her rucksack, and Helena trudged up to the bedroom she had shared with Nick. She almost expected him to be in there, lying on the bed with a *Sunday Times* magazine propped on his knees and a cheeky grin on his face, as if nothing had happened.

She paused in the doorway as Charles threw open the curtains to let in the remaining daylight.

'Thanks, Charles,' she said. 'Thanks for bringing my things up.'

'It's nothing,' he said. 'Come down and have some tea and tell us about your trip . . . and what happened.'

'I will,' she replied quietly.

As Charles shut the door, she looked around. The first thing she noticed was her beloved but neglected cheese plant, and she went to the bathroom with it, leaving it in the sink to have a much-needed drink. Back in the room, she surveyed her books. They lined an entire wall, a strange combination of chemistry, romantic poetry and novels, some in Greek and others the English classics that Sally had encouraged her to read. Little by little, during the previous year, she had moved many of her possessions to the Ladbroke Grove house. On one of the lower shelves there was Nick's well-thumbed copy of Oscar Wilde's plays and a short biography of John Donne, but he owned relatively few texts for someone who had read English literature at Oxford. He had more records than books, and these were in an unruly pile on the living room floor next to the gramophone player, owned by Charles but shared by them all.

A pair of Nick's brogues stuck out from beneath the bed, and she knew without even opening it that the wardrobe was full of his shirts. What would she do with his things? She knew with certainty that he would not be returning to live with her.

All these thoughts were in her mind as she unbuckled her rucksack. Her desire to launder her clothes and wash away the dirt of these past weeks, so defiled by its last moments, was intense. She even thought of binning everything she had worn on the dig in order to get rid of the memories, to eliminate traces of Nick. But no, that was extravagant. A hot wash in Charles's twin tub would suffice.

For now, though, she couldn't face the task. The others were waiting downstairs and she needed to tell them that she and Nick had broken up. His crime would not be mentioned.

She removed the cap in front of the mirror and, with a slight change in the position of her parting, managed to brush over a section of hair to cover the mark on her face.

As she went out onto the landing, she could hear Charles on the phone in the hallway. She paused. The slightest movement would make the floorboards creak.

'Maybe best tomorrow, then?' he said in a low voice.

There was silence for a few moments.

'Right-o. Right then. Okay. Midday. Don't be late. Bye, old chap.'

She heard the receiver being put back on its cradle and held her breath for a couple more seconds. She knew who Charles had been talking to.

Steam rose from the five mugs of tea on the kitchen table. The chipped china was reassuringly familiar, along with the dim grunginess of the kitchen, with its chaotic stacks of magazines on every surface and a pile of dishes from the previous night still in the sink. It felt like a student house but for the four oil paintings at the other end of the room and the glass-fronted cabinet displaying a porcelain dinner set.

The four of them were waiting for her.

'So, Helena, tell us everything. What's happened? Why isn't Nick here? You two had a row?'

Charles's line of questioning was breezy but well-meant, and Helena gave short answers.

'Yes,' she said. 'Blazing.'

'So you split up?'

'Yep. It's over.'

Edward had less affection for Nick than the rest.

'To be truthful, I never liked him much,' he said bluntly.

'Ed!' berated Charles.

'Well, he was an incorrigible flirt – every girl in the English faculty, his tutors, the librarians, kitchen staff . . .'

'Honestly, Helena doesn't need to know that now,' reprimanded Charles.

'Don't worry, Edward. I know what you mean,' Helena said to reassure him. 'He paid more attention to the other girls on the dig than to me.' She would allow them to think that their split was the result of an infidelity.

Without thinking, she tucked her hair behind her ear and inadvertently exposed the mark above her right eye. It had gone from bright red to bluish-purple, and spread.

Sally seized upon it immediately.

'What's that mark? Helena? Did he hit you?' she demanded.

'No.'

'Are you sure? Really?'

Sally clearly didn't believe her. Nor, from the expressions on their faces, did the others.

'I tripped on the last day of the dig. It's nothing. Uneven ground, lots of loose stones . . .'

'You poor thing, that looks really bad,' said Caroline. 'I've got some arnica in my room. Shall I get it?'

Helena's eyes began to smart with tears.

'It's probably better that Helena knows a few home truths about him, isn't it?' suggested Sally.

'The truth can be painful,' Charles said with a frown.

'I can take it,' said Helena, suddenly eager for their candour. It might not lessen the pain she was in, but she needed to hear whatever they had to say. 'I realise that I was very taken in by him . . . I was pretty stupid actually.'

'Because you only met him at the end of Oxford, you didn't know what he was like as an undergraduate,' said Caroline. 'We all thought you had changed him and that he was going to settle down.'

'He was a tireless womaniser, I'm afraid,' said Edward. 'His nickname was Byron.'

'That's no surprise.' Helena laughed bitterly. 'Reciting Byron is his party trick, as you can imagine.'

'And he wanted people to think he was aristocratic,' said Charles. 'Nicholas Hayes-Jones isn't his name. Close, but not exact. He's Nick Jones. Born in Hayes, Middlesex.'

'Who cares really? None of that matters to anyone. But it did to him,' said Sally. 'He always wanted to hide his background. And he felt inadequate because he'd been to a comprehensive.'

'But he told me he'd been to public school. And his father was a judge . . .'

'None of that is true,' said Charles.

'His father was a postman,' Caroline told her. 'Mine worked in a warehouse, so maybe that's why he once confided in me.'

'I taught him how to do up a bow tie in our first week. After that, he was in black tie all the time,' said Edward. 'He loved acting the toff.'

'And he is a very good actor,' Sally added. 'In every way.'

'That's definitely true,' Helena said, staring into the whirlpool she had created on the surface of her tea. 'Not sure why he doesn't become one. He's good at it.'

'I think what he wanted to change most was his financial status,' said Edward. 'He always had a nose for money.'

'That didn't worry me,' said Charles. 'I was aware of what he was about, but you make allowances when someone is such great company, don't you?'

'You're very forgiving, Charles,' said Edward. 'I know you never got his share of the bills from him, did you?'

Charles shook his head.

'That's why we all love you,' said Sally, kissing him on the cheek. Her boyfriend's generosity to his friends was legendary. He gave without taking.

'He apparently finished his third year owing the college more than fifteen hundred pounds,' added Edward. 'I don't think his father had a bean, so he couldn't bail him out.'

'Nick's a professional scrounger,' agreed Charles. 'He was invariably late with his essays and had to crib from ours most weeks. But there was one of those in every set. Someone who always needed to borrow lecture notes, or money, or a cummerbund . . .'

'Or a girlfriend,' Caroline chipped in.

Helena tried to smile, pouring more milk into her tea.

'Well, I'm under no illusions now,' she said. 'But I wish you'd told me some of this before.'

'We would have done, but we genuinely thought you'd changed him,' said Charles.

'One thing I never imagined was that he would be violent,' said Sally, looking at Helena's head.

'He wasn't. Really he wasn't. It was an accident.' She didn't want to be seen as a victim, and yet there had undoubtedly been savagery in their final moments together.

Sally still looked sceptical.

'Domestic violence is a crime,' stated Caroline. 'You could take him to court.'

Helena stared down at her lap. For the first time she noticed a bruise on her wrist and pulled down her sleeve.

'And something once happened that I've never even told you about, Edward,' Caroline continued. 'When we first moved in here and you were on a course, he tried to force his way into my room one night. He thought I was just playing a game, and wouldn't take no for an answer.'

'Why didn't you say anything to me?' asked Charles, horrified. 'I'm so sorry, Caroline.'

'I might be quite small, but I'm tough,' she replied. 'I threatened him. And he could see I was serious. He'd torn my shirt, though.'

'Oh my God,' gasped Helena. 'He's a monster. There's no other word.'

'I would have *killed* him,' added the usually gentle Edward with fury.

'I don't think so,' Caroline smiled, taking his hand.

The five of them sat silently for a while, shocked.

'I would have thrown him out there and then if I'd known,' said Charles. 'It's even worse than those paintings.'

'Paintings?' Helena asked.

Charles explained that a couple of small watercolours had gone missing a few months ago.

'I didn't even notice they'd disappeared at first,' he admitted. 'But there wasn't anyone else who ever went into my study. And it wasn't a break-in.'

'You really think that was Nick?'

'I have no proof, but he knew they were by Chagall. They were small and discreet but worth some millions.'

The vision of the broken figurine was clear and sharp in Helena's mind, but she wouldn't bring it up now. She wanted to work out what to do in her own time.

Charles interrupted her musing.

'He's coming by tomorrow to pick up his things,' he said gently.

'Right,' she said firmly. 'I'll be out. But I'll box his stuff up so it's ready.'

She helped herself to a custard cream from the packet on the table and bit off a corner.

'Ah, I've missed these!' she mumbled. 'Delicious.'

'We've missed you too,' said Sally.

Conversation moved on to what the others had been doing over the summer. Who was seeing whom in their circle, a couple in their year who had announced their engagement, some parties that were coming up, Sally's speedy promotion to account director, the demands of Edward and Caroline's law firms. Helena was happily diverted for a while and felt secure for the first time in days.

It was gone ten in the evening and Charles uncorked a bottle of wine. And soon a second.

Edward had made spaghetti Bolognese and ladled generous portions into bowls. Helena managed to eat a mouthful but no more than that.

By midnight, Sally's head was slumped on her boyfriend's shoulder.

'Maybe it's time for bed,' Helena whispered, getting up. 'See you in the morning.'

Edward gave her a hug and Caroline repeated her offer of arnica. Charles remained pinned to his seat by Sally's weight, but squeezed Helena's arm as she passed.

'Sleep well,' he said.

That proved impossible. Helena was haunted by dreams of crumbling cliffs and avalanches of snow that turned red. Even more red than the earth they had been digging. In all these nightmares, she was running to escape, and four times woke up in sheets that were icy with sweat. Even though the tremor in Nisos had been relatively minor, her experience of the forces within the earth had haunted her.

The night terrors she had suffered so often as a child were back. She cried out, but in the rambling house, no one heard.

Chapter Thirty-Two

When she eventually woke up, the clock on the bedside table told Helena that it was 8.30. She lay there a while, exhausted but determined not to drift back to sleep and into the realm of disturbing visions and panic.

It was only October, but the summer was long gone and the wooden floor felt cold underfoot. She had forgotten the sudden chill that arrived with a London autumn.

She had gone to sleep in her underwear and was now shaking with cold. She threw on an old T-shirt and reached into the back of a cupboard to find her winter coat.

Just as she was tying the belt, she heard a gentle knock on the door. It was Sally, holding out a steaming mug of tea.

'That's so sweet of you!' Helena said with genuine delight. 'Thank you, Sally. Really. It's something I missed! A strong cup of PG Tips. Greek coffee is a bit harsh first thing in the morning.'

Sally smiled. 'I've never tried it myself.'

'Believe me, it's bitter,' Helena said.

'Did you sleep well?'

'Not really . . . I think it's normal, isn't it? When you're suddenly back in your own bed. It takes getting used to again, somehow.'

'I suppose so. But are you okay?'

'Why don't you come in?'

The two girls sat on the edge of the bed and Sally put an arm around her friend.

'So what did he hit you with?'

'He didn't, Sally. And that's the truth, I promise,' responded Helena. 'But let's say that Nick is not who I thought he was. And when he comes to collect his things, I won't be around.'

'I totally understand that, Helena.'

'He's coming at twelve, isn't he?'

'Yes. Charles will be here when he arrives,' Sally confirmed. 'He's taking the morning off. And I've rung in sick.'

'All his stuff will be in the hall, so there's no need for him to come upstairs.'

'We won't let him,' Sally said firmly. 'God knows what else he'd pinch.'

Helena stood up, catching a glimpse of a tramp in the mirror: shaggy unbrushed hair, bruised face, tatty winter coat, bare feet. She must smarten herself up and go out.

The shower ran as tepid as usual but the pressure was enough to wash away the grains of Greek dust that still clung to her. A residue of reddish soil gathered around the plughole as she shampooed her matted hair for a third time.

She dried herself quickly, then wound her hair into a bun and ran across the chilly landing into her room. Still wrapped in a towel, she found an old cricket bag of Nick's and began to empty the drawers of his clothes. His shirts went on top of his crumpled T-shirts, then his shoes. Before zipping it up, she slipped in his copy of Jack Kerouac's *On the Road* and Dante's *Inferno* from a bedside drawer, books that she had seen in his pocket but never in his hands. There were three suits: morning dress, a dark suit that he had worn for formal dinners at Oxford, and an evening suit shiny with wear at the knees and elbows. She carried them downstairs on their hangers and dumped them on a chair in the hall.

'Let me come and get the other things,' said Charles, appearing out of the kitchen.

'It's just the one bag,' replied Helena. 'But what about his records?'

'I'll put them in a box before he comes.'

'Great.' She forced a smile. They could dispose of the vinyl, but the songs he had played over and over again would always remain with her.

Dressing quickly, she grabbed her coat and purse and left the house. It was almost eleven. Nick was invariably late, but it would be typically perverse of him to change his habits just for today.

She took the Underground to Marble Arch and wandered into Hyde Park. There were a handful of nannies pushing prams, and a party of small boys in grey blazers were being marched through the park, but few others apart from the gardeners who were trimming hedges and picking up litter. For an hour or more she walked clockwise around the park, noticing little but the melancholy of the fading flowers and the leaves that were just beginning to turn. She was glad of her winter coat, already nostalgic for the warmth of the Greek early autumn, where the days held their heat until late evening.

Her watch must still be on the bathroom shelf, but she guessed it was gone two. She had barely eaten anything since the meagre plane meal the day before, and hunger had begun to taunt her.

She bought a ham sandwich, all that was on offer from the kiosk, and wandered towards the Serpentine. The only vacant bench was next to one with a couple on a lunchtime tryst. Helena was glad when the besuited grey-haired man and the girl in a short brown coat and thigh boots who giggled like a child eventually left. She was in no mood to witness love.

The geese gathered round, noisily demanding her food. Simply to get rid of them she hurled the dried-out bread as far as she could, and they snatched at it greedily, squawking, pecking, violently flapping their wings. They repulsed her with their aggression.

Once they had divided the spoils, the geese took to the water, and the sense of being alone in front of this huge sweep of still grey pond now overwhelmed her. The screech of gulls above only reminded her all the more strongly of how far away were those idyllic days of skinny dips in the Aegean, when the sun had scorched their skin as they lay on the sand.

She stood up, but immediately felt faint. The motion of the journey and the anxiety that had accompanied it – the nausea of the ferry, the rumbling of the Greek bus and the polluted air of the overheated plane – returned to her. She closed her eyes to regain her balance, clutching the back of the bench to steady herself.

'Are you all right, dear?' asked an elderly woman who was wheeling a man of similar age through the park. 'Can I help you in any way?'

'I'm fine, but thank you,' she managed to reply.

'Did he hit you?' the woman asked with concern.

Helena's hand went automatically to her bruise. 'Oh, no, no. I fell.'

'A beautiful girl like you. You shouldn't put up with it.'

Helena was not going to dissuade her.

'I wonder . . . do you have the time?' She was desperate to be at home, lying on her bed, staring quietly at the ceiling, thinking, being calm. Had she killed enough time for Nick to have come and gone?

'Bert, dearest, can you give this young lady the time?'

The elderly man held out an emaciated arm, and his wife (Helena assumed her to be so, at least) drew up his sleeve an inch or two to reveal a watch, then stooped to read it.

'It's just after three,' she said brightly.

Helena managed a thank you before they continued on their way. She noticed the woman rearranging the invalid's blanket as they walked. How did people retain such a cheerful demeanour with adversity such as this? It was evident from the man's limited motion that a stroke had taken away his power of speech. She thought of her deaf and voiceless friend at the kiosk. The previous day had been traumatic, but nothing compared with the suffering of these people. Life was much crueller to others.

A while later, she used the phone box outside the Underground to call Charles and Sally.

'It's all fine,' said the reassuring voice at the other end. 'He came a couple of hours ago and took his things. You won't bump into him.'

She bought a ticket and was soon travelling home, alone in the carriage apart from some schoolgirls whose chatter and laughter made her smile.

She found her friends at the kitchen table.

'He's gone?'

'Yes,' said Charles, looking her straight in the eye.

'Tea? Coffee?' asked Sally.

'No thanks,' Helena said wearily. 'I want to finish unpacking.'

She took off her shoes and sat on the bed, ready to curl up for a sleep. After such a disturbed night, all she wanted was rest.

Her rucksack was still propped against the wall where Charles had left it. Only when she had unpacked would the trip really be behind her. She hoisted it onto the bed and began to pull out T-shirts, bikinis and faded jeans, so ragged they were almost beyond saving. She had repacked roughly after her discovery on Nisos, and everything felt like a souvenir of those past months, all now so tainted by memory.

Further down inside were toothbrush, hairbrush and the remains of shampoo.

She carelessly tossed the rucksack back into the corner, where it landed with an audible thud. She must have left something inside. She tipped it upside down on the bed, coating everything with sandy soil.

Something wrapped in the page of a book – she recognised it immediately as a page of Byron's poetry – landed on top of the pile of grubby clothes.

With her hands shaking so much she could barely manage to control them, she unfolded the paper. Inside was a piece of cream-coloured stone, just a few inches long. In utter disbelief and horror, she turned it over in her palm. It was the lower section of the broken figurine, from mid-shin downwards.

She gently touched the precious downward-pointing feet and ran her finger along the neat incisions that indicated straight childlike toes. Even this small piece of it had a mesmeric beauty.

Then a sudden fury gripped her from the inside. How dare he do this? He would have known the horror that this twisted act of revenge would instil in her. How sly to implicate her in his theft, and how inordinately vicious. There was a knot in her stomach. The dregs of the tea that Sally had brought her that morning were still on her bedside table, and she reached out. Anything at all would do to moisten her dry mouth.

She slid the marble fragment under her pillow, then bolted down the stairs, anger fuelling her flight.

'Charles! Sally!'

Sally appeared at the living room door.

'What's wrong?'

'What's *wrong*?' Helena could hardly contain her fury. 'I'll tell you what's wrong! You let Nick go into my room! Why? *Why* did you let him?'

Charles was now standing next to Sally, looked bemused. He had never seen Helena angry like this.

'But we didn't. He didn't go upstairs. At all.'

'Are you sure?'

'Absolutely certain,' said Charles firmly. 'He came to the door. We had a farewell Scotch in the kitchen for old times' sake, he picked up his things from the hall floor, just where you left them, and then he was gone.'

'Really? He didn't go upstairs at all? To the bathroom maybe?'

'I promise,' said Charles, slightly defensively. 'I wouldn't lie to you, Helena. I was with him all the time.'

She was still shaking.

'Look, what's this all about? What's happened? What's going on?'

'I can't tell you now, but I promise I will one day.'

She had already turned her back on them, and was at the top of the stairs even before their questions tailed off.

She realised that Nick must have found her bag on the boat and hidden the piece of figurine inside during the crossing. She felt more betrayed than before, and was fuelled by an even greater anger. His original plan had been for her to smuggle the whole thing, and even when she'd discovered it, he'd still made her a partner in his crime. How would she ever explain why she had this object? Nobody knew of its existence, but it was beyond justification if anyone found it. And beyond excusable.

She suddenly remembered the first dig, and the gift she had carried for Charles. She was sure now that it was a decoy and that she had been used as a mule to carry something else as well.

On the floor where she had dropped it was the wrapping Nick had used. She picked it up and read some of the lines. They were from *The Curse of Minerva*. In the margin, he had scribbled: *A little reminder of our secret xx*. What a sick joke to use Byron's diatribe against Elgin.

The translucent marble seemed to glow against the deep navy of her pillowcase, and she gazed for one last moment at its simple beauty before wrapping it again. The only place she could hide it was back in her rucksack, so she stuffed it right down inside with the ragged jeans on top, then fastened the buckles and stood on a chair to put the bag on top of the wardrobe. She did not want to see it, think about it or even know that it was there; she would bring the broom up later to push it to the back.

Hoping she could finally rest, she lay down, but the orange glow of the London sky filtering through the curtains kept her awake. Perhaps she had grown too accustomed to sleeping behind the heavily shuttered windows in Kolonaki, or in the ink black of a Nisos night.

This eerie toxic light cast strange shadows around her bedroom, creating silhouettes on the walls. The asymmetrical shape of the back-pack became a creature ready to pounce, and a slight stirring of the curtains from a breeze caused everything inanimate to move and breathe.

Even when she closed her eyes, Helena could feel the unwilling presence of the marble fragment, a beautiful but menacing hostage. It should not be there. She buried her head under the sheets to block out the light and eventually fell into a fitful sleep that lasted until morning.

Nightmares haunted her. She was desperately searching for her mother, but Mary McCloud had been abducted, Helena had been given false leads, and time was running out. She was the sole person looking. Her father had vanished and nobody else seemed to care. She was paralysed by anxiety and fear, and when the front door closed with a bang, she woke up, tears running down her cheeks. There was no point in analysing the dream. It was obvious to her where such a fear had originated. The lies and dishonesty of Nicholas Hayes-Jones had wreaked havoc on her peace of mind. Like a Greek tragedy, there could be no happy ending to this story.

In those first moments of waking, still drowning in the desperation of the dream, a word came into her mind: *Ekdíkisi*. Revenge.

It was what had fired Medea, a woman so crazed with anger that she took the lives of her own children to satisfy it. Nick must have it in his vocabulary too, even if it was just from playing Jason. He had performed the role of a man confronted by the rage of a woman, and now he would experience it in real life.

Something had snapped inside Helena when the statue broke, and triggered a rage that could only be calmed by retribution. She had a sense of being so profoundly Greek in that moment that she was almost afraid. As Mihalis had often said, her Britishness was only one half of her. Her psyche was equally Hellenic.

Nick had made a fool of everyone he came into contact with: housemates, archaeologists, herself and no doubt countless others in

349

his life. This charismatic chancer was a con man, habitually stealing, smuggling and seducing.

Though her future felt uncertain, at this moment Helena had never felt a greater sense of purpose.

Part Four

Chapter Thirty-Three

The nightmare about her mother had left Helena feeling deeply unsettled, so a few days later she took a train to see her father. Hamish McCloud was keeping himself occupied with work and accepting more invitations as the months went by. The garden was immaculate, with regiments of winter vegetables already planted and a display of bright dahlias filling the beds, their dramatic gold and crimson heads waving like balloons.

Over a Sunday roast, Helena told him all the news she felt was necessary.

She had already decided to keep her descriptions of the dig as bland as possible, and said little about Nick except to tell Hamish that they had gone their separate ways. She could see that her father was not sorry. Perhaps he had better instincts than she had imagined. Once that news was dispensed with, she enthused about her days in Athens and her new friendship with Mihalis and his set, and how she was discovering different parts of the city.

Hamish was glad to hear that she was returning to Athens reasonably soon to do a final clear-out of the flat and get it sold. He was keen for her to secure her nest egg. Neither of them mentioned her longer-term future, both accepting that present projects were enough. Hamish had no intention of nagging her about what she was going to do next, appreciating that time would help her decide.

When Mary had died, happiness had felt like something that neither of them would ever experience again, but Helena could see that her father was finding contentment, and was glad.

'All the veg were from the garden,' he said as they were leaving for the station. 'I've picked you some to take back to London. And a few flowers.'

'Someone's got green fingers,' said an elderly woman passing through her carriage as Helena settled herself into a seat. She indicated the mass of curly-petalled scarlet blooms that lay next to her, their stems tightly wrapped in foil.

'My dad,' Helena replied, smiling.

'Well, they're almost as beautiful as his daughter,' the woman said. 'You've got the most spectacular hair I have ever seen. The colour! The waves! You lucky girl!'

As the woman receded down the train, Helena looked at the back of her head. She could see the scalp through her short, thinning hair. It had taken Helena most of her life to accept how she looked, and at this moment she castigated herself for being so unappreciative of her untameable mane. Even if friends might have reason to lie, strangers did not.

She caught sight of her reflection in the grubby train window and did not look away. Any flattery from Nick over the past months had ultimately meant nothing, but these few words from a stranger had had real sincerity. Her self-esteem, so badly knocked by him, grew again just a little.

A week or so later, Helena was back in Athens. The days were noticeably shorter, but the late October temperatures were mild. The pavements were littered with bitter oranges from the overburdened trees that lined the streets, and at dusk, swallows gathered noisily on the telegraph wires, thousands, hundreds of thousands perhaps, ready to leave for warmer climes. The pavement cafés were still full, but only with locals now. The tourists had mostly gone, and Helena could feel the Athenians' pleasure in having their city back.

As she walked up the street, she contemplated how much her sense of belonging had grown since her childhood trips, her Greek more fluent, the city's streets mapped inside her head and, most importantly, she had friends.

On her first night back, she went to see Mihalis. He was just pulling the shutters down outside the shop.

'Eleni *mou*! You're back! Give me five minutes!'

She strolled a short distance away, remembering that Giannis Ligakis's shop was just round the corner. It was still open, so she hung back and watched people going in and out. They were all respectable in appearance, rather like the owner himself, but Helena knew all too well that dressing in Savile Row did not make someone trustworthy.

Suddenly Ligakis emerged, and Helena stepped back into a shop doorway to avoid being seen. He would recognise her. No one ever forgot her hair. She watched him lock the door top and bottom, and then, to her relief, he marched up the hill towards Lycabettus.

Mihalis was waiting for her outside the hardware shop.

'Wednesday! Early closing! Where shall we go?'

'You're asking me?' Helena laughed.

He put his arm through hers. 'Your first night, you get to choose,' he said.

'Exarchia, then.'

'Right answer,' he quipped.

They spent the whole evening together. They collided with some of Mihalis's friends from Polytechnic days, went to one or two bars, and ate *gýro*, kebabs, from a takeaway. As they sat on some steps, chips and tzatziki falling from their pitta breads and onto their jeans, Helena told Mihalis that she had split up with Nick but was back to finish clearing the flat and put it on the market. She did not mention her other reason for being there, wanting to forget for a moment the piece of marble that she had carried back through customs in her shoulder bag, her heart palpitating with guilt and anxiety.

For the first time in memory, the pattern of academic terms did not structure her life, but she had a new aim: 'being Medea', as she thought of it.

In addition, she had the goal of freeing herself of the oppressive apartment.

At ten o'clock the following morning, she was standing outside Anna Morakis's shop, gazing in at a pair of stone lions, half life-size, facing each other snout to snout.

'Can I help you?' asked a voice behind her.

She spun round to see Anna's brother, who was rattling a bunch of keys. He was in a bright blue shirt, and she noticed that his thick hair was still wet from a shower.

'*Kaliméra*,' she said. 'We met before?'

'Of course. Sorry, I'm a bit distracted today.'

'I was waiting for your sister,' she told him.

The door was wide open now.

'Come in then. She shouldn't be too long.'

His tone was brusque but not unfriendly. Professional, Helena decided, as she followed him inside.

'Was there something you were interested in?'

'Not exactly, but she came to value some things for me and I wanted to follow up.'

She watched him as he got the shop ready for the day, pulling up the shutters and taking some items out of a safe to put them on display.

'Do you want me to find her valuation?'

He was sitting behind a desk now, and Helena could see a strong family likeness. She recalled Anna's dark brown eyes, almost black hair and thick lashes, and noted that this man had the same. Like his sister, he was slim, but had broad, athletic shoulders.

'No, really. It's fine. I could come back later?' Helena said, slightly flustered, feeling suddenly awkward beneath his gaze.

The bell behind her jangled.

'Helena!' said Anna. 'What a lovely surprise. I thought perhaps you had sold to another dealer.'

'No, no,' Helena replied. 'I went away for a while and just got back to Athens.'

Anna was even more chic than Helena remembered, in a very fitted cream suit, the jacket edged in black. From her days in the haberdashery shop, she remembered similar pearly buttons that were faux Chanel. Somehow she knew that these were the real thing.

Anna sat at her desk and Helena took the seat opposite. Haris disappeared into the back office.

'He's the artist in this business,' Anna said. 'I do the business with the art.'

'I see,' said Helena, without meaning it.

The two women exchanged pleasantries for a while.

'So, were you happy with my offer?' Anna asked. 'I could improve on it, but not by a huge amount.'

'It's fine, absolutely fine,' Helena replied.

There was a moment's pause.

'And those other . . . pieces. The Meissen. I had some thoughts,' said Anna.

'That's not really why I'm here.'

'Would you like me to come round?' suggested Anna helpfully, consulting her desk diary. She imagined there was some furniture she had missed. 'I could call early evening?'

'No. No need. It's something small. I have it with me.' Helena felt a desperate need to share what had happened. 'I need to tell you about it first,' she said with urgency.

In a low voice, so that Haris would not catch a word if he emerged from the office, she told Anna the story of the broken figurine. She had to trust somebody, and if this was an error, so be it. Her instincts had been wrong about Nick, but she had not entirely lost faith in her own judgement.

Anna leaned forward to catch every word, but expressed no surprise at any point.

'We have come across this before,' she said when Helena had finished. 'But to use a lover as the means to smuggle . . . that is the worst part of your story.'

Helena flinched at the reminder of Nick's vindictive behaviour.

'May I see the piece he planted on you?'

'Yes,' said Helena, leaning down to retrieve it from her bag. It was still wrapped in the page of Byron's verse, and she placed it carefully on the desk in front of Anna, reluctant to touch the marble herself.

'That's almost definitely the real thing,' said Anna, picking up a magnifying glass to examine it. 'We would have to get the soil analysed, and those encrustations.'

'I *know* it's the real thing,' emphasised Helena. 'I was probably not far away when he pulled it out of the ground. And I saw it whole.'

Guiltily she wrapped it up again. She did not want to look at it.

'So you have seen other things stolen from excavations?' she asked.

'There are many looted treasures out there, but we have a reputation for turning them away these days, as I told you,' said Anna. 'In spite of that, we get some odd characters who come in with objects that have been deliberately broken so that they can be more easily removed from a site.'

'Why would they bring them to you?'

'Because everyone in the business knows that my brother has a skill. He mends and restores and makes things new. That's what I meant by him being an artist. He has a talent. And he's been practising it from a young age.'

Helena leaned forward.

'Our father had a customer here one afternoon who had come in to have an Etruscan vase valued. It was what they call a *krater*.

It was beautiful and quite rare, and our father had just given him a verbal valuation of several million drachmas. Haris came in from school, and as he walked past the desk, for some reason he turned, and knocked it off with his bag. I was already in the office doing my homework. I heard the crash and then lots of shouting.'

Anna paused to brush a stray hair from her face.

'Haris was mortified, my father was beside himself and the owner was screaming at both of them. It was a terrible accident. But what could my father do? He had to pay him exactly the money he had just valued it for. And it was a really beautiful piece.'

Haris came out of the office and heard the tail end of the conversation.

'Let me guess,' he joked. 'You're telling her about my childhood misdemeanour.'

'We laugh about it now, but at the time, it was a catastrophe. Let me finish telling the story, Haris.'

Helena could tell that these siblings had a long-standing habit of joshing with each other.

'So, our father promised to pay this man, and he was always as good as his word. There was no question of it. He had a week to come up with the cash.'

'Your poor father,' interjected Helena. 'And awful for you too, Haris.'

'Thanks, Helena,' he smiled. 'There wasn't much sympathy for me at the time.'

'While my father went upstairs to tell our mother, Haris picked up the pieces.'

'Twenty-three of them,' said Haris firmly.

'Stop interrupting, Haris!' said Anna, with an older sister's bossiness. 'We ate supper in silence that night and our mother didn't say a word to Haris for two days. I told them that we had put the pieces in a box.'

'Am I allowed to speak now?' Haris interjected.

'No,' Anna answered, determined to continue. 'Our father sometimes mended things, so he had a few tools and the right adhesives, but it was obvious that this was going to be beyond his capabilities. What we had really done was take all the pieces upstairs to Haris's room and set them out on his table.'

Haris was finally given permission to take over the story.

'As Anna passed them to me, I arranged them on the desk, trying to make sense of them while I could still remember what went where.'

Helena tried to imagine them, two children colluding in the semi-darkness, attempting to right a wrong.

'Since I was small, I had made aeroplanes. The kind you buy in kits and stick together and then paint.'

'He was really good at it. Unbelievably patient!'

'Some of the aeroplane parts were minuscule, much smaller than any of the vase pieces. So I just got on with it. I didn't think about whether it was the right thing to do. I knew how long to leave the glue to set and how to make the joins vanish. I did it in sections and then finally pieced them together.'

'I told our mother that he was making a present for her, to say sorry for what he had done,' said Anna, reminding her brother of the role she had played. 'And I asked her not to go into his room.'

'The last pieces to go on were the handles,' Haris continued. 'Luckily they had come away intact.'

A note of pride came into his voice.

'Ten days later, on a Saturday morning, I carried the vase carefully downstairs before our parents were out of bed and put it on display in the shop window.'

'It was his version of a practical joke,' said Anna.

'When he opened up, our father didn't notice it. There were plenty of other things in the window, and some larger pieces of furniture obscured his view in any case. I lurked about in the office all morning pretending to do my homework, desperate for him to spot it.'

Haris's eyes were gleaming. He had Helena's full attention, speaking in the present tense as he relived the day.

'At around two in the afternoon, our father gets the keys out of the drawer ready to close for the day – he won't reopen again in the evening because it's a Saturday. At that moment, somebody comes in. A man. Tall. Silver-haired, in a very expensive-looking coat. I've left the office door open and I hear him say the word "vase", in English, but with an American accent. He pronounced it like "haze". This guy beckons my father over to the window to point something out to him. I'm standing watching them. Then our father lifts the vase from the window.' Haris was now miming his father's actions. 'He's holding it up, examining it closely, shaking his head. He carries it over to his desk and the buyer scrutinises it with a magnifying glass that's hanging from a gold chain round his neck.'

Anna took over now to do an impersonation of the customer.

'"Aaa haive never seeeeen a more be-yootiful vase",' she drawled. '"Aather in Idaly or Greece or anywayer in the wurrld. Maa waafe collects. Aa think she would lurve this piece. The paintin' on it is ex-quisite."'

'He was from New Orleans?' joked Helena.

'No,' Haris said. 'Anna's terrible at accents. She wasn't even there. I think he was Californian.'

They all laughed. The situation he was describing was already turning from tragedy to comedy.

'I can see that my father is trying to keep himself calm,' continued Haris. 'He points out to the customer that it's had some repairs.'

'"Aa can see thay-at."'

'Anna, do stop!' said Haris, poking his sister gently. 'I don't think I can stand it.'

The three of them were smiling, as Haris took charge of the story, dropping the impersonation.

'This guy actually says to our father that the repairs in no way detract from the beauty. The restoration actually *adds* to the vase's charm and its authenticity. If it was whole, he says, it would just look brand new, and he wants his friends to know that this is the genuine article. The immaculate restoration is part of its appeal, in his mind.

'Of course, the next question is the price. My father, who has gone really pale, has to sit down for a moment to look through his records, although the amount he paid for the vase is etched in his mind. What he is really doing is composing himself. I'm now standing at the door of the office, watching him flicking through his card index system to kill time, and I can see he has a dilemma. Should he make a profit? Because it's clear that he can.

'"Three million five hundred thousand drachmas," he says.

'It's precisely the amount he gave to the original owner the previous week. Without a moment's hesitation, the American accepts. He does not demur or negotiate, simply smiles as though he's got himself a bargain.'

Haris continued the story. '"I can pay you by banker's draft or cash, dollars or drachmas, whatever is best for you," he says. "My chauffeur is outside and I can send him to the bank. I cannot even tell you how delighted my wife is going to be with this. Would you be able to wrap it very carefully? It will be going with some other antiquities that I am having shipped to our new place in California. And it's so beautiful, I don't want *anything* to happen to it."

'His appreciation of the piece is immense. As my father boxes it up, prepares a receipt and certificate of provenance and so on, the American notices a small piece of Roman glassware, which is something he himself collects, and he has that wrapped too.'

'It's like a divine visitation!' said Helena, beaming. 'Did this *really* happen?'

'It's totally true,' confirmed Anna. 'And it gets better.'

Haris stood back to let his sister finish the story.

'The driver came in with the dollars and to fetch the two parcels. The buyer shook hands with my father and then he was gone.

Once he had driven off, my father literally sat at his desk and wept, with relief, and pride too. He didn't ask for an explanation. For some reason, we don't know why, the dollar dropped over the next few days, and when my father banked the money, he found he had made a good profit. Not a huge one, but the exchange rate was better than normal.'

'I wonder who the man was?'

'We don't think it was Getty, but he was someone a bit like that. Somebody who loved beautiful things, who wanted to possess them and didn't care how much they cost,' said Haris.

'And that's how my little brother found his vocation in life!' Anna concluded.

They all laughed.

'What a strange and mysterious thing it is when someone falls in love with an inanimate object,' said Helena.

'That's the business we're in,' said Haris. 'And that's the thrill of it. You never know when someone is going to find something irresistible.'

If she had not been staring at what was on the desk, Helena would have noticed him gazing at her.

'Haris sees things quite romantically,' said Anna. 'Beauty is in the eye of the beholder, is what he means.'

Haris leaned forward.

'What's that?' he asked, peering at the scrap of marble.

'Helena brought it in. Have a look. We need your opinion.'

Haris smoothed out *The Curse of Minerva* beneath the piece of figurine. Then, from a drawer in the desk, he took out some white gloves, and from a top pocket removed what looked like the spectacles worn by watchmakers, with highly powerful lenses. Gloves on, he bent in close without saying a word, before picking up the Cycladic feet as though he was handling something as delicate as an eggshell.

The silence went on for what seemed a long while. Anna was restless. 'Would anyone like some coffee?' she asked.

Neither Helena nor Haris replied.

'Interesting,' said Haris at last.

'Interesting?' quizzed Helena.

'I saw the rest of this a week ago. A man brought it in. Three sections. Clean breaks, just like this. Same colour, size, shape. The same figurine. But missing the feet. No doubt whatsoever.'

'Who was he?' demanded Helena.

'First of all, where did you get this?' She detected a more formal tone in Haris's voice.

'She didn't steal it,' Anna insisted. 'It's a long story, and we'll tell you later.'

'Please tell me what he looked like,' persisted Helena, her voice betraying her anxiety.

'British. Aristocratic. Reasonably well dressed. Around twenty-five. Good-looking. Fair-haired. I think you British would call him "posh",' replied Haris. 'I told him we don't deal in such antiquities, meaning of course that we don't touch loot. It was clearly smuggled and very recently broken. I told him I only repair ceramics.'

'Did he give his name?'

'Something like Nigel Parker-Jones. Yes, that's what it was.'

Nick. Obviously Nick. Nobody knew him in Athens, so it must have seemed safe enough to find a restorer here. She was shaken to the core by the idea that he had stood in this very room not long before. One day she hoped to confront him, but not yet.

She pointed at the little feet. 'Would you mind keeping that here, in your safe or somewhere?'

'That's no problem. And if it suits you, I'll drop by later to work out what size lorry we'll need for your removals,' Anna said.

Haris had already disappeared back into his workshop, but all three of them knew that the conversation about the figurine was yet to be finished.

Helena was lost in her own thoughts as she made her way back to the apartment. Though shocked by the thought that Nick had already been looking for a restorer, she felt happy to have confided in Anna, who she imagined would tell Haris in due course. She felt so much less alone.

The side streets were still quite empty, and she stepped off the pavement almost carelessly, only just stopping in time to miss being hit by a car. It seemed to have appeared out of nowhere.

The next moment felt as if it was happening in slow motion. As she stepped back, she saw two faces through the windscreen of a red sports car. Nick's head was turned towards Arsenis's in brotherly intimacy and Arsenis was leaning towards Nick, so neither would have seen her. The flash of Nick's white teeth told her he was laughing. In a second, they were gone.

She sat down on the pavement, her legs shaking so much she couldn't stand. The two men must have recognised a kindred spirit that day when Arsenis took Nick to the museum, or perhaps it even went back further than that. She felt utterly deceived. Nick had known from their first meeting that she had a connection with Greece, that she spoke Greek, that she was fairly green and innocent. And the inheritance of the Athens flat must have given him ideas about her wealth.

The two people, the *only* two people she loathed in all the world were allies. Her desire for revenge only strengthened. She was resolved now. Like the goddess Nemesis, she must take action.

On her way back to Kolonaki, Helena devoured two sugary pastries. She needed one for comfort and the other for energy. She still had something to deal with in the flat, and could put it off no longer.

Chapter Thirty-Four

Back in the apartment, Helena gathered some cleaning materials from the kitchen and braced herself. It was time to clear her grandfather's study.

The stink of Stamatis Papagiannis's past assaulted her as she opened the door of the windowless room. The wood panelling had absorbed the smell of his tobacco and the rug was yellowed with nicotine.

The desk was huge, nine feet by three, and it looked to Helena as if her grandmother had not touched it after his death. There was a reverence with which his personal effects were still neatly laid out: a silver fountain pen and inkwell, both now tarnished, and a large leather blotter. The heavy cigarette lighter she had been made to use sat next to a box engraved with his name. She lifted the lid and saw a neat row of his favourite brand of cigars inside. There was a second silver box with a more ornately engraved lid. When she opened it, a rancid smell released itself into the air. The wooden lining of the box had absorbed the scent of tobacco over many years and was now sour. The smell of this room brought back all too vividly the terrifying childhood encounters she had had to endure all those years before.

Perched on the edge of Stamatis Papagiannis's green leather chair, she studied the photograph that sat in front of her. A typed caption told her that it had been taken on Makronisos on 24 March 1949, when her grandfather had escorted King Paul and Queen Frederika on their visit to the euphemistically described 'correction camp'. Stamatis Papagiannis stood next to the smiling couple, clearly proud to be showing them around the brutal island of exile. Helena placed the photo face downwards with disgust.

The desk had four drawers on either side, and she knew from having tried before that they were locked. Vainly she ran her hand along the back of each shelf of the bookcase in search of the keys, before concluding that their hiding place would be more subtle than that. Perhaps they were even in a pocket of her grandfather's uniform, which had already been discarded. There was nothing she could do about that now.

If she thought about it for too long, she was not even sure that she wanted to know what was inside the drawers, but curiosity proved an irresistible impulse. Unsentimental about the furniture itself, and spurred by impatience, she went to fetch the tools that she knew were kept in an old bucket under the kitchen sink: several screwdrivers, a wrench and two hammers, one with a hefty claw.

She carried the whole bucket to the study. A gentle approach with a screwdriver did not work. Clearly more force would be needed. She inserted the sharp edges of the clawed hammer into the top of the drawer and wood veneer started to come away. For a fleeting moment, she recalled Giannis Ligakis's interest in the desk, and the sum he was prepared to pay, but this did not deter her. She would not even sell that man a cup and saucer. Using more violence increased her pleasure in the task, swinging the hammer towards the drawer as though she was trying to chop down a tree, and hacking at the front panel until the mechanism itself was smashed.

The drawer opened with a satisfying twang. Inside, she found two large leather-bound notebooks, one with a black cover, the other burgundy. They were ledgers of some kind. Opening them, she saw neat entries in her grandfather's hand and surmised that they had been written with the very pen that sat on the desk. He had always used black ink, of which there was still a trace in the well.

Similar headings appeared at the top of each page in both books:

NAME

PETITIONER

REQUEST

LOCATION

DATES

ACTION

GIFT/DATE RECEIVED

DATE TRANSFERRED BY AP to GL

SUM/DATE RECEIVED

The entries themselves were not all perfectly legible, but she soon got the gist.

'AP to GL. Arsenis Papagiannis to Giannis Ligakis?' she murmured. This must have been the date on which Arsenis gave something to Ligakis to sell.

Occasionally there was a gap in time between when something was received and then transferred.

In the burgundy notebook, the requests generally referred to army promotions or transfers from one place to another. The family name of the person making the application seemed to match that of the person for whom promotion or transfer was being requested. Every action resulted in the receipt of a gift. Sometimes there was a brief description of an object and its value.

She looked at one random example out of the thousands, so she could visualise the stages of the process. The father of Dimitris Halkidis had requested his son's posting to Thessaloniki on 4 June 1953. Transfer and promotion took place 3 September 1953, and was thanked with the gift of a fourth-century BC vase, received 6

October 1953. The vase was then transferred to Ligakis 2 January 1954. Sold for a sum of 500,000 drachmas on 30 March 1954.

She now understood that in receiving payment in the form of gifts, Stamatis Papagiannis had successfully whitewashed his corrupt actions. In her mind, there was also no doubt that his nephew and Giannis Ligakis had colluded.

The entries in the black notebook were very different. Requests related to a third party who seemed unrelated to the petitioner, and the locations were not always places that Helena recognised. She did understand the word *exoría*, exile, however.

The value of the objects here seemed to be considerably larger than those in the burgundy book. In this ledger, payment was often in precious gems, and many entries described antiquities. *Set of gold jewellery 2nd century* BC, *Attic Greek rhyton in shape of ram's head 5th century* BC, *Egyptian figure of falcon 3150* BC were just a few of the things listed. Many were of such great age that Helena could not begin to imagine why they were not in a museum.

Entries in the burgundy book began in 1935, when she calculated from what her mother had told her that Stamatis Papagiannis was already well on his way to seniority in the army. In the black book they began in 1944, when he was put in charge of prison camps. Many places were listed, some on the mainland, but the names repeated most often were Makronisos, Leros, Yiaros, Ai Stratis, Ikaria and Anafi. She deduced that these were all names of island prisons, and now she wondered if she would recognise any names of individuals. She ran her finger down the list of victims on the first few pages, fearing that sooner or later she would find Mihalis's family name, and Petros next to it. She kept an eye out for the name Lefteris too, wondering if the kiosk owner had also been a victim of her grandfather.

Both the notebooks had entries well into 1971, and it was clear that Stamatis Papagiannis's connections had given him power over people's lives right up until his death. There were hundreds of names in each book, men who had benefited from his corruption and others who might well have died because of it. Helena was over-whelmed by the sheer scale of these operations, but now that she had begun to destroy this desk, she felt compelled to continue.

She had only hacked into one of the desk's eight drawers. She jimmied open the remaining three on the left and found each one stuffed with correspondence. The mostly handwritten letters were almost illegible, but a cursory glance showed her that most began with the same words: *Sas efcharistó.* Thank you. She read a couple all the way through:

General Papagiannis,

We wanted to express our sincere gratitude for the transfer and promotion of our son, Constantinos. He is doing extremely well in the ministry.

Kind regards from myself and my wife,

K. Livanis

General Papagiannis,

We are most grateful for your help in cleaning up our neigh-bourhood. Our business is thriving now and the tone of the area has greatly improved now that the communist presence has been removed.

Many thanks,

K. Karvounaris

Two letters were enough. She had no need for any more evidence of her grandfather's sickening activities. The first related to an entry in the burgundy book, the second to the black book, and the latter proved that her grandfather had facilitated the removal of leftists and their imprisonment.

She wondered if he had kept this correspondence in order to incriminate the writers in the future. She would not put anything past the man. Now there was the question of what she should do with the letters herself. Most had been written years before and the authors might be dead by now. Should she keep them? Hand them over to someone?

There was no question of disposing of the ledgers. The burgundy one established that Stamatis Papagiannis had ruthlessly abused his position of power. The second told her that he was a crueller man than she had ever imagined.

Pieces of the desk lay around the room like debris from a shipwreck. Remembering that Anna was due soon, she abandoned the idea of tidying up. There were the rest of the drawers to be tackled and she went at it with gusto, feeling a massive surge of gratification as she swung the hammer with great force.

The top drawer on the right rattled like an old utensil drawer as she opened it. It held a jumble of metal cups and bowls, random coins, pieces of gold jewellery such as rings and bracelets. They were all dulled by age. She scooped them out in handfuls and laid them on the leather surface of the desktop, planning to take a closer look at each one later.

She had begun to pull out the drawer below when she heard the doorbell. Anna was here. She hurriedly put the ledgers and letters back inside the half-destroyed drawers.

'I'm glad you're here,' she said. 'I need some company. There are a few more things to value.'

Anna followed her into the study.

'Oh my God, Helena! That desk was an antique!' Anna surveyed the splinters of broken wood and the array of sharp tools with bemusement.

'I know it looks a mess, but I couldn't find the keys,' Helena explained hastily.

'You could have picked the locks?'

They laughed. The mess was almost comical.

'Even my brother couldn't glue this back together!'

Anna's eye was drawn to the desktop and she picked up one of the coins.

'Can I call Haris?' she said. 'This is more his period. Byzantine.'

Helena had no real sense of what that meant; everything on the desk looked like junk to her.

Haris must have sprinted. Five minutes later, Helena heard his breathless voice on the intercom.

'Come up!' she said eagerly. She had not expected to see him so soon.

'This is a grand place you've got,' he commented politely. 'And my sister says you've found some interesting things.'

Helena showed him into the study, where Anna was looking down at the contents of the drawer. She had spread the items out a little.

'*Theé mou!* My God!' he exclaimed. 'I didn't expect this!'

As he picked the pieces up one by one, his amazement seemed to deepen. '*Den to pistévo, den to pistévo!*' he kept repeating, shaking his head. 'I don't believe it!'

'Anna said it's Byzantine?'

'I'm certain that some of these go back to the fourth century,' he replied. 'This is really incredible. Astonishing!'

Helena could see that he was totally immersed in the pieces, but she needed his help.

'Haris,' she said, 'can you give me a hand here?' She held out the hammer and pointed to the undamaged drawers.

'I think there might be another way.' Haris rummaged in the tool bucket and pulled out a small screwdriver. In a matter of seconds, they heard the lock click and the next drawer opened.

'I preferred my method,' said Helena, laughing. 'Not so elegant, but . . .'

They were all smiling as Haris went back to the collection of artefacts.

This drawer was heavier but tidier, and neatly packed with boxes, which the two women piled onto the desktop. Anna opened the first and took out a jewelled chalice.

Helena was overwhelmed by the scale of the discovery. She

went into the kitchen to fetch water from the fridge, and then stood at the sink rinsing some glasses, absently staring at the water gushing from the tap. Had her grandmother been ignorant of the existence of these objects, or had she simply turned a blind eye? If the latter, she might well have been both ashamed and afraid of their implications.

It was too late for her grandfather to be punished, but there were two people who were still alive and, she was certain, culpable.

When she returned to the room, Anna and Haris were standing over the Byzantine collection on the desk.

'Some of this goes back to the third century after Christ,' Haris told her. 'You have amulets, rings, coins, buckles, seals. I would say much of it comes from Constantinople. Virtually everything here is gold. It's a treasure trove.'

Anna was holding a necklace of finely worked chain to her chest.

'Look, Helena!' she said excitedly. 'Haris says that the stones in this are probably sapphires and emeralds! Maybe sixth century.' She replaced it gently on the desk.

'And this is truly extraordinary.' Haris held a cross that covered his entire palm. It was decorated with enamel figures on back and front: Christ in the middle and saints on both sides.

'Do you know why it has a hinge?' he asked Helena.

'It opens, I assume,' she answered.

'Shall I?'

Anna nodded.

Helena watched as Haris, his brow creased with concentration, carefully eased open the cross. They all knew that it could break, but the risk was justified by a need to know if there was something inside.

The three of them stood close, holding their breath as the two parts came away from each other.

They all stared at what lay in the palm of Haris's hand. It was a fragment of something dark, jagged-edged, organic. A sliver of wood.

'Do you think . . .?' asked Anna.

'I want to believe it is,' whispered Haris.

'Part of the True Cross,' Anna murmured.

'You mean from the Crucifixion?' asked Helena.

Anna nodded.

'Shall I close it now? Everyone seen enough?' he asked, looking at the two women. 'I don't think it should be exposed to the air for too long.'

He laid the cross carefully on the desk again. All three of them were silent for a few moments, heads bowed as if in prayer.

Anna broke the spell.

'If you put all the pieces of the supposed True Cross together, you would have enough wood for a ship,' she said cynically.

'I don't care. Imagine the people who have held this over the past thousand years, the depth of their belief and what their faith gave to them,' said Haris, with reverence.

'Whether or not it's really a piece of the Crucifix, this is more than simply a reliquary containing a fragment of wood, real or fake. It has absorbed something from everyone who has held it, looked upon it, revered it. It's not true of every object. But it is with this one. I can *feel* it.'

Helena looked down at the cross and knew that she agreed with him. It was an object that touched her deeply too – a crime to have been lying in the darkness of her grandfather's desk for decades.

'You can't put a price on something like that, Anna,' he went on. 'It should be in a church, where people can feel the faith of their ancestors.'

'I admit it's beautiful,' said Anna.

'But it has *animus* too, doesn't it?'

'Okay, Haris,' Anna laughed. 'Enough for now. Helena didn't invite us here to listen to us bickering!'

In fact, Helena loved listening to the discourse between them, even though it reminded her of what she had missed as an only child.

'Two more drawers to go!' she said cheerfully.

Haris picked the lock of the third drawer. It was hard to pull out because of the weight inside, but he eased it open by a few inches.

Helena dipped her hand in and blindly picked up the first thing she could reach, handing it to Anna.

'Now here's a surprise,' said Anna. 'We've gone back a few millennia now.'

Helena stared at the object, wide-eyed.

'Looks a bit familiar, doesn't it?'

She took it from the palm of Anna's hand. 'A head,' she said, 'Cycladic.'

Haris stepped forward to see. 'She's beautiful,' he breathed. 'Harp-shaped.'

'What else is in there, Helena?'

For the next five minutes, brother and sister watched incredulously as she mechanically removed one piece after another, in varying shades of marble from almost white to dark sand: feet, ankles, feet still connected to shins, single limbs, whole torsos, sections of neck, parts of pelvis. The final drawer, the one beneath, contained a similarly random selection of body parts, none of them more than a few inches long. There were some objects shaped like animals, too, and various pots also made of marble.

Nothing really surprised Helena now. After the first few pieces, she hardly glanced at what she was removing.

Anna had laid them out in neat rows on the desk, and some of them almost disappeared against the faded leather surface.

'How sad they look. How lost,' said Haris, surveying the jumble of broken pieces.

With a restorer's instinct, he began to move them around to see if any of the parts might fit together.

'All widows,' he muttered, surveying the collection. 'All broken a long time ago – see the erosion on the edges? All kinds of different marble here too. Very mixed.'

Helena slipped out of the room. These strange misshapen pieces of marble had reminded her of something. Suddenly, all these years later, they made sense.

On her first adult visit to Athens, she had chosen to sleep in her mother's childhood room. She had found it somehow comforting, and felt closer to her there. Nobody had gone into the guest bedroom where she had stayed as a child for a very long time, except perhaps Dina, who had flicked a duster over the surfaces in her last months in the apartment.

Perhaps those jagged lumps she had gripped so tightly that terrible evening of her grandfather's saint's day were still hidden in the bedside drawer where she had left them.

She was not disappointed. Right at the very back, behind an Enid Blyton book, were the two oddly shaped stones. She took them back to the study and showed them to Haris.

'Are they . . .?'

'Just add them to the collection,' he said, giving them a superficial glance. 'They're part of something Cycladic, without doubt. But I can see they aren't parts of the same figurine.'

Helena put them on the desk, where they immediately got lost in amongst the rest.

'You look really pale,' said Anna with concern.

'Do you mind if we go into the other room for a moment,' she asked. 'It's so stuffy in here.'

The sight of those once perplexing pieces had all too vividly reminded her of her childhood trauma. A combination of exhaustion, dust and the harrowing revelations of the afternoon was beginning to overwhelm her.

In the drawing room, Anna pulled across a curtain to shut out a shaft of low sunlight.

'I'll be fine in a minute,' said Helena, sinking into a sofa.

Haris attempted to be jovial. 'There's enough in there for a small museum,' he quipped.

'A slightly strange, eclectic one,' Anna added.

The two collections were indeed strangely disparate, with thousands of years separating one from another.

Anna and Haris were both full of questions about how and why these things had been locked up in the darkness.

'I could name it the Museum of Murder,' said Helena sardonically. 'Or the Criminal Collection.'

She noticed the look of apprehension on Haris's face, and felt an urgent need to distance herself from the objects.

'Stay here for a moment. I want you to see something else.'

She fetched the two ledgers from the study, and Anna and Haris joined her on the sofa, one on either side. Beginning with the burgundy one, she showed them the entries, page by page. Occasionally one of the items under *GIFT/DATE RECEIVED* corresponded with something they had seen in the study. One of the gold crosses was certainly described.

'You don't seem to be surprised by any of this,' Helena said to Haris.

'By what? That people paid bribes to get their sons promoted? It's nothing new. That kind of behaviour probably goes back to Alexander the Great.'

The black book provoked a much stronger reaction. It was not only the greater value of the gifts (many of the golden Byzantine treasures and Cycladic pieces appeared as entries) but the reason for the payments.

'Makronisos . . .' Anna said almost inaudibly.

'And Leros,' whispered Haris. 'The worst. I see what you meant by a Museum of Murder now.'

'Even for those who survived, it was a living death while they were there.'

Helena ran her finger down each page, every so often noting other matches with something in the study. On one of the later pages, she spotted the name of Mihalis's Uncle Petros. His sanity had been traded for the torso of a Cycladic figurine.

It took them an hour or more to reach the final page.

Helena felt secure, shoulder to shoulder with Haris on one side and Anna on the other. Sharing the weight of all this made it more bearable, and there was a moment when she began to turn the pages more slowly, simply to prolong the closeness with them.

'All these things were currency,' said Haris.

'For money laundering,' added Anna.

'There's nothing actually wrong with trading in antiquities for profit, but this is much more than that. It's theft, it's looting. It's people's lives.'

'It's evil on every level, isn't it?' Helena was not looking for an answer.

Now that the sun was no longer shining directly into the room, Anna got up to let in a little more light. Haris remained sitting with Helena for a moment.

'Do you know the Greek word for "bribe", Helena?'

She shook her head, looking straight into his eyes.

'*Doro-dokía*,' he said.

'*Dóro*. As in gift?'

'Exactly. If it's an *objet d'art*, it feels like a gift, doesn't it, and it keeps your conscience clear. If you accept money, it's far more incriminating. But it's still a bribe, whatever changes hands.'

'And what could be the reason for him keeping all those things in a drawer?'

'Anna?' Haris deferred to his sister.

'Because if they're stolen, it's much better to wait until the heat has died down before you put them on the market or smuggle them out. And with the Cycladic fragments, perhaps he was getting different parts at different times so that they could gradually be pieced together. That's when you get the optimum value.'

'It looks as if none of the ones that were in the drawers when your grandfather died were ever going to form a whole.'

'For some reason that gives me great satisfaction,' said Helena. 'That he may never have had the pleasure of holding a complete one.'

'And even judging from this list, he only ever received fragments,' said Haris.

'But what am I going to do with all of it?' She was overwhelmed by the implications.

'What you have in there is worth a lot,' said Anna.

'But I don't want any of it. None of it belongs here.'

'And now that it's not properly locked up, I would suggest it doesn't stay here.'

'Is there any chance . . .?'

'Of course,' Haris said. 'There's plenty of room in our safe. And it would take a mastermind to crack the code.'

They went back to the study. Helena surveyed the piles of goods. It was too late to repair the harm that Stamatis Papagiannis had done to innocent people, but it wasn't too late to see his collaborators brought to some kind of justice.

'Why don't you take all the gold stuff away today and I'll pack up the rest and start bringing it over in the morning,' she suggested.

They agreed on the plan, and Anna and Haris left for the shop.

That evening, having securely locked the flat and fastened the padlock once again, Helena strolled up to see Mihalis.

'Do you need some more polish?' he joked.

'Not at the moment.' She attempted to smile. 'But I do need a glass of wine.'

'Meet you in twenty minutes. The café on the corner of Exarchia Square?'

Half an hour later, they were sitting enjoying the cool evening air. A carafe of chilled retsina and a bowl of olives sat in front of them.

Helena was impatient to tell him about the ledgers, and the fact that she had found his Uncle Petros's name. He was one of the people on the left who had been betrayed and arrested without real justification.

Mihalis took the news calmly. He did not blame Helena. It only added to his hatred for a regime that had damaged his family so much and left the ugly legacy that lingered to this day.

'Panos's uncle didn't appear anywhere in the list,' Helena confirmed. 'But I want to make amends to your Uncle Petros. I mean it. Somehow.'

She then launched into a catalogue of all the things she had found in the drawers, some of them matching entries in the ledgers: vessels, goblets, crosses, marble torsos, brooches, bowls, rings . . .

'It sounds like the flea market in Monastiraki,' said Mihalis. 'Piles of old junk.'

'No, really the opposite,' Helena said emphatically. 'Byzantine gold and ancient Cycladic treasures.'

'Really?' he queried. 'And how do you know they're genuine?'

'I had some experts with me who identified them,' answered Helena. 'They're really knowledgeable people. They have a shop not far from yours, actually. Anna and Haris Morakis.'

Mihalis nodded knowingly. 'Yes, I know them. Brother and sister. Both a few years older than me.'

'Did you go to the same school maybe?'

'No,' he scoffed. 'They went to one of the best schools in the country, Athens College. But I think they're good people and my father knew theirs.'

'They're very nice,' confirmed Helena. 'And really helping me with all of this . . . mess.'

'There are plenty of strange individuals in that business,' he continued. 'But the Morakis family has a clean reputation. And if my father and theirs drank their morning coffee together, there was definitely trust between them.'

'It seems a very small world,' Helena said. 'Does everyone know everyone here?'

'Not really. People talk about six degrees of separation, but I reckon it's only three or four in this city. You should think of Athens as a small town, or even a collection of villages.' Mihalis poured the last dregs of the wine into their glasses. 'And Kolonaki is one of those.'

'It certainly feels like it,' she said. 'People don't seem to move far.'

'That's true for most,' confirmed Mihalis. 'And even if they do, they never forget the past.'

Chapter Thirty-Five

Helena woke the next morning regretting the amount of retsina she had drunk. Someone was knocking very persistently on her door. She suddenly remembered that Anna and Haris had promised to return.

Bleary-eyed and still in the white T-shirt that she was wearing as a nightgown, she opened the door to the immaculately dressed Haris.

He was holding two coffees and had a large leather weekend bag thrown over his shoulder. It was already ten o'clock, but it was obvious from her state of dishevelment that she had been asleep and he politely apologised for waking her.

'It's me that should apologise,' she gabbled. 'I overslept.'

'One of us had to stay at the shop, so I was dispatched to collect the rest of the . . .' He hesitated for a moment, clearly unsure how to refer to the motley collection of tainted goods.

'Hoard?' Helena offered. 'It's so kind of you. I really do appreciate it.'

'And I brought you a coffee.'

'Manna from heaven,' Helena said, smiling. 'Shall we go and drink it on the balcony? It's such a beautiful day, and the sun reaches it at this time of morning.'

Seated opposite Helena on a wicker chair, Haris tried not to stare at her. She seemed completely unaware of how she looked, her tangled auburn hair almost down to her waist and her long freckled legs stretched out in front of her. Her total lack of self-consciousness and vanity were extraordinary to him. His girlfriend of three years, soon to be his wife, considered every detail of herself, from coiffure down to polished toenails, before she would even think about leaving their apartment for work. It was impossible not to appreciate the result, and he felt proud that he was with a woman whom other men admired as they would a work of art. Helena, however, was different. Her emerald-green eyes needed no embellishment, and the beauty of her hair resided in its wildness and colour, both refreshingly natural.

'Look, um, I really appreciate what you and Anna are doing here,' she said.

'We know you do,' Haris answered. 'It's a horrible situation. And you seem very alone in it.'

'It's not only the mountain of stuff from the past,' she explained. 'There is something more recent too.'

'Anna mentioned that something had happened with your friend.'

'He is not my friend,' Helena said forcefully. 'Not any longer.'

'I didn't mean . . .'

Suddenly appreciating the sensitivity and quiet intelligence of this kind person, she regretted having snapped.

'The point is,' he continued, pretending he had not noticed, 'even though some of those things had been in the drawers for some time, they could be evidence of an active theft and smuggling ring.'

'But the feet in your safe are from a much fresher theft, aren't they?' suggested Helena. 'And if we can link Nick with Arsenis and then Ligakis, maybe we can get some kind of justice for the past, as well as put a stop to what's happening in the present.'

Haris leaned forward. 'Anna and I want to suggest something. It could be the only way to gather evidence of what might be going on now. We want to visit the island where you were excavating. Will you come with us?'

Helena hesitated. Nisos. A place of such mixed memories: love, pleasure, discovery, happiness, but finally utter disillusion. Now, though, it might help her on the path to revenge.

Haris seemed to notice her moment of uncertainty.

'Helena, it's in the interests of us all to stop people stealing what belongs here in Greece,' he urged. 'It's in the interests of the country, of archaeological study, of the whole of civilisation, for that matter. And yours, because you are Greek.'

She needed no more persuasion.

'Yes. Of course. I would love to,' she replied. 'When?'

'There's a national holiday coming up next week and we can close for three days. Can you be in Athens until then?'

'Yes,' she said eagerly, certain that there was nothing in her life that was more important. Any trepidation fell away when she noticed his smile.

Before he left, she asked him a favour. Would he remove the portrait from the wall in the drawing room, because she could not reach it. In a trice, he had done so.

'Where do you want it?' he asked.

'In the study,' Helena replied.

He carried it through for her and she asked him to lay it face down on top of the broken desk.

'*Efcharistó*, Haris,' she said.

'A pleasure,' he replied. 'It should have been removed long ago.'

Helena used the days leading up to the Nisos trip to clear what was left in the apartment. She kept only some basic furniture: bed, bedside cabinet, in which she had stored the ledgers along with the letters, now tightly bound together, a couple of chairs and the kitchen table, where the memorabilia of her mother and Andreas sat. For now, the Meissen also remained, safe in its walnut cabinet. A team from the Morakis shop carefully dismantled everything else, and over a period of days, a pantechnicon took away the chairs, tables, bedheads, wardrobes, mirrors, sideboards, a chaise longue and numerous other pieces. Finally the broken desk was transported to a dump, and she asked the slightly bemused driver to take the portrait with it.

The apartment now seemed even larger than before, and she wandered from one empty, echoing room to another. One ghost, at least, seemed to have gone.

Every other evening, she met Mihalis and Panos and mingled with their friends, listening to live music in small cafés or sitting inside tavernas long into the night as the Athenian autumn finally cooled.

Real-estate agents had come to value the apartment, and Helena appointed someone who was personally known to Anna Morakis.

'He was a classmate,' Anna told her. 'And is less likely than most to do any dirty dealing.'

On 28 October, Óchi Day, the commemoration of Greece's defiant rejection of the Italian demand to enter the country in 1940, Helena's bag sat ready in the hallway. She was glad that this was the weekend for their trip, as the sparse and lofty rooms were beginning to make her feel lonely.

At 8.25 a.m., she looked over the balcony rails and could see Haris standing below. This was a different kind of Greek, one who arrived early. She dashed inside, locked up and took the lift down.

He was already holding open the passenger door of a slightly dented grey Mercedes-Benz. In her excitement, she embraced him. It was a brief gesture, but she sensed him pull away. Perhaps she had been too informal, but surely in making this journey they had crossed the line between business acquaintanceship and friendship? Anna certainly thought so, because she leapt from her seat in the back to give Helena a hug.

'Kaliméra,' she said, smiling. 'It's so lovely to be going on a trip. We haven't been to an island for a couple of years.'

The Morakis siblings looked as if they had stepped from a magazine feature on how to dress casually, both of them in chinos and white shirts, packet fresh, and suede loafers. Anna had a pink cashmere pullover draped over her shoulders. Helena inevitably felt scruffy next to them, with her favourite jeans, appliquéd on the back pockets, bleached almost white by the sun and a cheesecloth shirt that had seen better days.

Haris had stowed Helena's bag in the boot and the engine was running. They had to be at the port of Rafina by eleven. The ferries were now working to the winter schedule and only ran to Nisos twice a week. It was one of the more remote islands and the journey would take at least seven hours, particularly if the Aegean was going to be rough later in the day. The ferry would stop at six other islands on the way.

'There's always plenty of food in the cafeteria,' Haris told her as they joined the queue of cars waiting to board. 'But do you have something to pass the time? There's no reading matter on board. Last week's newspapers tucked in a rack if you're lucky.'

'I've brought a couple of books that belonged to my mother,' Helena told him. She had the volume of Cavafy's poetry and the Kazantzakis novel in her shoulder bag.

Responding to the shouts and gesticulations of the team in charge, Haris parked the car. It stalled a couple of times while he was doing so.

'She's on her last wheels,' he joked. 'She belonged to our dad, so I'm too fond of her to say goodbye. But she does let me down occasionally, I'm afraid.'

'Hope she behaves herself on this trip,' quipped Anna. 'I did say you could drive mine.'

'I had her serviced last week,' he assured them both, taking the key from the ignition.

They squeezed themselves between the rows of vehicles and went up the steps to find a place in the lounge.

Haris and Anna were immediately absorbed by what they were reading. Anna was browsing a publication on furniture from the Napoleonic period, and Haris was studying *New Techniques in the*

Restoration of Roman Glassware. Helena had Cavafy lying on the low table in front of her and a small dictionary on her lap. She was reading 'Ithaka', perhaps the poet's best-known work, and jotting unfamiliar words into a notebook.

'Tell us if anything needs translation,' said Anna.

'I'm fine so far,' Helena smiled. 'It's all making perfect sense.'

> *Me ti efcharístisi, me ti chará*
> *Tha baíneis se liménas protoeidoménous.*

> With what pleasure and happiness
> You enter harbours for the first time.

Every hour or so there was the great commotion and excitement of docking, and the words of Cavafy's poem came alive.

Some of the islands were even smaller than Nisos and depended entirely on the ferries for their survival. Helena went on deck to watch as labelled crates were offloaded, everything from toilet paper to building materials, from canned tomatoes to gas canisters. Most islands were self-sufficient in only one thing: goats. Milk and cheese were the sole commodities they did not need to import. During the half-hour the ferry was docked, a few women came on board selling packets of dried herbs or mountain tea, sometimes jars of honey or capers. Then over the tannoy came the five-minute warning for departure, and they scurried off again.

Helena was fascinated by the apparently treeless isles. Why had people first settled on these barren outcrops of rock? she wondered. And how had they survived in such an inhospitable environment? What had inspired them to create objects of beauty such as the elegant figurines that still held their allure five thousand years later?

The three of them drank plenty of coffee to punctuate the journey and ate several toasted sandwiches, and eventually Haris put his book aside and dropped his guard. The formality that had felt like a barrier between him and Helena evaporated, and he began to talk about the things he had restored that had given him the greatest pride.

'After that Italian *krater*, my father put me to work on some porcelain. It was very fine work. The thickness of the pieces can be paper thin. You can read your love letters through your Meissen, did you know that?'

'I don't think I've ever had a love letter,' Helena laughed. 'Or any Meissen.'

'Not quite true,' he corrected her. 'You do have Meissen now. Plenty of it.'

'But still no love letters!'

Haris raised his eyebrows. 'I find that hard to believe,' he teased. 'Anyway, I managed a few plates. And then groups of figures started coming in. They were so elaborate. Dancers, trios of *putti*, classical tableaux like Europa and the Bull, animals of every kind.'

Anna leaned in. 'He was brilliant at it. And collectors and dealers all began to hear about him.'

'So, there were no more model aircraft?' Helena asked with a smile.

'Never again. I was piecing all these tiny porcelain fragments together instead. There was a queue of jobs, but to be honest, I liked plates and bowls better than china ornaments. Those were fussy.'

'You didn't have a choice?'

'Not really. I finished my school work first and then got out the adhesives! It was very satisfying.'

'And the rest of our father's business benefited, because it brought different people in to the shop,' added Anna.

'Then one day my father handed me something wrapped in brown paper. Seven small pieces of marble. Heavy. It felt very different. You know it yourself – you've felt that weight, haven't you, Helena?'

She nodded, her memory taking her back to the moment of discovering what Nick had planted in her rucksack.

'It was Cycladic and what is known as a violin-shaped figurine, with a long, slim neck and tiny waist, from around 3000 BC,' continued Haris. 'It had been intact until the previous day, when a museum curator had dropped it on a stone floor.'

'The man was absolutely beside himself when he brought it in,' Anna confirmed. 'His job was at stake, of course.'

'It wasn't a massive challenge because the breaks were clean,' said Haris.

'Don't be so self-deprecating.' Anna scolded her brother even while giving him praise. 'It was impossible to see the joins once you had finished it. She was perfect. Whole once again. The museum never knew.'

Helena was touched by the pride that Anna showed in her brother. 'The point is, Helena,' he said, 'it felt really worthwhile. I had seen those figurines in museums and for me they represent a kind of perfection that has never been achieved again, even when Picasso, Mondrian and other artists like them tried to emulate that primitivism five thousand years later. Their work was not original. What I held in my hand was a prototype. Pure and beautiful. Simple as they are, these figurines have great power.'

'I agree with you,' said Helena. 'I first saw them when I was a teenager. They made a big impression.'

'I wouldn't collect them,' he said. 'For me they are almost sacred and shouldn't be kept by a few rich people in their homes.'

Anna had curled up on her seat and was now dozing. Haris returned to his book. While he was oblivious to her gaze, Helena observed him. He was undeniably attractive, and as she watched his eyes flicker across the pages, she realised that his quiet intelligence made him even more so.

With her two companions opposite and the gentle rocking of the boat, Helena felt a surge of contentment. Here in the middle of the ocean, with the soothing sound of the waves and the gentle progress towards their destination, she began to wish that this journey would never end. Through a porthole, she could see the setting sun, and glancing down at the poem in front of her, she murmured some lines to herself:

Allá mi viázeis to taxídi diólou,
Kalýtera chrónia pollá na diarkései.

But don't hurry the journey in any way,
The longer it lasts, the better.

Haris looked up. 'It's beautiful to hear you reading in Greek,' he said. 'And I was feeling the same. That I'd be happy for this journey to last for ever.'

She was relieved that the words resonated with Haris, given that she was responsible for bringing him and his sister on this seemingly interminable trip to Nisos.

She smiled. 'Do you mean it?' she asked. 'I was feeling a bit guilty about how long it was taking.'

'It was our idea to come,' he said. 'Why don't you read me some more?'

He moved to sit closer so that he could look over her shoulder as she read a few more lines of the text. The few moments of gentle intimacy were precious to her, and she felt a pang of regret when the ship sounded its horn to signal its approach into the port.

Chapter Thirty-Six

It was nine in the evening when they drove off the ferry and towards the village. An unfriendly wind had whipped up since they arrived, and fine rain was beginning to fall.

'There should be a spare anorak on the back seat,' Haris told Helena as the drizzle gave way to a downpour. 'I always throw in extra waterproofs if I'm going to the islands in winter.'

Helena had only experienced Greece in summer, always leaving before the sudden October drop in temperature and the cold humidity that could penetrate the bones. She realised now that the thick stone walls of island architecture had been built not only to keep the heat out, but also to withstand the harsher elements. She snuggled into Haris's rusty-brown jacket and put the hood up, enjoying the subtle scent of him.

'Let's try the taverna that used to feed the archaeologists,' she said, pointing in the direction of Marina's. 'Hopefully it'll still be open in the winter.'

Light glowed through its steamed-up windows, and two old men eating at separate tables, heads bent over their plates, glanced up when Helena, Anna and Haris walked in.

The owner came out from behind the bar to greet them. He was glad of some more business on this wild night, and listed his dishes of the day. They ordered enthusiastically. He failed to recognise Helena with her hood up and a scarf concealing her hair.

'My wife could make up a couple of bedrooms,' he offered, when they enquired about somewhere they could stay. 'Shared bathroom, but there's not much choice at this time of year. Maybe one other place in the north of the island.'

'I don't suppose you have a third room?' Anna asked. The patron had assumed that either she or Helena was Haris's partner.

'We'll see what we can do. Food first?'

They made quick work of a goat stew, despite its chewy texture, and the fresh bread to soak up the sauce and dip into olive oil was delicious. A carafe of red wine soon disappeared, and they ordered another.

There was a log fire burning in the corner, and they sat by it to finish their wine, warmed by alcohol, the crackling olive wood and the hospitality,

Haris found himself staring at Helena again, her cheeks glowing pink from the warmth. In his imagination, she was Hestia, goddess of the hearth and fire, who was always pictured with flaming red hair. He was increasingly mesmerised by this half-Greek girl with her other-worldly look.

Helena was lost in her own thoughts. From the moment she had set foot on Nisos again, recollections of Nick had flooded back, in particular her arrival on the two previous occasions. Looking back, she realised that there had been an unidentifiable sense of unease despite his honeyed words and convincing ardour. Only now did she face the reality that her insecurity was well founded. Naïvety or inexperience; it did not matter what it was called, but anger simmered inside her. She did not forget for a moment why they were here. She wanted to punish her 'uncle' and Nick for their cynical crimes, and the image of Nick's wide smile through the windscreen of Arsenis's car only strengthened her motivation.

Anna jolted both Helena and Haris out of their daydreams.

'We only have two days here,' she said. 'So we should make a plan.'

The taverna was empty now, but even so, they spoke in low voices. If there had been any kind of illegality on this island, somebody in its small population must have been involved.

'I think we should work out if there is anyone we can really trust,' said Haris. 'And also if there is anyone who is still stealing or smuggling.'

His sister giggled.

'I know it sounds simplistic, Anna. But what are the other options?'

'There might be a third category,' Helena offered. 'The ones who know it happens but pretend not to notice. I wouldn't trust them either.'

'I suggest we go to bed now and get up around eight,' said Anna. 'Then we'll have plenty of time to see the archaeological sites and get to know the island.'

The following morning, the taverna owner made each of them a strong, gritty coffee. In broad daylight, he remembered Helena from all the meals he had served to the archaeologists, and was curious about her return. It was unusual for anyone to come at this time of year. She kept her story simple, saying that she had loved it so much on the island that she wanted to show it to her friends. Any other explanation would have prolonged his interrogation.

By nine, they were ready to leave. There was only one main road, and it followed the circumference of the island. The sole decision required was which direction to travel. Anna favoured anticlockwise, as it would bring them to the far west in the late afternoon, and she wanted to watch the sun dipping below the horizon.

'With this rain, we're unlikely to see it,' Haris pointed out. 'But as you wish.'

Helena navigated them to the first of the archaeological sites where she had volunteered. It was not far out of town, up on a hill, and was fenced off with a large notice in Greek warning against entry. The gate was easily climbable, and there was no guard. From what Helena could see, however, nothing looked very different from how she remembered it on the last day. She recalled the professor being reasonably certain that this area had given up all its treasures.

It was the second site that was still a work in progress when they left, and the richer of the two in terms of what it held. It was here that Nick must have found the figurine.

On this remote hillside, rain slicing horizontally into their faces, Helena suggested trespass.

'Unless we lift the tarpaulins, we won't be able to tell if there has been any more digging.'

She knew that all the tombs had been re-covered with earth before they left, so further and more recent excavation would be obvious.

They carefully stepped across the muddy earth, incriminating themselves with footprints, and approached what Helena knew to have been a wealthy cemetery. As they walked around the edge, everything looked intact at first, with the flapping plastic sheeting apparently still in place. Only at the far end did they see that it had been slashed across.

Helena quickened her pace, filled with dread as much as excitement. The others followed.

They all stood around a large fresh mound of damp soil. Whoever had been responsible had left evidence of his favourite cigarette brand, *Karélia*. Twenty or thirty butts were carelessly scattered about, and the empty packet was not far away. The hole was at least four feet deep and the surface area was around eight feet by six.

'Too lazy even to replace the dirt,' said Anna scornfully.

'Yes, but look!' said Haris. 'They've left something.'

He had noticed a small marble fragment sticking out of the discarded soil and was now excitedly scrabbling around it with his bare hands. In a matter of seconds, he had retrieved some sizeable chunks of marble bowl, as well as a torso and several small legs from figurines.

The two women watched him, speechless.

'If they didn't bother to take these,' he said, lining up the pieces on the ground next to him, 'I suggest it was because they found something more significant. Something whole, perhaps something much bigger.'

He got up, covered in mud. The pieces on the ground were being washed by the rain.

'What do we do with these now?' said Anna, feeling like a tomb raider herself.

'My suggestion is that we bury them over there in those trees, make a note of exactly where, and convey the information to Helena's professor. That will keep them safe from whoever did this digging. They will be properly noted, and when the dig is resumed, they can be easily found. Perhaps the rest of this bowl is still in there somewhere.'

Helena nodded. They could not become guilty of the same crime that they were trying to prevent.

Rain continued to fall, so once they had buried the pieces, they retreated to the car, turned the heating to maximum and attempted to dry off.

As they drove northwards, the rain slackened off a little. At one point, a shaft of sunlight broke through the clouds and a spectacular rainbow arced across the sea, its hues stronger and more jewel-coloured than any Helena had ever seen.

'Everything is so extreme here,' she said, smiling. 'Look at that. One minute the sky is grey, and the next you get a psychedelic light show. So beautiful.'

'"Somewhere over the rainbow",' Haris sang quietly.

Helena and Anna joined in, and by the time the song was over, the skies had cleared. To the left of them, the rocky, barren landscape had not changed, but to the right, the ocean stretched away to the horizon, a vast stretch of cerulean blue.

'I'm starving,' said Anna from the back seat.

'There's a village in the north,' said Helena, looking at the map. 'Shall we eat there?'

Just as she said this, the road curved left and Haris slammed on the brakes as a fifty-strong herd of goats appeared in front of them.

Bells jangling noisily, they trotted down a vertiginous path towards the sea, where copious quantities of herbs sprouted from the rocks.

By the time the village came into view, Helena's stomach was rumbling as loudly as the distant thunder. Rain was returning.

The little port was crowded with brightly coloured boats bobbing on the restless water, and Haris parked opposite, outside a row of what were clearly fish tavernas in the summer. Their shutters were down, with the exception of one, and the two women ran in to avoid a heavy downpour.

'*Eíste anoichtós gia fagitó?*' Anna asked the patron whether he was open and serving food.

It had been too rough for the boats to go out the previous night, so there was no fresh fish, he explained, but his aunt had brought some kid down from the mountains. 'It will be delicious,' he assured them.

As he said this, Haris walked in shaking his hair out like a puppy, and grinned.

'*Pináo san lýkos,*' he beamed. 'I'm as hungry as a wolf! I've been wanting some more *katsíki* since we had it last night!'

His exaggerated enthusiasm for more goat was met with a disapproving glance from his sister. Helena did her best to suppress her laughter. The comic moment was a surprise.

The meat was even tougher than what they had been served the night before, but they put on a convincing performance when the owner enquired if they were enjoying their lunch.

Over the next hour, as they sat over their meal, the whole community streamed into this small venue. Some twenty or so rough-skinned fishermen were enjoying their day off. The forecast had told them that they would be back out at sea early the following morning, so they were making the most of today, joking, drinking and playing *távli*. Their chapped fingers endlessly tossed the dice, and counters clattered up and down the board. They seemed not to notice the strangers in their midst, until Haris got up to pay the bill. Then one of them beckoned him over and vacated his seat, indicating that he should take his place in the game. Haris accepted the challenge and sat down.

Tempted as she was to go over and watch, Helena was conscious of the invisible line that divided the room between male and female.

'Haris isn't just playing *távli*,' said Anna enigmatically. 'He's up to something.'

'But you'll miss the sunset!' said Helena, as she saw him starting a second game.

'Never mind,' Anna answered.

They were both quiet for a moment while the taverna owner cleared their plates.

'I feel like we're getting somewhere,' Anna said. 'We've already identified illegal excavation, haven't we?'

'All we really proved was that the sites should be under guard the whole time,' said Helena with frustration. 'And that some people have no integrity.'

'Or perhaps they are in dire need of money,' said Anna sympathetically. 'It's a pretty basic way of life here, and if there is treasure in your back yard, it must be tempting.'

She ordered another carafe of wine. Her brother was driving and it was clear they would not be leaving soon.

Helena began to open up to her about her past few years: the death of her mother, meeting Nick, and how she had slightly lost her way at Oxford because she was distracted by love.

Anna was a sympathetic listener, but she also shared some pain in her own past, in particular a tempestuous marriage to a shipowner's son that had ended in bitter acrimony when she failed to produce a child.

'That's cruel,' commented Helena.

'It's why so many women have a child before marriage here,' said Anna ruefully. 'To make sure they can fulfil their obligation. And if they can't . . .'

They talked for a while about the differences between British and Greek society, how the role of women was gradually changing in Greece, even if a little later than in Britain.

All the while, Helena kept one eye on Haris, losing count of the number of matches he played. As one man lost, another was waiting to challenge him. Shouts occasionally went up from the corner in which he was playing, and a few of the fishermen had gathered around to watch. At one point, money was put on the table and a larger group assembled.

The two women continued chatting, with Anna admitting that she was happy again now and enjoying her independence. She was doing a part-time degree in art history and the business had become a great passion for her.

Aside from her immediate aim of exposing the looting and theft of antiquities and bringing the perpetrators to justice, Helena confessed that she was slightly uncertain about her future.

'You know you could combine that incredibly impressive degree of yours with this new interest in ancient objects,' Anna said thoughtfully, sipping her wine.

'You think so?' asked Helena.

'One of Haris's friends has just finished a course in archaeological science. He has learned all these new techniques that allow him to establish the origins of any piece of pottery. He says it has revolutionised our ability to reach conclusions on ancient societies – deciding whether there was migration, for example.'

'Sounds much more exciting than a job in the pharmaceutical industry,' responded Helena with enthusiasm.

'It's something called petrography,' continued Anna. 'I can't begin to explain it to you, but you should look into it. This guy was a chemistry graduate like you.'

Helena was interested, but suddenly distracted by a thickset bearded man coming into the taverna and people parting to let him through to the *tavli* table. Judging by the noises of encouragement and applause, the impromptu tournament had turned into a keenly fought contest. From the crowd that now gathered, it seemed that this man might be the reigning champion.

Around nine o'clock, when the sun had long gone down, Haris got up. He had lost the final game and was a few thousand drachmas down. Still smiling, he shook hands with everyone. His good-natured defeat had made him popular, and when he slammed a few more notes down onto the counter to buy drinks for them all, he became their hero.

Helena and Anna were more than ready to leave. They went out into the windy night, and Haris quickly started the car and put on the heating.

'Well,' he announced as he pulled away, 'that was very interesting. And very useful.'

'I told Helena that you were up to something,' Anna said. 'Not just having a game of backgammon!'

'That guy was really tough competition,' Haris smiled.

'What were you actually doing, then?' asked Helena impatiently.

'I dropped into the conversation that we're in the antiques business,' he explained. 'And they made the assumption that we're here to buy . . .'

'Clever you,' said Helena.

'I didn't disabuse them.'

As he drove, carefully negotiating the hairpin bends of the dark, damp road in the bulky car, he shared what he had learned.

'They weren't very forthcoming, but they could smell money,' he said.

'The car? Your watch?'

Haris wore an antique watch that had belonged to their father, and any car that was not an agricultural truck made an impression in this fishing community.

'It just took a few casual questions,' he said. 'I gathered that some of them dig and others do the smuggling with their boats. They tend not to use the main port down south to get things to Athens, but take the goods to one of the bigger islands, from where someone transfers them by ferry. It's too small here. The man I was playing against last seems to be the lynchpin and the main contact for customers. The others in effect are just his workers.'

'*Lathranaskafí*, an illegal dig,' reflected Anna. 'It all sounds very organised.'

'And if there is someone unscrupulous on such a dig, these men are very useful traffickers.'

Helena remembered the time, late at night, when she had seen Nick with two men and he had explained the situation away.

'It didn't seem to occur to them that I might disapprove of any of this,' Haris said. 'They simply saw us as potential customers, so I said we might come back another time and we left it at that.'

It was now raining heavily, and the rapid back and forth of the windscreen wipers struggling against the deluge precluded conversation. Every mile or so, they passed a roadside memorial for a fatal accident, where a small oil lamp burned next to the icon of a saint. Getting them safely back to Marina's demanded Haris's full concentration.

Piece by piece, Helena felt they were gathering evidence of the illegality that Nick had been caught up in. She was waiting for the moment when she would use it to trap him.

Chapter Thirty-Seven

When she threw open her shutters the next day, Helena was surprised and happy to see a clear sky. She rested her elbows on the ledge for a while, taking deep breaths of fresh autumnal air. Despite the sour memories she had of Nisos, she was forming new ones with new friends.

For some reason, there was no one in the taverna to offer them coffee, but she knew of a café on the other side of the village that might be open.

As they strolled along the seafront, past small shops boarded up for winter, a shuttered taverna, and a dilapidated kiosk that looked as if it might lift off in the wind, a bell began to toll, slow and insistent, as if to summon them.

They wove their way through labyrinthine alleyways not even wide enough for a car. All the houses were simple dwellings, single-storey, painted white and mostly with peeling blue paintwork and shutters that were kept closed at this time of the year. A terracotta pot or two on a window ledge was standard for every home, and everywhere Helena looked, there seemed to be a cat.

They continued walking until they found the source of the melancholy sound. It was a small whitewashed church, outside which a throng, perhaps the whole population of the town, was gathered.

Helena hung back, self-conscious to be intruding in a place where everyone mourned. Even their jeans and waterproof jackets seemed garish next to a congregation dressed entirely in black. She noticed that men, some of them even burlier than the fishermen from yesterday, as well as women were dabbing at their eyes with handkerchiefs.

Gradually the crowd began to file in and out through the low door.

'They're just going in to pay their respects by the coffin,' Anna explained.

It was impossible for them all to be inside at once. The chanting of a priest was broadcast to the outside, and the sound ricocheted off every wall.

'I feel like a voyeur,' said Helena. 'Shall we keep going?'

'I'll be surprised if your café is open,' moaned Haris, 'if everyone's in church.'

'He's not worth knowing until he's had some caffeine,' Anna told Helena as they continued their stroll.

Soon they found themselves on the other side of the village. As Haris had feared, the café was closed. Waves were splashing over the esplanade and clouds were gathering again.

An elderly woman feeding a straggle of cats on her doorstep looked up as they passed. She was the only human being they had seen since leaving the church, and she was dressed in a flimsy floral dress, apparently oblivious to the cold and the grief of her neighbours.

Helena was still wearing Haris's anorak for warmth, but the hood was down and her hair had fluffed out in the humidity.

'I remember you,' the old woman said, showing the dark spaces of her toothless mouth. She plucked at one of Helena's ringlets with her swollen fingers, gnarled with arthritis. '*Ti ómorfi pou eísai.* How beautiful you are.'

As she spoke, the door of the neighbouring house opened.

'*Poios írthe*, Katerina?' asked a thin voice. 'Who's there?'

A face peered round the door, a mirror image of the first woman, with the same hooked nose, short silver hair and diminutive stature.

The only noticeable difference was their eyes, and the fact that this one was wearing a plain blue dress.

'One of them is a fiery-haired goddess, Popi. She has the pale face of a nymph and sea-green eyes. The others are strangers.' Katerina was still holding Helena's hair, as if she were a dog on a lead.

'Tell me about the others,' demanded Popi.

'Mainlanders. But they're handsome enough,' Katerina said, before launching into a rapid torrent of island dialect that Helena had no hope of understanding.

Popi opened her front door wide. She had a white stick in her right hand and stepped adroitly over the threshold to fondle Helena's hair.

'I have only seen hair curled like this on one of my vases,' said Katerina to her twin. 'Like a maiden's ringlets, coiled springs of pure copper.'

Helena stood there patiently, touched by the way the woman explained the world to her sightless sister. She suddenly remembered Elpida telling her about a blind woman who had heard some looters talking.

The two sisters were chatting to each other as if the three outsiders could not hear, but Anna had picked up on the reference.

'Your vase?'

'One that our father found,' Katerina explained. 'When we were children. And this korítsi, this girl, looks like someone from the past.'

'We both have vases,' grinned Popi. 'We couldn't let those people take everything, could we?'

If by 'those people' she meant the archaeologists, perhaps there was a need to say that they did not remove things for their own gain, as these octogenarian residents of the island might imagine. The importance of academic study might require explanation for someone whose father and grandfathers were here long before the arrival of foreigners from countries they could not even imagine.

'Do you have a nice collection, Kyría Popi?' asked Haris innocently.

'*Nai! Fysiká!*' she answered. 'Yes, of course!' as if it was a matter of pride. 'We both do, don't we, Katerina?'

'Yes. I have nice ornaments too,' nodded Katerina. 'But we don't show anything to strangers.'

'She's not a stranger, though,' Popi stated. 'The red-haired one.' With those words, she vanished into her own house.

'Will you come in?' asked Katerina, pointedly addressing Helena only. Without waiting for an answer, she unlatched her flaking blue door.

Helena gave Anna and Haris a slightly apologetic look before stepping into the darkness. She heard the door close behind her. There was a single window, and its shutters were tightly closed. Katerina opened them enough so that light filtered in to show two shelves inset into the walls. They were packed with objects.

'I keep my bowls here,' she said, beckoning Helena over. Her collection also comprised a selection of other ancient pieces carved from marble, including vases and jugs, and two particularly elegant items: marble goblets with flared stems. Helena remembered that they were known as *kylikai*.

Though flabbergasted by what she saw, she praised everything with muted admiration.

On the other shelf, arranged in rows, in the same way that Helena had lined up a collection of china animals when she was a child, were several primitive zoomorphic shapes made from clay. A ram, several oxen, some pigs, some doves and a pair of hedgehogs.

Katerina took one of the hedgehogs down and allowed Helena to examine it closely.

'It's so sweet,' smiled Helena, holding it gently, astonished not simply by the presence of this antiquity in such an unexpected setting, but because all the objects were perfectly preserved.

'Popi wants you to see her collection too,' said Katerina.

As Helena turned to leave, she paused. Sitting on the kitchen table atop an elaborate lace cloth was a bowl filled to the brim with small pears. She ran her hand over the rim to feel its texture. The simplicity and grace of its shape seemed very modern, but instinctively she knew it must be many thousands of years old. That this clay treasure had survived at all was miraculous. For it to be in domestic use many millennia later and remain unblemished was magical.

She followed Katerina outside, surprised to see that she left her door wide open, and looked around her. There was no sign of Haris and Anna. They must have gone for a stroll.

The old lady stepped around two huge rusting tins that had once contained feta cheese but now overflowed with basil, and ushered Helena into her sister's house.

Popi was sitting at her kitchen table listening to the wireless. Over the crackling airwaves came the sound of cheerful island dance music, violins and lutes. Hearing the sound of the latch, she got up and clapped her hands with glee.

'*Kalós orísate, paidí mou,*' she cried. 'Welcome, my child! *Neró gia to paidí!*'

Her twin dutifully brought a jug of water to the table along with a grimy-looking glass.

'*Kátsete!*' ordered Popi over her shoulder as she tapped her way across the room towards some shelves similar to Katerina's.

Helena obediently sat down at the table and, in the small low-lit room where the old lady ate, slept and spent most of her waking hours, she waited on an uncomfortable straw-seated chair. She turned to see Popi taking something off a shelf and handing it to her sister, who brought it to the table.

'Here you are,' she said, as though giving an ice cream to a child.

Helena tried not to overreact. In her hands she held a small violin-shaped figurine. From the professor's lectures, she knew it was one of the earliest types. It was around four inches high, pristine.

Katerina continued going to and from the shelves, taking statuettes from Popi and passing them to Helena. The next one had a rounded abdomen, indicating her fecundity, and after that was one with a series of horizontal grooves meant to suggest post-partum folds.

'She's had a baby?' Helena queried.

'How would we know?' asked Katerina. 'We never had children.'

Then came a figure that was clearly male, some kind of hunter with carefully incised marks carved diagonally across his body. Helena recalled being told that such lines indicated a baldric, a belt over one shoulder that held a sword.

'What do you think of our *agalmatákia*?' asked Popi, referring to these treasures as 'little statues'.

Her visitor was lost for words, but after a moment she managed to speak.

'They are beautiful,' she said. 'But tell me, how did they come to be here?'

'*Archaiokápiloi!*' declared Katerina. 'Illegal excavators!'

The sisters took it in turns to speak, sometimes narrating their story with hesitation and a little caution. Helena got the impression that they had not told it to many people. Their collection was a completely unique and secret one, perhaps even more so than the private ones owned by the ultra-rich and scattered all over the world. Between them they described how, when they were little girls, around five years old, men had arrived from other islands. They first came for a few weeks, and after that returned each year for many years.

These men asked their father to help them dig things out of the ground, and offered to pay him so well that he could not refuse. It made the difference between his daughters having shoes or not. One day he hid a figurine inside his shirt and brought it home. The next day he came with another.

'These *eidólia* were our dolls. And we made clothes for them,' said Katerina.

Their father told them that the men had found a whole cemetery, and there were many of these dolls and hundreds of bowls, cups and animals. To the girls it seemed wrong to dig up people's graves and take away the treasures they wanted to have in the afterlife. So they asked their father to bring home as many objects as he could, intending to put them back into the ground when all the strangers had gone.

Popi made an interjection here, explaining that their mother had died in childbirth. They were sometimes taken to her grave and always imagined her sleeping underground next to her favourite possessions. It was for this reason that they so disapproved of this grave-robbing.

They were saving these treasures for the island and for the dead. But once the *archaiokápiloi* stopped coming, the archaeologists began to arrive, and they took things away too.

'That's why we have kept our collections. We treasure them for our own *tópos*, our place, where they were created, and for the dead who wait for them,' said Popi. 'One day, all these people will stop coming to dig.'

Helena sat for a while reflecting on their logic. Perhaps they were right, and the *eidólia* and vases truly belonged beneath the ground.

'We are sure that these little figures were buried to keep the deceased company,' added Popi. 'It must be so lonely under the soil.'

Helena thought about her own mother. She admired the certainty of Popi's theory. The old woman knew as much as anyone about the purpose of these mysterious marble figures.

Surely somebody on the island was aware that they had these objects and would have talked about them? Were they not vulnerable to theft?

When she asked this, Katerina laughed.

'That would mean someone entering the homes of Popi and Katerina Theodorou!' she said.

'We're safe from that, *paidí mou*,' Popi confirmed. 'No one would even think of it.'

It was a puzzling statement.

'We were outcasts from the day we entered the world,' said Katerina. 'A girl child is a curse on an island like this. And worse, there were two of us. And our mother was dead before Popi's first cry.'

'Two female births. One death.'

'A triple curse,' confirmed Popi. 'No guns of celebration were fired for us. Just a bell that tolled for the wife of Pavlos Theodorou.'

She explained how their grandmother had stepped in and brought them up on a diet of folklore, superstition, primitive cures and practical handicrafts. They were shunned by the rest of the islanders, who did not want them close to their own children, and so they had never attended school. Even now, they knew that there was a funeral happening, but they would not have been welcome there.

'There are fifty churches on this rock,' said Popi. 'We have a key to one, and we go there to remember our loved ones. We don't need a priest to do that.'

Katerina found a small carafe in the dresser. It was filled with a red liqueur, and she poured three shot glasses.

'*Stin ygeiá mas*,' said Popi. They all clinked their glasses together and drank.

Having grown up in her cosy Suffolk home, Helena could not imagine life here all year round, and she asked them what it was like.

'The winter is hell,' said Popi. 'Everything damp, even the wood, cold sheets, walls dripping, rough wool scratching your skin, your hands raw.'

'But then it's summer!' chimed in Katerina. 'And summer is heaven. The hillsides covered with flowers, sweet breezes, the *kypos* full of vegetables, the trees laden with fruit, the vines heavy with grapes.'

'You'll have me moving here,' laughed Helena.

'Well, you can stay with us for the afternoon if you want to be helpful,' said Popi. 'End of October is when we have to preserve everything we grew in the summer to get us through winter. We have to bottle it, or salt it, or boil it. I say "we", but I'm not much help. I can deal with the dried herbs, but not much more.'

'She started losing her sight twenty years ago,' explained Katerina. 'That's why we moved all the figurines in here, because they are wonderful to touch. And a few other things.'

She got up and fetched a flat circular object from the shelf.

'It's like a frying pan, isn't it?'

Popi took it from her and showed Helena the surface. It was decorated with perfectly executed spirals. She ran her fingers over them as if reading Braille.

'When the window is open, I can hear the sea, and when I touch this, I can watch it too.'

'More cherry raki?' asked Katerina cheerfully.

Helena politely declined.

'I'm going back next door then.' Katerina stood up. 'I've got work to do.'

'Stay, stay a little,' Popi urged Helena.

Helena replaced the figurines where they had come from and sat down again.

'The *archaiokápiloi* are back now,' said Popi casually. 'I don't think our dead will ever be safe.'

Helena leaned forward. 'Why do you say that?'

'Because when you are blind, people imagine you are deaf too. And when you are old *and* blind, they also think you are stupid. And they say things you aren't meant to hear. It was in the summer, before the weather turned. The archaeologists were still here. I know their voices. I can detect bad intentions in any language.'

Helena felt it right to reveal that she had been a volunteer on the dig, even though she did not want the old lady to see her as one of those who removed the island's riches.

'Well, if you spent some time here, you must know that row of benches facing out to sea near the harbour. That's where I often go to sit when it's fine. A few days running there were some rough-voiced people talking with the smooth-voiced. The rough voices were speaking in Greek and the more educated person, a man, was doing his best in beginner's Greek too, with that very particular accent that the British have. And I would say he was young.'

None of this was solid evidence, but even the reference to his basic Greek made Helena suspect it had been Nick.

'He was telling them that he needed a boat, to transport something. He said it was urgent. I was there again a few days later and they told him he had to go up to the north of the island. It was the only safe place and there was someone up there who would help him. It's the same old story,' she said. 'There are still people stealing from the dead.'

Helena glanced at her watch, worried about how long Anna and Haris had been waiting for her outside. It had been more than an hour.

The presence of these ancient objects, some of them still in daily use, gave a sense of these two women living outside of time. If the Theodorou twins had claimed they were five hundred years old, Helena would have believed them.

'I must leave you,' she said decisively. 'I'll come back and say goodbye before we go tomorrow.'

'You can't go empty-handed,' Popi protested, bustling around her kitchen.

She pressed on Helena bunches of dried herbs and a jar of honey, with full explanations of the therapeutic benefits of each.

'It's all I can give you,' she said apologetically.

'These are riches,' said Helena. 'Thank you.'

She left humbled by the old lady's generosity. During the periods she had spent on the dig here, she had not properly encountered the *filoxenía*, the hospitality, that characterised small islands, places where people possessed so little but gave anything they had.

She walked towards the seafront and spotted Anna and Haris at a café near the harbour that had opened now the funeral was over. The sun was briefly showing itself, so they were sitting outside.

'Those women,' she told them, 'were both the poorest and the richest people I've ever met in my life.'

She described everything she had seen.

'Those things belong to them,' said Anna. 'Nobody has any greater right to have them than they do.'

'The archaeologists would obviously disagree with that,' said Haris. 'But the looters are depriving everyone of knowledge and heritage.'

'This little place is being squeezed of its treasures, isn't it?' said Anna.

'And what will happen when Popi and Katerina are no longer here?' Helena asked.

'That collection is totally unknown, as far we can tell,' Anna said.

There was silence for a while, as they walked westwards along the cliff away from the town. The sun would be setting in another hour.

The path took them out of sight of any dwellings, and the only sound was the bleat of goats and the jangle of their bells.

'Look,' said Haris. 'There's our dinner!'

'Very amusing,' said Anna. 'But I have a feeling . . .'

'Maybe we'll get the eyeballs tonight,' he said.

The rains had intensified the strong smell of oregano in the air. As ever, the aroma reminded Helena of her mother.

An hour into their walk, they stopped to sit on the steps of a tiny stone church built next to the path and facing out to sea. The sun was sitting on the horizon, balanced like a ball, and the sky was streaked with pink that reflected in the waves.

Very slowly, the sun went down.

Only when it had completely disappeared did anyone speak.

'You know how many times that has happened in the lifetime of those figurines?' Hari asked. 'More than two million. And if they are loved and looked after, there will be millions more. Long after we are gone, they will be here. If they haven't been obliterated in some way.'

'I really believe there is something special about them,' said Anna. 'Maybe it's to do with the mystery. But the idea of stolen ones being shown off in a rich man's house, displayed like hostages, is utterly wrong.'

The taverna surprised them that evening with *pastítsio*, a dish of home-made pasta with ground lamb. Brother and sister argued over whether there was some goat mixed into it, Haris insisting that there was.

'There's nothing else on the menu. And you'll be eating all your favourite dishes in Mistrali with Persephone tomorrow night,' scolded Anna, mentioning both Haris's favourite Athens restaurant and his fiancée in one breath.

It brought Helena back to reality. She felt a violent and involuntary contraction in her stomach at the mention of a girlfriend, and was angry with herself for it.

'I want to talk about what we need to do next,' Haris said hastily.

When the taverna owner came to clear the plates, he brought them another carafe, one they had not ordered.

'For the young archaeologist,' he said, indicating Helena. 'From her friends at the bar.'

Helena looked over her shoulder. There was something distinctly menacing about the three men who were staring back at her. One of them made a gesture at her, but in the gloom of the taverna, it was hard to interpret it.

She turned back to the table. 'That makes me uncomfortable,' she said. 'They remember me from the dig and are making a point, I think. Maybe they know I wouldn't have come back without a reason.'

'They're pretty rough-looking, aren't they,' said Anna in a low voice. 'I'm glad we have Haris with us.'

'I'm sure one of them was in the other village playing *távli* yesterday,' said Haris. 'Just raise a glass to them and smile. Then let's go to bed.'

'It's undrinkable anyway,' said Anna. 'Like lighter fuel. So, I think we've got their message.'

On the narrow landing that led to their rooms, they stopped to have a conversation.

'It's a small place,' said Haris. 'And stealing treasure is big business – and a lucrative one.'

'I'm glad we're leaving tomorrow,' said Anna. 'See you in the morning.' She disappeared into her room, leaving Haris and Helena alone.

'Sleep well, Helena,' said Haris.

Helena knew she would not sleep well without asking one question.

'When you said it was big business, what did you mean?'

'There are millions – and I mean dollars, not drachma – to be made from looting,' he said, holding her gently by the shoulders. 'And I don't want you to come to any harm.'

'So those men downstairs won't like it if they think we're on to them, will they?'

'Exactly.'

'I'll lock my door, then,' she promised.

'*Óneira glyká, Elenáki,*' said Haris affectionately, wishing her sweet dreams.

In the morning, Helena decided to take a brisk stroll through the village to say goodbye to her new friends. Anna and Haris accompanied her. The shutters on both houses were still closed. She didn't want to wake the sisters, so she scribbled a note and slid it under Katerina's door.

'We must memorise the route to them,' said Anna, noticing that every small nameless and numberless street looked the same. 'Otherwise we'll never find them again. Every house is identical.'

'I won't forget the size of those *máti*,' laughed Haris, pointing at the huge ceramic blue eyes set in the lintels, one above each door. 'Those two must think they need to ward off a lot of evil.'

Rough seas meant that the ferry came in late. Anna took a seasickness tablet and found somewhere to pass the journey, but

Helena and Haris struggled up on deck to watch Nisos recede from view.

As Helena reflected on the very mixed and extreme experiences this island had given her, the wind gusted violently and she felt Haris put his arm around her to stop her falling.

'It must be at least an eight!' he said, his words carried away on the air. At her quizzical look, he added, 'On the Beaufort scale.'

'Yep, rough,' she said, gripping the rail.

'Did you find what you were expecting?' he asked her. 'Did the island give you a marvellous journey?'

Helena smiled. They both knew he was paraphrasing Cavafy's poem.

'Yes,' she answered. 'What about you?'

'I'm so glad we came.'

They stood for a few more moments, and then a huge wave surged up and splashed over onto the deck.

'Better get inside,' he said. 'Before we're swept overboard.' Holding Helena firmly by the hand, he led her to the door that took them into the lounge.

She took half of one of Anna's pills to stave off nausea, and was soon asleep.

Many hours later, Haris leaned down and gently touched her hair.

'Come on, sleeping beauty,' he said. 'Time to wake up.'

'We're there?' she said sleepily.

Flustered and perturbed to find that they were already approaching Rafina, she sat up and saw that Anna and Haris had already gathered their things. Anna was immaculate again, with tidy hair and a fresh blouse, Haris was in a sports jacket, car keys in hand.

Helena had strong feelings of disappointment that their trip had come to an end, but hid them well, especially when Haris dropped her at the door to the apartment.

'Don't forget we have a safe packed with your possessions!' he laughed. 'We need to decide what we're going to do next. Not just about your treasures, but other things too. Will you come in to see us in the next few days?'

He gave her a quick hug, then picked up her bag and carried it into the hallway.

There was a brief but awkward moment between Helena and Haris and then the lift arrived, its doors slid open and then it took her away.

It was past ten in the evening when she put her key in the door to the apartment.

When she flicked the switch, some of the lights fused, but she had no idea where the board was, so decided to go straight to bed. She did not need an excuse, but she'd go and see Mihalis as soon as he opened tomorrow. Some fuse wire should do the trick.

As her head sank into the pillows, she lay for a while thinking of Haris. She assumed that Persephone was the girl she had seen him with at the Dalaras concert, and tried not to picture what they might be doing now. Instead, she made herself think of Mihalis's uncle. Petros Pavlidis had been on her mind during the weekend. The injustice that he and many others had endured must continue to drive her on to find the figurine and to link it back to Arsenis and hence to her grandfather and his nefarious past.

Haris had already described how Nick had come into their shop with the broken figurine. Suppose he had now managed to get it mended elsewhere, and it was complete apart from the feet, what would his next step be? Obviously to sell it. But where?

Chapter Thirty-Eight

Helena slept well and woke early. In the echoing flat, the cupboards were denuded save for a few grains of coffee in a rusty tin. She dressed and went out, greeting Kýrios Manolis as she left.

Athens was looking beautiful in the dawn light, and the city seemed still and calm by comparison with the tempestuous Aegean. She walked the familiar streets of Kolonaki, avoiding Ligakis's shop, and began to feel regretful that she would be leaving the city once the flat was sold. There was nothing to anchor her here.

It was an hour or so before Mihalis's shop would be open, but the cafés had been serving for some time. People were refreshed after the three-day weekend, and she overheard many greetings of 'Kalí evdomáda!' as people cheerfully wished each other a good week.

She took Skoufa Street, which was long and straight, and followed it up towards Exarchia. She was hoping to find the café where Mihalis and Panos had once taken her for fresh fruit juice and warm apple pastries, away from the businessmen, ministry bureaucrats and government workers who tended to take their morning coffee in Kolonaki Square. In her canvas shoes, filthy from the Nisos mud, and with her hair still tangled from the wild sea wind, she felt more out of place than ever among men with polished shoes and smart suits.

'Helena!' From a pavement café that jutted across the street, she heard her name being called. It was Haris.

She showed her surprise to see him here. Surely Kolonaki was his more natural habitat?

He had pulled out a chair for her.

'I know you think I'm a Kolonaki man, but it's full of our customers and people I know, so I prefer to come here and read my paper in peace.'

She noticed that he had a copy of *Ta Nea*, the centre-left daily newspaper, in front of him. The right-of-centre *Kathimerini* was the one more commonly seen in Kolonaki.

The waiter brought her a Greek coffee *skéto*, without sugar.

'I saw you coming from right down the street,' Haris confided. 'And took the liberty of ordering for you.'

A plate of miniature pastries, including *milópita*, apple pies, then appeared on the table.

'You ordered perfectly,' Helena said. 'And you even knew that I was hungry!'

While she was eating, Haris picked up his newspaper. He went through it until he found a particular page and folded it back to show her. It was the report of an auction that had taken place in New York only three days before. The headline, English even in the Greek newspaper, was *MILLION DOLLAR DOLL*.

'That's what you meant by big business,' said Helena, her eyes widening as she read the article. 'Incredible.'

She was staring at the image of a figurine, restored but very chipped, one leg missing from the knee downwards, wide-hipped, inelegant, and with nothing like the refinement of the one Nick had stolen.

He nodded. 'And the problem is that nearly everything coming onto the market in this sector has no real provenance. It says something like "anonymous owner", "private collection". Everything is vague and so much of it is illegal.'

'And the people who buy don't care?' asked Helena. 'Is that how the price gets so high?'

'Yes. And there are so many people who have to be paid on the way,' said Haris. 'During the journey from the soil to where it ends up in an auction house in New York, it goes through so many hands. Let's say it passes from the *tymvorýchos*, the grave-robber who is paid to dig in Nisos, to someone like your old boyfriend, then to a fisherman, then to somebody who smuggles it to Athens, then to another middleman, then perhaps to a restorer, then to someone like Arsenis, and then to Ligakis, who contacts a potential buyer. At some point it might be stored for a while so that it doesn't come too fresh to the market. And then perhaps it's sold to a private collector, or even goes to an auction house. Up and up and up it goes until it finally achieves the highest possible price that anything like it has ever fetched.'

Both of them looked down at the image in the newspaper.

'One million dollars,' Helena murmured. 'With all those people taking their cut.'

'And it belongs to the island where it was found. To Greece. To all of us.'

Haris summoned the waiter.

'More coffee?' he asked.

'Yes please.' Helena was in no hurry.

'Look, Helena, I know very little really. But I do understand the rich. I have studied their behaviour my whole life. It hasn't made me want to be one of them. You can see I read the wrong newspaper for that,' he joked. 'Something I do know is that most of them want to show off to each other. There is no point in being wealthy unless you demonstrate it to your peers. It's like a flashy car. You don't just keep it in a garage, you drive around the streets in it, hoping to get noticed. Even if something has dubious provenance or several stages back it was stolen, you'll want to display it somewhere. Things always show up . . . sometime, someplace.

'The other thing I know is that beauty is something the rich want

418

to possess, and even if they regard themselves as honest, they will pay anything to lay their hands on it. Beauty is irresistible to some. It's driven plenty of men to foolish acts, hasn't it?'

Helena nodded. 'So they say,' she murmured, her mind wandering now. Seeing that picture of the inferior figurine sold for a record price at a big auction house had given her an idea. Nick surely would have thought of it too. He, or someone else, would take the figurine, probably restored by now, to an auction house and find the highest bidder. White's. That was where it could be going. And with the feet, she might be able to prove that this was not something found decades ago that could therefore be legally sold, but something on which the soil was still fresh.

'I need to go back to London,' she said.

'London?' To Haris, the statement seemed to come out of nowhere.

Helena thought she detected a note of disappointment in his voice, but chose to dismiss it.

'I think he'll try to sell the figurine through an auction house.' She did not even want to say Nick's name now.

'Yes,' agreed Haris.

'And London would be one of the best places.'

'Almost certainly,' he confirmed, chewing thoughtfully on a pastry. 'It's too dangerous and too noticeable to be sold here.'

'And what I'm thinking is that with the help of the auction house, we can be ready to trap him,' said Helena. 'I know someone with contacts at White's, in London.'

She was getting excited now. 'He's a friend.'

'But he might not go to that one,' said Haris. 'Unless . . . unless you can persuade White's to put on a sale of Greek and Roman artefacts. And then I calculate that our seller won't be able to resist.'

'Well, that's what I will ask them to do,' Helena said with determination.

The waiter brought them both another coffee.

'Something else is on your mind,' she said. 'What is it?'

'The bigger picture, Helena. All those other objects we have. And the ones written down in the ledgers that we don't have. All that illegality and theft can't go unpunished.'

'I agree. This is not just about me and . . . him. It's about Mihalis Pavlidis's uncle and so many others.'

'Exactly, and if we want to prove more than the theft of this one figure, we have to involve some other people. We need them to look into where all those objects given to your grandfather went, don't we?'

'Yes, yes, of course we do.'

'That has to be the police here in Athens. There is a special team that deals with stolen and looted antiquities.'

'As there should be in a country that has so much of value,' observed Helena, flicking a ringlet out of her face.

Haris could see the commitment in her eyes. He found himself comparing this girl with his fiancée, who was cool and organised and rarely displayed any fervour for anything at all. Helena, by contrast, was like a fire besides which he felt warm and alive.

'The police,' she asked, 'will they be helpful?'

'I know some of this team personally,' said Haris. 'And yes. What they do is a vocation. These guys don't go into the force to give out traffic fines. And they regard the crimes they solve as serious. People who traffic antiquities are often the same ones who traffic drugs and people.'

'So I need to speak to my friends and you need to speak to yours,' concluded Helena.

'And they should talk to each other too,' said Haris. 'The Greek police and the British. I'll give you a name when I have spoken to them. You might have to do some translating, as their English isn't always the best.'

She thanked him.

'And I suppose we have to go our separate ways for a while.'

Once again Helena thought she picked up a hint of regret.

'For a few weeks we will be like cats waiting for the mice to come out of their hole,' she said. 'And I hope it *will* be weeks, not months.'

Haris gestured to the waiter for their bill.

'Don't forget your evidence for White's,' he smiled, counting out some notes. 'You should have it with you.'

'The feet! Of course!' she laughed. 'Is it okay for me to come to the shop in an hour or so? I'll grab my things from the flat, go to a travel agent and come on my way to the airport.'

They got up and walked away from the table, but not before Helena had noticed the waiter's gratitude for a very generous tip. Only once had Nick paid for her coffee, and she recalled how he had meticulously picked from the saucer every last coin given as change.

Chapter Thirty-Nine

The house was empty when Helena arrived back at Ladbroke Grove. It was seven in the evening and no one was back from work. She went up to her room, where Nick's ghost had not quite disappeared, and dumped her bag on the floor, then went down to the kitchen.

She smiled at the sight of her flourishing plant on the window ledge. It was now cared for by Caroline and a dozen new leaves were unfurling.

An old copy of *The Times* lay on the table. Someone had been trying to finish a prize crossword. Helena's mind had been so focused on what was happening in Athens that she felt very out of touch with everything in Britain. She scanned the headlines: *UNEMPLOYMENT STILL OVER THREE MILLION; TROUBLES IN IRELAND CONTINUE.* The story that captured her attention was not a domestic one, though. It was about a forthcoming trial for war crimes: *ISSUE OF ARREST WARRANT FOR BUTCHER OF LYON.*

Klaus Barbie, a former Gestapo chief currently living in Bolivia, was wanted in France to face trial for the murder and deportation of thousands of men, women and children between 1942 and 1944. The story made Helena reflect. Forty years after the event, the need to achieve justice was still fresh and strong. The passage of time did not diminish the act, she thought to herself, her mind drifting to her grandfather.

The door slammed. Sally bounded in and threw her arms around her friend.

'Hels! So sorry I wasn't here to welcome you! You didn't even ring to say you were coming today! God, I'm dying for a gin and tonic.'

Once Sally had shared some gossip about university friends and told her about a new account she had won for the agency, she drew breath.

'Tell me about you! How was Athens?'

The door banged again. This time it was Charles.

He kissed Sally and then embraced Helena before sitting down. Sally was pouring him a generous measure of Gordon's.

At least, Helena thought, I won't have to explain everything twice.

Over the next hour, she shared what had happened, beginning with what she had kept back when she returned from Athens the previous time. The theft of the figurine was shocking enough, but her revelation that Nick had buried the feet in her rucksack disgusted them.

'I think I was ashamed to have been so taken in,' she confessed. 'I felt angry, with myself as well as him. That's probably why I didn't tell you.'

She then explained about the ledgers, the contents of the desk and her uncle's involvement in laundering antiquities for her grandfather.

'And now Nick has formed a friendship with Arsenis,' she told them. 'And I am certain that they're dealing in looted goods.'

'It's me who feels stupid now,' said Charles. 'I knew he was a bit of a rogue, but an out-and-out criminal? I suppose after those Chagalls I should have guessed.'

'He should be brought to justice,' Helena stated plainly. 'But it's not just personal revenge.'

'Being treated like that would be enough for me,' said Sally. 'He should be locked up and the key thrown away.'

Charles wanted to know more about the ledgers, and Helena described how her grandfather had traded favours and betrayals in exchange for valuables, and people had gone to prison, even died, as a result.

'The uncle of a friend of mine in Athens is in a psychiatric hospital because of what the junta did to him. My grandfather was given a lump of marble in exchange for sending him to Makronisos, a brutal prison island. I can't give him his life back, but I can make amends, make things better for him than they are now. And if I can find any others like him, I will do the same.'

'You're right to want this,' said Charles. 'But how are you going to go about it?'

'I have some new friends in Athens, antique dealers, who are helping me. They know their way around the system there. But I also need *your* help, Charles.'

'Happily, my dear Helena. Tell me what I can do.'

Charles needed no persuading. His anger at Nick's theft of the paintings was enough, and the value of Marc Chagall's work had been steadily rising of late, which had made it worse.

'We need an auction house on our side,' Helena told him.

'I'll ring Hugo and set up a meeting at White's,' said Charles without a moment's hesitation.

The following afternoon, Helena found herself in the unfamiliar surroundings of the chairman's office at White's, the pile of the cream carpet so deep that her feet sank into it almost up to the ankles.

She and Charles had to wait while Hugo White finished talking to some staff, but it gave her plenty of time to survey the room. There was a dark oil portrait on a wall behind the desk, the same size as the one of her grandfather, but this man looked positively genial. He was holding a skull, which seemed macabre but was, according to Charles, a family joke.

'He was the founder,' said Charles. 'Lovely chap.'

On a side table there were some familiar objects: four Meissen figures, allegorical representations of the seasons. Charles picked one of them up to examine it closely.

'Ghastly stuff,' he said. 'Not my taste at all.'

Helena smiled to herself.

At that moment, Hugo White hurried in, a slim figure in a pinstripe suit, around forty years old. He went straight to his desk.

'Oh my God,' he said. 'Awful, aren't they, Charles? They're here for me to give a second opinion on the value. They were the old boy's pet hate, and personally I wouldn't pay ninepence for them.' As he spoke, he indicated the man in the portrait behind him. 'I do try to keep some standards in taste around here, but these are worth tens of thousands, maybe more, so I don't really have a choice, do I? Think of the commission.'

So far he appeared not to have even noticed Helena.

'Dear boy,' interrupted Charles. 'Let me introduce.you to Helena. She needs your help.'

Hugo sat behind his desk and moved some other *objets d'art* out of the way so that he could see them both.

'So, Helena, what can I do for you? Got some Picassos for me, have you?'

Helena kept her cool.

'Better, I think,' she said, determined not to be patronised by this chum of Charles's. Even though it must be obvious that she was not the type to own valuable paintings, she needed to ignore his flippant manner and find a way of holding his attention. If she did not make him take her seriously, the opportunity would be lost.

'Does it concern you,' she asked him sternly, 'that many antiquities that get into the art market are stolen or looted? That countries are being robbed of their culture and history just to satisfy rich men's cravings?'

Hugo got up, came round to the other side of the desk and sat on a chair opposite them. His jovial manner vanished. He realised he was being challenged by this young woman and perhaps should listen to what she had to say.

'What are you implying?' he asked.

'That there is sometimes collaboration, and that dealers and auctioneers turn a blind eye to where things have come from.'

'I know that happens,' he said. 'But not here, I can promise you.' Helena saw him glance at Charles, as if for support.

'It's true,' said Charles. 'White's does have a good reputation.'

'Anyway, what's your point?' asked Hugo. 'You said you had something better than a Picasso.'

'Something more important, at least,' Helena said.

'Excellent.' Now it was his turn to try and make a good impression. Perhaps he had underestimated this friend of Charles's with her provocatively wild hair.

'How long have we got?' Helena asked him. 'What I am going to explain to you needs time.'

Hugo looked at his watch. 'Plenty,' he said. 'It's almost six, though. Shall I get them to bring us a sherry?'

A silver tray arrived with a decanter and glasses and Charles poured for them all.

'Nicholas Hayes-Jones . . .' she began.

'God, yes! I remember that name. Friend of yours from Oxford, wasn't he, Charles? Awful man. He was supposed to come and help out as a porter at some viewings, but he rather made a show of himself. Very charming and all that, but he was overfamiliar with a few people – not just women, but men too – and it didn't go down too well.'

'I'm sorry, Hugo. And it was so good of you. He needed work and was genuinely interested in the art world.'

'All well and good, but one of the people he tried to seduce was my wife!' Hugo's face reddened with anger at the recollection.

Helena and Charles exchanged a look. She was confident now that she was not going to lose Hugo White's interest.

For an hour, Helena talked. She told Hugo about the excavation and the figurine, then took a small box from her bag and handed it to him.

'Open it,' she told him.

Hugo went back to his desk and put on a pair of pristine white gloves taken from his top drawer.

'Ah, beautiful,' he said with appreciation, lifting out the feet. 'Like a ballerina. I can picture the rest . . . left arm resting on the right, long legs and neck, head tilted serenely.'

'Yes, yes. Exactly like that. And she was so beautiful,' gushed Helena, impressed with Hugo's knowledge and his reaction even to this small piece.

'I've only ever seen a whole figurine in a photograph, but I can tell just from these feet what a pretty creature she was.'

He produced a high-magnification jeweller's loupe from his top pocket and meticulously examined the piece for a few moments.

'This is real enough,' he said. 'No doubt about it. The break is clearly new. And we have some soil still present, which will prove where it has come from and that it has been recently excavated. Even if the rest has been cleaned up, this is our evidence.'

Almost with reverence, he replaced the object in the box and removed the gloves.

'Do you mind me keeping this here?' he asked.

'Please do,' Helena said. 'It's not mine, after all. And it will be safer with you, won't it.'

Hugo's appreciation of what was in the box had reassured her, and she was aware that his interest was very palpably increased by a personal distrust of Nick Jones.

She went on to give him details of everything that might be useful.

She mentioned Jones's connections with a dealer called Giannis Ligakis and his associate Arsenis Papagiannis, and suggested that this might be his route to bringing the figurine to the market. Perhaps other items had passed through the auction house in the past from the same dealer.

Victoria Hislop

Ligakis's name did vaguely ring bells for Hugo, and he promised to get someone to go through the records to find out. It was quite possible that the dealer could have used a bank account in a different name, but he would do his best. He told Helena that he would need to involve the police, both British and Greek.

'We must live up to our name, mustn't we?' he joked.

The important question for Helena was the date of the next sale when such an object might be auctioned. Hugo knew it without needing to look it up.

Hugo White had left Eton and joined the family firm when he was seventeen. Twenty years on, he knew the business inside out, from every sale date to prices achieved at each one of them and the name of every member of staff. Over the past hour, Helena's opinion of him had completely changed, just as his had of her.

'It's in a few months' time. Greek and Roman antiquities. The experts in that department are putting together the catalogue now. As far as I know, we haven't got anything Cycladic in it. But pieces can be submitted at the last minute.'

'Is there any chance,' asked Helena, 'that you could make the sale sooner? We need him to submit the figurine here and not anywhere else.'

Hugo paused to consider. It was quite a thing to ask. He flicked through a large desk diary for a moment or two before replying.

'Helena,' he said finally, 'it's one hundred per cent in our interests to stop this kind of looting, so I am going to make this happen.'

'Thank you, old man,' said Charles, pouring himself another sherry.

'I tell you what,' added Hugo. 'To give us more chance of reeling him in, I'll get the marketing department to put a couple of ads in the Greek press to promote the forthcoming sale. That's perfectly normal. They always attract buyers and sellers. We've got quite a few shipping families who like to come to London for a few days to stay in the Dorchester and shop in Harrods, and then they come and bid for a few bits and pieces for their island homes.'

Helena could imagine some of the old-style Kolonaki types doing that.

It was now almost 7.30. Hugo stood up.

'Must go,' he said briskly. 'Have to get to a dinner. Lovely to meet you, Helena. Charles, lunch at the club soon?'

Moments later, Helena and Charles were out on the pavement.

'That went well,' Charles told her decisively. 'He's with us, completely. And he won't let us down.'

'I think he dislikes Nick as much as I do,' she said, smiling.

The following day, she rang Haris to tell him about the meeting at the auction house and the chairman's promise to bring the sale forward.

In turn, Haris described his cataloguing of the Cycladic pieces from her grandfather's desk. With few exceptions, their edges showed that they had been broken in recent decades, suggesting it had been done to make it easier to smuggle them. Frustratingly, as he had suspected, none of the pieces seemed to be part of the same figurine.

'As though your grandfather was given not just pieces of a jigsaw but pieces from different jigsaws,' he added.

'Maybe he and Arsenis were waiting for some matching pieces,' mused Helena.

'And maybe anything complete had already been taken elsewhere or sold?'

'We're going to find out, *Hári mou*,' she said.

As she replaced the receiver, she realised that she had slipped into a more familiar tone with him.

Haris began to go through the Byzantine treasure trove next, and there was always something to tell her. Each piece was so different, and complete in itself. He was trying to establish provenance before even attempting to ascertain value.

Quite often they chatted about nothing in particular. How was London? How was Athens? Small talk with Haris never seemed insignificant.

One evening, he gave her the name and number of Giorgos Kourtis, a contact at the Greek police.

'Get your friend at White's to contact him to tell him what's happening,' he said.

Helena also spoke with Anna.

'Haris is working really hard on your grandfather's collection,' Anna related with enthusiasm. 'He's identified several exact dates and origins of the Byzantine pieces. We suspect that many were stolen from churches. There's definitely some loot from Cyprus.'

'That's no surprise,' said Helena.

'And when you come back to Athens, I'll value your Meissen. I've done some initial research from the notes I made, and I think it's going to bring in a huge sum.'

Very early one Saturday morning, before anyone was up in the Ladbroke Grove house, the phone started ringing. Helena dashed downstairs to answer it. It was Anna.

'Helena!' she said breathlessly. 'I have just seen Arsenis in the street. He was with someone younger. About your age. Blond and slim. Definitely not Greek. The sort that turns heads. You know, very good-looking.'

'Oh.' Helena grimaced. 'Sounds like Nick.'

'I thought as much. Haris wasn't with me, but he says the description exactly matches the person who came with the broken pieces. Anyway, I followed them. They went into Ligakis's shop.'

'The thought of the three of them . . .' murmured Helena. 'Horrible.'

'I just thought I should let you know.'

'Thanks, Anna.'

Like every other conversation they had, the call ended with Anna's expression of hope that Helena would come back to Athens soon. She often added that Haris was looking forward to seeing her too.

Mihalis, when he called, also urged her to return.

'I will, Mihalis! I'm impatient too. I can't even tell you *how* impatient. But I have to wait. I've got to be by the trap.' She had described what she hoped would happen at the White's auction.

Conversations with him always followed the same pattern: the musicians they had seen, a new plan for the shop, Panos's projects, updates on the *paréa,* who had all asked after her. Even though she had never met him, Helena always enquired about his Uncle Petros. The answer was the same each time: he was living in his own world, stable and calm thanks to the drugs but on a very spartan ward with ten others, many of whom were very disturbed. Helena thought of the money she was going to make from the Meissen sale. She knew how she was planning to spend it.

Trying to lift the mood of the conversation, Mihalis described to her the sweet scent of baking *kourampiédes,* a crumbly seasonal shortbread, that filled the streets of Kolonaki in December. Helena yearned to be there. It was too long since she had seen her Greek friends, and the sense that they were waiting for her exerted a strong pull.

One night in mid December, the Ladbroke Grove house was full of university friends who had come for pre-Christmas drinks. Above the noise, Helena could hear the phone ringing and picked up. Someone was asking for Charles. Above the hubbub, all she could hear were the words '*Must* speak to him.' It sounded urgent, so she went in search of him, scanning over the crowd in the kitchen, on the stairs, in the drawing room. That was where she saw him, holding forth with a group around him, just as that first time she had set eyes on him after *Medea*. She pushed her way through, jolting Edward and Caroline's glasses.

'Sorry, sorry, sorry! Have to get to Charles.'

She interrupted him mid-anecdote. 'Phone!' she called above the noise. 'Urgent!'

Charles assured his audience that he would be back soon, and hastened to the hall, his face lined with anxiety. Nobody liked to take an urgent phone call. It suggested accident or death.

Helena went to the kitchen to get another glass of wine, then returned to a conversation she had been having.

Back in the hall, Charles had put the phone down.

'Helena!' he boomed, his face beaming. 'We're on!' He came over and gave her a bear hug. 'They've brought the sale forward. It'll be the first one of the new year. Beginning of January.'

'That's wonderful!' she said.

Charles had grabbed a glass, and the two of them made a toast.

'To Hugo, our hero.'

She rang the Morakis shop early the following day, eager to share the news. Haris was not there, and Anna mentioned that he had needed to take some time off.

'He'll be happy, Helena. I promise to tell him when he gets back.'

She did not ask where he was, but felt a sense of desolation.

Despite her growing emotional connection with Athens, Helena wanted to spend Christmas and New Year with her father.

This visit to Suffolk was the first for several months. She found Hamish excited to see her, the house decorated and everything ready for their few days together.

By a crackling log fire on Christmas Eve, she told him the truth about Nick, why they had split up, the story of the figurine, her discoveries in the Kolonaki flat, her plans to try and resolve everything and to make amends to at least one person whose life Stamatis Papagiannis had ruined.

As a GP, Hamish was an exemplary listener. He sat quietly as his daughter told him what had been happening. He gave no diagnosis, just a conclusion.

'You're doing absolutely the right thing pursuing this,' he said. 'And your mother would have been very proud of you. It's as if you're settling something in her place and because she couldn't.'

'We haven't seen it through to the end yet,' she said quietly.

'But that's our hope, Dad. And yes, above all I want some kind of justice, retribution, I don't know what to call it really. It involves people who are mostly dead now, but not all. There are three criminals who are very much alive, including the new recruit.'

'Yes. That Nick person,' Hamish said, with uncharacteristic vehemence. 'He deserves whatever is coming. Mostly for how he treated you.' His inherent kindness did not extend to someone who had been cruel to his daughter. 'And believe me, love doesn't always end that way,' he added.

'I know that, Dad,' Helena said, sipping the aromatic mulled wine she had made for them.

For the next few days, they enjoyed long walks together, drinks with neighbours, creative dishes made with the leftovers of a turkey rather too large for two, and some favourite films from Hamish's growing video collection. There was not a moment, though, when Helena forgot the forthcoming auction. The hours were ticking by.

On 4 January, she returned to London. As she said goodbye to her father at the station that afternoon, she promised to keep him fully informed.

Helena's housemates were at home when she got back. All four of them had returned to work that morning. They were sitting round the kitchen table sharing a bottle of wine, and wished her warm New Year's greetings before briefly exchanging tales of family Christmases.

'And now,' said Charles, 'something we've all been waiting for!'

Helena suddenly noticed the A4 envelope in his hand. The White's logo on the outside. She almost snatched it from him and, with sweating palms, pulled out a thick, glossy brochure: *White's Ltd Auctioneers. Greek and Roman Antiquities.*

On the cover was an image of a Roman bust. A general, apparently.

Her hands were shaking so much that she could scarcely turn the pages.

After a lengthy introduction by Hugo White and advertisements for other forthcoming sales, there it was, on page nine, the image of a footless figurine. She bit her bottom lip, attempting to control her tears. A flood of bad memories swept over her, and tears she had not shed at the time flowed down her face. Sally handed her some tissues. Helena's reaction needed no explanation.

It was so strange to see the figurine again, whole but not quite. In the photograph, it was hard to make out any joins, so whoever had put it together had done a reasonable job. But Helena could picture it smashed to pieces, and there was still a tiny chip out of the head. And of course, no feet.

On pages ten and eleven, there were close-ups. The angle of the head, the suggestion of pregnancy, the slimness of the legs. The history of it was predictably vague: *From the collection of a private owner. Purchased pre-1960. Probably found in Naxos.*

Charles had already looked at the brochure, but Helena laid it flat on the table for the others to see.

'I can understand exactly what the fuss is about,' said Caroline. 'She literally gives off an aura, even on the page. Something. The power of the feminine, maybe.'

The others murmured in agreement and with admiration.

'But how you could loot it . . .'

Everyone in the room had a personal interest in the fate of their former university friend. Nick Jones had betrayed, cheated or robbed each one of them in some way.

'Only a few more days to go,' said Charles.

'Yes. True. I'm getting a bit nervous, to be honest,' replied Helena. 'It means Nick might be around somewhere. I don't believe that he'll be able to resist being in London.'

Her first call was to the Morakis shop.

'It's happening,' she said breathlessly. 'Charles just brought home the catalogue. Eighth of January. White's. *She* is going to be there.'

'Great. That's great,' said Haris. 'I'll tell Anna. Keep me posted. Sorry. Gotta go. Bye.'

Helena felt that she had been dropped from a great height. Haris's curt response was not what she had expected. There was not a trace of enthusiasm in his voice.

She called Mihalis and got the reaction she needed.

'That's fantastic news!' he said. 'But are you sure it's the same one? What are they estimating? Will you be there in the room? Aren't you a bit nervous?' Questions spilled out of him and she tried to answer them.

'There's a plan in place,' she assured him. 'She'll be safe at last.'

Before picking up the phone to speak to her father, it rang. It was the real-estate agent in Athens, calling to say that a Swiss buyer had shown strong interest in the Kolonaki flat at the asking price. Helena felt an unexpected sense of loss, especially when the agent advised her that she should make herself available to sign some papers because this buyer was in a hurry. She was almost relieved that she had an excuse not to go to Athens immediately. The antiquities sale was happening in a few days' time, but she assured the agent that she would contact him very shortly.

Once the conversation had finished, she called her father.

'Dad, how are you?'

'I'm fine, darling. I've got my planting done early so that I'll have seedlings by mid March. The apple trees are pruned and ready for spring. It all looks pretty dead at this time of year, but it'll come to life in a month or so. The horticultural society has made me president for the year, so it's going to be a busy one.'

His kind, confident voice always gave her hope that there were more good men in the world than bad. She still had doubts sometimes.

'That's great!' she said. 'I heard from the Greek estate agent today. It sounds as if the flat might be sold.'

'Marvellous news!' he responded. 'But believe me, given how long it took to put it in your name, it might be a little while before you get the funds. Have you thought where you might buy?'

'I haven't really. I'll let you know what happens,' she said. 'But more importantly, the figurine, the one I told you about, is in the auction at White's in a few days' time.'

'So soon! That's good news, sweetheart. But take care. Anything to do with crime always has some danger attached.'

'I know, Dad,' she said. 'I promise to be careful.'

She began to count the days. The night before the sale, Charles took her to the evening viewing.

The auction house was situated in the same street as several gentlemen's clubs and some tailors and milliners displaying the sign 'By Royal Appointment'. The building fitted well with its Establishment neighbours, with exceptionally beautiful young women behind a large reception desk to welcome visitors, and slim young men with cut-glass accents to escort them wherever they wanted to go, catalogues tucked under their arms.

A bust of the founder stood on a pillar in the centre of the marble-floored circular foyer, and around the walls were highly polished glass-fronted cabinets containing first editions of Dickens. These were the White family's personal collection, Charles informed her as he strode through, greeting almost every member of staff by their first name.

In the next room, people were sitting on deep leather sofas and talking in low voices. From there, one carpeted room led to the next. It was an environment suggestive of luxury and wealth, a world with which Helena was very unfamiliar.

In Room 5, the forty lots coming up for auction were displayed. The items ranged from the early Cycladic period to the Roman, but there was one object that seemed to be attracting more attention than any other. A crowd of more than twenty people were gathered round to take a closer look.

'It's the figurine,' breathed Helena.

She was centre stage on a plinth, supported upright.

'I can't believe Nick won't come,' she said under her breath.

'I wouldn't put anything past him,' Charles responded. 'But it's at his own peril, isn't it?'

Charles was known to the assistants, and was invited to handle the figurine, the privilege of any potential buyer, who was entitled to scrutinise for blemishes, authenticity and so on. He passed it, with extreme care, to Helena.

Already unsettled at the thought that Nick might be in the building, Helena trembled as she held the doll, the bitter memory of the last time it was in her hands even more vivid. Any residual doubt she might have had evaporated at this moment. The weight, the width, the length, the figurine's gaze. It was absolutely the same, unique piece.

Now that she was looking at it in real life, she saw that the joins were almost indiscernible. Nevertheless, she wondered how much better a job Haris would have done. She had thought of him every day with concern since that strange call. Something was wrong, and she could not work out what it might be. It constantly nagged at her.

Hugo White breezed in as they were about to leave. He greeted many of the clients in the room and then approached Charles and Helena.

'Shall we have a quick chat in my office?' he suggested.

They followed him upstairs. He did not invite them to sit. He clearly wanted to be brief.

'It's all set up,' he told them. 'Spoke to that chap in Athens. The one whose name you gave me. Something like Curtain? His English wasn't bad, and he's already in touch with his London counterpart.'

'Kourtis,' Helena corrected him, recalling the name. 'Giorgos Kourtis.'

She hardly slept that night, tossing and turning, dreaming and worrying.

It felt as if everything whirled around her, and every time she rationalised one anxiety, another emerged: whether the sale would go as planned, the potential presence of Nick the following day, Haris's froideur, the idea that she might have to meet Arsenis again, selling Kolonaki, poor Petros Pavlidis, what her future held. A migraine hovered.

Chapter Forty

Sally gave Helena the run of her wardrobe that morning.

'You'll have to dispense with your bohemian look for once,' she told her friend as she dashed out for work. 'Be more Bond Street, less Kensington Market.'

Helena laughed. She knew exactly what Sally meant. An image of Anna came into her mind: neat, chic, pearls.

She picked out one of Sally's corporate outfits and held it up against herself. It was a little on the large side, but it would do. She did up the buttons of a purple silk shirt dress, cinched it tight with a gold belt around her waist, tamed her hair into a bun and put on some make-up. Her long, slender feet just about squeezed into a pair of Sally's high court shoes, even though they were a size too small. Finally she put on a tailored red coat. It was rather short on her, but the overall effect was striking.

'Gosh, Helena!' said Charles in admiration. 'You should dress like that more often.'

'I don't think so,' said Helena, grinning.

Around midday, Charles, in suit and club tie, drove them from Ladbroke Grove and parked in Pall Mall. He then marched her into a nearby pub, where he insisted that she drink a double whisky to calm her nerves.

'I'll be nervous until it's all over,' she said. 'Suppose there's someone in there with a bottomless wallet. This time tomorrow our girl could be in New York.'

'Helena, it *won't* happen. It's all going to be fine. She's going to lead the authorities to find these people. Trust me. And I mean that. What you will see happening won't really be happening.'

'But the auction house will lose so much commission if it's not properly sold!'

'We have Hugo's word, Helena. Stop worrying. Please.'

Helena swallowed the last of her whisky.

'Let's go,' Charles said calmly. 'We're using a different entrance that leads straight up to the offices. We can't be in the room, in case one of your Greeks turns up.'

'Or Nick, I suppose,' said Helena.

'He has the temerity, but after his behaviour with Hugo's wife, he'd probably be kicked out anyway.'

As they approached White's, they could see that the main entrance was thronging with people.

'It's not always like this,' said Charles. 'There's lots of excitement today, I can feel it.'

Helena followed him to a discreet door. He pressed a buzzer and they went in.

'Let's go and see our friend on the third floor.'

At the end of a corridor, past various departmental offices – Impressionists and Modern, Old Masters, Islamic Art, Ancient Sculpture, Ceramics and Glass, and so on – they came to Hugo White's office. The door was open.

'Come in, come in!' Hugo greeted them warmly. 'Not long now, eh?' He seemed to be as excited as Helena was nervous.

The previous time she had been in his office, she had not noticed the wall of screens at one end. This was where Hugo led them now, so that they could watch the sale going on. There were nine CCTV cameras in the sale room, some of them facing the audience, one of them directed on the auctioneer, another on the lot under auction.

'It's almost better than being in the room,' said Hugo. 'You miss nothing.'

Her eyes moving from one screen to the next, Helena was soon enthralled by the black-and-white images.

With the sound on, they could hear the hum of conversation and snatches of muffled dialogue. Many people, predominantly men, greeted each other, most already acquainted in this world of wealth and privilege. All the seats were soon taken, and perhaps forty or fifty people were left standing at the back, crammed together and chatting as if they were at a cocktail party.

'Dealers, curators, collectors, they're all here today,' Hugo explained. 'The usual faces.'

At right angles to the audience was a selection of White's experts behind a row of telephones, ready to take bids from those who could not be physically present at the auction.

'Usually overseas buyers,' said Hugo.

'That's Jeremy, in the middle,' Charles told her. 'Old Masters. Excellent chap. Great friend of my late uncle's.'

The auctioneer himself then appeared. He was handsome, suave, ready to perform. Climbing up to his slightly elevated position on a stage at the front, he announced the commencement of the sale, clearly familiar with many in the crowd that he was playing to. The chatter in the saleroom stopped immediately.

A porter stepped forward with the first item and held it up to be viewed. The auctioneer gave a brief description and bidding began.

'Starting at fifteen. Fifteen in the room. Thank you, sir. Sixteen? Sixteen against you, sir. Try seventeen. Seventeen . . .'

And so it went on as two men battled it out for the vase, with discreet nods of their heads to confirm agreement to the ever-rising prices.

'Twenty. Twenty against you, sir. Twenty-five? Thank you. Now at twenty-five thousand. Thirty? No? Are you sure? Really sure?'

The auctioneer's tone was jovial, amused. 'Fair warning,' he said, lifting his gavel in the air and holding it there for a few suspenseful seconds.

'Going, going, *gone!*'

The gavel came down with a bang, and he moved on immediately to the next lot, and then the next. Helena was astonished by the speed with which things went under the hammer. Bidding for the first half-dozen lots went at breakneck pace, reminding her of the television commentary for the Grand National. There was jewellery, rare terracotta vases, a statuette of Cupid with a goat, another vase, and the bust of a Roman general. Most of them were sold well in excess of their estimates. One of the cameras showed how the crowd at the back was swelling.

Even the heat in Hugo's office was rising. Helena took off her coat, to reveal the bright purple dress with its outsized shoulder pads. The contrast with her hair was eye-catching, and Hugo glanced at her admiringly.

Half an hour or more went by.

'It's in reverse chronological order,' Charles whispered. 'Archaic next, when he's done with the Roman. Then he'll finish with Bronze Age.'

Helena's attention on the screen with the auctioneer drifted occasionally, and she also spent time studying those showing the audience. She could not entirely banish the thought that Nick might be there. Or Ligakis or Arsenis Papagiannis. All of them brazen, all of them emboldened by having ducked and dived all their lives.

'You, sir, another fifty? Twenty-five?' The auctioneer was trying to encourage one of the bidders to go up.

'No? We have two hundred and fifty on the telephone. Two hundred and fifty thousand. Fair warning . . . Going, going . . . gone!'

As the items became more ancient, the prices got higher and rose in ever larger increments. Even when it was something in which she had no interest, Helena felt her heart racing as people paid out sums for statues and pots that were more than enough to buy a three-bedroomed house.

There was a very brief interlude, and her eyes shifted again to one of the lower screens. Someone caught her eye. A man: tall, slender, in suit and tie, short back and sides, steel-rimmed spectacles. The image was indistinct and it was nothing like Nick. And yet it bothered her. The way the woman he was talking to tipped her chin to listen to him reminded her of the semi-adoration he could arouse.

'Charles . . .' she said, wanting him to look too.

'She's coming, Helena!' he said in a stage whisper.

'At last!' said Hugo, standing up and strolling to his desk.

Although its photo had appeared quite near the beginning of the catalogue, the item they were waiting for was going to be the last lot to come up.

Helena's heart pounded as the figurine was carried in by a porter and held aloft like a trophy.

The auctioneer opened at three hundred thousand pounds. The amount achieved in New York for her 'sister' had no doubt influenced the starting price.

A man in a shabby oversized coat had slipped in the side door five minutes earlier. Even on a screen it had been impossible not to notice someone of his great height. He was wearing a cloth cap and took a seat that must have been reserved for him in the front row. The cap came off to reveal a shiny bald head.

His large hand rose in the air.

'American,' muttered Charles, recognising him.

'We have four hundred. Five. Five hundred. Do I have six hundred? Gentleman at the back? Thank you sir, six hundred. Seven hundred? Seven hundred. Eight hundred? Thank you, sir. Nine? We have nine here in the front. Nine hundred.'

There was a pause for just a fraction of a second, almost as if the auctioneer himself doubted that anyone would agree to a seven-figure sum for this beautiful but broken marble artefact.

'One million? One million from the gentleman at the back.'

Helena glanced at a different screen. Another man, dapper in broad pinstripes, was determinedly bidding against the first.

'That's a French dealer,' Hugo told them from his desk.

'Hugo! Charles! What's happening? They're going to take her.' Helena was panicking. What had Charles meant by 'Trust me'? The bidding was running away.

Despite their assurances, she could not believe that there was no possibility of the plan backfiring.

Hugo was now on the phone, having a muttered conversation.

'We have one million,' the auctioneer's voice boomed.

It now seemed like a battle of wills between the American and French bidders. One million pounds for the Cycladic figurine. One million two hundred and fifty? he suggested to the American, who lifted his finger without a moment's hesitation.

There were some suppressed gasps around the saleroom, and in Hugo White's office too.

'One million five hundred? One million five hundred thousand? Sir? One million four hundred then? Do we have one million four hundred?'

The price was sticking. The French bidder was standing down.

'Oh my God, Charles.' Helena felt sick. She looked down at her hands and saw that her knuckles were white. The American and the Frenchman were genuine bidders. Where was the fake bidder?

'On the telephone now,' said the auctioneer, projecting his voice above the hubbub, 'we have one million four hundred.'

Helena now focused on the screen that showed the experts who manned the telephones. Charles's friend Jeremy had his receiver to his ear and was simultaneously communicating with the auctioneer and talking to his customer.

'One million five hundred?' The auctioneer addressed the bidder in the front row.

He tipped his head in reply.

There were a few more sharp intakes of breath from the audience as the price climbed. It seemed that the American was willing to go to the moon for this ancient piece.

The bidding quickly reached two million pounds. It was getting noisy in the room now, as it always did when records were being broken.

'Two million two hundred thousand? Sir? You're out? Against you on the phone at two million. Are you sure?'

The American shifted in his seat.

'Last chance,' teased the auctioneer. 'Big decision. Two million one hundred, perhaps?'

The American could not resist. His hand went up.

'We have two million one hundred. In the room. On the phone, two million two hundred?'

Jeremy nodded.

'So. For the Cycladic figurine. Two point two million.'

The auctioneer re-engaged with the American bidder.

'Not yours, sir. I'm back with the telephone at two million two hundred thousand. Two million three hundred?'

The American was immobile for a moment.

'Take your time, sir.'

The auctioneer knew exactly how to coax a little more from customers. At weekends, he went trout fishing and his expertise in balancing patience and persistence was as legendary mid-stream as in the auction room.

'I've got to bring the hammer down . . . Last chance.'

Within a few seconds, the American's hand went up.

'Thank you, sir. And on the telephone, do we have a little more?'

The knife-edge bidding now began to go up by increments of fifty thousand. When it reached two and a half million the whole room was silent. At that moment, it seemed that the American would be taking the figurine away. The amount seemed inconceivable.

'Thank you very much. Can we go a little higher?'

The auctioneer was addressing Jeremy, whose hand was cupped over the mouthpiece.

He was muttering inaudibly.

'Do I have two million five fifty?'

Jeremy nodded.

'So, just a little more. Another fifty? Last chance? Hammer is up . . .'

The auctioneer directed his words to the American.

The smooth, bald head dropped. He had reached his limit. He would not outbid Jeremy's client.

The auctioneer took a breath. Charles squeezed Helena's hand.

'At two million five hundred and fifty thousand pounds . . . on the telephone. Going! Going! Gone!'

Helena heard the gavel come down with a bang. At the same moment, Hugo dropped his phone back on its cradle.

The saleroom erupted in applause. The telephone bidder and the figurine were getting a standing ovation. Jeremy's unseen client had secured the Nisos loot for an almost unimaginable sum.

'Happy now, Helena?' boomed Hugo from his desk.

She looked round to see his smiling face.

'It was you!' She was shaking her head with disbelief and relief.

She hugged Charles, laughing and almost crying at the same time.

'You're right, Hugo is a hero!' she said, turning to take Hugo's hand. 'I am so glad that's over.'

The headache that had plagued her since the morning lifted. She could now allow herself to imagine Nick at this moment. He might already know how much money the figurine had fetched and would be imagining that he was now a wealthy man. Dare she even hope that instead of a cheque, he might soon receive an arrest warrant?

'I'm just popping down there,' said Hugo. 'Back in ten minutes.' He disappeared from the room.

Helena turned back to look at the screens. She saw the American leaving, his head like polished bronze visible above the crowd, and had already spotted the Frenchman slipping out through the door.

Everyone in the sale room was now standing, milling about, discussing what they had just witnessed. Helena leaned close to see if she could spot that figure in the steel-rimmed glasses again. Instead, she saw another face in profile. He looked familiar, but she dismissed the idea. There had been many dark-haired men in the room, very possibly some other Greeks.

A few moments later, there was a sharp knock on the door and Jeremy walked in.

'Jeremy! Congratulations! Excellent job!' praised Charles. 'This is Helena.'

Jeremy shook her hand.

'Even the auctioneer had absolutely no idea what was going on,' he told them. 'Everyone in the room had to be convinced, otherwise the whole thing would have felt fake.'

They were all dry-mouthed for one reason or another, and Charles served them iced water from a jug on Hugo's desk.

'It was brilliant,' said Helena, gulping hers back. 'I almost feel sorry for those disappointed bidders. Particularly the American. He desperately wanted our figurine.'

'Don't worry about him,' said Jeremy. 'He has plenty of toys to play with already and more money than he knows what to do with.'

Hugo walked back in holding something wrapped in a black silk cloth. He laid it on his desk.

'Gather round, everyone.'

Pulling on a pair of white fabric gloves, he opened one of his desk drawers and produced a small box, from which he removed the marble feet. Then he unfolded the cloth to reveal the figurine and laid her flat.

Helena, Charles and Jeremy all leaned forward.

Hugo carefully placed the feet next to the severed ankles. The edges met exactly. There was no light between the pieces.

Whole again, thought Helena, her eyes misting. Thank God.

'This beautiful sculpture is not going to America, Helena,' he said. 'But she will need to travel to Greece.'

They all took a seat. Helena in particular was eager to know what happened next.

'So who is expecting the cheque?'

'The man you mentioned, Giannis Ligakis, is already a suspect of the art team in Athens, but he has always covered his tracks. The Ligakis shop in Kolonaki has connections with a Swiss-based outfit, and the art team believes that he sometimes trades through them. This time, though, it looks as if he didn't. The figurine was delivered to us by a very smooth-talking chap. His English was so elocuted that my staff knew he was foreign even before they took his name. The girls on reception are not just pretty faces. They make a note of everything.'

'Show them the photo, old chap,' said Jeremy.

'Ah yes, CCTV. Very useful. With millions of pounds' worth of art and sculpture passing through every month, we try to keep an eye on the reception area,' said Hugo. 'Multiple eyes, in fact. Mostly it's just a deterrent. But we do have an image.'

From an envelope, he produced a grainy black-and-white photograph, which he slid across the desk towards Helena.

The slicked-back hair, the neat moustache, the double-breasted suit were familiar.

'I'm sure that's Arsenis Papagiannis,' she said. 'Giannis Ligakis's friend. Accomplice, I should say.'

The notion of that man in London made Helena feel distinctly queasy.

'So now he comes to pick up the money?' she asked.

'Not cash in a suitcase,' laughed Hugo. 'The seller will be expecting a bank transfer. But we can procrastinate for a short while. Not too long, though. We don't want him to become suspicious.'

'I am aware you missed out on a big commission for this,' Helena said. 'On two and a half million . . . '

'Don't even think about it, my dear,' he said with a dismissive wave of his hand. 'It's a short-term loss, but a gain in the long run.'

'What's next, then?' she asked eagerly.

'As I said, this fine sculpture and her feet have to be taken back to Athens. From my conversation with the police here and that Curtain man, I understand this is the evidence they have been waiting for. The British police will take it over there tomorrow, with paperwork and information provided by us. The soil analysis alone should be adequate proof that this is a looted piece. It's more than enough reason for the team to take a very close look at the Ligakis premises.'

'Do you mean raid the place?' asked Charles.

'I imagine so. And even if they find nothing else, Ligakis will have to face the consequences of trying to sell our little goddess.'

Helena was wondering if Nick was going to get away with it after all. Her story about what had happened to the figurine was only her word against his. He had gone into the Morakis shop to enquire about repair, but even that would be hard to prove.

'The police art team in Greece is excellent,' said Jeremy. 'We've worked with them before. The truth is that they have much more incentive on all this than us. Without strong prevention, the country will literally be bled of its treasures.'

Helena stood up to shake hands with Hugo and Jeremy. She was eager to call her friends in Athens to tell them what had happened.

'We'll probably all go to my club for a drink,' said Charles. 'Hope you don't think that's unsociable?'

'Your gentlemen-only club?' laughed Helena. 'It's a hypothetical question, isn't it!'

Leaving them to chat, she walked down the several flights of stairs and back across the tiled foyer. The place was almost empty now, and the sound of Sally's borrowed heels clicking on the marble flooring echoed around her.

She stood for a moment on the steps of White's, relieved to be outside the overheated building. It was dark now, but the shops selling high-end fashion and jewellery were dazzlingly lit. The chilly January air grazed her cheeks.

Right opposite was a branch of Yves Saint Laurent for men. In the window stood a row of four dummies, faces chiselled, uniformly dressed in jet-black knee-length coats, heads tilted at an identical angle to balance Spanish-style hats, wide brims, shallow crowns. They appeared to be striding out of the window towards the street, their sharp, padded shoulders and purposeful stance making an arresting tableau. Helena was reminded of a 1960s Beatles album cover. Then she observed something strange. A fifth dummy, identically dressed, was standing just outside the door, same coat, same hat, black, chic, minimal, facing in the same direction.

To her astonishment, it began to move, turning down Bond Street towards Piccadilly. There were plenty of other people in the street, on the way home from office jobs, going to meet friends, or shopping. None of them seemed to have noticed this walking mannequin.

Rooted to the spot, Helena suddenly realised that it was a man. Of course it was, she scolded herself. Perhaps that migraine had left her vision blurred.

As he marched away, he took off the hat that had kept his face half concealed until now. Even though his shock of blond hair had been lopped and closely trimmed, she was fairly certain it was Nick. His slim build and the way he walked were distinctive, but when he removed a pair of spectacles from his pocket, she knew for sure that he had been in the sale room. His chutzpah was almost absurd.

For a split second, he glanced over his shoulder in the direction of White's, and she shrank back. He appeared not to notice her, and she hoped that Sally's clothes and today's unusual hairstyle were a good enough disguise.

She was almost glad to be wearing these ridiculous, stupid shoes, otherwise she might have run after him screaming 'Thief!' He deserved to be in handcuffs. All kinds of humiliation and revenge came into her mind.

Helena knew she must let him go for now, however, and watched as he disappeared into the night, like Nosferatu in his long black coat. Both self-control and silence gave her power.

Chapter Forty-One

A moment later, Charles and Hugo pushed through the shiny glass doors of White's. They were surprised to see Helena still there. Hugo shook her hand again, and Charles hugged her and kissed her cheek.

'See you later,' he said, as both men set off towards their club.

Helena suddenly felt drained of all energy. The rushes of adrenaline during the sale and the horror of seeing Nick had left her totally exhausted. Desperate to sit for ten minutes to think and regain her composure, she hobbled towards a narrow side street where she had spotted a small café.

Apart from one table, it was empty, so she sat by the window, gave her order for tea and fruit cake, and then slipped into the ladies' while she waited, leaving the White's sale catalogue on the table.

When she reappeared, she could not hide her spontaneous feeling of joy at seeing Haris sitting at her table. An unexpected day had given her yet another surprise.

'Haris! You're here! In London! Do you know, I thought I saw someone who looked like you earlier, but I told myself it couldn't be. But it was you after all. I am so happy to see you. Why didn't you tell me you were coming?'

Her effervescence was immediately flattened by his unsmiling reaction.

When the waitress approached with Helena's tea and asked if her friend would like something, Haris waved her away. Helena was dumbfounded by the tone of his voice and his manner.

'I was going to ring you tonight,' she said. 'To tell you what happened. It went perfectly!'

'It didn't look as if it did,' he said cynically.

'Haris, please tell me what's happened. What's the matter?' She put her hand on his.

'Don't,' he snapped, pulling it away.

The couple at the other table were looking at them with curiosity, as people did when there might be someone else's marital altercation to enjoy.

Helena fished in her purse for some coins, put them on the table and got up.

The waitress was bringing the slice of cake.

'Sorry,' said Helena. 'But we have to go.'

Haris followed her out into the street. Helena remembered how shy and introverted he sometimes appeared. Perhaps a glass of wine would help him relax. She put his arm through his and, as authoritatively as Charles had done with her earlier in the day, took him in the direction she wanted to go. The blisters on her heels were raw now, but there was an old-fashioned basement wine bar with barrels for tables not far from the café.

After crossing a few streets and turning left into an alley, Helena could see it in the distance. Haris had freed his arm from hers and fallen into step with her.

'White or red?' she asked him as they stood waiting at the bar. It was a busy time of day.

'Like you, I prefer white,' he said, without expression.

They carried the bottle to one of the barrels and sat down. Haris poured and they both sipped.

Neither wanted to be the one to speak first, but Helena gave in.

'How is everything in Athens?' she asked stiffly, her excitement at what had happened with the figurine now falling away. 'Anna? The shop? All well?'

'Business has been a bit slow,' he replied. 'But Anna is fine. We'll need to take your grandfather's hoard to the police soon.'

'Of course,' she responded. 'That's what I wanted to tell you – that I will come to Athens in the next few days.'

'Oh,' Haris said, with apparent lack of interest. 'And how is the flat sale going?'

'Some progress.'

'Tortuous business in Greece,' he confirmed.

There was silence for a moment.

'I'm selling too,' he told her.

Helena was puzzled.

'I originally bought my place with my fiancée.'

Helena felt slightly dizzy. Maybe because she had not really eaten all day.

'Buying somewhere bigger?' she managed to ask.

As she took a gulp of her wine, she managed to spill some on Sally's dress.

'God, I'm so clumsy,' she said with exasperation, dabbing at it with a napkin that Haris fetched from the bar.

'Somewhere bigger then?' she had to repeat.

'No.'

'Oh.'

The conversation was becoming progressively more awkward, monosyllabic.

Both of them finished their first glass of wine and busied them-selves cracking open peanut shells. Helena poured them each another glass.

'We've split up,' said Haris bluntly. 'I met somebody else. And I realised that I loved the somebody else more. So I couldn't continue with Persephone because I had to be honest with her. It was painful. But easier because I was truthful with her – and myself.'

He was gazing at his feet while he was speaking, and Helena looked at him. He continued staring at the ground.

'Then I realised that the somebody else had somebody else. Though in fact it doesn't make any difference,' he said, now looking up to meet Helena's eyes. 'I would still have had to leave Persephone.'

'It all sounds really sad,' said Helena, feeling that she was expected to respond in some way. 'I'm so sorry.'

There was another silence.

'Look, do you mind if I let down this ghastly hairdo?' she said. 'It's so tight and I'm certain it isn't helping with my headache.'

Her unruly hair tumbled down.

'Let's talk about the auction,' she said brightly.

Haris still seemed withdrawn, but Helena was determined to try and cheer him up.

'The plan went exactly as I described to you on the phone,' she told him, leaning in close in case anyone else should hear. 'They wanted some genuine bidders, major figures, to battle it out. Which is exactly what happened. And then at the last minute they brought in the fake phone bidder.'

Her elation failed to infect Haris with any kind of enthusiasm. But she persisted.

'To be honest, Haris,' she whispered, 'I thought it had all gone horribly wrong. When it got to two million, I thought maybe White's had backed out of the plan because they wanted the commission. Who could blame them really?'

He sipped his wine thoughtfully, staring at her.

'Even though Charles had *promised* me, and Hugo White had sworn he wouldn't let me down, I didn't really believe it. I was shaking like a leaf, until I realised that it had been Hugo on the phone after all. And almost the best thing is that Ligakis, Papagiannis and Nick will be expecting to split around two million after the various commissions.'

'That's quite a pleasurable thought,' commented Haris.

There was another long silence. Helena cracked nut after nut.

'Anyway, it all sounds great,' said Haris. 'I'm glad it went well.'

'But it's not over yet. Tomorrow the figurine will be taken to Athens by the British police and handed over to your friends in the police there.'

'I suppose it should lead them to Ligakis.'

'And to Nick Jones and Arsenis Papagiannis, I hope.'

The wine bottle was almost empty now. It did feel as if Haris's mood had thawed a little. Helena had to conclude that he was low on account of his break-up. It was natural.

'Will you take me to meet them?' she asked. 'Kourtis sounds very involved in what's happening.'

'Of course I'll take you,' he said. 'We'll go there with the Byzantine collection and the Cycladic pieces. I've already alerted them that they're on the way.'

'Great.'

'And you do realise that they will be expecting us to give evidence if all this goes to trial?'

'I want to,' Helena said determinedly. 'I want to stand in court and describe what Nick did. Mostly because he doesn't think I'm capable of it.'

'I'll be there with you,' said Haris, almost warmly. 'I will testify that he came into the shop with all the pieces.'

'Well, not quite all of them,' laughed Helena.

'That's true,' said Haris, smiling for the first time that evening.

'And the good thing is that there are still traces of soil on those feet. It's conclusive proof of where they came from.'

'Another drink?' Haris asked.

'I think I've had enough,' said Helena. 'I'm pretty tired. Not much sleep last night.'

'And I'm taking the first flight back tomorrow,' said Haris. 'So I could do with an early night.'

Helena felt his eyes on her as she put the blood-red coat back on.

She caught sight of herself in the mirrored wall of the bar. It was an even more dramatic combination with the purple dress now that her hair was loose.

They climbed the spiral staircase to the pavement.

There was a flower stall opposite, and the owner was packing his buckets of buds and blooms into a van for the night. Haris ran across the road, made a purchase and returned with a bouquet. To Helena's astonishment, he put it into her hands.

'I'll see you soon, Helena. Call me when you get to Athens.'

For the second time that day, she watched a man walk away until he was out of sight.

A black cab swung round the corner, yellow light shining. She threw out her hand, took off Sally's shoes and climbed into the taxi in her stockinged feet.

'Ladbroke Grove, please,' she said.

The driver winked. 'Someone's got an admirer.'

For the next twenty minutes, she sat gazing at the perfect white roses. By the time she had reached her destination, they had filled the taxi with their intoxicating scent.

Chapter Forty-Two

Helena arrived in Athens three days later, glad as always of Manolis's friendly presence in the hallway.

She went through the rigorous process of unlocking, and then relocked from inside, still nervous that Arsenis might try to enter. She slept badly that night in the echoing apartment, and promised herself that she would get on with the legalities of selling as soon as she could.

The following morning, she called the Morakis shop to let them know she had arrived.

Anna picked up. From the acoustics, she could envisage Helena alone in the huge empty flat, and suggested that she should come and stay in her apartment.

'Get here around six,' she told her. 'I'll be home by then.'

Helena welcomed the invitation with alacrity and repacked her bag, stuffing the letters to her grandfather and the ledgers on top. They would be safer out of the apartment, and she would need to show them to the police.

From its elevated position in the attractive neighbourhood of Mets, Anna's fifth-floor apartment had a spectacular view over the city. She had furnished it in a simple, modernist style, which surprised visitors given the generally baroque nature of everything in her shop.

The first thing Helena noticed when she arrived were some men's shoes in the hallway. Perhaps Anna had met someone in the past few months.

Anna saw her looking at them and soon disabused her.

'My brother's,' she said, matter-of-factly. 'He's moved in.'

'Oh,' Helena said. Thinking of the roses now wilting in Ladbroke Grove and, remembering her confusion that evening, she felt her pale complexion redden.

It was an unusually warm evening for the time of year, and they were able to sit on the terrace in their coats to enjoy a glass of wine. The city's lights twinkled below them. It was the first time Helena had been in Athens during January, and Anna explained to her that there were often unexpectedly warm days during that month,

'*Alkyonídes méres*, halcyon days,' she said brightly, topping up Helena's glass. 'It happens almost every year, a sudden burst of warmth in the middle of winter that can go on for a few weeks.'

'It's wonderful,' Helena said. 'Like spring!'

Helena did not ask, but Anna volunteered information on Haris's newly single status. She described watching the final disintegration of her brother's relationship with his fiancée over the past two months. To most, the couple had seemed an ideal match, and the wedding photographs against the sunset on an island would have shown the perfect bride and groom, beautiful, polished, both of them dark and glossy-haired with symmetrical features. The date, pencilled in for the following year, had been erased, she told Helena. She admitted that she had never thought Persephone interesting enough for Haris and believed that her vanity had already become tiresome. Apparently she had been very spoiled by wealthy parents.

'It seemed quite sudden in the end, though. And Haris won't even tell me what the final straw was,' she said. 'He simply moved out of their place. Just like that.' She snapped her fingers to demonstrate.

'Relationships can end as fast and furiously as they began,' Helena offered.

'Let's change the subject, though,' said Anna briskly. 'He'll be in soon and he would hate to think we've been talking about him.'

'It must be nice having a sibling that you get on with so well,' said Helena. 'And that you even enjoy working with.'

'Here in Greece, it's pretty standard to keep business in the family,' Anna told her.

Looking out across the city on this balmy night, Helena happily listened to her talking about their shop.

Panayotis Morakis had set up his art and antiquities business way back, and Anna and Haris had willingly taken it over. Their father had told them to keep everything above board, and not to make the mistakes he had made when he began. Customers trusted the provenance and source of anything they bought from the shop, and it thrived that way. It did not, however, stop looters approaching them occasionally. A few years before, they had been offered some grubby-looking beads, so freshly looted from a tomb that they still bore traces of soil. Haris had talked to the police art team, who raided the home of the person who had brought them in. Soil samples were matched with a particular archaeological site, and the beads were identified as part of a stolen gold funerary hoard dating to the twelfth century BC. The team managed to retrieve the rest.

'You have to share information quite subtly to protect yourself,' said Anna. 'It can be very dangerous crossing paths with the looters and traffickers. They only care about money, and human life is pretty cheap to them.'

'I think Arsenis Papagiannis and Nick Jones probably fit very well into that world,' Helena commented.

'It's worse in Italy,' said Anna. 'There have been a few unexplained deaths there recently, two archaeologists and even a member of their art squad.'

The conversation came to a natural end as Haris arrived home. The women went back inside. It was too cold to sit outside now.

There was a moment of awkwardness between Helena and Haris, but it soon passed.

'Anna told me she had invited you to stay,' he said. 'Good idea.'

Helena cooked a simple meal of pasta, and while they were eating, Haris explained what was planned with the art team. A junior member was coming to the shop the following day at eleven.

Many people wasted the team's time by contacting them with something that turned out to be perfectly bona fide, and they liked to ask a few preliminary questions before inviting them to headquarters.

Helena, of course, must be present for the meeting.

The next morning, at around 11.30, a skinny man, around forty years old, arrived at the shop. Angelos Vellopoulos was a relative newcomer to the team, and neither Anna nor Haris had met him before. He had a neat moustache and a serious demeanour.

'Vellopoulos,' he said, holding out a bony hand to Haris.

Anna locked the shop and the three of them went into the back room, where Haris had already laid out the Byzantine treasures and the Cycladic fragments on different tables, covering them over with cloths.

'Ashtray?' Vellopoulos asked.

Haris gave Anna a look, but obliged, and the policeman lit up.

'I won't keep you for long,' he said, inhaling. 'Just wanted to check a few things. I know your father was a friend of the team.' He looked at Helena as he said this.

'Not mine,' she smiled. 'Anna and Haris's.'

'Ah, right. So who are you?'

'Helena McCloud.'

'Right.' Hearing this very Scottish name in a perfect Greek accent confused him considerably.

'I know you are acquainted with Kourtis,' he said to Haris. 'But let me tell you about me.'

461

Helena put her hand in front of her face to conceal a smile. Vellopoulos reminded her so much of Peter Sellers.

'Born and grew up on a small Cycladic island. Hand to mouth in the fifties and sixties, and no chance of anything getting better. Then came some outsiders, probably from Athens, but to us it was like they were from Mars. They were looking for old stuff. We all had a few bits and pieces and they bought what we had, but they wanted more.'

The story sounded familiar to Helena.

'Well, my grandmother supposedly had a gift for finding water with a split rod. It was useful when the animals needed to drink. Even if people called her a witch, she didn't care. She preferred to call herself a water diviner.

'One day my father borrowed the rod to see if he could do it too, but instead he found a grave. A really old grave. Or so he said. He did it a few times, and there was always stuff in these graves. So when the foreigners came again, someone told them about him, and my father found a few more. For money, of course. I think it's more likely that he just knew the kind of locations where they would be. I don't think it was magic, but does it matter? It seemed like money for nothing.'

By now, the story had engaged them all and even Haris had lost his look of mild impatience.

'Then I got involved. I did some of the smuggling to take items to the right people in Athens. Lots of to and fro on the ferries during my teens and twenties, hiding things in crates of olives or grapes. Not easy, because we weren't exporting much from the island, but I was good at it. Always had a story to deflect suspicion of why I was travelling so much. I never knew where those pieces of magic stone, whole dolls sometimes, went to. Never knew . . .

'Anyway, after a few years, I heard what sort of prices rich people were paying. There must have been something on the radio. And I realised that my father and I were like slaves to these people! They were the ones with Rolexes, not us.'

'More than likely,' nodded Anna.

'And whether it's drugs or antiquities, the pattern is the same. The non-elite are exploited for the profit of the elite. It doesn't matter if it's a tomb-robber or a peasant picking coca leaves, the profits only go to the exploiter.'

Vellopoulos had become progressively more emphatic and political in the telling of his tale. One cigarette already lay stubbed out in the ashtray, and he now lit another, as if he needed to calm himself. The room was filling with smoke.

'I realised I could earn more money working for the government, where I'd get a pension, job security, health insurance, perks, a nice office. And that's what I decided to do. Steady job for life, and I send money home to my father. He's happy. And I'm motivated. They're bad people. I'm not. And I can sleep at night.'

'Sounds like it was a good decision,' said Helena encouragingly.

Vellopoulos drew deeply on his cigarette, flapping his hand pointlessly to get rid of the smoke.

'And that's the hierarchy in looting and trafficking,' Anna said to encourage him. 'The difference in pay between the job that you were doing and what the man in the suit gets is huge.'

'Yes. I might be relatively new in the department. I might be a humble islander. But I know my stuff,' he concluded triumphantly.

Helena liked the man. She could detect that he often felt patronised, and sympathised.

'So what have you got here?' he said, taking out a notebook and licking the tip of a pencil.

Like a magician, Haris drew the cloth off the Byzantine pieces. He had cleaned most of them, and they glistened. Those in pristine condition looked spectacular now.

'*Panagía mou!* By the holy virgin!' Vellopoulos rapidly crossed himself a dozen times. 'No, no, no, no! How could they? How could they?'

he whispered. He crossed himself again, tears in his eyes. '*Gamóto!* Thieves, robbers, looters, whatever you want to call them. This is not just a crime. It's a *sin*! This is blasphemy. Against the Church and the holy saints.'

'Indeed,' agreed Anna, nodding sagely.

'And then *these*.' Haris lifted the second cloth.

Vellopoulos glanced at the fragments. He had no need to touch a single piece and took less than three seconds to survey the whole collection.

'This has got to stop,' he said. 'Those pieces are probably even from my own island.'

'And where is that?' asked Helena to be polite.

'Ammos,' he said. 'Beautiful little place. Have you been there?'

Yes, thought Helena, I have. But without waiting for an answer, Vellopoulos gathered cigarettes, lighter and notebook and put them back in his pocket.

'I'll tell you something,' he said, addressing his audience, 'I'm looking forward to this one. We'll get them. Don't you worry.'

Even before they had a chance to explain anything about the origins of the hoard, he was on his way out.

'Very nice to meet you all,' he said. 'Tomorrow afternoon, right?'

Haris unlocked the shop door to let him out, and then returned to the office, where Helena and Anna were laughing.

'Now, there's a man who loves his job,' he smiled.

Helena helped Anna rewrap and box all the pieces, and one by one handed them to her to store in the safe. Just as they finished, the bell above the door clanged and Anna went out to greet a wealthy-looking couple who wanted to browse.

Haris had locked the ledgers and letters in a desk drawer and gone back to his work restoring a Roman vase. He had a book in front of him, open at a page showing a similar item.

Helena watched him for a while, fascinated by the size of the pieces he was gluing, many of them less than half the size of her little fingernail and having to be picked up with special tweezers. It was clear that he needed to concentrate and did not want to talk.

She whiled away the afternoon in the National Archaeological Museum, revisiting her favourite exhibits and standing for a while in front of a small collection of Cycladic figurines and pots.

In the evening the three of them went for dinner in Mets, and Helena was relieved to find that Haris's mood seemed very different from when he had been in London.

She slept very lightly that night. Was it excitement for the following day? Or because she knew that Haris was lying on the other side of the wall? She could not decide.

Chapter Forty-Three

The stark concrete building in Alexandra's Avenue that housed the *Ellinikí Astynomía*, the Greek police, bore little resemblance to the Oxford equivalent Helena had once visited. Its architecture was brutalist, and she was glad not to be entering the huge and intimidating twelve-storey structure alone. She wondered how much crime must be committed in this city to justify such an edifice.

With their father's name, Haris and Anna were welcome visitors. Giorgos Kourtis, head of the art team, a jovial bear of a man, was there to greet them when the doors to the lift opened on the sixth floor. It was a Friday afternoon.

'Going on vacation?' he chuckled when Haris emerged with a holdall in each hand.

They all laughed.

'Not at the moment,' replied Haris. 'But somebody might be going on a long holiday to prison after you see all this.'

They followed Kourtis into a meeting room with a huge table in the centre and he used the phone to summon Vellopoulos. Haris introduced Helena and explained briefly and rapidly the background to her story, starting with the ledgers that listed all the bribes her grandfather had taken, the related correspondence, and the collections of objects that they had found in his desk. The latter were merely those items that had not yet been passed on for sale.

'Mmm, Stamatis Papagiannis. I remember that name. The army and the police had strong connections then,' Kourtis said, making reference to the junta period. 'And I've been around a while.'

Helena continued with the details, naming Arsenis Papagiannis and describing his connection with Giannis Ligakis. Kourtis reacted to their names too. They were both known to him.

'Ligakis is a classic type,' he said disdainfully. 'He looks like a gentleman, but his father sold *kouloúri* off a barrow. We keep an eye on his shop, but he's a wheeler-dealer and protects himself. He must have plenty of middlemen to keep his name clean.

'And how does your grandfather's collection relate to the Cycladic princess that was brought over from London? The one from White's.'

'Arsenis Papagiannis delivered it to London for the sale, but technically he was doing it on behalf of Ligakis,' Helena explained. 'It was taken illegally from an excavation in Nisos by someone called Nick Jones, who often uses the name Nicholas Hayes-Jones.'

'I understand,' said Kourtis. 'So we've got a couple of old hands who we've been wanting to get hold of for a while. They're a slimy pair, always slipping through our net. *And* a new recruit. Excellent!' He rubbed his chin with satisfaction. 'If we can sweep them all up together, I could retire.'

He wandered across to the window to gaze out, as if to daydream about that moment, and then came back to reality.

'So, let's see what you've got then.'

Vellopoulos pulled a black felt cloth out of a corner cupboard and spread it across the table. Helena wondered whether it was to protect the shiny wood or the fragile pieces that she was about to lay out.

She unzipped the first bag and one by one took out the thirty or so Byzantine treasures. On the plain black background and with the sunlight pouring in through the windows, the gold gleamed and the jewels sparkled.

Kourtis said nothing, and such was his nonchalance, Helena wondered if he had seen it all before.

Vellopoulos stood by an open window and smoked, occasionally looking over his shoulder to watch Helena at work.

When everything was laid out, Vellopoulos took a last drag of his cigarette, then tossed the butt out of the window and slammed it shut. He and his boss now stood side by side looking over the display.

'Nice, isn't it?' said Vellopoulos, crossing himself.

'It's spectacular, nothing less than spectacular.'

Kourtis picked up one of the crosses on a chain, and to Helena's astonishment put it round his neck and went to admire his reflection in the window.

'None of this is legal,' he said bluntly.

This seemed to be stating the obvious, but Helena, Anna and Haris nodded as if he had said something profound. He continued.

'But it wouldn't have been so easy to get rid of, which is probably why Stamatis Papagiannis kept it. Quite hard to disguise holy pieces if you are trying to smuggle them.'

He wiped his sweaty forehead with a handkerchief.

'Vellopoulos, get the camera, would you?'

Another member of the team was brought in to label and catalogue the pieces, and Vellopoulos methodically photographed each one from several different angles.

'We'll get our colleagues to start matching with the lists we have of stolen goods. Could be from churches or museums. Some of these things might even be from Constantinople. Definitely some from Cyprus. There was plenty of looting there even before '74. We've known people dress up as priests and come through the border wearing stuff like this.' Kourtis pointed to the ornate cross he was wearing. 'It's worth a fortune. Millions and millions.'

Once he was done, Vellopoulos rested the heavy camera on the table and sat down.

'Coffee, anyone?' asked Kourtis. Without waiting for an answer, he left the room.

Time was passing, so Helena started to unpack the bag of marble pieces at the far end of the table. Vellopoulos was leaning out of the window again to smoke. The sun was coming straight in now, and the temperature in the room was becoming unbearable.

'Do you mind if I shut the blinds?' asked Anna. She began to play with the twisted strings and with great difficulty managed to lower the dirty slats, which now cast horizontal stripes across the room.

A breeze caught the window and it banged shut on one of Vellopoulos's fingers.

'*Na sou gamíso!*' he swore crudely.

Kourtis was just walking back into the room with five paper cups of coffee, most of which had already slopped onto the tray, and a large box of *bougátsa*, rich, creamy pies.

'*Éla moré!* Come on, mate!' he scolded. 'Mind your mouth in front of the ladies!'

As he put his afternoon snack down, he spotted the Cycladic display.

'*Panagía mou . . .*' he breathed. 'Astonishing.' He was staring open-mouthed at the translucent marble, glowing and dramatic against the black cloth.

'A day like today makes it all worthwhile,' Vellopoulos said triumphantly, looking at the spoils on the table. 'You've got the lot here. Even parts of a stargazer. Very early.' With reverence he picked up one piece. 'And this is part of a violin-shaped figure,' he said knowledgeably.

Putting her down again on the black cloth, he selected a badly chipped pair of legs, some feet, an abdomen with folded arms and a torso with neat breasts. He put them close to each other, as if attempting to match them, though they were clearly all from different figures.

He seemed only to address Helena now, as though he thought the Morakis siblings might not need the lesson, and his face became more sweetly serious than before.

'Look, Kyría Helena,' he said, indicating the relevant part of the body as he spoke. 'The feet and legs give her the power of movement.

The breasts and arms and abdomen give her powers of love and reproduction. The head, if only she had one, would unite her senses and give her intellect.'

Kourtis was tucking into his second pastry and listening respectfully.

'And what do you have? Venus! Gaia! The Panagía! You have something that represents *all* of womankind, Kyría Helena.' Vellopoulos paused to cough. 'The best of humanity!'

Helena nodded.

'And what's my point?' He paused for a fraction of a second, not really intending for them to answer. 'My point is this. We know that some of these got broken in the past. They say it was a ritual; maybe it was a display of grief. Who knows? But! But if someone breaks one *now*, this is not a ritual, it is desecration, it is vandalism! Look! Imagine one of these complete, with a head, with a heart and body and legs! All united! Imagine the beauty, Kyría Helena!'

They all focused on the shattered pieces. The light coming in through the slats of the blind were creating stripes across Vellopoulos's face, but it only added to the slightly surreal nature of the moment and the transition this man had made from smuggling islander to passionate spokesman against looting.

'Their greatest beauty is when they are whole! And home!' he said with rapture.

'Thanks, Vellopoulos,' said Kourtis, as though talking to a child. 'I think our friends get the picture. And I don't think they disagree.'

'Whole, and home,' Helena repeated quietly. It was exactly how things should be. Even if something was in a museum, it should still be close to where it had been discovered.

The same colleague as before came in to label and catalogue, and Vellopoulos took several photographs of each piece. It was a painstaking but necessary process.

He picked up one piece after photographing it and pronounced it fake.

'Made with decent marble and good tools,' he said. 'Polished with hay to make the surface look authentic, but no. I don't think it's real.'

Haris took a closer look.

'I think you're right,' he agreed, acknowledging that Vellopoulos had spotted something he had not.

He was equally impressed when he noticed Vellopoulos turning pieces over to check the alignment of the groove representing the spine. Sometimes this helped match two pieces.

'While he's doing that,' suggested Kourtis, stuffing another pastry into his mouth, 'why don't you tell us more about those record books.' He ran a greasy finger down one of the pages. 'The problem here,' he said, crumbs flying, 'is that this is mostly historic.'

Helena felt a jolt of disappointment.

'Some of these entries are from decades ago, and looking at this column, it appears that he got rid of most things he was given. That's what these ticks show, doesn't it?' he said, turning the ledger so that she could see.

'Yes, I think so.'

'The pieces on the table here are just the ones he happened to still have when he died. Which was sudden, you said?'

Helena nodded.

'In this job, you learn a lot about the behaviour of the rich, the criminal and the criminally rich,' said Kourtis. 'And I can tell you that they all have one thing in common. Arrogance.'

With the exception of Vellopoulos, who had finished taking photographs and was once more hanging out of the window to smoke, they were all sitting at the table. The big man rocked back on his chair before concluding:

'And they say that an arrogant man feels immortal, even on his deathbed.'

'That would fit my grandfather,' said Helena, with conviction. 'He always acted as though he was invincible, and there was nobody to contradict him. He would never have been able to imagine the injustice of death for himself.' She did not bother to hide her deep loathing of Stamatis Papagiannis.

Haris looked at her. Every day he saw some new expression on Helena's face that made her even more attractive to him, even if, as now, it was fury. He resisted the urge to reach out and touch her slender hand.

'So apart from locking his desk, he didn't really cover his tracks, did he? These books list every act of corruption and betrayal,' said Kourtis, sounding almost impressed by the sheer volume of Papagiannis's crimes.

'It's too late to get him, of course,' he added, stating the obvious. 'All these things were in a dead man's desk. There can be no retribution for him.'

Stamatis Papagiannis was gone. That was unalterable. Most people did not even remember him now. The regime he had supported was long since discredited, its key participants in prison for life.

'Even if he was alive, there is no appetite for punishing historic crimes in this time of *metapolítefsi*, political change,' said Kourtis. 'There is only a desire to look forward, not back.'

Helena could not sit still any longer. She was restless, full of pent-up frustration. She wanted to know that those who *were* still alive would be punished. Surely some of her fish were on the hook?

'But Arsenis Papagiannis's initials are there – and Giannis Ligakis's!' she cried out.

'Yes, yes! Calm down, young lady,' Kourtis told her.

She did as she was told, quietly furious. Nobody ever told Medea to calm down.

'Everything will happen in good time,' he said, pushing the ledgers back towards her. She left them there a moment before reluctantly putting them in her satchel.

'We might need them in the future,' he said. 'Let's do things in order.'

Helena nodded, remembering the relatives of those murdered by Klaus Barbie who had waited so long for justice. To unpick the details of the ledger would be a labour for another day, but it was something she vowed to herself that she would undertake.

'What we can do immediately is get these photographs distributed to museums, archaeologists, experts, and see if they can identify anything. And then, as our philosopher friend Vellopoulos put it, we will ensure these treasures go home and are on view to be studied and enjoyed.'

The labelling and photography were completed now, and Kourtis glanced at his watch. The traffic from Alexandra's Avenue was becoming noisier by the minute, with people eager to get home to start their weekend. The regular sound of horns blaring came through the open windows. Helena felt his impatience to join the exodus from Athens.

Haris leaned towards him.

'Haven't we forgotten something?' he asked.

'Oh yes! Yes!' Kourtis said, smiling. 'My colleague here hasn't seen her yet. Shall I have her brought in?'

Like obedient children, the three of them murmured their acquiescence.

He used the phone to summon a junior to bring the Nisos figurine from his office.

'This, dear Angelos, is a rare beauty,' he said.

He handed the box to Helena, allowing her the pleasure of unwrapping and revealing the figurine. She gently placed it on the table, and then took the feet out of tissue and fitted them on the legs. Against the black cloth, the effect was dramatic.

Vellopoulos was dumbstruck.

'So there she is,' said Anna, who had not seen the figurine before either.

Helena noticed Vellopoulos biting his knuckle. He appeared to be struggling with his emotions.

'*Panagía mou, panagía mou*,' he muttered. 'Truly a goddess.' He turned away to conceal his tears, nervously smoking out of the window for a few moments.

Anna used the time to take a closer look at the figurine.

'That break,' she said. 'Really fresh and new. Perfect in court.'

When Vellopoulos returned to the table, Anna spoke to him for a moment, describing the figurine's strange odyssey.

Meanwhile, Kourtis told them that Hugo White had already given him the full details of the bank account into which payment was supposed to be made.

'For me, this is the best part of the evidence,' he said, brandishing a copy of the document. 'It's a Swiss account and one that we have traced to Ligakis. I think that just about concludes things for today.'

Helena could see that he was definitely thinking about his weekend now.

Vellopoulos was examining the little feet under his magnifying glass with a broad smile on his face.

'*Málista*,' said Kourtis decisively. 'Right. We now have the opportunity to take a close look at Ligakis's premises.'

Helena tried to hide her elation.

He got up. 'I'll leave Vellopoulos to clear up. All this will be kept safe,' he said, halfway through the door. 'I'll call you on Tuesday afternoon and tell you the plan. We'll need to sort some paperwork before then.'

She noticed a button pop off his shirt, and bent down to pick it up off the floor. Even during the course of the afternoon, his stomach seemed to have expanded.

'Can't seem to keep the weight off since I stopped smoking,' he said, taking it from her and slipping it into a pocket.

Unobserved, Haris and Helena exchanged a smile.

Helena, Haris and Anna chatted for a few minutes more with Vellopoulos and then left. Moments later they were outside on the pavement. It was ten minutes past five and almost dark.

'Hungry?' asked Haris.

They had missed lunch, and none of them had taken a pastry.

They walked along in the wintry dusk towards Syntagma. No one spoke for a while.

Helena's sense of relief at how well the meeting had gone was immense. Having the authorities on their side gave her courage. Nick Jones's name was now recorded in that forbidding police head-quarters, and both the British and Greek police were aware of him. She was moving closer to her goal.

'I really thought that some of that cream was going to fall on a figurine,' laughed Anna, breaking the silence.

'He definitely showed more interest in the *bougátsa* than the Byzantine pieces,' said Haris.

'Vellopoulos is the one who looks in need of some calories,' commented Helena. 'He doesn't look like he's eaten a decent meal in days.'

'I suspect he burns up a lot of energy,' Anna suggested, 'with that passion for what he does.'

'And there's no time for eating when you smoke that much,' observed Haris.

'But what devotion to his work!' commented Helena. 'And womankind.'

'In a somewhat theoretical way, I think,' added Haris.

They headed towards a small restaurant Anna and Haris knew in Monastiraki. With its white linen tablecloths and long-stemmed wine glasses, it was very different from the places Helena had been with Mihalis, but the menu was broadly the same. The owner knew the Morakis siblings and gave them the best table on his rooftop terrace. It was the magic hour and the sun was almost down.

'I'm going to order our favourite wine,' said Haris. 'I think we should celebrate.'

'Isn't it a bit early for that?' Anna said cautiously. 'Perhaps we should wait to see what happens next.'

'But it's *this* moment I want to celebrate,' he insisted. 'I want to celebrate that we met Helena, that we are sitting here together, that tonight there'll be a full moon.'

'That's more than enough,' Anna agreed, summoning the waiter. 'Can we have the Santorini Assyrtiko, and really chilled, please.'

'It was our parents' favourite too,' said Haris, as he poured. '*Stin ygeiá mas.* To our health. And to the future.'

As they raised their glasses, he looked first into Anna's eyes and then into Helena's.

Helena tried not to analyse what lay behind those words. The future. Next week when the Ligakis shop was searched? Next month when she ought to return to London? Next year? Perhaps it did not matter.

She glanced towards the horizon. The finest sliver of silver, the very top of the moon, had begun to emerge over a distant hill.

Chapter Forty-Four

Anna left early the following morning for the baptism of a friend's child in Aegina, a few hours away. She would return late Sunday evening. It would be the first time that Helena and Haris had been alone together for more than an hour or two.

The smaller of the guest bedrooms, where Helena was sleeping, was next to the kitchen, and she was woken by the sound of the coffee grinder. It was only eight, early for a Saturday, but the aroma was impossible to resist, and she got out of bed and wrapped a towel around herself to go to the shower.

Haris held a mug out to her as she walked into the kitchen, trying not to look at her wild dishevelled hair and long bare legs.

'*Kaliméra*,' she said.

'Do you have plans today?' he asked.

'I wanted to meet Mihalis tonight to tell him about the meeting with Kourtis,' she said. 'But apart from that, no.'

She sipped her coffee.

'This is fantastic,' she smiled.

Haris ignored the compliment.

'I'd like to take you to Sounion to see the Temple of Poseidon,' he said. 'And it's a glorious day, so we could even swim on the way, if you're up for that?'

'I've never been there and it's meant to be beautiful,' Helena responded. 'And I'm well used to chilly water. Only problem is, I don't have any swimming things.'

'We'll borrow something of Anna's,' he said. 'She won't mind.'

They left around ten and were soon out of the city and driving along the coast road. The beaches were deserted.

'Our parents used to bring us here when we were children,' said Haris, taking a right, then a left, and then several more turns onto progressively narrower lanes. 'We called it "the secret beach". It's where we both learned to swim.'

Eventually they could go no further and he stopped the car. They found themselves in a small, peaceful cove where the only sound was the gentle lapping of the sea rolling over the pebbles, wearing them smoother and smaller as the centuries went by.

Helena had put one of Anna's bikinis on under her clothes and was soon in the water. It shelved steeply almost immediately, and she plunged in, shrieking at the shock of the chill.

Haris followed, his athletic limbs still tanned from the previous summer, and soon caught up with her.

'It's so invigorating!' she cried. 'But I can see why you learned to swim. You had to!'

They swam out beyond the cove and into open sea, where the waves began to bash their faces.

'Say when you've had enough, Helena.'

'It's feeling a bit more like Scotland out here,' she spluttered. 'I can take a few wintery waves because I learned to swim in the Atlantic, but I'm happy to go back.'

Out in the depths, they paused for a moment. Haris seized the opportunity.

'Helena, I have to ask you,' he said. 'Was that a new boyfriend with you outside White's that day?'

Helena spluttered, simultaneously laughing and swallowing a mouthful of seawater.

'What? No! He's my best friend's boyfriend.'

So this had been the reason for Haris' frosty behaviour.

She took his hand and pulled him closer.

'Haris,' she smiled, 'I can't believe you were jealous of Charles.'

Treading water, they kissed tenderly, only moving apart when a strong wave splashed over their heads.

'That was so salty!' grinned Haris, kissing her once more. 'Perhaps we should go back now.'

'Let's race!' challenged Helena.

They were a few hundred yards from the shore, but for both it was an effortless distance.

Haris had laid the towels out on the beach to warm them in the sun, and soon they were both drying in its rays.

Helena lay stretched out beside him, her eyes closed, enjoying the heat on her face.

Haris looked down at her, bewitched by this girl with the mass of tangled hair. His ex-fiancée never swam in the sea, because she did not want to look a mess for the rest of the day, so he always left her on a sunlounger and went alone.

He turned his gaze to the ocean and saw a flash of turquoise. A kingfisher, swooping down to catch his breakfast.

'Helena, you must see this.'

She sat up and watched as the little bird returned. Then another appeared, flashing this way and that.

'*Alkyóni*, kingfisher,' he said. 'After whom these warm days are named. I'll tell you the myth in the car.'

They were both dry now, and quickly dressed before setting off.

Dalaras was singing on the radio and Haris joined in, his voice rich and tuneful.

Inside your heart let me fall . . .
Among the waves in the sea.

Helena looked at him, and for a second he took his eyes from the road ahead and glanced at her. He reached out his hand and she entwined her fingers with his.

Several songs later, they reached Sounion, their hands still pressed together.

There were only a couple of coaches in the car park and most of the tourists were getting back on board. They would have the site to themselves, at least for a while.

Helena had not expected the magnificence of the now roofless temple. Its position was commanding, its mighty rows of golden pillars majestic from every angle. Whether she looked at it against the sky or against the sea, it took her breath away.

'What do you think?'

'Not sure I think anything right now,' she answered. 'It's more about feeling sometimes, isn't it?'

Haris took her hand again, emboldened perhaps by their solitude, and led her to the steps of the temple, where they sat to face the sea.

'Helena, I thought I was in love once before,' he said. 'But I was mistaken. And I'm afraid of myself now.'

'I thought the same,' said Helena. 'But it was simple delusion and I don't know if I can trust my judgement any more. I got everything so wrong.'

'Maybe it's *all* a fantasy,' he said. 'And you just have to choose whether to go with it or not.'

'And make a terrible mistake?'

'You stopped me making one of those, Helena.'

'I'm glad.'

'The thing is,' he said turning to her, 'if I *am* in love with you, how do I know it's real?'

'I could ask the same,' she replied.

'I suppose this could be a mirage of some kind?' suggested Haris.

'Even with my degree in chemistry,' said Helena, smiling, 'I can't produce scientific evidence. There's no formula for creating love through carbon bonding. No putting it on a Petri dish.'

'I know,' he said, laughing. 'And even what they call the chemistry between people can be self-deception. So strong, then it suddenly vanishes in a puff of smoke.'

A big group of schoolchildren had turned up and they were running up and down the steps. Their teacher was attempting to tell them about Poseidon.

'Real love is the kind that lasts, isn't it?' Helena said. 'But how can you know that at the start?'

'You can't,' Haris reflected. 'Our parents were in love for a long time. And yours?'

'Until death parted them, yes.'

'Same as ours.'

He got up, taking her hand. He wanted to show her more of the temple. He pointed out where Byron had carved his name into the stone in curly childlike letters.

'Supposedly one of the great lovers of history,' Helena said, looking up to see the famous graffiti. She knew many of his poems but only this single fact about his life.

'A thousand lovers,' said Haris. 'But no one true love.'

'And a vandal,' Helena apologised.

They walked hand in hand over the uneven ground, pausing to look out to sea again.

'That island over there,' Helena said, pointing at a long stretch of land close to the coast. 'Which one is that?'

'That's Makronisos.'

'Oh my God,' she breathed. 'It's so close.'

'You know about it?'

'It's where Mihalis's uncle was sent . . . and Lefteris in the kiosk. And the composer too.'

The divinity of the temple and the ugliness of the island were a disturbing juxtaposition. A place of such cold brutality and bitter memory, so close to this beauty. Helena stood and stared at it for a long moment, reminded of her thirst for revenge.

For the rest of the weekend, Haris and Helena did not spend a moment apart. They discussed everything from favourite songs and films to memories of the moon landing. They slept together, ate together and laughed together. They told stories of their childhoods, both of them grateful for the stability they had been given. Helena told him about her visits to Athens as a little girl, and her fondness for Dina. They even went for a run.

She told Haris that Nick Jones had also been at the auction. She had wanted to forget that dark vision, but it no longer seemed fair.

'I can't believe we were in that room together,' he said quietly. 'He must have been standing somewhere at the back.'

'He was,' Helena confirmed. 'And you know what he did? As soon as the auction was over, he crossed the road and bought the most expensive coat in London. He imagined the money was already in his pocket.'

Haris could see that she had no wish to say any more, and they changed the subject.

She told him about the course in bioarchaeology that she had been mulling over, and they discussed when and where she might do it. Both of them were certain that they did not want to be separated for any length of time.

On Monday morning, the real-estate agent was on the phone early, pressurising her to sign the preliminary paperwork which Helena had asked the solicitor to send to Anna's home.

'I couldn't help overhearing that conversation,' said Haris. 'You don't seem enthusiastic.'

'For some reason I'm not. Can't really put my finger on it. Maybe it's having to read this infernal contract,' she said, waving the brown envelope in the air. 'It would be pretty impenetrable even in English.'

'I'm happy to take a quick look later, if you want me to?' said Haris. 'These things are normally fairly standard, but Greek law is different from English, so you want to be aware of any strange clauses.'

He needed to be at the shop, as his customer was waiting for him to complete the restoration of the Roman vase.

'Why don't you come with me, Helena?' he asked. 'I've got a whole library of books in the office. Some of them are on archaeology and you might find them interesting. You could even start learning how to tell the fake from the real.'

She laughed, accepting the invitation eagerly. Tuesday afternoon, when Kourtis had said he would have news, was more than twenty-four hours away, and she needed to distract herself.

That evening, they met up with Mihalis and Panos in a bar. Haris and Mihalis were already acquaintances because of the hardware shop, and there was immediate rapport between the four of them. Although his architectural style was relatively minimal, Panos had once bought what he called a 'signature piece' for a client in the Morakis shop.

Helena gave them a moment-by-moment account of the auctioning of the figurine, with Haris adding things he had noticed from being in the room itself. Their friends were riveted, asking lots of questions, listening patiently to the answers.

They then described their meeting with the police art team.

'I love the idea that this man Vellopoulos is a reformed *tymvorýchos* himself.'

'That's probably why he is so committed. He's like an ex-alcoholic, evangelical about his sobriety,' said Haris.

The four of them had finished a second bottle and it was time to leave. Helena was keen that Haris should read the contract of sale that night, knowing that the agent would be on the phone again if she did not sign soon.

Anna was already in bed when they got home. Haris sank into one of her generous white sofas and began to flick through the pages of the contract. Helena wandered off to call her father. It was two hours earlier in the UK, so she knew he would still be up and keen to hear her news.

When she came back into the room, Haris had finished reading.

'Come and sit next to me,' he said, patting the cushion next to him.

Helena snuggled up close.

'I don't think you'll want to sell it to this person.'

'Why not? The money is okay, isn't it?'

'The amount, yes. But not who's buying it. Look.'

Helena's eyes went to where his finger pointed.

'It's being purchased in the name of a Swiss-based company and is being handled through a bank. Which is also the address for correspondence.'

'Démontard & Cie, Banquiers Privés,' Helena muttered under her breath. 'Hugo gave Kourtis the same details for the auction proceeds.'

'Unlikely to be a coincidence, don't you think?'

'Very unlikely.'

'So that was your supposedly desperate buyer,' said Haris. 'Ligakis. Maybe with Arsenis.'

'Perhaps they think the desk is still there, with everything inside?' Helena speculated.

'And the ledgers,' he pointed out. 'That's what they would really want to get their hands on, isn't it? They obviously don't know what has happened to any of your grandparents' furniture yet, as it's in storage at the moment.'

'But they must be anxious,' she mused.

'They should be,' he agreed. 'And no wonder they've been in a hurry.'

'It's almost a relief, Haris. I didn't feel quite ready to sell it for some reason,' Helena said.

'That's understandable. You shouldn't feel under pressure, *kardiá mou*.'

Helena loved this term of affection that he had started using for her. My heart.

Chapter Forty-Five

On Tuesday, Helena went to the Morakis shop again. There was one book that had particularly interested her, and she happily spent the entire morning reading it and making some notes. It was on various analytical techniques for ceramics. It included one that had been developed to characterise the composition and identify the original source of pottery used in particular sites to establish provenance. If it was found that this differed from the local raw material, it helped to establish the changing patterns of trade and migration.

Up until now, Helena had felt that her lack of qualification in history would hold her back from pursuing archaeology as a career, but such techniques were very scientific. She recalled her mother mentioning something about it all those years ago, and now realised that this kind of research must call for chemists. When she saw an equation on one of the pages, it felt familiar and she smiled in recognition at the symbols. It concerned a way to explore compositional similarities and dissimilarities between different pots.

$$MCD_{pq} = \frac{1}{n} \sum_{i=1}^{n} x_{pi} - x_{qi}$$

This and terms such as 'neutron activation analysis' and 'atomic absorption spectrophotometry' excited her.

The phone in the shop rang quite frequently, and she jumped every time. She was desperate to hear from Kourtis.

At five o'clock, when Haris answered it, she had almost given up.

'I'll pass you to Helena,' she heard him saying.

With a shaking hand, she took the receiver and held it so that he could hear too. It was Vellopoulos.

'It's arranged for tomorrow. Ten o'clock in the morning. Stay out of sight of his shop. I will call you when we are out of there.'

The line went dead. Helena and Haris looked at each other, and then both of them went into the main part of the shop to tell Anna.

'I don't know how I am going to get through the next twenty-four hours,' admitted Helena. 'The temptation to sneak round the side streets to spy on what's happening might be more than I can resist.'

'But if Arsenis even glimpses you, it might be a disaster,' said Anna strictly. 'My suggestion is that you just spend the day in Mets. With Haris.'

The three of them passed the evening watching a film together, a comedy with Aliki Vougiouklaki, a childhood favourite of Anna and Haris. They kept off the subject of the impending raid. Helena had no idea whether Nick was in Athens, but she could not imagine why he would have hung around in London rather than being with his new friends, or however he thought of them. She did not know whether to pray, or ask the gods to be on her side. These days, she was thinking more about the Greek gods and goddesses, Nemesis in particular.

The next day, she and Haris did as Anna suggested.

When they got up, Haris told her that he had an idea about where they could go for a stroll. It was a quiet village not far away.

'It's somewhere I often go to think,' he said.

They drank coffee and then strolled hand in hand down the road.

'I thought you said it was a village?' she queried. 'I assumed we were driving somewhere.'

'Ah, no. You'll see.'

They soon came to some huge gates and wandered through.

'"The First Cemetery",' Helena read.

'The village of the dead,' said Haris. 'And a very tranquil one in which to spend eternity.'

There were long, narrow avenues criss-crossing each other, with splendid white marble graves on either side, some of them watched over by life-size statues.

'That's very beautiful,' Helena said, stopping at one with a sleeping woman.

'It moves me more than any other,' said Haris. 'It was made for Sofia Afentaki, who was only eighteen when she died. Yannoulis Chalepas was one of our most talented sculptors. She looks so peaceful, doesn't she?'

The folds of the flowing gown were perfectly executed, and her serene face and relaxed body were so lifelike that Helena could almost imagine her chest was rising and falling.

'When you see such a representation, you view death in a different way, don't you?' Haris said.

'Yes, simply as a long slumber.'

'Maybe you know that Hypnos and Thanatos were twin brothers in mythology?'

'Sleep and Death,' said Helena.

They continued their walk. Many of those buried here were the departed great and good of Greece, writers, poets, politicians. They lay beneath ornate headstones and statues, well-tended oil lamps and sprays of fresh flowers.

'I do sometimes wish my mother was in a Greek Orthodox cemetery,' said Helena. 'They are more celebratory, less gloomy than Protestant ones.'

'When did your mother die?' Haris enquired.

'End of my first year at Oxford. She was only forty-nine. All very sudden.'

'I'm sorry,' he said simply, squeezing her hand. 'And your father?'

'Very much alive,' she said, smiling. 'And I know he will enjoy meeting you.'

They sat down on a bench and Haris told her about his and Anna's parents, who had both died in their fifties, their father in a car accident, their mother of heart failure shortly afterwards. They were buried in a humbler cemetery than this one.

'But this place doesn't make me sad,' he said. 'I come here to contemplate life, not death. Does that sound strange to you?'

'Not at all,' agreed Helena.

'It reminds me to make the most of the life I have. *Carpe diem* and all that.'

Helena smiled. On whatever paths that motto had led her, she was sure she was on the right one now.

Afterwards, they went for lunch, but Helena could not eat. She kept glancing at her watch.

'It's around four now, isn't it?' said Haris.

'Just gone.'

'I am sure Kourtis will have wrapped things up by now,' he said. 'Shall we go home and call him?'

Within ten minutes, they were back in Anna's flat. Helena almost ran, Haris only just managing to keep up with her.

As they got in, the phone was ringing. It was Anna, who was still in the shop.

'Vellopoulos just called. They want us all at Ligakis's shop,' she said breathlessly. 'Get in a taxi and I'll see you there.'

The taxi driver took it very literally when they told him they were in a hurry, racing towards Kolonaki at breakneck speed. They flashed past the apartment on Evdokias, then turned left the wrong way up a one-way street, made three more sharp turns and screeched to a halt outside Ligakis's shop. There was a small crowd on the pavement trying to see what was going on inside.

A cordon had been placed across the premises and two policemen were on duty at the door. Anna stood next to them, and when she explained who Helena and Haris were, they were all allowed inside.

The Ligakis showroom was slightly larger than the Morakis one, and like theirs it had a desk centrally positioned and an office at the back.

'Some very smart furniture he's got here,' said Anna with grudging admiration. 'Look at that chaise longue, it must be eighteenth century. And the Roman bust . . .'

They went through into the office, where Vellopoulos was rifling through a filing cabinet. Kourtis was at the desk, drumming his fingers.

'There you are,' he said, as the trio walked in. 'What a day we've had. Take a seat for a moment, and my friend here will tell you what's been happening.'

Helena smiled to herself. There was only one chair apart from the one Kourtis sat in, so Anna took it and the other two leaned against the desk.

Vellopoulos began.

'So, we arrived on schedule, four of us, and I told Giannis Ligakis to keep his shop closed for a while so that we could take a look around. I explained that there was a new regulation: all premises like his needed to have a routine annual survey, as stolen goods sometimes got dumped on shops like his. "We know you're a clean business," I said to him. "There's nothing to worry about."'

He drew deeply on a cigarette.

'For an hour or so, all dressed up in suit and tie, he sat at his desk coolly working on his accounts and going through auction catalogues as if he didn't have a care in the world. I had someone keep an eye on the door, just in case he decided to go for a stroll, and we started to take a little poke around. Nothing abnormal at first.'

'Angelos, stop teasing and show them.'

From the look on Kourtis's face, Helena could tell that something exciting had happened. He seemed far more animated than on the previous Friday.

'Come on, then.'

The three of them jumped up and followed Vellopoulos to the back of the shop.

'One sharp-eyed chap of ours noticed this shelving,' he said. 'See how it has a small gap down the side? It doesn't look quite right, does it?'

He proudly slid it to one side to reveal a door, the lock on which had been forced so it was easily pushed open. Ligakis had apparently denied all knowledge of it so had not volunteered a key.

They followed him through and into a huge space. Floor to ceiling there was semi-industrial shelving, each shelf filled with boxes. Vellopoulos did not give them time to look closely. He was more interested in showing them the extent of the premises. Spiral staircases led up to two similarly laid-out floors.

'He's got a sizeable inventory, old Ligakis,' said Haris.

'This isn't the half of it,' said Vellopoulos. 'Keep following me.'

None of them spoke. They were focused on keeping up with the policeman. They returned to the shop through yet another door hidden behind a display case, then climbed some more stairs into an expensively furnished salon, with gleaming marble floors, white leather furniture and coffee table books illustrating various collections of sculpture and Roman antiquities. Helena noticed a fridge, and shelving above it holding cut-glass champagne flutes.

'It's like a rabbit warren!' Helena said, as they descended once again to the shop and out into the street, where Ligakis's neighbours were still exchanging gossip. Vellopoulos yanked up a lever, opening the door to an underground garage, its single space used to house Ligakis's Alfa Romeo. Inside, a trapdoor led to a larger area, with a further staircase going down to yet another floor.

The underground area had been turned into another warehouse, with rows of floor-to-ceiling shelving filled with labelled boxes and objects wrapped in paper, often yellowing newsprint. Every few moments there was a flash of light. Two experts from the art team had already begun the process of unwrapping, photographing and making notes on every single piece stored in this room.

'Had to make a start,' said Vellopoulos. 'It's going to take months to sort the whole lot.'

Haris went across to see what was on the table.

'Etruscan *krater*?' he said to the photographer.

'And not even a chip off the rim.'

'Aladdin's cave was empty compared with this,' Helena commented.

'We did a quick count and reckon there are over eight thousand boxes of different sizes. And some might hold more than one object. We'll need to identify if any of these things were stolen, smuggled or illegally excavated.'

'I suppose you can't make assumptions,' Anna suggested.

'We can't. But in my mind, I'd be surprised if they weren't,' said Vellopoulos, leading them out. 'I took one look at that Ligakis this morning, all smug with his silk tie and gold cufflinks. And you know what I thought to myself? Guilty as sin!'

Helena was keen to see Ligakis tried for what he had done, but it was not really him that interested her the most.

The four of them returned to the office, where Kourtis was leafing through a file. On the desk in front of him was a sizeable box.

'So, what do you think of Mr Ligakis's haul?' he asked.

'*Ekpliktikó!*' Haris said. 'Beyond belief!'

'It feels like Christmas,' said Kourtis. 'And you don't even know the best part. You haven't told them, have you, Angelos?'

Vellopoulos shook his head.

'Look at this.'

Kourtis opened the file in front of him and turned it to show them a photograph of a man standing in a museum next to a display of ceramics. Among them was a distinctive vase that bore an image of an octopus. On the back of the photo was a date, 2 May 1975, and the number 31.

Arsenis had not changed much.

'These fools have incriminated themselves, you know. And very tidily.'

'What do you mean?' asked Helena.

'It looks like they've done all the work for us. I brought one of the boxes down from upstairs, and noticed something like a catalogue number written on the outside: *NC1975/31*. I went through the files and found this one for 1975, and then spotted the number on the back of this photo. Presumably it was the thirty-first item taken that year. NC is North Crete, I think.'

He started to take something out of the box.

'See this?' said Vellopoulos cheerily, picking up an old piece of newspaper that had been used for wrapping. '*Kathimerini* front page, 20 May 1975. All good evidence.'

The small vase Kourtis brought out was in perfect condition and was decorated with the image of an octopus, its tentacles wrapped around the circumference. There were other sea creatures floating nearby, and the liveliness of the undersea world was vividly captured.

'If I remember rightly,' said Kourtis, 'early summer of 1975 was when a robbery happened in one of the smaller museums there. Before your time, Vellopoulos. They almost cleaned the place out. Must have got everything away on a night ferry before anyone even noticed it had been broken into. Half the contents of the museum just vanished. And it's always been thought that everything ended up in a private collection abroad.'

No one would ever have seen an image of this octopus and forgotten it.

'The challenge now is to match every item in the store here with stolen pieces or looted sites. If everything matches up as neatly as this . . .'

Helena, Anna and Haris were incredulous.

'Has Ligakis been charged yet?' Helena dared to ask.

'He started to get annoyed when we were asking for various keys, denied all knowledge of these rooms and got really angry when he saw our man slide that shelving across and smash the lock. Tried to leave the office to intervene, but one of the chaps guarding him stood in his way. Ligakis took a swing at him. There was a lot of weight behind that punch and our man got a nasty black eye, even worse because of that signet ring he wears. It was enough to give us an excuse to charge him. For now it's for violence against the authorities. But there's going to be a lot more later.'

Helena liked the idea of Ligakis being behind bars already, but what about Arsenis, and most importantly Nick?

'Arsenis Papagiannis?' she asked.

'That's probably enough to bring him in,' agreed Kourtis, looking at the photo in front of them.

'But if they're as close to each other as I think they are, when Arsenis is charged, that's going to alert Nick, isn't it? He might disappear.'

Haris could hear the hint of dismay in Helena's voice.

'We'd better get going then, hadn't we?' said Vellopoulos. 'We have to actively search for something on that Englishman.' He gave his boss a direct look.

'I'll make an exception and stay late,' said Kourtis. 'This has certainly been one of the most surprising days of my career.'

'So you'll sign off the overtime?'

Kourtis nodded.

It was half past five.

'The file we need is for Nisos, last year,' said Helena. 'That's when he took the figurine.'

'It's very unconventional to allow civilians to help,' Kourtis said. 'But go ahead. Just don't mess up any of the evidence. The judge will want every last scrap of it.'

⊚⊚⊚

There were six filing cabinets, three drawers in each, and the trio made a start. Many locations had several files, and chronology was not as strictly adhered to as they had hoped. Occasionally Anna could not resist and spread out the whole contents of a file, even though it was from the wrong island, or concerned the mainland, or even Italy. There was one with the name of an ancient site in Sicily, which the looters appeared to have stripped bare, posing in their pits with various finds. Those same finds then appeared in photographs showing them inside crates that had probably passed through this very shop.

'I've just realised why all the photos are Polaroids,' she said. 'So that they're not seen by a third party. They're cunning, these people.'

Mainly they worked in silence. The only sound in the room was the rhythmic flick of paper and card as they went through the files.

'Nisos!' Anna suddenly cried out.

'Bingo!' Helena responded, to the total bemusement of the Morakis siblings.

Helena and Haris stood one on either side of her as she turned over the photographs and relevant notes. So far, the dates were all in the 1960s.

'There was clearly plenty of looting going on even then,' said Anna. 'Exactly as the elderly ladies told you.'

She turned more pages. The dates were still from way back.

'Look, why don't you do this?' Anna suggested, knowing that Helena would want the satisfaction of finding the figurine among these records. The two of them swapped places.

When they got to the end of the file, it had still only reached the early seventies, but it did prove what the elderly ladies had said, and what Haris had concluded after his *tavli* marathon.

They went back to their respective filing cabinets and resumed the search.

The files were tightly packed, and more than half an hour went by. Three drawers each, but still nothing for Nisos in the 1980s. They all moved on to their second cabinet and began again.

At one point, Vellopoulos came into the office.

'All well here?' he asked, blowing smoke rings. 'It's a party upstairs! You would not believe what we have. We've asked for reinforcements. This place needs extra protection. Twenty-four hours. We've nowhere at headquarters to store this much loot.' He disappeared through the door concealed by the shelving at the back of the shop.

'Do you think he has a wife?' asked Anna. 'The way he talked about womankind, I'll never forget it. So wildly reverential.'

'She'd have to like the smell of tobacco, wouldn't she?'

Half an hour later, Helena pulled a file from her middle drawer, and held it tightly with both hands.

Haris put his arm round her waist and Anna leaned in to see.

1980– was written neatly on the buff cardboard cover. Helena opened it up.

'Oh my God,' she almost screamed. Her reaction was involuntary and visceral.

Grinning out at her as he looked straight into the lens was an all-too-familiar face: sparkling eyes, perfect teeth in a wide mouth, a thatch of sun-bleached hair. She slammed the file shut, put it down, nauseous and angry, and marched outside to get some fresh air.

Haris came out to join her.

'Sorry, Haris, even seeing that face . . .'

'I can understand it,' he said gently.

In her haste, she had not even taken in the other details in the image.

'It's all the evidence they'll need,' he told her. 'He's holding the figurine. And there's another photograph of him crouching down in the pit next to it even before it's removed from the ground. That shows the original find spot.'

'He's delivered his own sentence.'

'Let's hope so,' said Haris. 'He must have had a collaborator to take the picture.'

'He would have charmed someone into it,' Helena said. 'But I doubt they'll be able to track her down.'

They returned inside, where Kourtis and Vellopoulos were now back in the office.

'Will they be arrested?' asked Helena.

Vellopoulos's smile was affirmation.

'We have issued the warrants. Arsenis Papagiannis's address is known to us and we've been keeping a close eye on it. He hasn't been there for a week or so. Nick Jones. Any idea?'

Helena had to suppress a laugh.

'Sorry, no. No idea. Could still be in London. That's where I last saw him. The two of them could be living it up for a few days there. Just speculating.'

'That makes sense. You know Papagiannis has a pied-à-terre in Mayfair?'

'I had no idea,' said Helena. 'But it doesn't surprise me.'

Some of the photographs had been laid out on the desk.

'I forgot to tell you the other thing I know about the rich and the criminal,' said Kourtis triumphantly.

'And what's that?' asked Haris politely.

'That they are compulsive show-offs. It's not enough to have something. You have to be *seen* to have it. For most people, there's no point in having money or *objets d'art* if you don't display them. And many criminals incriminate themselves that way too. Those photographs of Papagiannis and that blond one are a gift.'

Haris appeared to be taking in Kourtis's latest insight into human psychology, but his mind was elsewhere and Helena could see it.

'What is it, Haris?'

'I'm thinking,' he said, 'that they will be assuming that Ligakis has the money in his Swiss account by now and should have given them their share for the sale of the figurine. When they don't receive it, won't they come and find him?'

'So that tape needs to come down straight away,' Vellopoulos said. 'Bit of a giveaway.'

'We'll have our men on watch outside tonight, and waiting inside tomorrow,' said Kourtis, 'so that we're ready.'

'I want to be here too,' said Helena firmly. 'I know how greedy they both are. They'll come. I'm sure of it.'

The new security team arrived, and Vellopoulos volunteered to stay overnight in the shop to help guard the premises.

'Nobody waiting for you at home, Kýrie Vellopoulos?' Helena asked him quietly.

Shaking his head, he pulled the shutters down and locked the door from inside.

Chapter Forty-Six

Although Helena had misread Nick Jones in so many ways, she had correctly identified one of his main weaknesses. Greed.

She got up early the following morning and arrived at the shop by 7.30, buying a coffee on the way for Vellopoulos. He was awake, so she only had to tap lightly on the door.

'Hard to sleep on that funny old couch thing,' he said, pointing to the ornate chaise longue that Anna had admired so much. Half of his legs must have hung off the end, and he looked exhausted.

At nine precisely, three additional policemen arrived. Two of them had been told to dress like typical customers, and had put on the suits in which they had got married. They would stand around in the shop. The third was going to sit in the office with Helena and Vellopoulos. He was in plain clothes, but his whole demeanour was unmistakably that of a policeman, something that even a monk's habit would not have concealed. He had two pairs of handcuffs ready.

Anna and Haris would be waiting at their shop for news.

Helena was watching through a crack in the door that led to the shop, and just before ten, she spotted Arsenis Papagiannis peering through the front window. She was relieved to see him, but at the same time experienced a huge wave of bitter disappointment. Where was Nick?

If Arsenis was arrested, Nick might slip away. He was capable of vanishing, changing his looks, changing country, changing identity. She'd put nothing past him.

Her uncle came in and started pretending to browse, clearly put out that there were two other customers in the shop already. If he was going to have a confrontation with Ligakis, it would be better for them to be alone.

'Where's the blond one?' whispered Vellopoulos.

Helena shrugged her shoulders.

Arsenis Papagiannis started to pass the time of day with the two policemen in the shop. Helena prayed that neither of them would say anything that would give them away. She had been told they were from the art team, but she did not really know how much knowledge that meant they had.

The situation was not how she had imagined it, but she told herself that if they arrested her uncle, at least that would be one of her goals fulfilled.

When it looked as if Arsenis had tired of conversation and was going to walk straight into the office, she heard the blast of a car horn. She glanced across to the front window to see a bright yellow sports car outside on the street.

The sound distracted Arsenis too, and he turned around and started to walk out of the shop. The bell clanged as he opened the door, and Helena's heart sank. They would have no Arsenis. No Nick Jones.

She exchanged a glance with Vellopoulos, who looked equally crestfallen.

But just at that moment, she caught sight of the man on whom she wanted so deeply to take revenge. As Kourtis had said, there was no point in being rich and having money unless you showed it off. It made perfect sense that, as well as an expensive coat, Nick would buy a flashy car that everyone would notice, and if they had not, then he would trumpet his arrival with the horn. It also made sense that he would be confident enough to buy these things in advance of receiving a cent.

Arsenis came back into the shop with Nick, and the two men marched towards the office. Clearly they had planned to arrive together and Nick had been a little late. The decoy customers stood and watched them.

Nick's expression when he walked in and saw Helena was one she would never forget. This time it was she who was grinning and Nick who displayed a look of horror.

The arrest itself was simple. Neither of them had a chance with four policemen there. Nick did not even attempt to talk his way out of it, and soon they were both handcuffed. There was no question of trusting either of them.

Helena looked into his bright blue eyes. They did not smile, or cry, or plead. She imagined them as a pair of blue glass marbles, displaying no emotion.

'There's no need to ask you why, is there, Nick?'

'You didn't even try to understand,' he snapped.

It was strange to hear that voice again and to find it so lacking in charm.

She was reminded of the last time they had met, and how his face had been contorted by rage. At this encounter, she felt proud and strong, in control of the situation, happy to see him in the hole he had dug for himself and not to reach out a hand. This was revenge.

'I understand something that you can't begin to, Nick. That stealing something from beneath the ground is a theft from the people whose country you take it from. A theft of their culture. And their story.'

'They're just stones, Helena.'

'They are sacred,' she snapped. 'Sacred statues that you swapped for a yellow Maserati.'

'Lamborghini,' he corrected.

Vellopoulos was getting impatient to take the two men to head-quarters. He did not want to waste any more time listening to this foreigner. He did not know what Nicholas Jones and Helena were saying to each other, but he knew that the man was a *tymvorýchos*, a looter, and that was enough for him to want him sent down.

'And this man you have colluded with,' Helena said, pointing to Arsenis Papagiannis, 'accepted bribes for destroying lives.'

Her so-called uncle remained silent.

A few weeks later, Helena and Haris attended the initial trial of Giannis Ligakis together. Anna agreed to stay at the shop.

Helena did not want to miss a single moment. They were on the steps of the court before it even opened and the first to take their seats. She looked as smart as she could in a black jacket that Anna had lent her, but the sleeves were too short and her hair was its usual wayward self.

Her only experience of trials was from television drama, but Haris explained the Greek process to her while they were waiting for everything to begin. An investigative judge, the *anakritís*, had already presented the defence to the public prosecutor and prepared the case for trial. The judge, the *dikastís*, and the public prosecutor then heard the case.

There might be witnesses, the accused might even make his own plea, but there would be no jury.

Kourtis had been waiting so long to find evidence against Ligakis that he had used all the resources at his disposal, including payment of overtime for every member of the team, to ensure that the process of object identification was completed. The antiquities dealer had handled more than five hundred items stolen from museums and many thousands more from excavations.

Helena stared at Ligakis each time he appeared in the box, recalling how patronising he had been towards her. He did not look at her once and his expression remained deadpan throughout. It gave her great satisfaction to think of the ledgers now in the safe possession of Kourtis. Whatever happened here, there were still those revelations to come.

The trial was quite straightforward. Ligakis had incriminated himself with so many well-catalogued photographs and a copious paper trail that the judge had no hesitation in sentencing him to twenty years in prison. In handling items stolen from the Greek state, he had robbed the Greeks themselves.

In the trial of Arsenis Papagiannis, the accused was charged with trafficking a large number of items and even shown to be sharing some business accounts with Ligakis. Papagiannis had travelled regularly to the United States as well as to England to smuggle illegal antiquities, and in fact owned not one but two flats in Mayfair. For this trial, Helena sat between Haris and Mihalis. The latter wanted to be there even though Helena had told him that the incriminating lists in the ledgers, including his own uncle's name, would not come up. Not this time at least.

'You bear responsibility for everything for which you have been accused,' the judge pronounced, giving Papagiannis fifteen years.

Helena wanted to applaud, but Haris was holding her hand so she could not.

'Just for being creepy towards you in the Archaeological Museum all those years ago,' Mihalis whispered, 'he deserves to go to prison.'

Helena stifled her laughter.

Neither Ligakis nor Papagiannis had made eye contact with Helena. She was relieved.

The second trials for these two would take longer to prepare. The ledgers were complex and historical, but Kourtis had agreed to delay his retirement in order to see the case through to the end. Helena was surprised when he told her his father had been a communist.

'It's best never to make assumptions or generalisations, isn't it?' she said to Haris, who nodded.

Finally came the trial she had been impatient for. At last, Nicholas Jones would be in the dock, answering to his real name, not a diminutive or a smarter version. When he walked in, as dapper as a banker in dark suit and tie, his hair shorter than ever, he looked directly at Helena and smirked.

She was glad to be wearing her mother's bracelet, and touched the small jewelled eye. Protect me from the devil's smile, she said silently to the sapphire *máti*.

Charles and Sally came from London. Charles had agreed to act as a witness. Not just to recall Helena's bruised face, but to describe Nick Jones's character and to mention his two missing paintings. Helena watched Nick closely during this part of the trial, knowing that for him it was the deepest humiliation to be rejected by the Old Etonian whom he had hero-worshipped and envied for his ease with himself and with life.

Some of the archaeologists from the Nisos dig had also flown over to play their role. Two gave statements. They were not conclusive proof, but they testified to Nick's patterns of behaviour and his relationship with a group of local men that had aroused suspicion.

Helena herself then appeared in the witness box. Once again she found herself face to face with the man she hated.

The figurine was brought out as evidence and the two parts were held carefully by Kourtis. Vellopoulos came in with the file and the Polaroids of Nick Jones.

Having confirmed that she recognised the figurine, Helena was asked to describe what had happened on the day they were meant to be leaving Nisos. She remembered it as if it was yesterday.

She was asked to identify a photo of herself she did not even remember being taken. Sally had photographed her bruised face. She was asked if there was anything else she would like to mention, and she described the night she had seen Nicholas Jones with two strangers down by the sea, along with his explanation, which was confirmed as untrue by the archaeologists.

Jones was an expert at playing a role, and at the beginning of his cross-questioning, for which he needed the interpreter, he maintained an innocent demeanour, suggesting that he knew such looting took place but his respect for Greek culture was too great to allow him to get involved. Sometimes his mask slipped, when something he said sounded truly hollow.

His problem was that the judge disliked him. Nick Jones was everything a Greek might resent: an apparently aristocratic foreigner coming into his country and stealing his heritage.

Helena listened carefully to the judge. His summing-up was measured. He had *dikaiosýni*, justice, on his mind. She still had *ekdíkisi*, revenge, on hers.

Nicholas Jones's sentence caused murmurs around the courtroom. Ten years. It was harsher than any of them had expected. A decade for an Englishman in a Greek jail. Jones went pale with shock.

'I wouldn't want to be in one of those even for a night,' murmured Haris.

Imagining what Nick would face, Helena almost felt sorry for him.

No, she told herself. Have no pity. Medea wouldn't have done.

Nick passed her, head bowed, eyes downcast, hands cuffed at the front.

It was he who was broken now.

Epilogue

Two years later

Helena throws open the doors to the balcony and begins to ferry out plates and glasses. She has to move a pile of her books from the table. For the past year, she has been doing a master's in ceramic analysis, and she is handing in her thesis next week.

It is nine in the evening, and through the leaves of their flourishing plants, the floodlit Parthenon seems to watch them.

'They'll be here any time now,' says Helena. There is excitement in her voice.

'I'll get some wine out of the fridge,' Haris says.

Her father arrived that morning and is still resting. Dina has been staying for a few days, at her own insistence sleeping in her old room.

A few moments later, the buzzer goes, and then several more times. Haris stands at the door to the apartment and welcomes their guests.

Anna has encountered Mihalis and Panos in the lobby and they come up in the lift together to the fifth floor. The front door is open, and as soon as they emerge into the flat, there are gasps of admiration from Anna.

'Panos! This is incredible. It's transformed!'

'The brief was to make it modern. All light and air. To make it unrecognisable from before,' Panos says, proud of his work.

'Well, you've achieved that. It's beautiful.'

'We got rid of that huge dining room and made it into two smaller

505

rooms – a little library and a new study. The old study is another bathroom now.'

Anna walks around admiring the simple furniture and the subtle colour schemes. Gone are the heavy drapes, dark furniture and ubiquitous gilt. In their place are neutral shades, with splashes of colour here and there, big comfortable sofas and soft lighting. The only antique piece is a cabinet made of walnut, the wood a work of art in itself.

Even though she has never met most of the subjects, Anna surveys with interest some photographs in modern frames: Mary McCloud and her brother as children, one of Andreas in his uniform, some of Hamish, Mary and Helena together, and one of Helena and her grandmother taken in the National Gardens when she was twelve. There is also one of Dina with Helena and Mary, taken in the village near Kalamata.

Hamish McCloud emerges from a guest bedroom and Panos introduces himself.

'I'm Helena's architect friend,' he says.

'You're Panos! I never saw this place before, but you have created a wonderful home here.'

'Helena seems very happy with it.'

'And I have heard so much about you all,' says Hamish. 'It's lucky you all speak English. I feel a bit of an outsider.'

'We'll teach you some Greek tonight,' says Panos, taking his arm. 'Shall we start with *krasí*?'

Hamish laughs.

'That's probably the only word I do know!' he says. 'Wine! My wife taught me that one.'

The two of them walk together through the drawing room and onto the balcony.

Anna carries an extravagant bunch of flowers presented in layers of net and ribbon fronds into the kitchen, which has been totally modernised. Something that Helena has not disposed of are her grandmother's giant vases, and she drops the bouquet into one of them, fills it from the tap and puts it on the white marble counter.

Haris is taking *spanakópita*, spinach pie, from the oven and cutting it into pieces.

'Didn't know you could make that,' comments his sister.

'Neither did I,' he laughs. 'But I'd never tried until today.'

'I finalised the sale of the Meissen today,' she tells him. 'By the end of the week it will be packed and on its way to the US.'

'That's great,' says Haris, scooping slices of pie onto a plate. 'It was the final shadow, I think.'

They both know that the sum will fund care for Mihalis's uncle and three other former camp detainees whom they have traced.

Clutching a gift wrapped in orange paper, Mihalis wanders towards the balcony, where Helena is standing with her father and Panos.

'You look like a goddess, Helena,' says Hamish, admiring his daughter in her long diaphanous green dress, her hair loose.

Helena smiles.

'It's a very caryatid style,' says Panos, referring to the sculptures of the maidens who support the entrance of the Erechtheion temple on the Acropolis.

'Caryatid?'

'Dad has never been up there,' she says to Panos, with her arm round her father.

'Really?' Panos responds with surprise.

'It's true,' Hamish confirms. 'But I will this visit.'

All four of them are now looking up at the Acropolis.

'Well, when you do go, you'll see five elegant figures, mighty and strong women but very feminine. And you'll see what I mean about Helena's dress. It's as if she's just stepped off the Acropolis, shaken her hair free and appeared right in front of us.'

Helena is laughing at Panos's flight of fancy.

'Perhaps she is the missing sixth caryatid?' he continues. 'Her sisters have been searching for her for so many years!'

Anna and Haris have gathered closer to the group and are listening. Hamish is enjoying the story.

'Where did she disappear to, this elegant lady?' he asks.

'She was *abducted*!' Panos answers dramatically.

'Elgin, Dad,' Helena interrupts. 'She's in the British Museum. With everything else he tore down and shipped off to England.'

Hamish shakes his head. He has recently read a piece in *The Times* about a new campaign, spearheaded by a Greek actress, to return the sculptures to Greece.

'She should live where she is meant to live,' he murmurs to Helena. 'Rather like my daughter.'

Helena smiles and hugs him tightly.

'Is that how it seems, Dad?'

'I miss you, Helena, but it does feel as if you belong here.'

The doorbell rings again and Helena hurries inside to answer it.

'Hels! You look fantastic! Oh my God, what a gorgeous place to live! I love it!' Charles is almost hidden behind an enormous plant, which he puts on the floor.

'I can't believe they let you on the plane with my cheese plant!' Helena laughs.

'It took a bit of persuasion,' he replies, 'but we told them that it had huge sentimental value and needed to live with its owner.'

Sally is hugging Helena and then hands her a bottle of wine, which she puts in the kitchen as they pass.

'I can't believe I've never been to Athens before,' Sally is confessing. 'We only arrived this afternoon, but I'm in *love* with it!'

'How's the Grande Bretagne?' enquires Helena.

'The same as it's always been,' answers Charles. 'Grand.'

Helena laughs, remembering her visit there all those years before with her *yiayiá*, and that first taste of Coca-Cola.

Haris puts on a cassette of his favourite music, and Dalaras's voice floats out from the drawing room and into the night air. He goes onto the balcony and hands around the spinach pie.

The guests are all outside now, sipping their chilled wine and silently admiring the view. No matter how many years most of them have lived in Athens or however many times they have seen it, not one of them fails to respond to the Parthenon's presence.

Mihalis wants Helena to open his housewarming gift before dinner and hands it to her. They all gather round as she tears off the paper and opens a box. Then she puts the gift on the table for them all to admire.

It is a perfect replica, constructed from a mould.

'It's absolutely indistinguishable from the real thing, isn't it?' says Hamish, admiring the copy of a Cycladic vase.

'It *is* real in its way,' says Haris, and a discussion begins over the difference between a fake and a copy.

Charles claims that originals in any art media always have an aura. 'I think I can spot a fake,' he says. 'It's something you can feel, even if it's expensively done and contains identical flaws to fool the viewer.'

'We'll put you to the test!' says Haris. 'I've got some things in the shop we can do it with.'

'You're on,' says Charles, and they shake hands.

Helena smiles to herself, thinking of one fake that her friend failed to spot.

Everyone is laughing. The conversation is convivial, the evening sultry, the wine refreshing, and old friends blend with new. Greek and English are rapidly translated for anyone who needs it.

Dina has prepared a spread of dishes that she is bringing to the table, and everyone showers her with compliments. Helena remembers the meal in her brother's restaurant in the Peloponnese. The same specialities are laid out in front of them now.

'But it's not wrong to copy a work of art,' says Anna, taking some *pastó* from a dish held out to her by Charles. 'It's a question of intent.'

'A fake is made to deceive and a copy is created to pay homage to the original,' offers Helena. 'But an original is sacred. It is more than the material with which it has been made.'

After Dina's desserts are served and glasses of *tsikoudiá* are poured, toasts are made to the happiness of Helena and Haris in their new home.

'It's midnight!' Haris cries out suddenly, noticing the time. 'It's the big day tomorrow! Just to remind everyone, be there by seven!'

As dusk falls, Helena and Haris run up the grand flight of steps into the museum and hurry down the empty corridors, passing the Mask of Agamemnon, passing the grave stele, passing Aphrodite.

They are following the arrows to a private opening of a new exhibition.

Suddenly they see her from afar and stop, breathless.

She is upright on a simple circular plinth, centrally placed in a spacious refurbished gallery and spot-lit from above. As they approach, they realise that the enigmatic Nisos figurine has already drawn a large crowd. It is the first time that Helena has seen her made whole again, and she slips through to stand close.

With her head tilted towards the heavens, the figurine seems proud. With her arms folded, she seems relaxed. With her diminutive ears, she seems to listen. With her pale eyes, she seems to be aware of the crowd.

Helena moves aside to make way for others to appreciate her.

She sees Angelos Vellopoulos, who is a head taller than anyone else in the room, and goes across to greet him and Giorgos Kourtis, without whom this event would not have happened. While Kourtis continues to cram his mouth with canapés, he tells Helena that he is now officially retired. He feels his life's work is complete, following the new cases against Giannis Ligakis and Arsenis Papagiannis, which have given them each an additional twenty-five years in prison, sentences they are unlikely ever to complete. Vellopoulos is excited to tell Helena that he has been promoted following the success of the prosecutions.

She looks around at all her friends who have been involved in the figurine's journey, and then at her father, who is staring at the little statue. She knows that he has an image of his wife, her mother, in his mind.

In display cases on the walls are more pieces, most of them fragmentary, that are also finds from Nisos. There are segments of other figurines, heads, torsos, legs, but nothing complete, along with many pots and pyxes. Of the hundred or so exhibits, half were recovered from Giannis Ligakis's warehouse, without details of their exact find spots. The other half, what is now known as the Carver Collection, comprises the more important pieces, all of them carefully identified and recorded. There are details about the precise depth at which the objects were found, and what has been learned about an ancient community and how they lived, whether they came originally from other places and if they brought with them different skills and materials. Among the items is the section of another figurine that the late Professor Carver found on that last dig.

The juxtaposition of the looted pieces and those carefully preserved and studied tells its own story.

'*That* can buy one man a fleet of cars or a luxury home,' says the museum curator in her speech to inaugurate the exhibition, indicating the Ligakis loot. '*This* gives us all a glimpse into how civilisation developed,' she says, turning to the other side.

The audience looks towards the Carver Collection and applauds with enthusiasm. The curator has not quite finished, though.

'And our beautiful figurine here tells us something even more important. She tells us that there will always be mystery. She tells us that for many millennia we have had a sense of the divine. We have always worshipped something greater than ourselves. And perhaps when we stop doing that, we cease to be human.'

Her words float in the air, and Helena thinks briefly of her grandfather and Ligakis, of Arsenis and Nick Jones. She is certain that they did not believe there was anyone or anything greater than themselves. That at some point they ceased to be human.

'She is in the place where she belongs,' concludes the curator, gesturing once more to the figurine. 'For everyone to see.'

Helena leans in very close to Haris, her lips brushing his ear. Only he can hear the next words.

'Safe and sound,' she whispers. 'Whole, and home.'

Acknowledgements

I would like to thank everyone who has been generous with their time and insight:

All those connected with The British School at Athens who have helped me during the course of writing this book, including Professor John Bennet, Professor Rebecca Sweetman, Dr Evangelia Kiriatzi, Dr Kostis Christakis, Gerald Cadogan, Professor Roderick Beaton, Lord Renfrew and Dr Michael Boyd,

All those at the Museum of Cycladic Art in Athens, including Deligini Prifti, Metaxia Routsi and Marietta Kypriotaki,

Professor Nikos Stampolidis, Director of the Acropolis Museum, for permission to reproduce part of his poem on the Birth of Cycladic Civilisation,

Dr Christos Tsirogiannis for his invaluable insight into the trafficking of looted artefacts,

Stelios Daskalakis, Museologist and Museum Designer, for his patience with my questions,

Giorgos Dalaras for his music and providing infinite joy both to my fictional characters and myself, Anna Dalaras and Minos Matsas,

Val Rahmani and Professor Richards for their advice on chemistry,

Lord Poltimore, Chairman of Sotheby's,

Field McIntyre for sharing her knowledge and love of Meissen,

Fotini Pipi, Thomas Vogiatzis and Popi Siganou for their help and guidance with Greek language and culture,

Eleni and Stelios Kteniadakis for their *filoxenía* in Crete,

Miltos Patronis and colleagues at the Hellenic Motor Museum,

Dr Anna Vasiliki Karapanagiotou, Director of the National Archaeological Museum in Athens,

Fellow members of the British Committee for the Reunification of the Parthenon Marbles, especially Professor Paul Cartledge and Marlen Taffarello Godwin,

Everyone at my wonderful publishers, Headline, especially Mari Evans, Patrick Insole, Caitlin Raynor, Bea Grabowska, Lucy Upton, Elise Jackson, Rebecca Bader, Isobel Smith – and my marvellous, one and only editor, Flora Rees,

Everyone who looks after me at Curtis Brown, especially Jonathan Lloyd, Liz White and Caoimhe White,

The London Library for the inspirational writing environment,

Emily Hislop for being my first reader and for her eagle-eyed editing, and to everyone in my family for their love and patience.